In the Company of Shadows

The Night's Road: Book Five

Darkness Beckons

Andy Monk

All rights reserved. No part of this publication may be reproduced, distributed, or transmitted in any form or by any means, including photocopying, recording, or other electronic or mechanical methods, without the prior written permission of the publisher.

Copyright © 2024 Andy Monk
All rights reserved.
ISBN: 9798339654438

Eight Hours Later

Part One

Brides

Chapter One

Thasbald Castle, Electorate of Brandenburg, The Holy Roman Empire - 1631

Beneath pink-tinged pennants of wispy cloud, the dying sun's light gilded the highest towers of Thasbald Castle in gold,

"Fucking grim pile of shit..." Lucien hawked up phlegm to punctuate his verdict.

He couldn't argue.

He'd thought Ettestein an uninviting-looking place, but even in the most flattering of light, Thasbald made it look like a cheery palace built for frivolity and frolics.

The castle sat bleak and alone amidst wetlands stretching from horizon to horizon; the road approaching it a causeway banked above bogs fringed with dead winter reeds.

Skims of ice still hardened much of the water despite the sun shining all day. Here and there, gnarled, twisted trees interrupted the flat monotony of the landscape. They put him in mind of anguished souls petrified in wood.

We're going to die in there... horribly, most likely

Thasbald certainly looked the kind of place well apportioned with dark, dank dungeons suitable for doing away with people horribly.

It sprouted towers, turrets, bastions and abutments like some bizarre spiky creature from an exotic shore. One that liked to impale its prey and carry a few dead things around on its back in case it fancied a snack later.

The walls were high and likely too thin to withstand modern canon fire. However, that would depend on whether you could get artillery anywhere near it in the first place. The surrounding ring of wetlands would play havoc with any besieging army. Perhaps that explained why Bulcher remained here, secure in the knowledge any foe would sink into his swamp before they could wheedle the bastard out of his prickly shell.

He pulled his horse to one side of the road and waited for Solace.

She no longer rode at the front of the column.

Hilde had hacked her hair short again. She might pass as a boy, swaddled in thick clothes, a scarf about her face and a woollen cap low over her eyes. If no one looked too closely.

"Won't Bulcher recognise you?" he'd asked her earlier as they ate a sparse lunch on the edge of the marshes.

"He saw me for less than an hour nearly two years ago; I doubt it."

"You made enough of an impression for him to hire the Red Company to fetch you?"

Her eyes hardened at that, "I think my father's insult made the biggest impression. He will not recognise me... until 'tis too late for him..."

"My lady," he said when she finally came alongside.

"Ulrich," she nodded, his name muffled by the scarf wrapped around her face.

"Thasbald awaits…" he said after urging his horse to keep pace with Styx.

"Indeed."

"tis a large fortress, my lady. Likely well garrisoned."

"I would imagine so."

"'tis not too late-"

"Yes, Ulrich, 'tis far, far too late."

He sighed to himself. He'd known it a hopeless tilt to try and change Solace's mind at the last minute, but a man shouldn't ride to his own death without comment.

"We will not die in there," Solace said as if reading his thoughts.

He would have asked if she'd seen that, but it was best not to talk about her *sight*, even amongst friends.

If they really were amongst friends.

Any number of their companions might consider a quiet word in the *Graf's* ear a more profitable option than trying to help seize a castle and kill its lord.

But Solace refused to heed his concerns.

Did her *sight* truly show them surviving, or had vengeance blinded her to common sense?

He did not know.

Still, he would follow her into the dark, grim fortress ahead. Honour bound him. By oath, by duty and by the fact he betrayed her family and had sworn never to do so again. Even at the cost of his own life.

Honour is the only thing that cannot be taken from a man. He can only give it away…

He'd given his away once. Helping, to his eternal shame, the demons of the Red Company gain access to The Wolf's Tower to save his own life. Whatever he did henceforth would never balance scales weighed down by the blood of innocents. So, he would follow, he would serve, he would obey, and he would die. But, in doing so, he would cling to what tattered remnants of his honour remained. And that would be something.

Wouldn't it?

They rode on in silence.

He would not change her mind.

She had her plan. He thought it madness but would do all she asked and pray it might work. Perhaps God would take pity on them. And wouldn't object to a few more corpses in a world already awash with blood.

As Thasbald loomed above them, the gates opened, allowing six horsemen to ride out.

"I assume we *are* expected..." he said out of the corner of his mouth.

Solace only stared ahead, though a hand snaked up to touch her throat.

Wendel's ashes.

She carried the remains of the fingers sliced from the demon's hand to send the face-changing monster spinning to his doom at the foot of The Grace Tower in Ettestein Castle. He did not know why she kept it, but her hand often sought it.

He resisted letting his own fingers brush the pommel of his father's sword, the closest thing to a lucky charm he possessed. He'd never died whilst holding it, so he guessed that meant it must be lucky.

Still, it is best not to touch your weapons when riding towards a castle. Especially one you wanted to fool into believing that you were their friend.

Bosko held up a hand to halt their column and await the riders.

Was there a chance the *Graf* might have become bored awaiting his child bride and married someone else? Even someone as monstrous and insane as *Graf* Bulcher wouldn't marry two women at the same time, would he?

That fancy didn't last long.

The Thasbald horsemen didn't send them away with a flea in their ear, telling them Lady Karoline was now surplus to requirements.

Instead, the lead rider reached across and shook Bosko's hand after reining his mount to a halt. They exchanged words and smiles before the riders wheeled their horses and led the column to Thasbald's open gates.

His heart sank.

And he couldn't shake the feeling of how much those open gates and raised portcullis reminded him of a gaping, fanged mouth.

One about to snap shut and swallow them...

*

A noble wedding was usually a matter of fuss and fanfare.

Her own – which she had once spent a substantial portion of her waking life daydreaming about – was going to be stuffed to the gills with it. *Graf* Bulcher clearly favoured a more understated approach to matrimony.

Nothing awaited Lady Karoline's carriage in the cobbled

courtyard before Thasbald's towering keep. No trumpets, no banners, no decorations, no garlands. No pageantry, no pomp, no... *anything.*

Would he have made more of an effort for me...?

She grimaced at the thought behind the thick, woollen scarf wrapped around her face. With dusk falling and swaddled in winter gear, no one would recognise Solace von Tassau, though it struck her as they rode through the main gates, she should have let Renard ride Styx.

The stallion wasn't a mount for someone trying to be inconspicuous.

She suspected it one of a million things she hadn't thought of. And when you set out to kill a lord and seize his castle, it would help your chances no end to think of everything.

I have no doubts...

No, if Thasbald was to be her tomb, her *sight* would have warned her. It might not tell her everything, show her everything, but surely, it would have had a thing or two to whisper about that.

It had told her about Madge and the Merry Gentlemen's attack. It had told her Bosko was Karoline's father. It would have told her if this was folly.

Wouldn't it?

As they waited before the closed doors of the castle's soaring keep, she tried to put doubt from her mind, as if the observant might notice it like the steam rising from Styx's back and wonder what the boy with the big horse had to worry about.

Renard glanced at her several times; she kept eyes front.

The men who brought them into the castle had dismounted, and so had Bosko. Everybody else stayed in their saddle.

No greeting party emerged from the castle, no servants, no... anybody.

"The *Graf* seems utterly overjoyed at his bride's safe arrival..." Renard said.

"I was hoping for feasting and celebrations," Lucien twisted around to face them, "getting pissed with company is so much more enjoyable..."

"You're not here to get pissed," she glared back at him.

"No," Lucien agreed, "but if there are merriments, 'tis important we fit in..."

She rolled her eyes.

Lucien laughed and turned back.

Renard shook his head and gave her a forlorn look.

The iron-studded doors of the towering keep swinging open curtailed further comment.

A grey-haired man scurried down the steps, fur-lined cloak flying in his wake, a heavy silver chain bouncing off his chest.

"Apologies, apologies!" he cried as he hurried towards Bosko and the Thasbald horsemen.

"The *Graf*'s steward?" Renard ventured.

"Or some such," she whispered back.

They were too far back to hear what else he said, but the *Graf*'s lackey appeared to be doing a lot of bowing and hand wringing in Bosko's direction. Which was what you paid lackeys for.

Do I kill them all?

The thought came clear, sudden and unexpected enough to chill her more deeply than the winter evening.

Of course not. Only Bulcher had to die. Others might have to, to achieve that, but, no, she didn't want any unnecessary deaths.

Why not? Everyone you knew died because of that man.

She shifted in her saddle; beneath her, Styx shifted too, perhaps sensing the dark thoughts.

She knew little of Bulcher. He'd not said much to her during their brief introduction, and she'd been too horrified by the sight of him to pay attention to the little he had uttered.

How many children did he have? Siblings? Extended family? Who else did he share Thasbald with? People he cared about? People he loved?

Shouldn't they die, too?

Didn't they deserve to die?

She blinked.

Everybody was dismounting.

She shook her head. Styx shook his in time and added a snort.

Renard's brows furrowed under his hat.

She flashed a reassuring smile and only remembered she still had a scarf wrapped around her face after her boots found the frost-flecked cobbles.

Thasbald stood stark against the darkening sky. Unlike Ettestein, the castle didn't perch atop a rocky outcrop, just a modest fold of land in the surrounding sea of marsh and bog. Yet it seemed to climb so much higher.

How long would it take a body to fall from its tallest towers before it hit the ground?

Renard leant in close, "My lady..."

"Don't call me that here. *Ever!*"

He nodded and backed away.

Servants had materialised and were scurrying to show riders where the stables were. Bosko and Lebrecht handed their mounts off and walked along the line with Bulcher's lackey to Karoline's coach. None gave her a glance as they passed.

A stable boy appeared in front of her. He gave Styx a wide-eyed glance, before ushering Renard, Lucien and her to come with him.

You want this one dead, too?

Lucien chatted amiably to the lad, who chatted amiably back.

Too many murderous echoes reverberated around her head to follow their conversation.

And she should be.

Every scrap of information was useful, even titbits discarded by stable boys, but her heart pounded too hard. Her mouth swam with the coppery tang of blood, and screams rolled out of her mind's shadowy corners.

I am not a monster. I am not...

The boy took them to the castle's stables. They were large and well-provisioned. Judging by their size, Thasbald could muster a sizeable force of horsemen. But was all of it in use?

She groped for a way to innocently ask, then stopped herself. She might pass for a lad, swaddled in cloak, scarf and winter gear; her hair might be cropped short, and Hilde had strapped her breasts flat with torn strips of linen, but nothing could disguise the femininity of her voice.

Save keeping her mouth shut.

Unlike Ettestein, no village sat within Thasbald's outer walls. The only visible outbuildings were the stables; much of the land between the outer walls and the soaring towers of the keep had been given over to pig stys. In fact, she thought it the largest pig farm she'd ever seen as they rode past to a serenade of oinks, snorts and squeals. She guessed Bulcher had a fondness for pork. Perhaps that was why he'd taken such offence at her father's insult...

With the horses attended to, they collected their gear and returned to the castle where servants awaited to show them where they were going to room.

Karoline, Lebrecht and Bosko were already inside, and servants were helping unload the coach.

Other than the stable lad, no one smiled at them or spoke to them. Everybody kept their head down and tried their hardest to avoid eye contact.

"A happy place..." Gotz noted as they followed a stooping old man into the castle.

The old soldier was right. Thasbald had a joylessness that hung about it like morning mist; cold, cloying and keeping the sun's warmth from the world.

"Everyone must be excited about the wedding?" Lucien asked the servant, who couldn't have flinched more if the mercenary slapped him.

"Of course..." the servant urged them on with a flick of a bony wrist.

She'd grown up in a castle. As much as she'd loved The

Wolf's Tower, she knew it was a stronghold and a projection of power and wealth before it was a home. Thasbald was those things, too, but nothing about it felt like a home.

Inside, it was dark, cold, damp. Nothing softened the stark stone walls. The ceilings were too low, the corridors too narrow, the air too stale. The castle pressed in on her from every side as their boots clipped bare stone.

No distant voices floated through open doors, no laughter, no shouts, no curses, barely a sound at all beyond their little group.

This is a tomb...

Only for Bulcher.

She concentrated on staring at Lucien's shoulder blades.

Imagination wasn't always a virtue.

The servant led them to a cramped, windowless room with six bunks. It smelt of musty disuse, and the whitewash on the walls looked tobacco yellow in the rushlights the bent-backed old man lit for them.

She assumed this was the part of Thasbald where Bulcher billeted his men-at-arms. Another thing they would need to find out very soon.

"Where might we eat, friend?" Lucien asked, positioning himself in front of the door before the servant could scurry away.

"The kitchens," the old man said, trying to move around the sizeable moustached obstacle.

"And where are the kitchens?" Lucien put a shoulder against the doorframe and beamed.

"The other side of the castle. Ask someone when you're ready; you'll never remember if I tell you."

"But I have an excellent memory!" Lucien leaned in and loomed over the man, "I'm renowned for it..."

While the servant trotted out a staccato list of directions she'd forgotten after the third left, she threw her gear on one of the lower bunks. How did she feel about sharing a room with four men, if you counted Hugo as a man.

What would Father say?! He would have hung any man other than Torben who entered her bedchamber.

Or a year ago, he would have.

This was the anniversary of his death. Her brother's abduction. Her home's destruction.

The smile behind the scarf withered.

"What's your name, friend?" Lucien asked once the servant had given his directions and started looking longingly towards the cold, dark corridor outside.

"Fux."

Lucien's eyebrows shot up, "Really?"

"Yes, now if-"

"Tell me, *Herr* Fux, when is the wedding?"

Fux scowled, "I do not know."

"But surely these things take planning and preparation? One of mine needed nearly a week. Had the Devil's own job finding enough beer."

"It will be soon, that is all I know. The *Graf* does not tell me anything!" Fux finished with a squeak.

"No... but there will be a feast? Guests? Music and merriments?" he loomed over Fux, who shied back a step as the mercenary growled, "Beer? There *will* be beer, won't there?"

"I don't know. My master does not like fuss. He just wants

matters resolved speedily."

Resolved speedily.

Bulcher was even less of a romantic than she'd thought.

"Hmpf!" Lucien leaned back and scratched his stubbly chin.

"Please, excuse me, I-"

"Where are our friends and companions roomed?"

"The soldiers on this floor. The better guests are in the Octavian rooms..."

"The *better* guests? Are we not-"

"Lucien..." Renard warned, perhaps sensing she wanted to.

"Well," Lucien shrugged and moved aside, "I'm not sure any house could have better guests than I."

"I'm sure," Fux mumbled, making a dash for freedom.

Lucien stepped back in front of him, "For I am none other than Lucien Kazmierczak, the famed soldier, adventurer and lover! You've probably heard of me."

"Erm... well... actually-"

"And let me assure you, great houses from Dublin to Damascus have welcomed me as the very best of guests..."

"Well-"

"So, *Herr* Fux, go get us a better fucking room and make sure there's some beer and food in it!"

"I'm not sure-"

Lucien stood aside before barking, "Go!"

"Yes, sir!!" Fux performed a little hop in time with his screech as he bolted from the room

"A man named Fux!" Lucien said, closing the creaking, ill-fitting door, "Who would have thought I'd have lived to see such a thing!"

Hugo laughed, Gotz smirked, Renard looked like he needed to empty his bowels.

"We're supposed to be not drawing attention to ourselves," she said, unwrapping the scarf from her face. The room was so cold she immediately wanted to wrap it back around.

"The suspicious thing would be *not* complaining about this freezing, pokey, shithole..." Lucien shot back with a grin, tapping a finger against his temple to signify the base cunning behind his argument.

Renard shook his head as he crossed the room to put his back to the door.

"What do we do now?" he asked, looking at her. As was everybody else.

"We find out as much as we can..." she met each gaze in turn, "...and then we absolutely ruin this fucking wedding..."

Chapter Two

Solace sent the four of them off to learn more about the castle, its garrison, and the wedding. And in Lucien's case, where the beer was.

He wanted to check on Hilde, but she was serving as Lady Karoline's maid, and he wouldn't get anywhere near the bride-to-be's rooms.

At every turn, he feared Bulcher's men would appear to seize them. All it took was one loose tongue. And even if he trusted all their recently expanded company – which he didn't – there were still the Vadians to worry about. If one of them mentioned the strange young woman who'd instigated the hanging of those Swedish soldiers and was now trying to pass herself off as a boy it would, at the very least, bring unwanted attention their way.

And if Bulcher became suspicious of these strangers who'd attached themselves to his bride's party…

Still, on the bright side, he'd become accustomed to living with fear.

There is no shame in fear. Only a fool never knows it. 'tis how one copes with it that marks the measure of a man…

Another of his father's homilies.

They had all sounded good until he'd reached enough of an age to realise the man who spouted them was a drunk who continually found new ways to disgrace himself.

He wanted to keep an eye on Gotz and Hugo as much as pursue intelligence for Solace. A coward and a thief. Neither gave sufficient confidence to trust his mistress' life with. But Solace thought otherwise, and Thasbald was a large castle.

In the end, Lucien and the boy went off in one direction, while he took the fat old soldier in another.

If Lucien and Gotz went off together, he suspected they would spend the night roaringly drunk.

"Where do you think you can find some beer in this place?" Gotz asked once Lucien and Hugo disappeared, rather confirming his suspicions.

"We're not here to drink the night away."

"Drinking loosens tongues. Always worth finding the beer when you're after information."

He glanced at the old soldier, "It'll just as likely loosen our tongues..."

"You have no worries with me. My capacity for beer is legendary!"

"I suspect you and Lucien are cut from the same block."

"Death is never far away when you're a soldier. Beer makes that reality less... sobering."

"Maybe from the same block as my father, too."

"He was a soldier?"

Their boots echoed down the deserted corridor as they talked.

"When sober enough."

The shadows hung heavy inside Thasbald, the air stale and greasy. The whole atmosphere of the place pressed down upon his shoulders. Perhaps it was because he knew a monster lived here. Not a monster like Saul the Bloodless and his ilk, but a monster, nevertheless.

"You're something of a gloomy fellow, if you don't mind me saying," Gotz looked at him as they turned into another deserted corridor.

"I'm a realist."

"Really?"

"We're all going to die."

"As I said…"

"Why did you stay?" he stopped and stared at the old man.

"Stay?"

"With us. After what Lady Solace told you."

"About demons? About vengeance?"

He nodded, "And don't tell me 'tis because you want to right wrongs."

Gotz's voice dropped, "Maybe it was that talk of silver and gold."

"More believable," he conceded, "but I don't think so."

"I'm not going to betray you."

He kept the man's gaze. Just.

Gotz's unkempt eyebrows shot up, "Now, don't tell me that thought hasn't crossed your mind."

"It has."

"And I dare say the fat piece of shit whose roof we're under might pay me well too. Despite the state of this place, I don't doubt he's a rich man."

"So, if you are motivated by money, that would be an easier way of getting it."

"Guess it would."

"You haven't answered my question."

"Nope."

"Why would that be?"

Gotz worried his beard with grubby fingers, "Because I ain't got no good answer for you. Curiosity, maybe. Your lady has something about her. Don't ask me what it is, because I don't know. But mainly, I think it's because I got nowhere else to go."

"I can think of plenty of better places to be than here."

"I'm old, Ulrich. Too old to still be fighting, that's for sure. But I got nothing. No woman. No children. No family. No friends worthy of the name. Spent my life drifting and concentrating so hard on staying alive that there was never much room left to do anything with the life I was working so hard on keeping. Maybe I just don't want to be alone. Dying alone... been thinking a lot about that recently. Maybe doing something that isn't for money, that isn't for someone else's greed or vanity or plain old-fashioned stupidity appeals..." Gotz's beard split to show the blackened remnants of his teeth "...or I'm just too tired to go out on that fucking road alone again to find a better cause to risk my worthless old hide for."

He wasn't sure what to say to that, so he said nothing.

Gotz patted his arm and started walking again, "C'mon, lad. We've got no time for this maudlin kind of shit. We've got a rich bastard's wedding to ruin, remember?"

*

"Why the hurry?"

"Perhaps he is madly in love?"

The cynicism dripping from Lebrecht's voice wasn't

typical, but he had been spending time with Lucien.

She sat on the edge of her bunk, hunched forward, hands clasped tightly together. The young nobleman stood in front of her. Despite the ruler straight back, high chin and steady eye, she sensed awkwardness and simmering unease.

Whether due to the prospect of murder and theft or being alone in a bedroom with her, she wasn't at all sure. Perhaps a little of both.

"We will have to act quickly then."

Lebrecht nodded, "'tis for the best. Less chance someone will-"

"Castles have their own ears."

He nodded again. Lebrecht grew up in a castle, too and knew as well as her, secrets were hard to keep when stone walls confined enough people.

She shuffled along the bunk and patted the thin mattress next to her.

Lebrecht's awkwardness bubbled from simmering to boiling.

"We should speak as quietly as possible."

As if to reinforce her point, the thud of iron-nailed boots came from the corridor. Lebrecht eyed the door until they passed.

Then he sat beside her.

Lebrecht smelt of scented oil and wore a clean shirt. He might even have found time to bathe, or at least wash. He'd packed a lot into the few hours they'd been inside Thasbald.

Bulcher and Karoline's wedding would be the day after

tomorrow. There would be no guests from outside. The ceremony in the castle's chapel would be followed by a celebratory feast for Thasbald's household.

"What did you make of the *Graf*?" she asked as he settled beside her. It was only the third time she'd been on a bed with a man in her life. The first had been Renard, when she'd warmed his freezing flesh after they escaped The Wolf's Tower and again in Madriel for reasons of exhaustion, expediency and necessity. The second had been the Imperial soldier who tried to rape her in Ettestein before the demon Wendel intervened and killed him. She did not like to think of it as saving her.

She resisted the urge to find the leather pouch of grey dust hanging from her neck.

And now here she was with Lebrecht, heir to the *Markgräfschaft* of Gothen. Young, handsome, a Prince of the Empire. The kind of man who, up to a year ago, she'd spent considerable time daydreaming about sharing a bed with.

Though never to plot murder.

A year ago...

Part of her wanted to bring down ruin on Bulcher tonight. It had an appealing poetry. But she planned to deliver justice to Bulcher after the wedding, and her *sight*, she thought, agreed, while Flyblown's mark remained cool and untroubled.

Sometimes, poetry had to wait.

"I met him only briefly," Lebrecht twisted to face her, the bunk's wooden frame creaking as he moved.

Flyblown's mark might be cool; her cheeks, however, felt

anything but.

"Long enough to form an impression?"

"I did count the rings on my fingers after he left..."

She surprised herself with a laugh.

"Anything else?"

"If Father tried to marry Sophia to him... I'd kill the bastard."

"Your father or the *Graf*...?"

That earned a grim smile.

"What did he have to say for himself?"

"Not much. He thanked us for ensuring Karoline arrived safely. He said we were welcome to attend the wedding and stay afterwards to recover from our journey. But the way he said it suggested he wanted us gone as soon as possible."

"And what did you make of him as a man?"

Lebrecht shook his head, "He made my skin crawl; there is something... *unclean* about him."

"That's how I felt, too. The prospect of being his wife..." she shuddered.

"Karoline is but a child..."

"She will not be his wife for long."

"No..."

"You could leave; I would not ask you to do something you object to."

"He is evil," Lebrecht said.

"Yes, he is. And insane."

Lebrecht's gaze fixed on the wall opposite.

"And Bosko, what did the Captain make of him?" she asked.

"Bulcher did not say a word to him. I think a lowly soldier

is too far beneath his station to bother with. Bosko looked troubled, though."

She reached over and took his hand.

Lebrecht's eyes darted to hers.

"Thank you."

He swallowed and found a smile.

She squeezed his hand.

He squeezed hers back.

"We might die doing this..."

"Yes," she agreed, "we might."

"If we succeed... even with the war... there are still laws. For men like Bulcher, at least."

"Does he have family?" she asked.

Lebrecht shook his head, "None here. As far as I know Leopold, his son, is his only relative."

"The people here, have you seen the look in their eyes?"

"Fear," he said, without hesitation.

She would have said haunted, but it was close enough.

"I don't think many will be sorry if he were no longer their lord," she said, "Bulcher has been the *Graf* of Thasbald for a long time."

"He is not a young man."

"But he isn't an ancient one either..."

"How long has he been *Graf* here?" Lebrecht asked.

"I don't know. But I remember my father saying Bulcher had been *Graf* since before my grandfather's time. I thought he did not look *that* old when I met him, but I was too repulsed and scared by the thought of having to marry him to give it much consideration."

"He could have come to the title as a boy..." Lebrecht

suggested.

"He could have, but *something* tells me otherwise... *something* tells me his business with demons goes beyond destroying his enemies." She felt Lebrecht's hand tighten on hers as she added, "I think he has sold his soul to them too..."

"Then there is even more reason to stop him..."

Lebrecht's thumb caressed the knuckle of her hand.

How often had she dreamed of sharing a bed with a handsome young Prince of the Empire? There were too many to count, though none of those dreams envisaged the bed being a bunk in a cold, dank soldier's billet that smelled of strange men's sweat.

'tis a year since I died...

She smiled and interlocked her fingers with Lebrecht's.

...'tis maybe a night till what remains of me dies too...

He leaned in, drawing closer to her in hesitant increments.

Why shouldn't I?

His lips came nearer, eyes brighter. Her heart, in return, beat all the harder.

Because if you let him use you, it will become more difficult to use him...

She teetered on the brink of his kiss, swaying as if buffeted by the wind, unsure if she wanted to fall into it or stagger backwards.

As it was, Hugo took the decision from her.

The boy burst into the room, wide-eyed and breathless; he slammed the door behind him as she and Lebrecht jerked away from each other.

"We've got a problem..." he panted.

She tried not to smile, knowing what Hugo would say next with absolute certainty.

No, we don't have a problem at all...

Chapter Three

They found Lucien in the servant's dining hall. A battered tankard in one hand, a droopy sausage in the other and a plump maid in his lap.

The maid was squealing, a couple of the Gothen men, Usk and Dreyfuss, were laughing hard enough to spray beer, Hugo didn't know quite where to look. The smattering of others in the room sported various expressions of annoyance, irritation and disdain.

Oh, for goodness sake...

He glanced at Gotz, who merely shrugged before lowering himself down next to Lucien and introducing himself to the girl, who was the jolliest-looking person they'd met in Thasbald by a long way. So jolly, in fact, her ample breasts were swinging around enough to present a danger to the unwary.

He eased down opposite the mercenary and started scowling at him.

"More beer!" Lucien roared. When the maid tried to wriggle out of his lap, he pulled her back down again, "Not you, me beauty, you're helping to make us feel welcome. Important work!"

The maid screeched with glee as if the oaf had said something funny.

He glowered all the harder.

"Cheer up," the maid said, noticing the sour expression, "there's supposed to be a wedding on, y'know!"

He squeezed out a begrudging smile.

"This is Edda..." Lucien pointed his sausage at him in a knowing kind of way. He assumed the buffoon was introducing the girl on his lap rather than the unsavoury-looking tube of gristle, "...she's been telling us all about the wedding, haven't you, my dear...?"

Edda squealed, shrieked and wiggled all at the same time.

He managed a perfunctory nod. Edda seemed a delight...

"Well, the *latest* wedding..." Edda gave him a big wink before sliding off Lucien's lap, landing on the floor with a thump and knocking the heavy table hard enough to rattle it, despite it being made from the kind of thick oak planks used in warships.

"Oops, look at me, fucking clumsy cow!" Edda bellowed, adjusting her cap, "I'll fetch you boys more beer; no one else lifts a bloody finger in this place..."

With that, Edda headed out of the hall with the grace and lightness of a bull in heat.

"Seems like a nice girl," he smiled at Lucien as the mercenary tore off a lump from his sausage.

Gotz leaned closer to Lucien, eyes wide, wiry eyebrows soaring, "Do you know if she whores, lad?"

"This isn't why we're here!" he glared across the table at them.

Lucien and Gotz gave him pitying looks. Once Lucien got the gristle down his gullet without choking, he asked, "It isn't?"

"No!"

"Why are we here then, son?" Gotz asked, eyebrows doing another jiggle.

When he said nothing, Lucien answered for him, "We're here to celebrate the marriage of Lady Karoline to the noble and esteemed *Graf* Bulcher, who has so graciously and generously invited us into his home for the duration of the nuptials. The world out there, the one we will be going back to shortly, is cold, wet, and full of people trying to kill each other. Food is scarce, and beer, if you can find it, is thin-"

"And even whores are hard to come by a lot of the time!" Gotz shook his head, mouth turned downwards in disgust.

"Exactly!" Lucien continued, "So, we should make the most of the good fortune that brings us into this welcoming house, enjoy the hospitality, bless the happy couple and wish them a long and fruitful marriage. Don't you think, Ulrich...?"

"Yes..." he managed to say through not quite gritted teeth.

"Excellent! Now start looking like you're fucking enjoying yourself!" Lucien beamed and tossed the greasy half-eaten sausage onto the table before him, "Remarkably, 'tis actually worse than it looks..."

"So..." he ignored the sausage despite his rumbling stomach, "...what has your new friend said about the wedding... the one we will enjoy celebrating so much..."

"You can ask Edda yourself..." Lucien said as the maid returned bearing half a dozen foaming tankards.

"There you go, boys!" Edda slammed the tankards down, "Get your fucking throats wet. We're all gonna be pissed soon, ain't we, you miserable bastards?" Edda didn't direct the question at them but the smattering of servants and soldiers still loitering in the hall, who responded with stony silence and disparaging glances rather than a rousing cheer.

Edda brushed Lucien's hands aside so she could plonk herself back into his lap. She was a hefty girl, and he thought he might have screamed if such a weight landed on his balls with so much force, Lucien, however, only grinned one of his infuriatingly know-it-all grins at him.

"Everybody looking forward to the wedding then?" he asked Edda as he helped himself to one of the tankards.

"Oh, yeah, much merriment and mirth, I'm sure!" Edda brayed, leaning across the table towards him, displaying the pale fleshy crevice of her cleavage with no obvious shame. She added in a lower voice, "Just like all the others…"

"Others?"

"Edda! What on Earth do you think you are doing?" A hollow-faced, long-boned woman, who he doubted had ever ventured onto anyone's lap, appeared at Lucien's shoulder.

"Just entertaining the *Graf*'s guests, *Frau* Bussler!" Edda shot back.

"If I've told you once, I've told you a hundred times, Edda, this is a reputable house. If you wish to work in a *disreputable* one, I have heard there are many in Hamburg catering to…" the woman ran an eye around the table "…low sorts…"

"Yes, *Frau* Bussler…" Edda disentangled herself from Lucien. She paused to offer the woman a half-hearted curtsey, before stomping across the hall to the kitchens.

Frau Bussler's beady eyes narrowed as they returned to

them, "I do hope you are not the kind of gentlemen who will mar the upcoming happy occasion with *rowdiness*..."

Everybody shook their heads and muttered, "No, ma'am," apart from Lucien, who just grinned and looked *Frau* Bussler up and down as if to see what she had to offer.

"We live with the grace of our lord and master the *Graf* here. Thasbald is a sanctuary and a haven in this terrible world. We will have no trouble here..."

"No, ma'am," they all replied again.

"Splendid. I'll expect no trouble then. I find trouble before a wedding *most* inauspicious..."

"We shall be good as gold," Gotz said, standing up, "we have had a long and fraught journey with little hospitality. Please trust we won't abuse the *Graf's*."

"Very well, I shall leave you on your best behaviour," *Frau* Bussler paused as she turned to go, "and please don't lead any of my girls astray. Life is complicated enough without having to deal with the *consequences* of straying..."

She treated each of them to an individual glare – even Hugo, who likely had little idea what they were talking about – before gathering her skirt, raising her chin and floating back across the dining hall.

Gotz leaned back in his chair, "Do you think she-"

"I'd very much doubt it," Lucien leaned over the table to retrieve his sausage.

"Dunno about you, but I wouldn't mind a bit of straying..." Dreyfuss swept back his long, greasy locks to seemingly better display his warts.

Am I the only man in the world who doesn't continually think with his cock?

Before he could remind his comrades they weren't actually here to drink and fornicate, a red-faced and flustered Hilde appeared. Rather than the travel-soiled clothes she'd worn since leaving Ettestein, she now wore a dress befitting one of Lady Karoline's maids. He assumed it was one of Elin's, but it fitted her exceedingly well; he couldn't help but notice.

Her appearance summoned a smile and dispersed thoughts of his lowly, base fellows and their lewdness.

The smile didn't last long.

Hilde crouched beside him and put her lips to his ear, "We have a problem..."

*

When she arrived with Hugo, Hilde and Renard were already in Karoline's quarters.

Fortunately, given the hour and the cold, there were few people about, and those who were didn't question why a lad might be walking around the castle with a scarf covering half their face.

Karoline's maid, Elin, gave her a suspicious look as she unwrapped the scarf. In truth, Elin gave her a suspicious look every time she laid eyes on her.

If there was one person in their company whose loose lips might endanger her plans, it was Elin. However, she rarely ventured far from her mistress and seemingly never took interest in anything other than Lady Karoline's well-being.

Which probably explained why the maid currently looked so fraught.

"What happened?" she asked.

"My lady met the *Graf* for the first time this evening..."

Elin wrung her hands, "...it did not go well..."

"Where is she now?"

"Locked in her bedchamber. *Mon Dieu!*" Elin exclaimed, "My lady is threatening to kill herself!"

"I thought you might want a word," Hilde said.

"I wanted to fetch Captain Bosko, but *Fraulien* Hilde thought you would know what to do..." Elin's hands fell from her face as the maid eyed her suspiciously again, "...do you?"

"I had an unwanted marriage proposal once..." she offered by way of explanation as she crossed the room.

Renard followed her.

"You and Hugo shouldn't be here," she said.

"Neither should you, being a boy..." he replied.

"Make sure no one comes in... or leaves."

He nodded and went back to the others.

She knocked on the bed chamber's door, "Lady Karoline?"

There was no reply.

"Please, open the door. Nothing is as bad as it seems..."

You are about to marry a vile monster, but, luckily for you, I intend to kill him before he can do you any harm...

A few snatched sobs floated under the door by way of reply.

She glanced over her shoulder to where the others stood watching.

"I can kick the door in?" Renard suggested.

She shook her head. The girl was already terrified

"Karoline, please, come to the door. You do not have to face this alone. I can help..." still nothing, "...I am your friend. And not your only one. As bleak as things may seem... you have choices... always..."

Something moved on the other side of the door. The squeak of furniture, footsteps...

"Celine...?" a small voice croaked.

"Yes. Please open the door. No one else will come in. I promise."

A long silence followed.

Then a shuffle, a scrape, a click. When the door cracked open, a pale, ghostly face peered out.

"I am sorry..." Karoline said, voice quieter than the shuffle, scrape and click that preceded it, "...I fear I am being somewhat silly."

She smiled and shook her head, "No, you're not. May I come in?"

The door trembled as if Karoline swayed back and forth between opening it and slamming it shut again.

In the end, Karoline faded back into the shadows, leaving the door ajar behind her.

She followed her inside, nodding at the watching faces across the room before closing the door after her.

A large four-poster bed filled the room. A fire glowed, and candles burned in front of a chipped looking-glass on the mantle above it. Otherwise, the room was bare, stark and bereft of decoration, much like the rest of Thasbald.

Karoline retreated to the bed; a hand wrapped around one of the posts as if she did not trust her legs to keep her upright.

She hurried over, took the girl in her arms and hugged her.

Sometimes, words were insufficient.

"I fear I may cry again..." Karoline breathed in her ear.

"And if you do, I will not let go until you are done," she whispered back.

For a heartbeat or two, Karoline just held her in return, then convulsed so violently she feared the girl was suffering a seizure. The tears came hard and continued for so long it seemed they would never stop.

How could one fragile little body hold so many tears?

The memory of her own tears reared out of the shadows. Those long, lonely months within the shattered remnants of The Wolf's Tower, her only companion too lost in his own pain, shame and grief to offer much actual company. Hour after hour curled alone in the dark, trying to stifle the sound so he would not hear. The darkness wrapped about her so thick with the stink of smoke she still smelt it from time to time and still wondered what portion of it was from her father...

She held Karoline. Made soft sounds in her ear and stroked her hair.

Had she cried since leaving The Wolf's Tower?

She didn't think so.

Those tears dried long before Morlaine arrived.

She doubted she would ever cry again.

That girl who wept in the smoky darkness was as dead as the girl who'd spent hours combing her hair and dreaming of handsome princes.

Eventually, the sobbing subsided.

She eased Karoline down to sit on the edge of the bed.

The poor thing looked wretched.

There was nothing to drink in the bedchamber, so she left

Karoline clutching her hands to get Elin to fetch some watered wine.

"Lady Karoline?" Elin asked as she returned to the bedchamber door with the goblet.

"I will do what I can to make things better," she said, taking the wine and then shutting the door before Elin could ask how on Earth she could do that.

"Drink this," she said, pressing the goblet into Karoline's hand. The girl, hunched forward on the edge of the bed, stared at it as if she were having trouble focusing.

"Will it help?" Karoline asked.

The bed creaked and groaned as she sat next to Bulcher's bride-to-be, "It will ease your throat."

Karoline sniffed up snot and took an unconvinced sip. When done, she held the goblet two-handed in her lap. Tiny ripples moved across the wine's dark surface.

"What happened, Karoline?"

"*Graf* Bulcher happened..."

The ripples grew, becoming wavelets lapping upon the goblet's rim.

"Drink more, please."

"I fear it will not help."

"No, it won't. But if you drink more, there's less chance of you spilling anything over your dress. Wine stains are so ridiculously hard to remove."

Karoline peered at her through puffy, red eyes. Then laughed. It wasn't a happy laugh. But almost all laughter is better than tears.

The girl took a long, deep draught. When she lowered the goblet, her hands were steadier. A little, at least.

She tried again, "What happened when you met the *Graf?*"

"Happened? Why, nothing much happened at all..." she snorted violently enough for snot bubbles to erupt from her nose, "...he barely spoke to me. We dined. Or rather he did. He sat at the other end of the table behind this mountain of food and just... shovelled it into his mouth. Occasionally, he would stop to throw some wine after it. And a couple of times, he did look at me..."

She reached over and placed a hand on the girl's wrist. The waves had returned to her goblet.

"My expectations were low. Extremely low. I knew he was old and fat and... not as handsome as one might hope for," Karoline turned to her, "...but none of that means a man cannot be kind, does it?"

"No. The ugly can be kind, the handsome cruel."

"But a man can be ugly *and* cruel?"

She nodded.

"Then I appear to have been particularly unfortunate..."

"Drink the rest of the wine."

Once Karoline drained the goblet, she plucked it from her and put it on the floor so she could hold the girl's hand.

"Are you not going to tell me the *Graf* deserves a chance? That he may be a better man than I give him credit for? That I should get to know him? That-"

"No," she squeezed her hand, "I am not. I am your friend, Karoline, so I will not lie to you."

"If I could run away, I would. But Father told me I must marry the *Graf* for the good of Vadia. I do not know the arrangements, but I believe the war has hurt our barony badly. Things are difficult..." she sniffed, "...so I must be brave. That is what Father said to me. I must be brave..." the girl's lip trembled, "...but I don't want to be brave. I think I want to die."

"Life is a gift from God, Karoline; it should not be tossed away lightly."

The cold press of a muzzle beneath her chin, squeezing the trigger, holding her breath, expecting the end, but nothing happening bar the empty hollow click of the pistol...

I chose death, but death did not choose me.

Because vengeance had already claimed my soul...

She closed her eyes and heard that click again and again, echoing as it would for the rest of her days.

"When the *Graf* finished eating, he came to stand over me..." Karoline was saying, she suspected the girl might have said more, but for a few seconds she'd been in another place, "...he just stood, looking down at me, his shirt was so stained, I think half of his dinner went over it..." she released a shrill, mirthless laugh before continuing, "...he is huge! I kept thinking, *he will crush me, he will crush me flat...* then he reached down and ran his fingers over my face... they were sticky with grease..." Karoline brushed her cheek, as if she could still feel the ghost of the *Graf's* touch upon her skin, "...he said, "You will do..." then he laughed and waddled off. He is so fat he can barely walk!"

Karoline's words dissolved into a spluttered sob as she shot to her feet, "He is *obscene!*"

"Karoline-"

"I cannot do this!" the girl cried, "I cannot!"

She stood and tried to hold her, but Karoline jumped

away.

"I have to go to the marriage bed the night after tomorrow!" her eyes stretched wide; she shook from head to foot, and one trembling hand swept back and forth in front of her face as if she'd found herself caught in cobwebs.

"I can help..."

"How? How can anyone? I have no choice. I am not a person. I am a commodity my father has traded. I cannot refuse; I cannot go home! Father told me I must do this. For the family. For Vadia. I must become Bulcher's... *thing!*"

"There is always a way. As I told you on the road before we arrived here. There are always choices, there are always alternatives..."

"But how can I possibly escape him?"

She quickly seized Karoline's arms, pinning them to the girl's side.

"By doing what I tell you to."

"But... you only want to see him to discuss business; that's what you told me as we travelled here!"

She stared into the girl's frightened eyes.

"I just need to be alone with him. And I've thought of a much better way than that..."

Karoline panted, a pitiful keening noise escaping the back of her throat.

"You can escape this by doing exactly what I tell you..." she squeezed hard enough to make Karoline gasp, "...you can escape this by marrying the bastard and going to his bed..."

Chapter Four

"Bulcher has had many wives, although it was tricky to pin down just how many. Karoline will be his sixth, at least…"

"What happened to the others?" he asked.

"None of them got to live happily ever after in the land of milk and honey."

"I guessed that. But what happened to them?"

Lucien slowly drew a finger across his throat.

"He murdered them?" Hugo's eyes widened.

"Oh, all natural causes," Lucien flashed a dark and blackened grin, "obviously…"

They were back in their room, recounting their discoveries. It was late; the castle silent, and the walls were thick. His eyes still regularly drifted to the door. He felt uneasy. But he didn't have the *sight*, so put it down to being a born pessimist.

Solace stretched out on her bunk, hands behind her head, eyes closed. Listening, but not participating.

"Life is often short…" he suggested.

"Particularly for those who marry *Graf* Bulcher," Lucien pulled a face, "according to what I've been told, they all died within a year of becoming the *Grafin*."

"Did any of them kill themselves?"

"You might have thought so, but no. It seems there's a lot of sickness in Thasbald... That's what people here say. The few prepared to talk, anyway. Mostly they mumble something about minding your own business and hurry off. Which is most unusual. People usually fall over themselves to talk to Lucien Kazmierczak!"

"Children?" Hugo piped up, swinging his legs from the bunk he sat upon, "Rich people like children; it gives them somewhere for their money to go when they die. With so many wives, he must have lots."

"A son, Leopold, off fighting the Turks somewhere on the border, but he's the only name I've heard mentioned," Lucien said

"Bulcher initially told Father he wanted me for Leopold; the toad only announced his intention to marry me himself when he rolled up to The Wolf's Tower the night he visited us..." Solace said without opening her eyes.

"You said *at least* his sixth wife...?" he asked Lucien.

The mercenary nodded, "There's rumours of more, according to Edda."

"A fine source of information, I'm sure."

"A friendly girl. The only one prepared to talk openly anyway."

"And a fine pair of big bouncy tits to boot..." Gotz sighed, seeming to forget Solace's presence.

"You noticed, huh?" Lucien looked sideways at the old man.

"Oh, yes. I've always been partial to a big bouncy lass."

He coughed. Twice. And nodded at Solace.

Neither man looked abashed.

Hugo, to his credit, blushed furiously.

"These rumours?" he asked, moving things on.

"No one knows for certain."

He raised an eyebrow, "No one?"

"Apparently, no one is left here from the time before Bulcher..."

"How long has he been here?" he asked.

Lucien shook his head, "Everyone I spoke to seemed rather vague about when he inherited the title..."

Silence hung in the room while they all turned that over.

"He must be very old..." Hugo screwed up his face, "...sixty?"

"I think he's a lot older than that..." Solace said.

"You've met him. How old does he look?"

"I thought him ancient..." a distant smile touched her face, but only fleetingly, "...around my father's age."

Solace's father had been in his forties.

"What are you suggesting?" Lucien asked.

"He consorts with monsters. With vampires... we know their blood heals; it can prolong life, too. 'tis conjecture, but... I remember when I met Bulcher. 'tis not the kind of thing a girl forgets. The possibility, however briefly, of becoming a creature like that's wife... Of all the things about him, the one that stuck most forcefully was his teeth. They were perfect. White, straight, unstained. They were not the teeth of a man of forty, let alone sixty or seventy. Or more. Amidst his grotesqueness I found that strange. 'tis only now, looking back, that I think it unnatural. Demon's blood wouldn't make him thin, but it would keep his heart strong, his vitality intact and..." she cast her eyes about the room, "...his teeth perfect..."

"So..." Gotz pushed himself from one wall to walk to another and lean against that instead. It wasn't a long journey, "...we are saying our friend marries women who are the heir to their estates; once they inherit, if they have not already, they conveniently get sick and die. We are also saying he drinks demonic blood to prolong his life?"

"Yes."

Gotz scratched his head, "Fuck me... what a fellow."

"Why kill them?" he asked, "Once a woman marries, all she has passes to her husband. He would take ownership of her estate immediately anyway..."

"Greed..." Solace said, "...Bulcher is a man of excess. Whatever he has is never enough. Once they are married, Karoline's father and brother will soon die. Her father is old, her brother sickly. As soon as Vadia is his, Karoline's purpose is served. She will follow his other wives, and he will find another. One set to inherit something he wants..." she coughed up a bitter laugh, "...and I thought him only interested in my looks..."

"But..." Hugo was still frowning, "... why hasn't anyone noticed?"

Lucien shrugged, "People die all the time. And the world has other preoccupations. Spread over decades..."

Silence hung about them before he brought up the thing tugging at his mind.

"And if he is prolonging his life by drinking a demon's

blood, that raises another question. Who is this demon... and where are they now...?" he asked

"He deals with the Red Company. One of them?" Solace said.

"I'm not sure I can see Saul hawking his blood for money..."

Solace spun off the bunk.

"No demon's blood will prolong his life when his head is at my feet."

"I suppose not... where are you going?" he asked as she grabbed her cloak.

"To see Bosko."

He made to join her.

"I will go alone."

"My lady?"

"His rooms are not far, I will not get into mischief, I promise."

"If you are seen... recognised."

"I will not be... you should rest. Tomorrow, I need you all to discreetly ascertain the strength of Thasbald's garrison and their disposition during and after the wedding," she said, wrapping her woollen scarf around her face.

"Bulcher has at least a hundred men-at-arms here," Lucien said, "but no more than one hundred and forty. A quarter will guard the castle during the wedding; the rest will be in and around the chapel. There will be a feast after the ceremony; the *Graf* has laid on wine and ale to celebrate. There will be pork, chicken and fish, plus other sundry treats. The celebration will go on all night. Sore heads are expected..." Lucien raised his eyebrows, "...is there anything else you'd like to know, my lady?"

"You have been busy..."

"All the real work happens where the beer flows most freely," Lucien grinned.

Solace headed for the door, "I'll have a list of what else I need you to find out in the morning..."

Lucien looked around the room after the door banged shut behind her.

"She's impressed, I can tell..."

*

She found Bosko still awake.

He'd been drinking heavily, too; the smell washed over her as soon as he opened the door.

"Huh?" he managed, frowning at her.

She did not wait for him to invite her in.

His room was small, but at least he had it to himself. Furthermore, the walls had no dampness, and the fire burned generously enough to hold back the chill a little. In other words, it stood several steps up the social ladder from the one she shared with her men.

Bosko lingered by the door, swivelling to track her as she crossed the room to slump into the solitary chair. A table sat beside it with a jug of wine, a small earthenware bottle of something else, and a half-full glass.

"Close the door," she said, reaching for Bosko's glass with one hand while she unwrapped the scarf from her face with the other, "you're letting the heat out."

"Make yourself at home... erm... please," Bosko closed the

door. Lacking a chair, he leaned against the wall by the hearth, "Can I help you, my lady?"

She sipped from his glass, winced and handed it back to him.

"Don't call me my lady."

"No?"

"Here I am no one."

Bosko knocked back the glass in one. He didn't wince, "I have little idea who or what you are. Or why you are in my rooms at this hour?"

"Has anyone here asked about me?"

Bosko shook his head.

"Good. As to why I am here..." she stretched her legs out in front of the fire, "... 'tis to ask for your help in killing *Graf* Bulcher..."

Bosko put the glass down. He looked like he wanted to fill it to the brim again. Instead, he straightened up and folded his arms. He opened his mouth, frowned, and then closed it again.

"You can't decide whether to ask me why I want to do that or why I think you would help me?"

"More or less..."

"I'll answer both together. We don't have much time. Bulcher is a monster. He had my father killed, he unleashed monsters that destroyed my home and slaughtered every man, woman and child they could find. 'tis a long story, but I will tell it if you'll listen. As to why I think you'll help..." she tilted her head, "...I think you'll do what I want because Bulcher intends to destroy your home, too. And kill your daughter..."

"My daughter?" Bosko frowned, "Why would Bulcher kill my daughter?"

"Because he's killed every other woman he's married."

The Captain's face crumpled around his bulbous nose, "I thought you were mad when you made us hang those Swedes. Now-"

"Don't waste our time; you know damn well what I am talking about. Karoline is your daughter. Perhaps you don't know about Bulcher. I do. And I'm happy to explain what will happen to her, *Freiherr* Hoss, her brother and Vadia over the next few months..."

She pushed the little earthenware bottle across the table, "...I trust this tastes better than the wine, Captain?"

"It does. But you must think I've drunk an awful lot of it if-"

"Stop protesting. You're not a particularly convincing liar. Perhaps 'tis the drink. Perhaps 'tis because you are an honest man."

"I am not lying; I have no idea what you are talking about!" Bosko pulled the stopper from the earthenware bottle and sloshed clear liquid into his wine glass. It wasn't water. *Obstler*. She could smell the spirit fumes from where she sat.

"Tell me Karoline isn't your daughter."

Bosko snorted, "Karoline isn't my daughter!" he knocked back the *obstler*. His hand shook as he did so. When he noticed her staring, he slammed the glass down and shoved the hand in his pocket.

"I am your friend, Captain. Karoline's, too. What I know will not leave this room. I understand the sensitivity of this, for both of you…"

"Where does this nonsense come from?"

"An impeccable source."

"Your source is flawed."

Even without the *sight*, she would have spotted the lie. A thin sheen of sweat dampened his scalp, his eyes would not settle, and his hands trembled. She supposed excessive drinking could do all that, but not in this case. He was lying. She was sure of it.

"Very well", she shrugged and rose to her feet, "perhaps I was misinformed."

"You were. And keep this stupid idea to yourself!"

She moved to stand before him. Bosko was only a little taller than her but stocky and heavy-set. Her palms itched.

"If Bulcher marries Karoline, her father and brother will die. I don't know when, but it will be soon. Karoline will then be Vadia's heir. As her husband, Bulcher will own everything she has. Once he has that, he will have no further use for her. Maybe she will catch a convenient fever or eat something that will rot her guts. Maybe she will take a tumble. You know how clumsy women can be… 'tis what Bulcher does. He has done it before. Several times. He tried to do it to me, but my father refused him. Not only refused him but insulted him. He called him a pig. Bulcher had him roasted alive over his own hearth with an apple in his mouth…" her voice wavered for a second, but only a second, "…he destroyed my home and had everyone in it slaughtered. He wanted to abduct me and... do with me as he wished, I suppose. I escaped. He thinks I am dead. It was my only victory. Until now..."

Bosko had edged away from her till his back pressed hard against the wall by the fire. She must have followed him, though she had no memory of it.

"You really are insane!"

"Perhaps..."

She pushed her hand flat against his chest.

"What... are you doing?"

Bosko had changed out of his travelling gear; he wore a shirt, waistcoat and long coat, a neckerchief stuffed into the top of the shirt.

Eyes finding his, she first pulled the neckerchief free, then undid the top two buttons of his shirt.

Bosko's eyes bulged.

Hidden under the neckerchief hung a silver chain; on the end of it, a plain, unadorned gold ring. She held it between her thumb and forefinger.

"A keepsake..." she said, "...from Karoline's mother..."

Bosko swallowed but said nothing.

She pressed the ring into the wiry hair of Bosko's chest with the palm of her hand and leaned in so close her lips almost brushed his, close enough to taste the *obstler* on his breath and the sweat slicking his skin.

"Tell me this is a lie, too..."

For a moment, all she could hear was his heart thudding.

Distantly, she considered the possibility of pressing herself against a drunk man alone in his bedroom was not prudent. But what was prudence when you pursued vengeance? Vengeance required sacrifice, vengeance required throwing the dice and hoping they landed where you needed them to, and vengeance required forgetting about the consequences of your actions. Vengeance required doing whatever was necessary.

"How could you know? Are you…" Bosko finally asked in a strangled, faraway voice, "…a witch?"

Inside her thigh, Flyblown's mark tingled. Almost sensually.

"I am no witch, Captain," she breathed, "I am vengeance."

She put her lips to his ear, "Tell me, are you Karoline's father…?"

He wrapped a fist around the ring on the chain when she stepped away from him. For a heartbeat or two, he held her gaze.

When he could hold it no longer, he nodded.

She smiled.

Then sat him down, poured him a drink and explained how he could save his daughter's life.

Chapter Five

He'd never been much of a one for weddings. He supposed he'd picked that up from Old Man Ulrich, who'd studiously avoided marriage.

As weddings primarily constituted an excuse for people to get horrendously drunk, he would have thought his father would have had more time for them. However, as far as he could recall, Old Man Ulrich did his utmost when one arose to avoid going. Even when the alternative was a chilly night on a wall or patrolling a perimeter.

This one, sadly, was unavoidable.

The *Graf* had invited the "brave souls" who'd ensured his "beloved's" safe arrival at Thasbald. He suspected that was more to do with ensuring the chapel wasn't empty for the ceremony than any actual gratitude. Filling a chapel with your servants was probably a last resort.

No family, no friends, no neighbours. No local minor nobles and dignitaries. No one. Just the more notable members of the *Graf's* household.

He eyed the other side of the dingy chapel's aisle. Notable members of the *Graf's* household apparently ran at a premium, too. His steward, a few retainers, officers of the garrison.

It was almost as if the *Graf* didn't want anyone to know he was getting married...

Marriage was a grandiose affair for the nobility. A way of preserving bloodlines, sealing alliances, an opportunity to show the world how rich and important you were, an excuse for excess.

Graf Bulcher just appeared to be in a rush to finish the whole thing with a minimum of fuss.

Even the chapel had the air of an afterthought. A boxy little room with unadorned stone walls and a single small stained-glass window so dirty it was hard to tell night from day. Candles burned around the altar, while the rest of the chapel remained shadowy and unlit.

He'd never met Bulcher before, though Solace's descriptions had left a vivid and unflattering portrait in his mind. The reality was still shocking. He wasn't quite sure if he'd ever seen anyone so fat. Resplendent in a suit of aubergine-coloured velvet, he might pass for a giant fruit that had spent so long overripening on the vine that it was in danger of exploding.

Completely bald, Bulcher wore neither wig nor hat. Given the flushed complexion, it looked like a second, smaller but equally overripe, fruit balanced atop the first.

"Fuck..." Lucien leaned in and whispered, "...he'll squash that girl like a bug."

The mercenary had gone to great lengths for the wedding, having shaved off his stubble, splashed water over himself and wore clothes not soiled by mud, sweat, beer or stains of uncertain origin.

"Quite the dandy," he'd noted as they made their way to the chapel.

"Important not to upstage the groom," Lucien confided,

spitting in his hand before trying to wipe down a few strands of the less well-behaved hair remaining on his head, "even more so the bride."

Lebrecht got to stand at the front. The privilege of rank. He'd even found a new outfit from somewhere, perhaps he never left home without a set of emergency fancy clothes, just in case. Rich people did shit like that.

A smattering of their company stood at the back. Bosko, looking listless and slightly vacant-eyed, plus a couple of his more presentable men-at-arms, Gerwin and Corcilius, represented Vadia. Lucien and he were posing as Lebrecht's lieutenants.

Since their arrival, only Lebrecht, given his station, attracted any attention from Bulcher. The *Graf* had whisked him away for a private audience and luncheon the previous day where, apparently, he'd fawned and slobbered over the young nobleman. The rest of them were underlings worthy of no more note than peasants.

The remainder of their company waited with the castle's household to celebrate the wedding. Bulcher had arranged a feast; a cow and a pig had been slaughtered, and enough beer and wine hauled up from the well-stocked cellars for everyone in Thasbald to drink themselves into oblivion. Apart from Lucien and Gotz, whom, he suspected, could down most of it between them and still keep going.

He tried to look bored or awed as opposed to someone nervously checking for signs of disaster.

A dozen Thasbald soldiers lined the back of the chapel, two more stood at the front, one on either side of the altar, another two, both huge brutes, never ventured from

Bulcher's shoulders. The *Graf's* Household Guard. Each man's uniform was clean and crisp; they all wore a cuirass embossed with Bulcher's arms and a helm with a purple plume. Purple, the colour of kings and emperors, which only the Household Guard sported in Thasbald. The choice of livery clearly said something about how the *Graf* viewed himself. Armour shone, buckles and buttons sparkled, and boots gleamed. To his eye, the rest of the garrison and household were dowdy and even a little threadbare. But it seemed the *Graf* spared no expense when it came to his personal guard.

He wondered how many of them would be shit-faced on the *Graf's* booze tonight? And whether the two brutes at his side would accompany Bulcher *everywhere* on his wedding day…

"Do you think she's run away, locked herself in her room or passed out with fear?" Lucien leaned in again, stifling a yawn.

Lucien wasn't the only one getting restless, though the groom sat calmly on the first pew, one great flabby arm stretched out along the back. Thasbald's pastor stood over the *Graf,* a small, nervous-looking man who nodded and laughed too much every time Bulcher opened his mouth.

He checked behind him again, in the manner of a man wondering where the blushing (and scared shitless) bride might be. His eyes skirted over the purple-liveried soldiers. All attention front, all motionless, ten holding pikes, two banners, one of Bulcher's, the other of Vadia. He thought a pike was overdoing it for a wedding, but he wasn't aware of the local custom.

He blew out his cheeks (like a man eager to get the boring bit of the wedding over with and hit the beer) and returned his attention to the altar.

The Thasbald men-at-arms all looked like they knew what they were about. No old timers, cripples, or boys. These were seasoned fighters in their prime. They would be tough to beat in a fair fight. Luckily, they weren't planning a fair fight.

Were they staring at him now he'd turned his back?

He tried not to tick off all the people who could have betrayed them on his fingers, only partly because he knew he didn't have enough fingers.

Would Bulcher have armed them with long, ungainly pikes if he intended the soldiers to leap into the congregation?

His gaze returned to the enormous man spilling off the first pew. The *Graf* appeared comfortable and relaxed, especially for an old man about to marry a fourteen-year-old girl. But Bulcher was a man with enemies, and they were strangers; only a fool didn't treat a stranger with suspicion if there were people out in the world who'd gladly slice his throat open. And he doubted very much Solace was the only one of them.

He'd checked their room multiple times. The walls were thick, as was the ceiling. He'd found no hollow spaces where someone might listen to their conversations. Castles were full of secret places, some for hiding, some for moving around unseen, some for spying. Thasbald was no different. But their rooms were for common soldiers, and he hoped any spyholes or listening posts had been reserved for where the important people slept.

Or the old man had grown complacent in his fortress out here in the marshes.

And how old was this old man?

If he didn't know, he would have said fifty at most, though with no hair to grey and all the blubber stretching away wrinkles, and he hadn't actually seen him up close... and... and...

Perhaps Solace was right, and Bulcher was drinking a vampire's blood to extend his life. In the end, it didn't matter. No vampire's blood would save him from what Solace intended.

He'd killed men. In Tassau, in The Wolf's Tower, in Ettestein. But they had all died in the heat of battle when the only alternative to killing was dying yourself. To watch a man go about his day, knowing that you were going to kill him, or at least play a part in his death... that did not sit easily. What honour is there in murdering a defenceless man?

Even one as monstrous as *Graf* Bulcher.

The chapel door finally squeaked open, interrupting his thoughts. A skittish-looking servant hurried down the aisle to whisper in Bulcher's ear. The *Graf* nodded and hauled himself upright with a grunt and a helping hand from one of the purple-liveried guards. The Pastor smiled, bobbed his head some more and backed hastily away. It took a moment for the *Graf* to get himself steady and you really wouldn't want to be in his way if he fell.

Around the chapel, the people who weren't already standing got to their feet.

After another few minutes of muttering and foot shuffling,

the door opened again, and Karoline appeared. Despite the veil covering her face, she had the air of a woman walking to her execution rather than her wedding. Head lowered, shoulders slumped, hands clutching a posy of dried flowers, she managed a couple of faltering steps before coming to a halt. Hilde and Elin were behind her. They exchanged a quick glance as if asking each other what they should do if the girl bolted for freedom.

Bulcher twisted around, eyes narrowing. He made an impatient gesture with a fleshy, bejewelled hand then turned back to the Pastor. If Karoline didn't hurry, the *Graf* looked like he'd send the two brutes who shadowed him to drag her screaming to the altar.

Bosko left his pew and hurried down the aisle. He didn't catch their eye as he passed.

As far as he knew, Solace hadn't told anybody else that she suspected Bosko was Karoline's real father; it wasn't the kind of rumour you spread lightly. It would cause almost as much fuss as murdering the groom...

Still, she'd said Bosko and his Vadians were with them.

Which meant more souls for him to mistrust.

Bosko leaned into Karoline, whispered something, smiled and stood at her side. She nearly dropped the posy in the process, which did have a suitably funereal air to it, but managed to find the Captain's proffered arm with one shaking hand.

The *Freiherr* Hoss had, apparently, been too weak and frail to make the journey to Thasbald to give his daughter away, the symbolic act of passing ownership of the daughter to her husband, leaving her to make her progress down the aisle alone.

Now, the man who *was* her father stepped in to do the task.

Karoline made her way to the altar in silence. The only sound besides the scuffing of leather on stone as they passed was the sniffing from beneath the veil.

Hilde glanced at him. She wore a new dress and a brightly white linen cap. She looked pretty. He smiled and stopped thinking about murdering the groom for a second or two.

Bulcher shot Bosko a curious look, the kind you might reserve for finding something unwanted floating in your beer. Karoline, he didn't acknowledge at all.

Bosko patted Karoline's arm, before retreating to the pews with Hilde and Elin.

The ceremony was short. The Pastor mouthed a few words about God and the sanctity of marriage, then got on with the vows. Bulcher's voice was oddly high-pitched for a man his size, but they still boomed loudly enough to echo around the chapel. Karoline, he couldn't hear at all. He assumed she said *yes,* and *I do* at the right moments. She managed not to faint, vomit or run away.

So, as far as weddings go, it went as well as anyone could have expected, allowing them all to get on with the more serious business of celebrating.

And, of course, the killing.

*

The dress was perfect. Plain and dowdy as any housemaid's, while the linen cap hid her shorn hair.

Hilde brought them down that morning, and she changed after the men left the room, save for Hugo who kept watch outside, just in case.

"How is Karoline?" she asked as she stripped and dressed quickly. Not through modesty, the room was freezing.

"Terrified," Hilde tried to poke some life back into the room's tiny and inadequate fire, "if that man gets his hands on her..."

"He won't."

The stoking paused, "Is this going to work, my lady?"

"Yes. And I've told you, don't call me that here. My name is Celine. Nothing else. Understand?"

Hilde looked over her shoulder, "Sorry... not done anything like this before."

"None of us have."

"I suppose..." Hilde rested the poker against the wall; there was no more wood.

"You should get back to Karoline; you need to keep her strong."

"Yes... Celine."

"Elin, can we trust her?"

"She dotes on Lady Karoline; she will say nothing."

"Keep an eye on her anyway."

"And if she does say something to someone?"

"Stop her..." she patted herself down.

"How should I stop her?"

She smiled coldly, "By any means necessary. Our lives depend on Bulcher suspecting nothing. All our lives. Including Ulrich's..."

Hilde nodded; she might have blushed, too, but the light was poor.

"Now, will I pass?" she stepped forward, straightening her

cap.

Hilde looked her up and down.

"As long as no one gets too close."

"Too close?"

Hilde turned her hands but held her gaze, "From a distance, you will pass for a maid. Just don't let anyone look you in the eye."

She raised an eyebrow.

"You're too bold of eye... servants spend half their lives getting shouted at, threatened, insulted, even beaten. Soon knocks any boldness girls might have out of them. If a servant can go a day without being noticed, 'tis generally considered a good day."

"I see..."

Hilde grinned, "Well, most of us, anyway..."

"That's good advice... thank you..." she smiled at Hilde and thought of her blood splashing onto a church's stone floor.

If I told her, I could save her...

"We should be going."

"Yes."

If I can stop this happening to you, I will...

The words came out of the darkness. The promise she made to the girl in her vision, dying on the floor in Magdeburg, neck opened by Saul's fangs. Before she'd known that girl was Hilde.

The promise jarred her. She'd made it in good faith to a stranger but was now prepared to use someone she knew for her own ends.

What am I becoming?

"Does this show?" she asked, avoiding Hilde's eyes as she lifted her left arm. The sleeve of the dress seemed loose enough to conceal the sheath and dagger strapped to her forearm. But it was prudent to double-check everything when you were about the business of murder.

Hilde shook her head.

She draped a shawl around her shoulders.

"Best we make a start then."

Outside, Hugo leaned against the wall.

"Seen no one," he said.

"You know what to do?"

The boy nodded.

She touched his arm, "If things go wrong, save yourself. Get out of here any way you can. No one will be looking for you."

"Nothing will go wrong."

"But in case it does. We wouldn't have caught you if you'd run earlier from *The Eagle's Claw*."

A slow grin spread across the boy's face to go with his quick shrug, "Things didn't work out so bad for me..."

She stood aside, "Go."

Hugo turned on his heels and padded off in the opposite direction.

"You like that boy..." Hilde said, voice low.

Did she? She really didn't know. The world had become populated solely with tools to use, or so it sometimes felt.

"Walk," she said by way of an answer, "best we don't talk..."

The household was busy. A wedding feast took considerable preparation. And not for family, dignitaries and nobility (as far as she knew, none of those were here) but for all the people under his roof, from the lowest scullery maids and stable boys upwards. Say what you like about the despicable, demonic blood-guzzling, murdering bastard, he looked after his own.

Perhaps it helped them turn the other way when his wives died unexpectedly…

In a world of want, fear and death, buying loyalty took a lot less. Food, warmth and security probably did it.

She kept her head down, but no one paid them any heed. If anybody asked, she was one of Lady Karoline's maids running errands for her mistress on her wedding day. No time to chat; there are a hundred things to do!

Nobody wanted to chat.

Voices were low, heads were down, laughter absent.

Bulcher might have their loyalty, but there was little joy in evidence.

Do they all know Karoline will be dead within the year?

Maybe sooner if Bulcher could dispose of *Freiherr* Hoss and her brother quickly. And any other distant male heirs that might otherwise emerge. Most of the Empire operated under Saric Law, which meant a woman only inherited land and title when the male side of the family was extinct.

As with her family. She had no cousins, uncles, or nephews however many times removed on her father's side. Not common, but not rare. Karoline's family would be much the same. And if the *Freiherr* did have any distant male claimants for his title… well, she wouldn't be surprised if the Red Company hadn't already dealt with them.

But that was going to change.

Bulcher would bring no more women to Thasbald, and Karoline would not die within the year.

Yes, that's all very good. But what about Hilde?

Would she die within the year?

The thoughts squirmed in her grasp despite her best efforts to strangle them.

This is not the time!

No, it wasn't.

One murder at a time, eh?

Hilde led her up to the floors that housed the better guests. Currently, that meant Karoline and Lebrecht. After the wedding, Karoline would relocate to accommodation close to *Graf* Bulcher's private rooms, for matrimonial convenience. No doubt, he intended to make the most of the girl before disposing of her.

Waste not want not!

The wedding was at noon, followed by feasting and celebrations. When done, Bulcher would take his wife to her new home. In the meantime, Karoline's possessions, all those trunks and cases from her carriage, would be moved from their current location to the *Grafin's* rooms. Located within the Silver Tower.

What was it with men wanting to lock women up in towers?

She supposed that was a question for the ages. In any event, she would be going with the trunks to the new *Grafin's* rooms... and when Bulcher arrived to consummate the wedding... well, he wouldn't be locking anyone else up in his Silver Tower again once she finished with him.

A shrill, almost screeching voice jolted her thoughts back

to her surroundings. One she knew well despite not hearing it for long. It stuck in the memory as it so ill-suited the huge body it belonged to.

She forced her right hand from reaching for the dagger concealed in her left sleeve.

Bulcher.

He crossed the corridor ahead of them.

Bigger and even more hideous than she remembered. Resplendent in aubergine-coloured velvet, jabbered away to a tall, spindly man as thin as the *Graf* was fat. Two soldiers followed in their wake, big, heavy-set men in helms, armour and purple livery.

None of them looked their way; two lowly maids were of no interest to them. Soldiers rarely saw women and children as threats.

"Celine...?"

She blinked.

Hilde was leaning across her, brow crumpled in concern.

Her heart hammered, her hands shook, nausea crashed over her, filling her mouth with saliva. She reached out, seizing Hilde's hand as the world spun nauseously around her.

She thought her knees were going to give way.

What an absolute delight you are, my dear...

Bulcher's words, from when her father had first introduced the toad, echoed. Once more clammy fat fingers encased her hand, again wet lips slobbered over her flesh, small, greedy eyes lingered and devoured, and that smell... oh God, she'd forgotten how he smelt... sickly perfumed oil, old sweat mixed with something she'd never been able to define, a stink of rot, decay, corruption like that huge, bloated body was already dead on the inside.

She doubled over and spat out a stream of saliva to splat onto the stone floor. Her gorge rose behind it, but she swallowed it down.

"My lady...?" Hilde was asking.

How many times do I have to tell that girl not to call me that?

Wiping her left sleeve over her lips and chin, she sucked in air through her nostrils.

How am I going to do this?

How?

Hilde opened the nearest door and bundled her in.

She found herself slumped in a chair by a dead fire in a room smelling of dust and disuse.

Hilde crouched in front of her.

"We can still walk away from this?"

When the world stopped spinning, she shook her head.

"No."

Hilde chewed her bottom lip and nodded.

I do that. Been trying to stop.

She swept the linen cap from her head to run fingers through her short hair.

"I will be fine. Don't worry. The sight of him... startled me..."

"That was Bulcher?"

"In all his glory..."

"Jesus, no wonder Karoline looks so ill..."

"He's done this to other women. He will do it again. We must stop him even without what he did to me and my people."

"Of course..."

"You don't look convinced."

"Haven't got no quibbles about..." her voice dropped even lower "...killing a slug like that."

"But?"

Her shoulder rolled, "Rich people's business..."

She raised her eyebrows.

Hilde shook her head, "No time for my crazy thoughts; we need to get you into the room before Karoline finishes with Elin."

"Yes..."

She rose to her feet, knees still wobbly enough for Hilde to grab her arm.

"Thank you."

If I can stop this happening to you, I will...

She shook the empty promise and Hilde's hand away, but before she could cross to the door, the girl's arms were about her, hugging her fiercely.

She stiffened and made to pull away. What did the girl think she was doing! Instead, she found herself folding into the embrace.

"Everything's going to end right, you see if it don't...." Hilde whispered in her ear.

The girl was shaking. So was she.

When was the last time someone hugged her?

She couldn't remember.

As much as part of her wanted to slap Hilde's face for the temerity, for a moment, just a moment, she felt safe. She felt warm; she felt someone gave a damn about her.

Then she saw Hilde in another embrace, hanging from Saul's arm, blood pattering onto crimson-washed stone.

She stepped away.

"Why did you do that?"

"My ma told us whenever someone we cared about needed a hug, we should never be afraid to give it..." Hilde's lip twitched, "...my family are all gone now, so... I have to find new people to hug..."

"You... care about me?"

"Of course. Ulrich cares about you, so I care about you."

Several things swirled about her mind, none of them much suited to a day when you set out to do murder. Least of all, the one that came closest to burning her lips.

Ulrich cares about me?

Instead, she mumbled a thank you and something else she could not remember the instant it left her mouth.

Concern remained etched upon Hilde's face.

If I make a mess of this, she'll die along with the rest of us. No wonder she's concerned about me...

"'tis just a moment. Fear... I suppose. Bulcher has haunted me for a year. Seeing him again, in the flesh..." she shuddered.

"There is a lot of flesh."

Her laugh took her by surprise. Hilde touched her arm again and gave it a little squeeze. More impropriety.

"Come, let us do this," she said, turning away to escape Hilde's large chestnut eyes. If she looked closely, she could see her own reflection in them. If she looked closer still, she fancied she would also see the fiery orange light of a dying city.

If I can stop this happening to you, I will...

The corridor was empty and silent. They hurried down it together.

Bulcher's stink lingered heavily enough for her stomach to turn again. But this time, her knees held firm.

They passed no one else on the way to Karoline's rooms.

She loitered outside, continually looking back and forth, while Hilde went in. A few seconds later, the door reopened, and the girl ushered her in.

Hilde pressed a finger to her lips, and they crossed to another room, where Karoline's trunks and cases were piled. Voices, small and uncertain, floated from the bedchamber. Karoline and Elin. It would have been easier to let Elin know their plans, but she wasn't sure if she could trust the maid. Karoline had not been certain either, so they told her nothing.

After closing the door carefully behind her, Hilde opened one of the largest trunks. A few dresses covered the bottom, otherwise it was empty. Save for a crossbow and bolts. Hilde pulled the dresses out.

She took off her shoes and threw them into the trunk. Bare feet were better for sneaky work.

"Good luck..." Hilde smiled once she'd climbed in after the shoes and then placed the dresses over her. When the lid closed, darkness rushed in.

She heard Hilde's footsteps cross the room, the door squeak open and shut.

All that remained was to stay quiet and wait for Bulcher's servants to take Karoline's belongings to her new home in the Silver Tower during the wedding.

Her fingers felt the sheathed blade buckled to her left wrist. She had hours yet. She would fill them imagining what that blade would do to Siegfried, *Graf* Bulcher...

In the Company of Shadows

Chapter Six

The wedding feast started early, and Bulcher had provisioned it generously enough to suggest it would go on late.

Their plan was fraught with danger, and if it went awry, it would cost them all their lives. Many things could go wrong, though he was starting to suspect what might scupper everything would not be a careless word, an observant servant, or a diligent guard, but the fact they would all get so pissed celebrating the wedding they might completely forget they were here to kill the groom.

He glared at Lucien, sloshing ale left, right and centre as he joined in yet another toast to *Graf* Bulcher's good health. Karoline's good health seemed far less important; the girl barely got a mention.

"Let us drink like 'tis our last night on Earth!" Lucien cried, swivelling around on the shared bench to envelop him in a fierce and rather fragrant bear hug.

"Stop looking so fucking miserable," Lucien hissed in his ear, "half the empire is starving, and they're giving us a feast. If you don't drink and keep looking like you've shat in your britches, someone will notice..."

In a loud voice, Lucien sat back and finished, "Don't worry; next time you ask her, make sure she's had plenty to drink. A girl is far more likely to say yes if she's pissed!"

Laughter rippled about them.

He picked up his own ale pot and lifted it in a mock salute.

They sat amongst Thasbald's soldiers and servants, who packed the Great Hall around long wooden tables. The happy couple occupied a far grander table along a wall festooned with the heads of dead animals, upon a platform for all to see through the palls of pipe smoke. The Pastor, Steward and more senior household members on either side. Lebrecht and Bosko, as *Freiherr* Hoss' representative, made up the numbers on the ends of the table. And that was it. No locals, dignitaries, clergy, or lesser nobles come to fawn before Bulcher, no greater ones to be wined and entertained at his expense.

They were in the middle of a war and travelling was dangerous, but it still struck him as odd.

Only Gotz sat with them. The rest of their company were spread around the hall. Ola and Enni, the two barmaids from *The Eagle's Claw* who had taken up with the Vadian men-at-arms, Egon and Hector, were here, too, somewhere. He prayed the beer didn't loosen tongues or provoke second thoughts.

"How long before everyone is drunk?" he asked.

"Soon enough!" Gotz hoisted his ale pot and tapped it against Lucien's.

He picked at some of the remaining food. There was meat for all, both freshly roasted and sausages of numerous kinds, sour red cabbage, kale stew, steaming vegetables, loaves of warm crusty bread, savoury dumplings, pickles and sweet treats aplenty. It kept arriving from the kitchens in endless waves.

He should be filling his face. It had been a long time since he'd seen so much food, let alone ate it. Thasbald's larders and cellars were clearly well stocked. Even with the amount Bulcher was eating.

Every time his eye fell upon the *Graf* (and he was a man who morbidly drew the eye), Bulcher was devouring more food. He ate whilst talking, he ate whilst laughing, and he ate whilst gesticulating. He'd probably take something with him to nibble on if he needed a piss, too.

He supposed you didn't end up Bulcher's size without putting in the hard work.

Lucien was right; he should be making merry like everybody else. But as everybody else was getting shit-faced, too, he wasn't quite sure whose attention he was in danger of drawing.

He assumed the *whole* garrison wasn't drinking itself into oblivion. That would be too easy but judging by the number of people jammed cheek by jowl into the Great Hall, there couldn't be too many left on the walls, let alone elsewhere.

Lucien hoisted his ale pot heavenwards once more.

"May the *Graf* be blessed with strong, healthy sons!"

Like his previous efforts, Lucien's toast was typical of the kind of well-meaning salutes drunks offered a matrimonial table, and given Bulcher's single heir, his absent son Leopold, he would have thought a welcome one. But the lifted cups and slurry cheers from the Thasbald men around them were half-hearted and hollow. Perhaps they were getting bored with toasting, but a few knowing glances flicked between their newfound friends.

He wasn't the only one to notice.

"Does the *Graf* not yearn for more sons?" Gotz asked the shaven-headed Thasbald soldier, whose face appeared frozen in a permanent frown, sitting beside them.

"All men want sons," the man, named Faro, shrugged and found something important to stare at in the bottom of his ale pot.

"The *Graf* only has one child, hasn't he?" Gotz pressed.

"The *Graf* has..." another soldier, a swarthy man with a long face called Assunto, began. Faro shot his comrade a dark look but confined himself to sloshing more ale into his pot, "...been most unlucky. He only has one heir. Leopold."

"'tis a hard world, full of sorrows," Lucien agreed before breaking out into another grin and hoisting his cup again, "which is why 'tis best to spend as much if it as drunk as humanly possible!"

That brought a more enthusiastic cheer from those in earshot; one ruddy-faced fellow even leaned over to slap Lucien on the back.

There was a trick to being popular; he suspected it partly involved drinking copiously, grinning like an idiot at every conceivable opportunity, laughing too loudly and the ability to conjure vast amounts of horseshit to fill in the yawning chasms that existed between all men. No doubt, there was more to it than that, and whatever all the arcane ingredients were, Lucien knew them intimately.

On the other hand, he simply felt more alone in a crowd than he did when he was on his own.

The laughter and voices buzzed around him. He tried not to appear annoyed or surly or uncomfortable. But didn't think he made much of a fist of it.

The conversation swiftly returned to more suitable subjects for a wedding feast – a joke about a milking maid with particularly large, rough hands – and he excused himself to piss.

He was pissing rather a lot, not because of a weak bladder but because, frankly, the company of the stinky barrels in the privy was better than that of most of the men around the table.

When he got back, fiddlers had struck up a jaunty, raucous tune, and people were on their feet dancing, which always made his heart sink further, though he doubted anyone here would try to make *him* dance.

On the top table, Bulcher clapped along, red-faced and jolly. He seemed to be enjoying himself.

A thought occurred. One he hadn't considered before.

What if Saul had been lying? What if the Red Company's assault on The Wolf's Tower had nothing to do with Bulcher? What if they were here to kill an innocent man?

Bulcher was grotesque and hideous, with a taste for excess and young girls... but had he really sent the Red Company to kidnap Solace and make her his bride? It was an awful lot of trouble to go to...

He squeezed through the drunken revellers, catching Usk's eye as he passed him and the Gothen soldiers hunkered together. They, at least, didn't seem to be out of their heads yet. Usk winked and grinned at him.

He nodded back.

A maid laden with ale pushed past him, avoiding the groping hands of the men packed on the benches with weary resignation.

He'd never been to a lord's wedding feast before; his father and he had always been far too lowly for their presence to ever be required or desired. In Thasbald, however, the *Graf* had invited everyone, regardless of their station.

What did that say of Bulcher?

He preferred the company of the lower sorts? His own class shunned him? Did it help to buy the loyalty of his household?

When he returned to their table, Lucien climbed to his feet.

"Now my weasel requires a shake," the mercenary said, entirely unnecessarily, before wandering off, bumping into everyone he could on the way.

He assumed, and hoped, that was an affectation rather than due to the fool really getting shit-faced. He slumped onto the bench next to Gotz, who was troubling the remains of a chicken bone.

On the high table, Bulcher still clapped merrily away; next to him, Karoline continued to stare ahead, blank-faced and dead-eyed.

"No sign of the nuptials commencing," Gotz said, attempting to retrieve chicken from between the blackened stumps of his teeth with his little finger.

The happy couple leaving to begin the happy coupling was the sign for things to start happening.

"Doesn't look in any hurry," he agreed.

"Guess he's paying for all this," Gotz examined what he'd speared out of his mouth, wrinkled his nose, then sucked it off his finger, "So, suppose he wants his money's worth."

"He was in enough of a hurry to get the poor girl here…"

Gotz chuckled, "Well, if it were me…"

"You'd already have her in your bed?"

"Along with enough ale and chicken to keep me going till dawn."

He raised an eyebrow.

"Well, midnight."

His other eyebrow joined the first.

Gotz started foraging on the other side of his mouth as he winked, "Alright, but she'd definitely have a couple of minutes to remember."

He snorted out a laugh.

"You never married?"

Gotz shook his head.

"Why not?"

"Either because I like women too much or not enough. Never been quite sure which…"

His eyes returned to the high table. Bulcher stopped clapping to shovel more food into his slobbering maw.

Perhaps he intended to ignore his new wife all night and not go to her chamber. Which would be a problem.

Gotz summoned his attention with a rap of a knuckle on the table.

Be patient, the old soldier's eyes said, as he sloshed more ale into both their pots.

He nodded his understanding, took a sip of ale, swilled it around his mouth before returning it to his cup as if taking a second.

And then went back to watching the man they were waiting to kill.

*

She tried to remain still, even when certain the rooms were empty. She'd heard nothing for what felt like hours, though, she was sure, time flowed slower when curled up in a dark box.

For a while, distant, muffled voices provided a distraction. She didn't hear Karoline speak once, although she was pretty sure the sobbing had been the bride-to-be's. But there had been nothing for some time now. Would the ceremony have begun yet? Bulcher strutting like a fat purple peacock with his latest bride. His latest victim.

And last.

Her hand stroked the polished wood of the crossbow's stock. Bosko had left the weapon in the trunk for her. She had her dagger, but Bulcher might find the crossbow more persuasive when she started telling him what to do.

Would she just kill him on sight?

Her fingers found the metal of the trigger. The bow wasn't loaded or wound. She wanted to neither shoot herself nor lessen the bow's tension, but she couldn't help but imagine the whoosh of it firing, the shudder in her hands and the wet slap of the bolt slamming into Bulcher's blubbery hide.

She mustn't.

She needed information.

She needed vengeance.

Killing the bastard quickly wouldn't achieve either satisfactorily.

Her hand moved, seemingly of its own accord, to the pouch around her neck.

She needed something else, too.

Explanation.

However puerile, repulsive, laughable or ridiculous, she wanted to hear Bulcher explain just why he unleashed those demons on her home. To take her as his wife? To repay her father's slight?

Was that all it had been for?

Surely, there had to be something more?

Didn't there?

Voices.

Her heart beat harder, her hand froze about the bag of grey dust. She even held her breath for a second or two, although she suspected that was taking caution too far.

The voices grew louder, a door opened, boots squeaked.

"Shit... *all* of this?"

"Yep."

"Fucking hell..."

The boots moved some more.

"Can't we just-"

"No. All of it. You heard Seck as well as me."

"The cunt."

"The cunt who pays us. And the cunt who'll flay our hides if we don't get this shit up to the Silver Tower before the *Graf* wants to make use of *his* new cunt."

Something creaked; she imagined one of the men sitting on a trunk. Not hers, at least.

"So, while everyone else is getting merry, we're-"

"If you don't like it, you can piss off and find something better. Out there..." she thought that likely accompanied by a nod or a thumb hitched towards the nearest window.

"Just don't seem fair, that's all..."

"What you seen of life to make you think any of it's fair? Come on, soonest we start, soonest we finish. They'll be plenty for us. The *Graf* doesn't scrimp on weddings. You gotta give him that."

That got a snort. Then a few curses she doubted they would ever knowingly utter in the presence of a lady, and the boots shuffled away.

She scratched the nose that hadn't itched until the two servants arrived.

The Graf didn't scrimp on weddings...

How many had he had?

She wasn't sure how much time passed before the men returned. Neither said anything more, and another of Lady Karoline's trunks headed off to its new home. This time, she counted slowly till they came back. 527.

Karoline had ten trunks.

Her turn yet?

No. They picked another. She didn't take it personally.

She got to 540 this time. They were slacking.

"Fuck, I need a drink," the whiny servant said. He had a nasally voice suited to moaning.

"Soonest we-"

"Yes, so you bloody said! Give me a minute, will you."

Boots scuffed, floorboards creaked.

"You seen the new lady?" the moany servant asked.

"No. Heard she looks half dead already, though," a laugh faded into a sigh, "Poor cow..."

"She isn't poor."

"You know what I mean..."

"All I know is what Seck wants. And Seck wants it

because our master wants it. So, get off your fucking lardy arse. This one next."

"Don't you ever-"

"No. I don't. And if you know what's good for you, you never will either."

A creak, a huff, a curse. Another trunk hauled away.

She started counting again, tapping out each number against the hilt of the dagger in her wrist sheath. How many times would she cut Bulcher with it later? However many. It wouldn't be enough.

Whatever could be?

What happens if I do kill them all?

She shoved the thought away. There was no point dreaming of a future she might never see. One enemy at a time. One slice of vengeance. That was all she could do.

Damn.

She'd lost count.

She wanted to stretch her legs, she wanted to roll on her other side, she wanted to hear Bulcher beg and scream. She forced herself to still. Discipline. Patience. They didn't have the shiny, bloody allure of vengeance, but she needed those qualities. Today and every other day. Till the very end of the Night's Road.

A door opened. Boots approached.

"This one," the older, less moany of the two men said.

"Can't we just dump a couple in the cesspit? She won't bloody-"

"This one."

A sigh. More shuffling. A grunt, and she moved.

"Jesus! What's in this!"

She went back down again. Hard.

"Full of gold and jewels, you reckon?" the moany one asked.

"None of our business, come on."

Hands clapped, then the world started moving.

She braced her bare feet against one end of the trunk and hands the other to stop herself from sliding around. Hilde had covered her with a couple of Karoline's dresses in case anyone decided to peep inside, but leather belts secured the trunk, so no one should.

Cold sweat slickened her skin. She gritted her teeth to ensure she didn't cry out whenever her head found the side of the trunk as the servants roughly manoeuvred their cargo along corridors and up stairs.

She didn't think she weighed that much, but the curses of the two servants suggested otherwise. Perhaps it was the crossbow? Absurdly, that made her want to giggle.

The curses kept coming, and for someone who'd grown up surrounded by soldiers, she was surprised to find several she'd never heard.

She hadn't counted, but it seemed a lot longer this time, and that was just for the two of them to get to Karoline's new rooms, let alone return to the old one, presumably due to her gigantic weight.

The cursing increased, and the trunk tilted as the servants manhandled it up one of Thasbald's spiral staircases towards the tower where Bulcher planned to keep Karoline for the rest of her, she strongly suspected, very short life. She'd fled Ettestein to avoid being imprisoned in one high tower, and here she was, smuggling herself into another. There was some irony there if she could spare a moment to think about it. As it was, she was too busy sliding around the trunk.

"They getting heavier, or you getting weaker?" someone laughed, a different voice. Guards always protected Bulcher's private rooms; the same would apply to his wife's. Hence, she had to hide in a trunk to enter unnoticed. She could have posed as one of Karoline's maids, but that would have meant trusting Elin not to blab or question what they were doing.

"We can manage, but thanks so much for offering..." the moany one grumbled.

Doors opened before she hit the floor again. This time, she stayed there.

The sound of panting echoed beyond the darkness.

Then something thumped on top of the trunk.

A servant's arse, most likely.

Slowly, she slid the blade from its sheath strapped to her wrist. Just in case.

"We'll be dragging this shit out of here again in a few weeks," the whiny one said.

A squeak as the servant moved atop of her.

"How many are there down there now, do you think?"

"How many what?"

A long pause.

"Trunks... what else?"

"You ask too many questions. Keep them to yourself. The *Graf* don't like questions about his business..."

Another shuffle.

"Yeah, I know..."

"Then keep it shut. Seriously, Luds, you don't want to end up going downstairs, do you?"

"Nah, course not... but what *is* downstairs?"

"Nothing. That's all you need to know. *Nothing* is downstairs but rats and cobwebs. What's downstairs, Luds?"

A drawn-out pause, then, in a small, nasally voice, "Rats and cobwebs."

"And don't you forget it. Now, c'mon... let's keep going. Hopefully, that fucker was the heaviest."

A door opened, and the voices faded.

After a while, she remembered to start counting again.

Chapter Seven

"And behold, joy and gladness, killing oxen and slaughtering sheep, eating flesh and drinking wine. Let us eat and drink, for tomorrow we die!"

"That sounds like it's from the Bible?"

Gotz nodded, casting bleary eyes around the surrounding bedlam, "Isaiah... sounds appropriate for this night, don't you think?"

"I didn't take you for a Bible man?"

Gotz smiled and turned those tired, heavy eyes in his direction, "Oh, there's something for everyone in there if you look. That's why so much blood gets spilt over it, I suppose."

He didn't argue. He knew enough of the Bible to avoid ending up on a pyre as a heretic or non-believer, but no more.

He let his eyes move over the throng to the high table.

Music played, people danced, and not just on the floor. Revellers sang heartily together, but not always to the same song. Toasts still rang out, though often so slurred and incoherent they could have been toasting the Pope, the Emperor or the King of Sweden as much as the happy couple.

Food had stopped appearing, maybe because they'd eaten the larders empty, maybe because the serving girls were now being wined, danced and groped around the hall rather than fetching it from the kitchens. The way things were going, he wouldn't have been surprised to see the tables cleared and the women stripped and thrown over them for the use of all and sundry.

And above it all, the sloshed ale and ever-thickening pipe smoke, the ribald songs and braying laughter, the whirling dancers and furious jigs, Bulcher remained, looking down upon the mayhem and smiling from ear to ear, domed pate glistening in the candlelight.

Someone stumbling into him jerked his attention away. He reached for his sword, despite not wearing it, fearing their plans discovered, as he twisted around to find one of the serving maids had bumped into him.

"'scuse me, gorgeous," she ran sweaty fingers through his hair before giggling and staggering on between the rows of benches.

"She had her tit out!" was all he could say to Gotz.

"I noticed that," the old man nodded, eyes still on the retreating woman, "do you think she whores?"

"I doubt she's in the mood for charging..."

Gotz sighed and rubbed his chin, as if wondering if they really needed to kill Bulcher and seize the castle *this* night.

Lucien returned with more ale. It seemed you had to fetch your own now the maids had joined the festivities.

"Some wedding, huh?" Lucien slumped down between them. Most of the Thasbald men seated on the benches around them had moved to the cleared area beneath the high table, where they could more easily slosh beer in their lord's direction, jig with the fiddlers and paw women.

"Almost seems a shame to spoil it..." Gotz helped himself to one of the ales.

He shot the old soldier a look and hoped he was joking.

Before he could say anything, Lucien nudged him with his elbow. *Graf* Bulcher was struggling to his feet. He would have thought him heading out for a piss at last, but he was ushering Karoline upwards too. The girl blinked a couple of times, then took the hand her new husband offered as willingly as anyone might their executioner's.

Karoline summoned a rictus smile from somewhere. It lasted only as long as it took for Bulcher's bejewelled sausage fingers to wrap around hers like a bloated, deformed spider consuming its prey.

Bulcher patted the air with his free hand.

The music stopped, and the voices faded to silence. All eyes snapped to Thasbald's lord in an instant.

Most drunks, in his experience, were not so easy to bring to order. But in Thasbald no one shouted, no one sang, no wit offered wisdom or matrimonial advice. Nothing. In a heartbeat, it turned from a festival to a funeral.

"My friends..." Bulcher said, "...'tis time to bid you all farewell for the night..."

His voice was too high-pitched and screechy for such a big man. It would have set his teeth on edge even if he hadn't known what kind of a man Bulcher was.

"...pray continue to enjoy the feast, drink and sing. We all return to our duties tomorrow, but tonight, we celebrate. My wife and I wish you all good cheer!"

Bulcher's steward applauded, which was the cue for everyone else to do the same.

"Drink and make merry!" Bulcher waved, leading the terrified Karoline along the table. The two household guards who'd stood at his shoulders throughout fell in behind them.

Two more Household Guards walked ahead of the couple as they crossed the hall. None of those four had touched a drink, and all had the air of men who knew how to handle themselves. Whatever else happened tonight, Bulcher wouldn't be the only one to die.

The Household Guards cleared a path, though even the drunkest drunks ensured they were well out of the way before the happy couple passed. Bulcher smiling broadly, the glassy-eyed Karoline shuffled at his side, her hand still engulfed within her new husband's.

On the top table, Bosko stopped staring. He was the only one not clapping. Lebrecht moved along to his side and slapped a hand on the Vadian captain's shoulder as he whispered something in his ear. Bosko nodded.

The time was here.

His stomach made a sick lurch.

Solace, all being well, waited in Karoline's chamber. He had begged her that he should go, but she refused. Bulcher was grossly fat. A huge man. Undoubtedly slow and weak, but Solace weighed little more than one of his legs…

The wedding party passed where they stood, and he clapped and cheered as enthusiastically as everybody else. Though he noticed many of the locals seemed to find reasons to turn their eyes elsewhere as Bulcher and his bride went by.

Karoline looked like some inoffensive little creature that

had inexplicably found itself in a bear pit.

The clapping continued until husband, wife, and the four soldiers passed through the big doors of the hall, opened by two more of the Household Guard, who followed their master and the other soldiers out into the flickering shadows beyond.

The clapping and cheering faded with them.

For one awful moment, he thought everybody would head off to bed themselves. Then, like a shuddering sigh of relief, the music started again, and voices filled the Great Hall to its high vaulted oak arches.

Lucien sat back down and reached for his ale pot. When he glared at him, the mercenary just shook his head.

Not yet. Wait. Be patient.

Someone might notice if they all went scarpering out of the hall in Bulcher's wake. He forced his knees to bend and wrapped fingers around his ale.

He wanted to ask how long but didn't. He knew. They all knew.

Instead, he tried to smile as Lucien launched into another ribald anecdote. Which, at least, ensured the locals would keep away from them for the next few minutes.

He'd known some slow time since riding out from The Wolf's Tower with Captain Kadelburg and the doomed garrison to investigate the fire in Tassau. But these seemed some of the very longest.

Despite himself, he threw back the ale. He felt stone-cold sober, so reckoned it would do him no harm. Once he cast it aside, he clenched the fingers of his good hand into a fist and squeezed as hard as he could.

I've fought before. I've killed before. But I've never done murder before.

Bulcher might be a monster, but how many men and women around him were, too? They appeared ordinary enough. But-

Lucien slammed down his ale pot and pushed himself unsteadily upwards, "I need some air and a piss!" he declared loudly.

"Your bladder's as bad as mine!" Gotz laughed, following the mercenary to his feet.

He found his throat too dry to say anything but followed them all the same.

Bosko and Lebrecht were no longer on the top table, nor were Paasche, Usk and the other Gothens at theirs. The Vadians had been on the other side of the hall and there were too many bodies between to see them. Laughter echoed around them; a knot of men danced a frenetic jig. They passed a kissing couple as they made their way to the main doors, the woman's arse plonked amongst the ale puddles of a long table.

Nobody paid them any heed. All the Household Guards, the ones on duty at least, had retreated with Bulcher. Only drunks and servants remained, and the servants were seemingly intent on catching up with the drunks as soon as possible.

How many of the garrison and household weren't in the Great Hall?

He supposed they'd soon find out.

Outside the Great Hall was a lobby area, and to their left sat an even bigger set of doors, the main exit of the Keep.

To their right, wide stairs swept up into the castle's heart, and other doors led elsewhere. One to a room full of barrels to piss in.

Swoon stood bent over, hands on his knees, strings of drool dripping from his lips onto a puddle on the flagstones.

"This one never could take a drink!" Usk shouted for all to hear, whilst slapping Swoon's back.

"Get the pup to his bed!" Lucien laughed equally loudly, "He's embarrassing us all!"

Bosko and Lebrecht were coming through the hall doors, seemingly deep in conversation.

"My Lord!" Gotz said, hurrying over to Lebrecht.

Behind them, the Vadians filed through the doors after their Captain in dribs and drabs. A couple looked edgy and nervous, but no one paid them any attention. Ola and Enni, were hanging on to the arms of Egon and Hector as they touched heads and giggled to each other. He assumed the girls had no idea of what was about to happen.

Hugo appeared, caught his eye and nodded.

Wickler and Harri led Swoon off, ribbing him for not being able to take his drink. They didn't head towards their rooms, though.

"Count to a hundred," Lucien said, "then we go..."

He nodded as the mercenary turned and stumbled off.

"Where are you going?" he demanded.

"Need a piss."

"Now?!"

"Never go to a fight with a full bladder..." Lucien said without looking back, "...first rule of soldiering, that..."

He rolled his eyes and started counting.

*

She somehow managed to doze. Waking disorientated in the cramped confines of the trunk, she initially thought she was in a coffin, buried alive by Saul for his amusement. Heart thundering, she sucked in deep breaths of musty air till her mind caught up with where she was.

She listened.

Nothing.

How long had she been asleep?

It could have been minutes; it could have been hours.

Bulcher could be heading up with Karoline this very minute. Or the ceremony might not even have finished yet.

She calmed herself.

It would take as long as it took.

She'd waited a year. A little longer wouldn't matter. Killing a man wasn't a thing you rushed. It needed to be done right. It needed to be done slow...

Her fingers found the blade on her wrist.

She smiled. She trembled. A little.

She waited.

Some point later, her mind had drifted a few times, so she wasn't sure how long exactly, a door opened. Footsteps creaked the boards.

She stiffened, hand wrapping around her dagger's hilt.

"My lady?"

Hilde.

"Yes..."

The trunk rattled as the girl unbuckled the leather restraints and opened the lid.

She blinked after Hilde pulled Karoline's dresses off her.

"Is something wrong?"

Hilde shook her head, "I brought some food, I thought you might be hungry?"

Hungry? The idea that she might need to eat seemed absurd. Her stomach, however, told her otherwise.

She winced and sat up in the trunk.

"No one else is here?"

Hilde shook her head, "There are two guards at the door to the stairs; they are too far away to hear us."

Hilde passed her a cloth bundle; unwrapping it she found chicken and bread inside. She climbed from the trunk and stretched her legs. She was in a tower room, surrounded by Karoline's luggage. A narrow window looked out on darkness.

"It's night?"

Hilde nodded.

She perched on one of the other trunks. As she devoured the bread and chicken, Hilde fetched her some watered wine from another room. She washed the greasy meat down gratefully while Hilde stood over her, candlestick in hand.

"I don't think they'll search the rooms before the *Graf* arrives..."

"I'll get back in the trunk. How much longer, do you think?"

"I don't know, my lady. The wedding feast was still going strong the last time I checked. Becoming quite raucous, in fact."

"Our men?"

"Fitting in. My lady... what we are doing-"

"'tis too late for doubts."

"I know. 'tis just Ulrich, I worry…"

"He will be fine. We all will be. Bulcher is a monster; the world will be better without him."

"Yes, my lady…"

Hilde stood over her as she finished eating.

When done, she knelt to sweep up any escaped crumbs. She doubted either the soldiers or Bulcher would come in here, but if they did, she didn't want them wondering why there were breadcrumbs on the floor.

Hilde dropped to her knees with her.

"Let me, my lady. Stretch your legs."

Hilde placed the candlestick on the floor and brushed up the crumbs with her hand.

As she worked, Hilde's eyes rose to meet hers.

"Sometimes, my lady…" the girl said, "…you look at me… strangely?"

"I do?"

Hilde nodded, letting her gaze return to the floor.

She waved the question away, "'tis nothing. You remind me of someone, that's all."

Her chestnut eyes lifted again, "I do? Who?"

Someone who is going to die on the 20th of May, neck torn out by a monster…

"I…" she unearthed a smile, "…don't know. 'tis why I keep looking, I suppose. I can't quite put my finger on who it is."

"No one special if she looks like me," Hilde laughed. The laugh sounded as false as her own smile had been.

She thinks I look at her because of Renard. That I'm somehow jealous of her! Silly girl…

Hilde spread the cloth and put what crumbs she'd found

onto it, then stuffed it into her apron once she'd risen to her feet.

"Is there anything I should know?" she asked as the girl fidgeted before her.

"Know?"

"Problems? Has anything gone awry?"

Hilde retrieved the candlestick; its light, dancing below her face, gave her features an unfamiliar aspect. Older, almost haunted.

"I don't think so. The celebrations continue. People are getting very drunk. The *Graf* is still at the top table. He seems to be enjoying himself..."

Why not? 'tis his last night on Earth.

"And Karoline?"

"She looks terrified. If you were not going to save her, I think she would have taken her own life. Or simply died from fear. Truly!"

She nodded and moved to the window. Between darkness and condensation, there was nothing to see. But it was preferable to looking at Hilde's face.

If I can stop this happening to you, I will...

"I need to attend the hearth, my lady..."

"Of course..." she didn't turn around but watched the reflection of Hilde's candle retreat in the glass till darkness consumed the room.

The urge to tell Hilde to build the fire high so Bulcher didn't feel the cold when she killed him struggled up her throat. Pursued by a laugh that she was absolutely certain would not have sounded sane.

What is happening to me?

She scooped up the wine and drained it as she followed Hilde out of the room. Telling herself it was because it would be useful to know the layout of Karoline's chambers rather than to avoid answering that question.

The rooms were comfortable, opulent even, if you were being charitable. They did not, at first sight, have the air of a prison. But they made her immediately think of the Sparrow Tower because that's exactly what it was. Lebrecht's father preferred locking her up in Ettestein's highest tower in preference to marrying her and giving her the army she needed to destroy the Red Company.

Karoline's deal was much the same.

Rooms in a high tower where she would be kept comfortable while awaiting her master's pleasure.

She walked around the rooms, noting the silken drapes, fine chairs and deep rugs, the small bags of herbs to scent the air and ward off evil spirits, the dried flowers in delicate vases, the wide hearths and brimming coal scuttles. She noted the bottles of wine, too, but discarded her glass before the temptation to refill it became too strong.

She found Hilde in the bedchamber. The bed was huge. She supposed it needed to be if Bulcher planned to spend time here.

"How many other women have lived in this prison?"

Hilde looked up from the fireplace she knelt in front of, a small shovel of coal in one hand, a poker in the other.

"My lady?"

"Bulcher's previous wives. The ones who died over the years. I wonder if they all got to enjoy the comforts of these rooms."

She stared at the bed and tried not to shudder at the images her mind conjured.

"The marriage bed is often a prison for a woman, isn't it, my lady?"

Her eyes snapped back to Hilde, still on her knees in front of the fire.

"I had not taken you for such a cynic?"

Hilde pursed her lips as she returned to the hearth to feed the flames more coal.

"I have eyes in me head. And a brain behind them. I see how things are for a lot of women..." she discarded the shovel and poked at the coals.

"I said I didn't think you were a cynic. I didn't say you were stupid."

Hilde laughed at that for some reason.

"My father were a cu.... bad man. Cruel and violent, especially to my mother. Her marriage were nought but a prison..." satisfied with the fire, Hilde put down the poker and climbed to her feet "...maybe if the war hadn't come, I'd have got a similar deal. But when you see a world with little but cruelty and violence, it makes you crave something else even more..."

Hilde brushed coal dust from her hands and held her eye.

She's talking about Ulrich, isn't she?

"Not all men are cruel and violent..."

Hilde smiled, "I know. Just can be hard to find them ones..."

Yes, she is...

Nothing came in answer to that. Just the image of Hilde dying on a church floor in a pool of her own blood.

Why would Hilde be in Magdeburg, Solace? Why?

Hilde tilted her head, "My lady?"

She was about to kill the man who ordered her father's death. This was not the time for anything else.

Because you take her there. Or send her there. She dies because of you...

She swallowed. Not sure what words were going to form upon her lips.

In the end, none did, as the door to the apartment opened and boots creaked the boards.

Bulcher! Already?

Her heart tried to claw its way up her throat, her right hand moved to the sheath strapped to her left wrist, her eyes bulged, sweat erupted on her brow.

She froze.

"What are you doing, girl?" a gruff voice demanded.

Hilde pushed her aside and jabbed a finger at the open door before hurrying out of the room.

"What's it to you?" she heard Hilde demand.

Easing the blade from its sheath, she slipped silently behind the door.

"You're taking your merry old time, girl?"

"The fires had all but burned down, sir. You want them half done and the *Graf* cold on his wedding night?"

The sound of shuffling feet. One voice, one set of feet. She turned the blade in her hand.

"'tis my job to make sure the *Graf* is safe."

Hilde laughed, "Safe he will be in this big castle, but he might suffer a chill if I don't get these rooms nice and toasty for him and my lady. Go back to sitting on your chair and let me do my job!"

"Sorry..." the voice softened, "...just checking you were all right."

"How sweet... now, off with you! The *Graf* and *Grafin* could be back at any time, and you shouldn't be in my lady's chamber."

"Yeah... sure..." the man, one of Bulcher's Household Guard presumably, muttered. The sound of feet retreated. Then stopped.

"You been drinking the *Graf's* wine, girl?"

She mouthed a silent curse. She'd left the wine glass on the table in the next room.

"He won't miss it..."

The footsteps turned back.

"You don't know the *Graf*... he don't take kindly to liberties."

"Ain't your wine."

"Ain't yours neither, girl."

"'tis only-"

The sharp retort of a slap followed by a gasp.

"No *'tis only* about it, girl! I'll have to let the *Graf* know... he won't be best pleased. Might as well pack your bag, you'll be out on your ear tomorrow. Just better hope he don't give you a whipping first..." boots squeaked over the duller thud of smaller steps, Hilde backing away from the guard, "...that's the punishment for thieving in Thasbald..."

"'tis only a glass of wine, sir!" Hilde repeated, voice small and frightened.

She turned the blade at her side again.

"Of course, a whipping is only for the first offence. If

you've pilfered anything else, he might have a hand off you..."

"No... really, I ain't had nothing but a splash of wine! Please don't tell..."

"Maybe I could overlook it. Just this once... but you'll have to thank me properly for such a kindness."

Clothes rustled.

"I can be grateful. Right grateful. To a fellow who can help me out..."

The guard chuckled. A dirty, throaty sound that made the blade spin faster in her hand.

More rustling. Then, "I gotta finish these fires. We'll both be for the chop otherwise... but I got a room above. Why don't you come later? My lady won't need me once she... retires... and I can show you how grateful I am..."

Another dirty chuckle that made her want to use the knife she'd been saving for Bulcher.

"When do you finish your shift, sir?"

"Midnight."

"Reckon I'll be in my room by then..."

Another rustle, followed by boots crossing the room.

"Hey," Hilde said.

"Yeah?"

"Bring some of the *Graf's* wine with you. I'll be thirsty."

The guard laughed, "I will. We can celebrate the wedding together!"

"That we can..."

A door opened and closed.

She let out a breath and moved out from behind the door and into the next room.

Hilde stood red-faced and flustered. The girl put a finger to her lips as she pressed an ear to the door.

Hilde blew out her cheeks and dropped her shoulders, "Bastard's gone... excusing my language."

"Bastard seems entirely the right word... I'm sorry, I-"

Hilde hurried across the room and scooped up the wine glass she'd so carelessly left in plain sight, "You ain't got nothing to apologise for, my lady..."

"I should have been more careful."

Hilde shrugged, cleaning out the glass with her apron before putting it back with the others on a side table, "Guess none of us have done anything like this."

"No..."

The glass replaced, Hilde turned her attention to the fire in the room, which had reduced to embers.

She stood over her, realised she still had the dagger in her hand and fumbled it back into its sheath, "What would you have done if... someone like that caught you pilfering for real?"

Hilde didn't look up from shovelling coal.

"Depends."

"Depends on what?"

"On whether he was the kind that *talks* or the kind that *does*. If he were the kind that just talks, which is most of them, I'd slap his face and send him away with his tail between his legs. If he were the kind that does..." she scooped another pile of coal from the scuttle before pausing to roll her shoulders, "...you do what you gotta do to survive."

"I see..."

Hilde snorted and threw the coal onto the fire, sending sparks dancing up the chimney.

"Don't suppose that's something you've had to worry about, eh, my lady?"

"No. I just had the man who owns this castle have my father murdered and everyone I knew slaughtered because he wanted to fuck me..."

Hilde looked sharply over her shoulder.

"Well, he wanted to marry me first, but it still boils down to the same thing, doesn't it?"

Hilde thought about that before nodding, "What men want to do with their cocks, eh?"

She twisted around and headed back to the room storing Karoline's trunks.

"I should hide in case someone else checks on you."

"My lady?"

"Yes?"

"Please make sure you do what you plan to do..." Hilde offered a tight smile, "...I really don't want that bastard coming to my room later."

Chapter Eight

He waited till the man stumbled back into the Great Hall.

Then nodded at Gotz, who grabbed one of the doors while Usk took the other and they pulled them closed. There was too much noise and debauchery going on for anyone to notice. In fact, he half wondered if they'd have been better off just leaving them alone to drink themselves into oblivion.

The doors, solid oak and as thicker than his fist, banged shut. Like most castle doors they could be barred on either side to slow down any attackers who breached the fortress. They slid the bars, plus heavy iron bolts at top and bottom, into place.

There were only two exits from the Great Hall; the other, smaller, door was on the far side and accessed the kitchens. He counted to a hundred to allow Swoon, Wickler and Harri to reach that door and seal it at the same time.

There must be the best part of two hundred people locked in the Great Hall; how many remained free in the rest of the castle, however, he could only guess.

As turning up to a wedding armed to the teeth might have raised suspicions, they were unarmed save for a few discreet daggers and eating knives.

Hugo had found a log store in a corridor just off this lobby and had quietly moved their weaponry there during the ceremony, concealing them in a basket of logs he ferried back and forth between their rooms and the storeroom. The thought of what would happen to them if anyone figured out what the lad was up to was just one of many things that had left him queasy.

He'd warned Solace they were placing a lot of trust in people they didn't know.

As usual, she'd ignored his advice completely.

"Any problems?" he asked the boy as he strapped on his father's sabre.

"If there were, we'd likely be in the dungeons by now," Lucien answered for Hugo, taking his own weapon belt from the boy.

"I'm good at not being noticed," Hugo grinned.

"Right," he said, buckling the belt on, "now be good at keeping out of trouble."

"Might be a bit late for that…"

A bit late for all of them.

He found his pistols and backed away from the door to load them.

The men around him were tight-lipped and stern-faced. They didn't look like they'd been drinking for hours, which was something at least. They all knew what would happen to them if this went wrong, and that prospect should be enough to sober any fool.

With everyone armed, they splintered off to their tasks, which whittled down to keeping the locked doors locked and dealing with anyone on the wrong side of them.

"What we gonna do when we open the doors?" Hugo asked, eyeing the Great Hall. He could hear voices on the other side and the occasional rattle, but without gunpowder or axes, it'd be a long time before anyone got through it.

"Ask Lady Solace, she deals with the problems..."

Leaving Bosko in charge of the main group, he headed up the stairs with Lucien, Gotz, Lebrecht and Usk. Between them, they would have to deal with Bulcher's Household Guard and get to Solace.

Hilde met them coming down the stairs.

"We are started?" she asked, red-cheeked and breathless.

"No turning back now."

"Bulcher and Karoline are in her chambers; I was dismissed for the night."

"And Lady Solace?"

"She is in the rooms... waiting..."

They followed Hilde back up the stairs.

"Guards?" Lebrecht asked from his shoulder.

"One at the bottom of the stairs," Hilde explained, lifting the hem of her dress as she hurried them into a long corridor, "two of the men who came up with them will stay outside her door. The *Graf* rarely goes anywhere without them, apparently."

"Are you going to kill them?" a small voice asked.

He found Hugo trailing after them.

"I told you-"

"Leave it," Lucien said, for once no grin on his face, "we need all the help we can get..." he slid one of the daggers from his belt and handed it to the boy.

He sucked on that for a few strides before looking back at Hugo, "We kill no one else if we can help it..."

The boy was pale in the flickering light.

Hugo had been with the Merry Gentlemen when they attacked the tavern they'd been spending the night in after meeting Karoline's party. They'd been, in part, trying to avenge the death of a woman in their group's father. A mad woman called Madge. Solace killed him when Styx kicked him in the head. Driven by vengeance, Madge had persuaded some of the Merry Gentlemen to help her fire the tavern and kill them all.

What are we doing now that is so different?

The thought tugged at him.

They strode through Thasbald with murder in mind, spurred on by Solace's all-consuming thirst for vengeance. Bulcher might be a monster, but were the rest of his household?

They were barely twenty in number; how on earth could they seize Thasbald as Solace wished without spilling innocent blood?

He'd left women and children to die in The Wolf's Tower. Fifty-six freshly cut graves sat in the mud outside Ettestein Castle because he'd pursued Wendel rather than sealing the castle. How many more dead would he leave here?

He cast an eye around the group. Did anyone else have doubts? If the others did, they were keeping them to themselves. His honour and oath insisted he do this, but what excuse did they have? The prospect of Thasbald's riches? Lucien and Gotz, perhaps, but Lebrecht was the heir to Gothen; he had far more to lose than he did to gain. But he'd seen how the young nobleman looked at Solace, and nothing blinded a man so completely as love.

Hilde held up a hand as another corridor splintered off

theirs

And why was Hilde here, doing this?

Love, of course, didn't blind only men.

"The stairs at the end of this corridor..." she pointed down the one they'd been walking, "...lead to the *Graf*'s private quarters; this one goes to the Silver Tower, where Karoline's rooms are... around the next corner we'll see the guard by the door to the tower's stairs."

He nodded, "You should go back-"

"No, I'm staying with you."

"Hilde, 'tis dangerous. I-"

"I know what we're doing. Nowhere is safe if this goes wrong."

He turned his eyes to the ceiling.

Lucien chuckled.

"Very well, but stay at the back with Hugo and keep each other out of trouble-"

"No."

He frowned, "No?"

"The guard will see you all lumbering down the corridor and raise the alarm before you get close enough. I can deal with him."

"Deal with him? How?"

She smiled in a way he didn't like.

"How far between the corner and the guard?" Gotz asked.

"Thirty paces," Hilde said, "maybe more."

Lucien blew out air, "She's right. Unless he's fallen asleep, he'll see us coming."

"And as Bulcher only went up those stairs not long ago, I doubt he's asleep," Lebrecht said.

He didn't like it. He didn't like the thought of Solace in a room with Bulcher. He liked the idea of Hilde *dealing* with the guard even less.

"Come," she waved them forward, "I will get him to turn his back to you; you'll be able to come up behind him while he's distracted."

"How-"

Hilde slid a dagger from his belt as they walked. She winked at him.

"tis a sound plan," Lucien said at his shoulder, "women are always a distraction..."

Hilde put a finger to her lips as they reached where the corridor turned.

"Wait here till the right moment", she said.

"How will I know when the right moment is?" he asked as she slipped the dagger into her apron.

She looked at Lucien, "When you know the moment is right."

The mercenary nodded and grinned.

He scowled, but before he could ask her what she thought she was doing, she'd gone.

When he tried to peek around the corner, Lucien clamped a hand on his shoulder and pulled him back.

"Give the girl a minute," Lucien breathed in his ear.

He listened to her footsteps, but they soon disappeared. He strained to hear voices but made out nothing above his own breathing.

When he glanced behind him, Lucien was pulling his boots off.

When he frowned at him, Lucien explained quietly,

"Squeaky..." after handing them off to Hugo, he added, "I'll deal with the guard; you all be ready to join me."

He wanted to protest he should be the one dealing with the man-at-arms, but Lucien was a better fighter than him. The truth might be shit, but the truth was always the truth, and only a fool ignored it. That had been another of Old Man Ulrich's favourite ale pot homilies.

He gave Hilde a minute, as best he reckoned it, before peeking around the corner.

This part of the castle was as poorly lit as everywhere else. A few rushlights flickered in sconces, creating wan little islands of light between the deep pools of shadow. The corridor ended in a door by which two lanterns hung. A soldier, in the purple livery of Bulcher's Household Guard, stood talking with Hilde.

The guard was tall and spare and loomed over her. As he watched, she smiled up at him and put a hand on the door, which must open onto the spiral staircase climbing the tower to Karoline's chambers.

She twisted around, putting her back to the door. The guard swivelled to face her.

As Hilde said, it was thirty paces to the door. A good thirty paces. How would she distract the man long enough for Lucien to get there unseen? A small table sat by the door, and on it a brass bell. If the guard got hold of that, their escapade was probably over before it had begun.

Hilde leaned back against the door. Smiling, she reached up, slung a hand over the guard's shoulder and pulled him to her.

Oh, that's how...

"Now might be a good time..."

Lucien was already moving. And for a big man, he moved quietly, especially in his socks. Though being downwind would be an advantage.

He watched; arm raised to keep the others back until Lucien got to the guard.

Hilde was clearly well-practiced at distracting a man. The soldier kept his back turned right up to the moment Lucien clamped a hand over his mouth and put a dagger to his throat.

He waved everyone forward.

By the time they'd all trotted down the corridor, Lucien had the man against the wall. Hilde, his blade in her hand, craning over Lucien's shoulder like she was eager to see how it performed.

"Are you-"

She nodded and grinned at him.

He took Lucien's boots off the boy and sent him back to the corner to keep an eye out. There were several doors along the corridor, hopefully, the rooms behind them were unoccupied, but they had no time to check.

"How many men are with the *Graf* upstairs?" Lucien asked. When the guard said nothing, he pressed the blade harder against the man's throat until his eyes bulged and beads of blood started trickling down his neck.

"I don't want to kill anyone I don't have to... so please don't give me a reason..." Lucien pushed a little harder.

"Whatever you do would be nothing compared to what he'd do to me..." the guard gasped.

"Son..." Gotz said, putting a shoulder to the wall, "...the

Graf isn't going to be doing anything to anyone ever again. So, trust me, you should be concentrating solely on your current predicament."

"Exactly..." Lucien said.

The guard's eyes swivelled one way and then the other, perhaps trying to figure out who represented the biggest threat. He quickly concluded it was the one holding a knife to his throat.

"Four..."

"Where will they be?" Lucien demanded.

"Two in the guard room on the next floor, two outside the door to his lady's chamber."

"And the rest of the Household Guard?"

"Celebrating the wedding... the late watch sleeping in barracks."

"Which is where?"

"The floor below the *Graf's* private rooms."

"How many?"

"Not many... five or six!" he squealed when Lucien drew a little more blood.

He looked back at Hugo, the boy nodded; no company yet.

"What... do we do with him now?" Lebrecht asked; the young nobleman was pale as ashes. Murder was a business that could leave you queasy.

"Slit his fucking throat," Hilde suggested.

"Take his helmet off," Lucien told Gotz.

As soon as the old soldier tugged off the helm, Lucien grabbed the man's greasy hair and smashed his head against the wall. The guard crumpled to the floor. Lucien stepped back, wiping his hands on his britches.

"Killing him would be safer," Hilde offered again.

He reached over and carefully retrieved his knife.

Usk checked the nearest door; the room was dark and empty. They dragged the guard inside, stripped him, tied him as best they could and stuffed his socks in his mouth.

"Killing him would have been kinder," Hilde wrinkled her nose from the doorway as Usk and Gotz worked.

"I didn't think you were so bloodthirsty."

She shrugged, "I didn't like him…"

He bit back on the petty urge to tell her she seemed to like him well enough a few minutes ago.

With the guard secured, Hugo pulled on the man's doublet, cuirass, weapon's belt and helmet. It was all too big, but so long as no one got too close, he'd pass muster, and suspicions wouldn't be raised about why the guard had deserted his post. Possibly.

"And if he wakes up and makes a noise?" the boy asked, tipping the helmet back so it didn't cover his eyes.

"Make him go quiet again," Hilde said before anyone else could speak.

"No one should come down here," he said to Hugo, "but if they do, come up the stairs and find us."

Lucien lightly rapped his knuckle on the boy's ill-fitting helm, "And lock the door after you."

Hugo nodded, sending the helm rattling about his ears.

Gotz turned down the wicks on the two lanterns, "Don't want anyone getting too good a look at you, boy…"

"How do we deal with the other guards," Lebrecht asked when they were ready to go.

"You deal with the two in the guard room, and I'll distract

the two outside Karoline's room," Hilde said, beaming as she held out a hand for his knife again.

She really was enjoying this all far too much...

*

She'd never been good at waiting.

Father had always said she'd wear a hole in the floor with all her pacing.

Given she was having to wait while hiding in a trunk, she wasn't currently endangering the floor, but she found it increasingly hard to stay still. She fidgeted and repeatedly rolled from one side to the other.

Numerous times she all but talked herself into getting out. Bulcher wouldn't be rifling through Karoline's luggage when he turned up for his first night with his new bride.

No, but a guard had already checked in here once; they might do again ahead of Bulcher's arrival. And then there was Elin; she might warm the bed or lay out food or... whatever servants did before their betters arrived for their wedding night.

No, it was too close now. Just wait. Just wait a little longer.

For vengeance.

For something to fill the emptiness, to absolve her guilt, to cleanse this rotten world of one sick monster.

Several times, she thought she heard voices or footsteps. On each occasion, she stilled her restless hands and treacherous body. But nothing else came. As she knew well, old buildings were full of trickery and mischievous noises. How many times had she laid awake as a little girl imagining the creeks and groans of The Wolf's Tower to be spirits, goblins, faeries or any manner of strange beasties?

I will know him when he comes...

There'd be no mistaking Bulcher. His foulness would taint the air, his existence an insult to God, his evil setting him apart from all else.

How many hours had she spent in that trunk since Hilde left? It felt an eternity, but she had no means of telling. Minutes and hours became meaningless in the dark, in the silence, in the solitude where all you had for company were thoughts of murder and grief. Thoughts of vengeance.

Finally, just as she somehow started drifting off to sleep, doors opened, voices, footsteps.

At first, she thought more guards were coming to sweep the room as she heard only male voices. Her heart quickened, and stomach rolled. One of them was Bulcher's. She'd know it anywhere. High-pitched and squeaky, with a wet echo that made her think his lungs were full of rot. It had played a prominent part in her nightmares after the *Graf*'s visit to The Wolf's Tower to run his piggy, lascivious eyes over her.

What an absolute delight you are, my dear...

A door closed.

The guards leaving?

She strained to listen; between the dresses over her head, trunk and intervening doors, she struggled to make out anything comprehensible, but now the only voice she could hear was the only one that mattered. Bulcher's.

Poor Karoline must be terrified.

She'd told the girl what to do. Promised her she'd save her from Bulcher, but with the prospect of being alone with the

Graf a mountainous flabby reality in front of her, Karoline's nerve could still fail. It-

She stopped herself.

There was no other way.

Wait.

Wait till Bulcher occupied himself.

Karoline had to be brave. Any suffering the girl endured would be much less than hers had been at Bulcher's hands. And all Bulcher's previous *Grafin's,* too.

She sucked in long slow breaths.

Her hand trembled.

It wouldn't when it did what she needed it to do, though. Would it?

I'm about to kill a man in cold blood...

No heat of the fight this time. No impulse. No instinctive reaction.

This was premeditated. This was calculated.

She was going to look a man in the eye and kill him.

And just killing him wouldn't be enough.

Would it?

She'd spent a year thinking about this moment. And here she was.

Shaking.

And feeling sick.

What am I doing?

A stupid question. It was only what needed to be done. If she wasn't prepared to do it, she should have stayed cowering in the ruins of The Wolf's Tower.

But what if it doesn't change anything? What if I still feel as empty as I did after killing Wendel? What if-

Oh, do shut up!

What if didn't matter.

The man who brought down damnation on her house, who paid demons to roast her father alive, who set in motion the events that resulted in her beautiful brother giving himself to monsters, was in the next room.

About to bed his new wife.

Who was fourteen years old.

And who, she didn't doubt, he'd discard as ruthlessly as all his earlier wives once he got hold of her family's wealth.

So, are you going to hide in this box all night asking what if questions?

Her fingers traced the outline of the blade attached to her wrist.

Or are you going to do what needs to be done?

A muffled laugh, wet and raucous, cut the silence. It wasn't Karoline's. No, she remembered well that Bulcher was a man who laughed hardest at his own wit.

"Go to bed you fat bastard..."

She doubted him the type who'd want to entertain his new wife with hours of anecdotes and banter before bedding her.

Unless, of course, he had no plans to bed her.

Perhaps such pleasures didn't interest him. Maybe it was only the money he wanted.

No, she couldn't see that. She remembered how his eyes devoured her when they'd met. It hadn't been thoughts of anecdotes and banter she'd glimpsed behind the narrow slits of Bulcher's eyes.

What an absolute delight you are, my dear...

And even if he was, the marriage still needed to be consummated. *Graf* Bulcher wouldn't risk missing out on inheriting Vadia for the want of fucking a fourteen-year-old girl.

So, she waited.

And prayed Karoline was brave enough to go through with this.

Bulcher's voice came a few more times, his laughter, too. Of Karoline, she heard nothing. Finally, a door closed. Then silence.

Which door, of course, was pertinent.

If Bulcher had decided to return to his own rooms for the night... she would need a new plan.

The urge to leap from the trunk came again. Replacing the one to stay hidden. The moment was important but later was better than sooner. Ideally, she wanted Bulcher distracted; if she caught him snoring with his business for the night done, so be it. Karoline wouldn't thank her for turning up late, but saving her from a short, miserable marriage and an early death would help the girl live with the unpleasant memory.

So, she closed her eyes and waited for the *sight* to guide her.

She didn't expect anything so tangible as a whisper in her ear *to go kill the bastard now*, but she opened her mind and decided to trust her instincts.

After all, her instincts were much better than most people's.

Her breath slowed, her heart calmed, the tremors dissipated, her stomach... well, she still felt she might throw up, but she'd live with that.

The decision to pull Karoline's dresses off her and slowly push open the lid of the trunk was not a conscious one.

She sat there, listening. The room dark and cold around her. One small window dusted the room with starlight, but there was little more to see than to hear.

Carefully, she climbed out. Pausing once both bare feet were on the floor. Bulcher would be too occupied to hear much. The guards were probably outside Karoline's rooms. Hilde said Bulcher went nowhere without them. They'd certainly never ventured far from his side during his brief visit to The Wolf's Tower.

This room opened onto the main living space, with the bedchamber to the right, the door to the short corridor, and the stairs to the left. The doors here were heavy and thick. The guards would not hear her footsteps. And if they heard a cry or even a scream... well, it was a wedding night...

She fished out the crossbow in the darkness, cranked, and loaded it. The mechanism was well oiled, and her fingers true. It creaked a little, but not enough to concern her.

Finally, she found the two leather belts that had fastened the trunk before Hilde opened it. She'd kept them with her in the trunk and looped them over her chest. They might be useful for the kind of work she had in mind.

Picking up the crossbow, she allowed herself two more deep breaths then crossed the room, slow and careful. She'd made sure the route to the door was clear with Hilde, but she wasn't going to take a single step for granted.

The dark suggestion of the door rose in front of her. No

light crept under it. Bulcher and his latest wife had retired. Still, she waited. Listening.

Nothing.

The door opened quietly. She'd checked that before, too. Whatever else you might say about Siegfried, *Graf* Bulcher, he kept his hinges well-oiled...

She stepped into the room, which boasted two narrow windows in its curved wall, both shuttered against the winter's night. Hilde's fire still glowed, wan orange light flicking shadows about the room.

Light stole beneath the bedroom door; Bulcher liked to see what he was doing.

So did she.

There was an alcove between this chamber and the exit. Light played under that door, too. Bulcher's guards.

The chances of them disturbing their lord on his wedding night seemed crushingly slim.

Unless something had gone awry with the plan to take the castle, of course. News of that would be enough for one of Bulcher's Household Guard to risk his life and livelihood by pulling his master off his new wife.

The *sight,* however, remained silent. Which she took to mean nothing was wrong. Flyblown's mark tingled. Warning her of something? But what?

She moved to the bedchamber door, one slow, careful step at a time.

Outside, she paused, listening.

She'd never had a... *wedding* night. Or listened to anybody else's. Leaving her somewhat under-informed as to what one should sound like.

And when would be the most opportune moment to interrupt one with a loaded crossbow and a blade.

Holding the bow one handed, she reached out for the door with the other.

Now was as good a time as any to find out...

Chapter Nine

The two men in the guard's room were not expecting trouble.

One had already pulled off his boots, the other squatted over a bucket in the corner. Both looked surprised to see them.

Neither made much of a fuss nor tried for their weapons.

Usk and Gotz bound and gagged them after they confirmed that there were just two more guards upstairs, outside Karoline's chambers.

The guardroom consisted of two large rooms which filled that floor. There were beds for six guards. To keep Bulcher's wives safe or to stop them from trying to run away?

He stowed his curiosity.

"Is the layout the same as this on Karoline's floor?" he asked Hilde quietly while Usk and Gotz worked.

"A corridor curves around the tower's edge from the stairs to the door to Karoline's chambers."

"And both guards will be outside?"

"I assume so."

"And above Karoline's floor?"

"Servants quarters and storage, then the roof."

"We need them away from the door. If we make too much noise, it could tip Bulcher off if Solace hasn't already…"

"Spoiled his night," Hilde finished for him.

"Erm... yes..."

"I can distract them, get them to come down here."

"No," he and Lucien said in unison.

He hoped the mercenary had a better idea because he didn't.

Lucien nodded towards the guards, "Wear the uniforms; the light will be poor. By the time they realise they don't know us, it'll be too late."

"But if we make too much noise..."

"We won't," the grin that accompanied Lucien's words wasn't a pleasant one.

"Should work," Gotz, straightened with a wince.

He glanced at Lebrecht, who, as a nobleman, would typically be in charge. The young man shrugged. He'd been quiet since they left the wedding feast and began this questionable escapade. Perhaps he was starting to question what he was doing. After all, he had a lot more to lose than the rest of them.

"Very well..." he agreed, and they begun stripping the two guards.

"Perhaps the young lady should wait in the other room," Lebrecht suggested after the clothes started coming off.

"No, no, my lord," she said quickly, "don't mind me!"

"Go watch the door," he said.

She shot him a disgruntled glare but did as he said.

Usk and Lebrecht were the best fits for the uniforms.

When handed the britches and doublet, the nobleman wrinkled his nose but started changing as soon as Usk did.

"Come on. Chop, chop!" Lucien hurried them along, "You

haven't got to pass a parade."

Usk responded with a broken-toothed grin; Lebrecht continued to look like he was wondering what he was doing here.

He checked the guard's bonds as Usk and Lebrecht pulled on their cuirasses. Gotz and Lucien helped them with the fastenings.

"No need for anything fancy," Lucien told the two men once decked out in the livery of Thasbald's household guard, "just get close enough to put weapons on them. The rest of us will be around the curve of the corridor. But if they make a fuss, don't be squeamish. Lady Solace is a resourceful girl, but best she's not left alone for too long, eh?"

He shot a final glance at the two bound guards, who glowered back before ushering the others out.

"All quiet," Hilde said as they joined her at the door.

The staircase was wide, as far as castle staircases went. Karoline's new apartment was on the next floor. He let Usk and Lebrecht go first. Usk was a brawler who he trusted could handle himself in any situation requiring wanton violence. Lebrecht, however, worried him.

He wasn't a coward and was a much sharper swordsman than him. But whether dark work they were doing here suited him was another matter.

Quietly, they headed up in grim-faced silence. Apart from Hilde, who looked like she wanted to whistle.

The door to Karoline's chambers wasn't visible around the curving corridor. But all of them tramping down there together, weapons rattling and boots thumping, would alert even a dozy guard something was off.

Lucien drew his sword and waved the two men down. He ensured Hilde was on the stairs and pointed for her to stay there.

She nodded. Though she still had his dagger and a look to suggest she fancied using it on someone.

Usk and Lebrecht headed off, disappearing into the thick shadows. The soldier sauntered casually, the nobleman walked like something metallic was up his arse. Beyond the corridor's curve came a flickering glow, presumably a lantern by Karoline's door.

"Is Lord Lebrecht...?" he asked Lucien without knowing how to finish the question.

The mercenary rolled his shoulders, "Who knows. Nobility. Too much time on their nanny's teat. Fucks them all up."

That sorted, Lucien stretched his neck left and right hard enough for bones to click.

He grimaced and began edging down the corridor, shoulder brushing the curve of the inner wall.

Ahead came voices.

Amiable at first, then querying. Then, the sound of scuffling and a muffled cry.

He ran, sabre drawn. At close quarters with walls on either side, his long dagger was a better choice. But Hilde still had it.

Outside the door to Karoline's chambers, Usk had one of the guards, the big brutes who'd shadowed Bulcher all day, up against the wall, forearm across the man's throat. Lebrecht stood over the other guard, panting, bloody blade in his hand.

He didn't need to check if the guard was still alive; the hole where his left eye used to be confirmed he wasn't. Quite how Lebrecht managed to stab him through the eye with so little noise, he wasn't sure, but he had no time for questions.

"Tie this one up with the two downstairs," he told Usk, nodding at Gotz to help the big Gothen man-at-arms. The guard was a hefty-looking lad, but he went meekly enough, Usk's hand clamped over his mouth in case he was the kind who put duty before life and thought about shouting a warning to his master.

He stepped over the dead guard.

Lebrecht stared at the door.

This wasn't the right moment to ask the young nobleman how he was. It wasn't the first man Lebrecht had killed, though he suspected it might be the first who hadn't been invading his home trying to kill him.

Hilde came down the corridor as Usk and Gotz hurried the surviving guard in the other direction. She glanced at the body but didn't say anything.

He should shoosh her back down the corridor, but just signalled for her to get behind them.

When he checked with Lucien, the mercenary made an after you gesture towards the door.

Which was when the screaming started inside.

*

A hefty door stood between her and the bedchamber, muffling the sound coming from the room. This was good. The business end of a wedding night was a private matter between husband and wife. Its noises were not for the ears of the world.

What was about to happen on Siegfried, *Graf* Bulcher's sixth, seventh, eighth, or however many-eth wedding night certainly wasn't going to be...

The possibility the door might be locked stilled her outstretched hand.

That would be... annoying.

But why lock a bedroom door in your own castle, surrounded by soldiers? Was *Graf* Bulcher the kind of man who would even allow his wife to have a lock on her bedchamber?

She pushed, and it swung open smoothly on silent hinges.

No. He wasn't.

Her feet took her forward equally smoothly. Her hinges were well-oiled too.

She took in several things almost instantly. Her mind needed to be as well-oiled as the rest of her now.

As she'd noted earlier with Hilde, the room was large, the outer wall curved with the tower's exterior serving as Karoline's bridal cell, the two interior walls straight, giving the room the shape of a fruit segment or a slice of cake. A huge, ornate bed with crimson silk drapes strung between four thick spirals of polished oak.

A multitude of candles burned, on the mantle before a looking glass, on tables, on a dresser, on hefty iron candlesticks scattered about the floor. Hilde hadn't lit them earlier.

Karoline stood by the bed, hunched forward as if trying to make herself smaller. The girl was shivering convulsively despite the blazing fire and the legion of candle flames. Her dress lay in a crumpled heap at her feet, some of her undergarments too, breasts no more than suggestions, nipples dark stains on a canvas of pale porcelain in the whispering candlelight.

In front of her, Bulcher sat in a throne-like wooden chair, back to the door, sweat glistening on the folds of fat creasing the rear of his bald head. His left arm hung languidly on one side of the chair, chubby bejewelled fingers holding a goblet by the rim. Wine sloshed inside, dripping onto the floor in time to the rhythmic movement the *Graf* was making with his obscured right hand...

Karoline's eyes widened, and she stepped back from the pile of discarded clothes before her.

"I didn't tell you to stop..." Bulcher said in a breathy pant.

Continue... she mouthed at the girl.

Karoline dropped her eyes and began trying to unpick the knot on the ribbon keeping up the silk stocking on her left leg with almost uncontrollably trembling hands.

"Keep your head up, my little pickle. I want to see your face..." Bulcher ordered, words wet and hasty.

What was he doing?

Whatever, it preoccupied him sufficiently to ensure he didn't realise he was no longer alone with his new wife.

This could have been me...

If Father hadn't refused him...

Carefully, she reached back with one hand and closed the door behind her. Wet, fleshy, slapping noises came from the other side of the chair. Enough to mask the door and her feet as one step at a time, she crept towards the monster who destroyed her life.

"Put your leg up on the bed where I can see it, sweetie," Bulcher was telling Karoline. The slapping sound becoming harder and louder. Bulcher raised the goblet and guzzled wine, hand and goblet flopping back down as Karoline, leg hooked up onto the bed, untied her stocking and began to roll it down her leg.

"Slowly, do it fucking slowly, sugar plum..." Bulcher squealed in his peculiarly high-pitched voice.

Karoline sucked in a wet, shaky breath through her nostrils, then peeled the stocking down her skinny alabaster leg; her head turned to look at Bulcher with rapidly blinking eyes. Her bottom lip quivered, and she clenched them tightly together.

A single tear rolled down her cheek as if seeing her salvation had broken the determination not to cry.

The meaty slapping noise grew more intense, louder, faster.

Bulcher let out a strange, strangled groan.

"That's my good girl..." he said through what sounded like gritted teeth.

Raising the crossbow, she placed the bolt against the side of his bald head.

Her eyes widened as she stood over Bulcher, whose britches were around the ankles of his bloated white legs while his right hand gripped his...

That's what one looks like?

"What the-" Bulcher began to splutter, snapping her mind back into focus.

"Don't move!" she pressed the metal tip of the bolt against the side of his head, "Don't speak!"

The goblet slipped from his fingers to thump onto the floor, otherwise, the *Graf* did as she said.

She couldn't help but notice that the thing in his right hand had shrivelled, like a little animal scurrying back under the safety of his bloated, overhanging belly.

"Karoline?" she asked without looking at the girl.

She got a thick, wet sniff by way of reply.

"Are you good?"

"I... didn't think you were going to come..."

Bulcher's eyes widened, "You are part of-"

"Quiet!"

She wanted to pull the trigger. Kill the bastard and be done with it. She resisted the urge.

Instead, she circled the *Graf's* chair, crossbow pointed at him. Bulcher's eyes followed her, but the only other movement was his chest's slow rise and fall.

She worked her way around until she stood next to Karoline, back to the wall, facing Bulcher and the door behind him.

Never keep your back to a door, first rule of soldiering, that...

Not that what she was currently doing counted as soldiering.

Karoline had scooped her dress off the floor and clutched it to her naked chest. She shook so hard her teeth chattered.

"This will be over soon..." she said, talking to Karoline, looking at Bulcher.

"What do you think you are doing?" Bulcher demanded.

"I need you to help me. Can you do that, Karoline?"

When she didn't answer, she risked a glance at the girl. Karoline managed a shaky nod.

"I'll see you hang for this..." Bulcher sneered, "...and you'll both be grateful for the noose when I'm done with you!"

"You appear to have forgotten the bit about keeping quiet."

"All I have to do is shout. There are two of my men outside."

"Call them then."

Bulcher blinked, and chuckled. At least, she thought it was a chuckle. It sounded a lot like vomiting, too, "You've got one shot in that bow, little girl..."

"True. And I won't be wasting it on either of them. Even if they kill me, I'd have rid the world of you."

The smile faded from Bulcher's fleshy lips, "You want gold?"

Something twisted inside her.

Amongst all the things that had been twisting inside her for the last year.

"You don't even recognise me, do you?"

Bulcher hoisted an eyebrow, moving his right hand from his lap to the arm of the chair, "Should I?"

"I didn't tell you to move your hand..." she jerked the crossbow, "...keep hold of your little... *thing*. I don't want to see it. And neither does Karoline."

Bulcher curled a lip, flashing perfect white teeth, before moving his hand back to his lap.

"Keep holding it!" she ordered Bulcher, "You wouldn't want to lose it, would you? It's so easy to misplace small objects, don't you find?"

Karoline snorted a little laugh.

When Bulcher's hand curled about his shrivelled cock Karoline almost vomited up the words, "There's my good boy!"

Bulcher's jaw jutted forward, and she thought he would try to stand up and come at them. Given the time it'd take him to haul his colossal bulk out of the chair and lurch across the room at them with his britches around his ankles, she reckoned there was a fair chance she could shoot, miss, reload and shoot him again before he could get his hands on them.

Though she doubted she'd miss such a big target.

The same thought possibly bobbed to the surface behind Bulcher's eyes, and he eased back and relaxed his shoulders.

"Tell me, who are you? What do you want? How much do I have to pay you to go away?"

"A year ago... demons destroyed my home, murdered my father, slaughtered my people. Sent by you. To bring me to you to make me your wife. You wanted me so much you did a deal with The Devil and washed my home in the blood of hundreds of innocents..." she took a step forward, hand shaking, voice trembling, "...and now you don't even recognise who *I fucking am!*"

Bulcher's brow furrowed before realisation lightened his face. Then he laughed.

"Solace von Tassau!"

"The very same," she swallowed, forcing herself to move backwards until the wall touched her shoulder blades.

Bulcher shook his head, the laughter subsiding, "I heard you died..."

"Hasn't anyone ever told you the Devil lies?"

"How remiss of Saul, what a naughty, naughty boy he is!" Bulcher giggled. Which wasn't the reaction she'd been expecting.

"They killed hundreds of people! Wiped out a whole village, slaughtered everyone in Tassau!"

Bulcher stared at her blankly, then rolled massive, fleshy shoulders, "What of it?"

Her finger twitched on the trigger. She wanted the bastard dead, but that wasn't it. She needed to hurt him too. To see him scream, to make him feel what she'd felt, what her father had felt, what the people of Tassau had felt.

Pain.

Given the amount of blubber on him, a crossbow bolt probably wouldn't kill him straight away.

"Karoline..." she said, forcing her fingers not to squeeze the trigger mechanism.

The girl was struggling back into her dress.

"Yes?"

"I need you to do something for me. Just one thing. Then you can go."

Out of the corner of her eye, Karoline nodded.

"The two belts slung over my shoulder. I want you to take them off me and use them to tie his hands to the arms of the chair. You think you can do that?"

Karoline swallowed and nodded again.

Once more or less dressed, Karoline took the two belts and then stood, staring at Bulcher, twisting the leather straps together.

"He's not going to hurt you..." she said.

Bulcher smiled, "Oh yes, I am. I'm going to hurt both of you."

"Be quiet!"

The *Graf*'s eyes, reduced to two black slits trapped between fleshy rolls of fat, fixed on her, "I was so looking forward to fucking you, Solace. When Saul sent word you were dead... well, it quite spoiled my morning, I can tell you..." Bulcher giggled again.

"Bind him!" she ordered Karoline, "then you can go, and you'll be free of him."

"Solace... Solace... pretty little Solace..." Bulcher slowly moved his massive head from side to side, "...really, what do you think you are doing? You'll never get out of here alive. You must know that. You should have stayed dead."

She hoisted the crossbow to her shoulder as Karoline began taking hesitant steps towards the *Graf*.

"And as for you, Karoline... *bad girl!* I will have to punish you, too. No more comfy bed for you. Straight down into the dark now..." he leaned forward sharply enough to make Karoline recoil, "...straight down!"

She shuffled to her left to maintain a clear line of sight, "Left hand flat on the arm of the chair, Bulcher..."

Bulcher slowly did as she ordered, uncurling his fingers one at a time.

Karoline swallowed, looped the first of the belt under the arm of the chair and back over Bulcher's arm.

"I must say," the *Graf* twisted another smile out of the blubber encasing his face, "I do like what you have done with your hair. Quite the boy you look. Not my usual bag, but still..." his eyes fell to his lap, where his right hand still held his cock. He squeezed it hard and shivered.

Karoline whimpered, hands shaking so much she fumbled the loop of the belt.

"Careful!" she warned as Karoline moved to retrieve it.

But the warning came too late.

Bulcher grabbed the girl, moving faster than she would have thought possible for such a big man. Karoline screamed as the *Graf* hauled her on top of him. Using her as a shield, he jumped to his feet, the chair toppling over and crashing to the floor.

"Guards! Guards!" he screeched, dragging Karoline towards the door without entangling himself in the fallen chair.

She tried to get a clear shot, but with Karoline squealing and thrashing in his arms, she couldn't risk using the bow.

Her stomach lurched as the door to the apartment crashed open, and boots thudded across the floorboards.

"An assassin! Come to do murder!" Bulcher shrieked behind Karoline. His ankle caught a leg of the chair, but he kept his balance.

Indecision stilled her. If the guards were about to take her, better she killed Bulcher and prayed for the best, but she'd as likely kill Karoline as the *Graf*. The girl was only a slip; there might be plenty of Bulcher to hit, but she was no crack shot and-

The bedroom door flew open, and figures poured in.

"Take that alive!" Bulcher screamed, one arm around Karoline's neck, the other raised to jab a fat bejewelled finger at her.

"My lord," one of the men behind him said, "your britches

appear to have fallen down..."

Then Lucien put a pistol to Bulcher's head.

Chapter Ten

Seigfried, *Graf* Bulcher glared at them as ferociously as any man with his britches around his feet and cock hanging out could.

They were lashing the *Graf* to the heavy chair by ankles and feet. Or at least Lucien was. His bad arm meant tying things was not his forte, while such menial work, even concerning a *Graf*, was a bit below Lebrecht.

Bulcher reserved the worst of his glaring for his fellow nobleman, which seemed a little off, given Solace was the one who wanted him dead.

Turning his back on the rest of the room, he joined Solace by the tower room's fireplace as Lebrecht, looking pale and awkward, stood over Bulcher and Lucien worked with a breezy, and inappropriate, whistle on his lips. Hilde had ushered Karoline out into the next room. Her sobs, in intermittent gales, kept tugging at him. He really should shut the door.

"The castle's ours, my lady... for now..."

Solace still clutched her crossbow; he was careful not to stand in front of it. Her eyes were restless, fingers twitchy.

"Good..."

"But for how long...? There must still be a few people at large. If any of them open the Great Hall..."

"We'll deal with it if it happens. Bosko will do his best…" her eyes returned to Bulcher while her finger played with the crossbow.

"But after…" his eyes moved to Bulcher for an instant, too, before bouncing to her, "…what happens then? Once we let people out…"

"It will be fine, Ulrich."

"We are going to let them out… aren't we?"

"Of course," she said, with the air of someone who hadn't thought much about anything beyond what happened next.

"Right, all done!" Lucien straightened up and patted Bulcher's cheek, "Nice and comfy, my lord?"

"Do you know what happens to people who cross me?" Bulcher said, voice rising even higher than usual.

"Yep," Lucien said, wiping his hands together, "that's why we're here…"

"I'll flay you alive…" Bulcher hissed. He seemed to be getting his tongue back.

"Yes, of course you will," Lucien said, with a jaunty wink, before turning to them, "We should check the upper floors, make sure they're clear…"

Solace stared glassily at him.

"My lady…" he whispered, deciding it not wise to nudge someone holding a loaded crossbow.

"Yes… check the rest of the tower," Solace said. Although her eyes clicked back into focus, her voice remained hollow.

Lucien glanced at him. He nodded.

"Come, my lord, best I don't go alone," Lucien said to Lebrecht when the nobleman stayed rooted to the spot, "the dark has always made me nervous…"

Lebrecht looked like he would argue. Then his eyes flicked to Bulcher. He mumbled something and hurried after the mercenary.

The young nobleman paused in the doorway.

"Solace..."

"Go," she said without looking at him, "I think it best."

Uncertainty played over Lebrecht's face. Lucien tugged his arm and closed the door.

Leaving the three of them alone.

"Perhaps you should leave too..."

He assumed Solace was talking to him not Bulcher, even though her attention was fixed on the bloated *Graf*.

"No."

Maybe it was the curtness of his tone, or the unfamiliarity of him refusing her anything or the way he crossed his arms (despite the pain) to signify he was going nowhere. Still, whatever it was, it was enough to tear her eyes from the man she'd spent the last year wanting to kill.

"Ulrich..."

She only said his name, but a single word can have a lot of meaning stitched to it if you say it a certain way.

She didn't want him to witness what she was about to do. It was a burden she thought she should carry alone; perhaps she felt she could not do what she needed to if he was watching. Maybe she feared it might poison their relationship, whatever their relationship was. Perhaps she feared his reaction. Perhaps she feared her own.

All those things might have been true and conveyed in how she said his name, slow and drawn out, and how she looked at him, eyes wide, lips parted.

But none were why he refused to leave.

Save her, and you save yourself...

She looked so lost he experienced the strangest desire to step across Bulcher and hold her till the tears came. Which was not what you would normally do with someone about to torture and murder a man.

She took a deep breath, and something seemed to fall behind her eyes, sealing in whatever vulnerability that had momentarily splashed, floundered, and flung out a despairing hand towards him,

Solace placed the crossbow on the bed before standing directly in front of Bulcher. Slowly, she drew a blade from the scabbard strapped to her wrist. The steel glinted in the candlelight. The dagger was thin, and even if he didn't know the hours and hours Solace spent running a whetstone along each edge, any fool could see how wickedly sharp it was.

Especially when shoved under their nose.

Bulcher's head went down to look at the blade and then back up toward Solace.

The *Graf's* giggle was so high-pitched and sudden it sounded like a startled piglet.

"Are you trying to scare me, my darling girl?"

"Where are the Red Company?" Solace twisted the knife back and forth. This time, Bulcher's eyes remained on his mistress.

"You'll be terribly dissatisfied if you are. Fear is unknown to me, sweet cheeks."

"How did you hire them? How did you contact them? How did you arrange payment?"

"So many questions. You ruin a man's wedding night and then nought but questions!"

Solace placed the blade flat against Bulcher's cheek. The nobleman didn't flinch.

"Tell me!"

"And not even interesting questions. How tiresome…" Bulcher yawned.

"If you don't answer me, I will start cutting bits of you off. Don't think I won't!"

Another giggle. Another startled piglet.

"Tell me, sweet pea…" Bulcher jerked towards her fast enough to make Solace take a step backwards, and he one forward, "…do you really think you can do anything to hurt *me?*"

Solace gave the dagger in her hand a few more spins.

"You might be rich and powerful," she said, "but you'll bleed just like anyone else. You'll feel pain, just like anyone else. You'll die, just like anyone else…"

Bulcher eased himself back, flexing his fingers. A smile broke the *Graf's* face. His teeth were as dazzling in the candlelight as his eyes were dark.

"Not everything dies…"

The dagger in Solace's hand stilled.

Bulcher's too-white smile stretched further.

"You thought I'd fear you, didn't you, my chick? That I'd cry and scream and beg? Like your father did? But that's the thing you learn with age and wisdom. Life is just full to the brim with disappointments…" the smile widened so far it seemed the *Graf's* waxy face consisted of nothing but two black slits above white, white teeth, "…for the likes of you..."

Solace swallowed. Sweat glistened on her face, the dagger in her hand trembling.

He wanted to pull her away from Bulcher, drag her kicking and screaming out of Thasbald, put her on Styx and ride into the night. Something about Bulcher, those eyes, those teeth, made him think they'd be far safer out there with the brigands and mercenaries and rampaging armies than in here with a fat man lashed to a chair.

He tried to catch her eye, but his Lady could see nothing but Bulcher. Her world had reduced to this room. He doubted her even aware he was still here.

For the last year, vengeance had gnawed her, consumed her like rats in the cellar, eating her, eating the soft parts and leaving the hard. Now the feast vengeance demanded sat before her, trussed up and at her mercy.

But for some reason the feast was smiling.

"Where..." Solace swallowed again, "...are the Red Company?"

Bulcher tilted his head to the left, then to the right, the flabby folds of his neck swelling and flattening as his head moved as far as it could one way and then as far as it could the other.

"Why did Saul lie to me about you, little bird? Such a shame... I would have delighted in gobbling you up..." Bulcher's teeth snapped together, loud enough to make Solace flinch.

The startled piglet's laugh filled the room again.

"I'd never have allowed you to touch me," the dagger spun faster in her hand.

"How ungrateful. I would have saved you from those oh so naughty, *naughty* vampires. The least you could have done was... become a woman for me, my little chicky-chick."

"I'd have killed myself first."

Bulcher's colossal shoulder rose and fell.

"You wouldn't have been the first. But I wouldn't have let you until after I'd had my fill of you..." a wet pink tongue slithered out from between those too-white teeth to wiggle at her.

"Why? Why do all that just to... just to... have *me?!*"

Bulcher's dark eyes peered back at her through slits of waxy skin. Then he threw back his head and laughed.

Not a high-pitched squeal this time, but a booming, room-shaking roar.

"What's so funny?" Solace asked, the cords in her neck straining as she loomed over the *Graf*. He moved to his mistress' side.

Bulcher's laughter subsided in juddering, spluttering increments till it trailed off in one final long exhalation.

"Tell me..." the little eyes buried in their dark slits slid from Solace to him, "...would *you* go to so much trouble just to fuck one little chicky-chick, eh?"

"I'm not mad," he said before he could stop himself.

"You think me mad?" Bulcher's eyebrows, so thin they must have been fastidiously plucked, shot up his shiny forehead.

"All those people died..." he ignored the shut-up look Solace flashed him, "...because of your lust. How can you *not* be mad?"

"Lust..." Bulcher repeated, another squeaking giggle

bubbling in the back of his throat.

"And because my father called you a pig!" Solace moved the dagger from one hand to the other and back again.

"I didn't dispatch vampires because your father insulted me. And I didn't send them for your cunny either, though I admit that would have been a sweet fancy atop the cake."

He could feel Solace trembling next to him. Something falling apart? Something trying to escape? He put his shoulder between her and Bulcher.

"Then why did you send them?"

Why did you send the masters to me?

They broke me.

They made me a lesser man.

They made me a coward.

They made me cast aside my honour.

It was no real realisation that he had almost as many reasons to hate Bulcher as his lady did.

"Why..." Bulcher's eyes flicked back and forth, "...I sent them for the silver, of course."

"What-"

The door flew open before Solace could finish the sentence, and Lucien rushed in.

"We have a problem," the mercenary said.

Bulcher vomited up another squealing giggle.

"Of course you do..."

*

The stars could be falling from the sky and the dead clawing their way out of the dirt for all she cared. She had Bulcher, the vermin responsible for all the ills that had befallen her and hers, where she wanted him.

He might not be begging and squirming yet, but she would cut that awful, screeching, squealing giggle out of his fat, hideous hide if-

Renard had taken her by the shoulder to move her towards the door.

"My lady...." he insisted.

His eyes were narrow, lips hard.

Looking down, she found the dagger she intended to slice Bulcher into tiny pieces with, hovered a hair's breadth from Renard's stomach.

How had it got there?

She sensed she'd said something, but she wasn't sure what. All she could hear was Bulcher's infernal, squeaking laugh. Even though the *Graf* had fallen silent.

Renard's gaze rose from the blade at his gut.

"My lady..." he repeated, more firmly this time.

"Yes... of course," she said, unsure what she was agreeing to.

When Renard put his hand on her elbow again and started manoeuvring her to the door, she twisted to stare at Bulcher. She could only see the back of his head. Thick sausages of fat, waxy skin, beads of sweat. His shoulders rapidly rose and fell as if he were panting, although he hadn't been when she'd been standing in front of him. Had he?

"He's going nowhere," Renard said.

She dragged her eyes from Bulcher's back to Renard's face, brow furrowed, lips puckered. Concern dripped off his face as pungently as the perspiration did from Bulcher's.

She didn't want to leave Bulcher. She didn't want to be

near him.

"Solace..." Lucien called from the doorway.

She nodded, sheathing the dagger as she stepped towards the mercenary. Then she swivelled away, hurriedly crossed the room, and scooped the crossbow from the bed.

Bucher's eyes weighed down on her every step of the way.

When she turned back, she expected the *Graf* to be looming over her, a mountain of greasy flesh, britches around his ankles, his *thing* poking out from beneath a balcony of fat, hands reaching out to-

Bulcher remained in the chair, bound and motionless.

Grinning and glaring as if amusement and hatred simultaneously pulled him in different directions.

"Always best to keep the bed clear..." Bulcher's right eye closed and opened in a laborious wink, "...you never know, eh, sweetmeat?"

Her fingers squeezed the crossbow's trigger.

About as hard as she could without firing the thing.

Bulcher's grin didn't falter.

Neither did whatever turned down in his eyes' deep, dark pits.

She forced her fingers away from the trigger and hurried out of the room, Bulcher's giggle serenading her every step of the way.

"What!?" she demanded as soon as Lucien closed the bedchamber door on the *Graf*'s infernal giggling.

"We have company," Lucien put his back to the door to ensure either Bulcher didn't get out or to prevent her from returning.

"Upstairs?" she asked, thrusting the crossbow at Renard.

"No, there was only her up there," Lucien nodded at Karoline's maid, Elin, who now sat with her mistress, pale-faced and wide-eyed. Karoline had stopped crying, at least, as she gripped Elin's hand. Hilde stood behind them, arms crossed.

Lebrecht warmed himself by the fire; Hugo, in his ill-fitting Thasbald uniform hanging from his bony frame, shuffling by the other door, was the only other person in the room.

"Soldiers came," Hugo blurted, "so I shut the door and locked it before they got to me!"

"How many?" Renard asked, discarding the crossbow on the table.

"Five, six... maybe more."

"How many?" Renard repeated.

Hugo took a breath, "Six... there were six. They were running, they shouted at me... I wasn't going to fool them... so I thought it best to... did I do the right thing?"

"Could you have fought them off?" Lucien asked.

Hugo shook his head.

"Then you did the right thing, lad. Don't fight when you know you can't win. First rule of soldiering, that."

"Will the door hold?" she asked Lucien.

"It's heavy and solid, but no door will hold forever."

"And there's no other way in?"

"No obvious ones, but castles are full of secrets..."

"So, we're safe for now?"

Lucien pulled a face, "There's something else to consider..."

Her hands were itching to get back to Bulcher as much as her feet were itching to keep away from him. Which was strange, given how long she'd waited, dreamed and prayed for this. She stilled her impatience.

"They go away," Renard said before Lucien could continue.

"Wouldn't that be better?" she asked.

"If they get through the door, it means coming up those spiral stairs single file. One of us could hold them. Six men aren't enough to take those stairs."

"However, if they head to the Great Hall…" Lucien said.

"But Bosko has more than six men?"

"Spread around the castle, and none of the spots are as defendable as here. If they can get to one of the doors and let the household out of the Great Hall…" Lucien explained.

"We're done for…" Renard finished.

They'd become good at finishing each other's sentences. It probably had something to do with the time they spent drinking together.

"And if it comes down to a fight, how do we know Bosko's men will be up to the task?" Lebrecht piped up.

"Then we keep them here," she said.

"We open the door and take them on the stairs?" Lucien nodded.

"No one dies unless we have no other choice," she said.

"What… other choice do we have?" Renard asked.

"We talk to them."

"Talk?" Lucien and Renard asked in unison.

They really had been spending a lot of time together.

"We tell them to lay down their weapons."

"We do?" Lucien looked amused.

"Tell them we are witchhunters and their lord has been consorting with demons. If they denounce Bulcher, it will demonstrate their innocence, and they will be spared."

"And if that doesn't work?" Lebrecht asked.

"Then you kill them."

The silence in the room was deafening.

Which she took as their agreement.

"Off you go," she said to Lucien, moving back to the bedchamber.

"Me?" Lucien said, making no move to get out of her way.

"Who else? You're good at talking."

Lucien didn't look convinced.

"The wise general always assigns their troops to the task best suited to their talents..." she smiled and patted the mercenary's arm, "...first rule of soldiering, that..."

In the Company of Shadows

Chapter Eleven

"You think that will work?" he asked once Lucien and Lebrecht left. Usk and Gotz were already down by the door if the Thasbald men managed to break through.

Hugo still loitered by the door. Karoline started crying again. Hilde was staring at him.

"'tis worth a try," Solace said, "Go with them in case the worst happens."

"My place is with you."

He expected her to tell him his place was wherever she told him it was, but instead, her eyes turned to Hugo, "Take the women upstairs; it will be safer."

Hugo stared at the three women as if Solace had just ordered him to herd ferocious beasts but eventually nodded.

Elin rose quickly enough to suggest she wanted to bolt out of the room to escape the lunatics. Karoline hesitated to glance at the door to the bedchamber before rising to her feet, taking her maid's hand and letting her lead her across the room to Hugo.

Hilde stayed put.

When he jerked his head towards Karoline and Elin, Hilde said, "My place is with you."

Again, he expected Solace to argue, but his mistress was already heading back to the bedchamber as if drawn by some dark magnetism.

"Don't come in..." Solace said, pausing in front of the door, "...unless things go badly downstairs, in which case... run..."

Hilde watched as Solace disappeared, leaving the door ajar behind her.

"Ulrich...?"

He should say something to reassure her. Or just hold her for a moment. But he'd never been a man of words or actions that didn't involve shot or steel.

Instead, he conjured a smile, hoped that was enough, and hurried after Solace. As always, no matter what, he knew his place was at her side.

He closed the door after him.

Part of him wanted Bulcher to have somehow freed himself so he could simply kill the bastard. However, he found Bulcher as they'd left him. Solace already standing over him again.

"Troubles, troubles..." the *Graf* sighed, "...oh, how they do circle and sweep..."

Solace slapped Bulcher's face.

"What damn silver?"

"I never thought you so feisty! What fun we will have together when you're in your rightful place, eh, sugarplum?"

He moved to Bulcher's left so his back wasn't to the door. Quite what he'd do if Thasbald men came pouring through it, he didn't know. Die with honour was probably his best bet.

After ensuring they didn't take Solace alive.

Bulcher's eyes, all but lost between rolls of fat, were fixed on Solace. They made him think of stagnant ponds deep in a black forest where the sunlight never fell, where things died, and the world rotted.

No, he couldn't let his mistress fall into this monster's hands.

One or the other of them wasn't leaving this room alive.

He pulled a pistol free, cocked it as awkwardly as he did everything better done with two hands and placed it on a chest of drawers by the wall.

The click of the mechanism drew those corrupt pools in his direction.

"Are you going to slap me, too?"

He replied by drawing his second pistol and cocking that as well. Keeping hold of that one, he put his back to the wall.

"You're a cripple," Bulcher said, the words a wet fleshy snigger, "why haven't you been put down?"

Solace hit him again.

"So very feisty..." Bulcher tittered, "...breaking the feisty ones is always so much more fun than the snivelling ones. Skinny-whinny Karoline wouldn't have lasted long at all. Though... longer than she will now."

Solace hit him again. She grunted as her hand slapped flesh, the blow hard enough to knock Bulcher's head to the right. But not to stop him grinning.

"Can't you do it any harder, my little bunny?" Blood trickled from the *Graf's* lip, "I rather like it..."

Bulcher's fat pink tongue slithered from between his lips to lick at the blood. He lowered his head whilst keeping his eyes on Solace.

"See?" Bulcher wiggled his eyebrows.

He followed the Bulcher's gaze along with Solace down to where the purple head of the *Graf's* now erect cock strained towards his lady.

Solace recoiled backwards as if she'd just been hit, too.

He pushed himself away from the wall, but Solace, attention fixed on Bulcher, held out a hand, palm up.

I can deal with this.

Solace dropped her hand and straightened her back. She was panting as if she'd just sprinted up the Silver Tower's steep, twisting staircase. She sucked air through flaring nostrils.

Then, she slid her dagger free of its sheath once more.

Her eyes fell to Bulcher's lap.

And she twisted the dagger back and forth in her hand.

Bulcher's piglet squeal echoed around the room again.

"Do you think I won't cut that... *thing* off you?"

The *Graf* chortled enough to make bubbles of drool erupt over his bloodied lip.

Solace took a step forward.

"You had my father killed. Roasted alive over a fire, with an apple in his mouth... do you really think there is anything I won't do to you?"

"Your father was a tiresome bore, my rose; he got what he deserved."

"For calling you a pig?"

Flabby shoulders twitched, "He had something I wanted. He wouldn't give it to me, therefore he had to die. 'tis how the world works."

"What did he have? Tell me?"

"I have told you. Silver. And you, of course, but chiefly the silver. Women entertain for a while, but silver! Ah, buttercup, silver never, ever bores."

"We had no silver, Bulcher. Tassau was not rich; what nonsense are you sprouting? Do you think that will keep you alive?"

"No..." Bulcher's tongue slinked along his split lip again, "'tis not lies that keep a man like me alive."

Solace placed the dagger against Bulcher's cheek; she seemed to be struggling to stay calm, "If the next thing out of your mouth isn't a proper answer, I swear I will cut something off you..."

"Your family's mines. That's why I sent the Red Company, darling girl, for the mines."

Solace's brow, slick enough with sweat to dampen her roughly cut fringe, crumpled, "But the mines are empty, worthless, exhausted generations ago!"

Despite the steel pressed to his cheek, Bulcher chuckled.

"So your father thought, and his father before him, but I understand differently. Rich veins are yet to be tapped, deep down, down, down in the dark. I have spoken to men who assured me that is the case. You will have to take my word on that, as I had those men killed so no one else discovered the true value of those *worthless* mines."

While Solace stared at Bulcher, he asked the nobleman, "If the *Freiherr* thought the land worthless, why didn't you just buy it for a pittance?"

Bulcher looked sideways at him, the blade shaking against his cheek.

"I tried, but he became suspicious. So I offered to marry his daughter to get the land, but he insulted me, so... what else was I supposed to do?" Another wet chuckle escaped the *Graf*.

Solace's face dropped, "You did all that... for silver?"

"Oh, my poor flower, I can see the terrible disappointment on your face! You thought I did it all for you. Alas, no! As sweet as your tight, juicy cunny undoubtedly is, you're not worth anywhere near as much as the Red Company charges, you-"

Solace slashed the blade across Bulcher's face, cutting his cheek open. Blood sprayed her hand. She staggered backwards, staring at the darkened steel she held before her.

Bulcher didn't scream, squeal, or call out.

He didn't even flinch.

He just laughed as the blood poured down the side of his face.

The man's erection, he couldn't help himself from noticing, was, if anything, even more pronounced.

"So..." he said, before Solace could do more with her blade, "...your plan was to marry Solace? That's what Saul told us. You would pretend to pay a ransom for her freedom, and she would marry you, and with the *Freiherr* and Lord Torben dead, you would gain everything Lady Solace inherited."

Again, Bulcher looked at him sideways.

"It appears Saul is a more talkative chap than I took him for. How odd. I'm usually an excellent judge of a man's character."

"He lied to you. He betrayed you. He took your money and broke your bargain. Not only didn't you get Lady Solace, but you also didn't get the Tassau mines either. So, tell us where the bastard is?"

Solace's eyes followed each drop of Bulcher's blood that fell from her knife, her free hand wrapped around the pouch holding Wendel's ashes hanging from her neck. She didn't seem to be listening to either of them.

"Oh no, Saul delivered. Saul *always* delivers..." Bulcher chuckled again. Dear gods, the man chuckled a lot. He'd never met a man so superficially good-humoured, but he would have bet however much silver the madman thought filled those mines that there was no laughter at all inside all that blubber.

"How?"

"He brought me the deeds and titles. A little judicious forgery, and those mines in Silesia now belong to me. I missed out on a wife, but..." the *Graf* turned his head towards him, the fact a bloody chunk of his cheek was hanging off didn't seem to be troubling the man in the slightest, "...there is no shortage of noble cunt in the Empire to marry..."

"And you've married a lot of noble cunts, haven't you, Bulcher?"

Despite what it did to his face, the *Graf* smiled, "I enjoy my pleasures. Why shouldn't I? I've earned them."

"Until you kill them," he said.

"Everything serves a purpose. Until it doesn't. I'm no different to most in that regard."

"Really, my lord?"

Another wet, shallow laugh, "When she has no more use for you, do you think she will keep you around? Perhaps she won't kill you; perhaps she will," Bulcher turned back to Solace, who still stood clutching the bag of ash about her neck, chest rising and falling like a little bird, "who can say? I fear your lady is a little..." the face split again into a bloody grin as Bulcher's eyebrows crawled up his bald head, "...disturbed..."

*

The *Graf* was speaking.

His lips, fleshy, wet and now darkened with blood, were moving; she could hear sounds she knew were words, but nothing comprehensible reached her mind. Had he started jabbering in a tongue she didn't understand? Something alien and barbaric, like the language of the Moors? Or maybe something arcane and demonic? He was a man who consorted with creatures from the pit.

But, if he was, so was Renard, as he was talking to the monster.

With her monster.

She squeezed the bag of ash she hadn't realised she'd been holding.

One of her monsters.

She had backed away from Bulcher, lashed by hand and foot into his throne-like chair, but, again, she had no recollection of her feet taking her anywhere.

The candles were growing dimmer. Or so it seemed. The darkness in the corners of the room thickening, swelling, consuming the light.

At first, she thought Lord Flyblown might be making an

appearance, but no forms, human or otherwise, coalesced out of the shadows. The darkness simply grew.

What had Flyblown said the last time she saw him? When they... no, when she hung those Swedish soldiers?

Darkness beckons...

Ah, yes, that was it.

She couldn't understand Bulcher's words, but Flyblown's came to her clearly enough.

Harden yourself, child. To destroy the darkness, you must become the darkness...

She swallowed.

Her grip on the leather pouch containing Wendel's ashes hardened sufficiently to whiten her knuckles.

She had waited a year for this. A year of hardship and grief, of ghosts and torments. A year for vengeance.

And now...

Now, it seemed the night was closing in on her. She hesitated as if upon the edge of an abyss. Elsewhere in Thasbald, men were fighting for her, or at least her promises, maybe dying. If they lost and Bulcher's men regained the castle... all this would be for nothing.

Why waste time? Why ask questions?

Kill him! Kill him! Kill him!

Blood trickled down the left side of Bulcher's face. She knew she'd cut him, cut him savagely enough for part of his cheek to be hanging like a half-carved slice off a side of roast meat. But she could not remember doing it.

He needs to suffer for what he did.

I don't want to do this.

Do I?

He destroyed your life, your family, your future.
He is the seed of your damnation.

The voices cried from the deepening shadows, flapping around her like invisible bats on leathery wings.

The dagger spun in her hand. Bulcher's blood wet her fingers. Upon her inner thigh, Flyblown's mark throbbed ever harder. A warning. But of what?

It didn't matter. Nothing mattered. Everything mattered.

Bulcher still squeaked alien words at Renard.

His... *thing* still protruding from under his great belly.

How much blood will soak me if I cut that off?

It would stop him laughing, wouldn't it?

Not that slicing open his cheek had.

How could a man still laugh after you cut his cheek open?

How can his *thing* still be engorged? And why was it even engorged in the first place? And for that-

"My lady?"

She blinked.

She couldn't see Bulcher anymore.

Renard had stepped between them, head tilted, stooped so his eyes were at the same level as hers. No shadows reflected in his eyes. Only the candlelight.

"My lady?" he repeated.

She blinked again.

"Yes?"

"Are you... unwell?"

"I have never been better..." she let go of the bag of demon ash. The dagger in her other, bloodier, hand still spinning. She stopped that, too and found a smile. If Bulcher could smile, so could she, "...why do you ask?"

"You do not seem quite yourself?"

As she was no longer sure who she was, it seemed a trickier question than it once might have been. So, she lied.

"I was just... gathering my thoughts."

Renard didn't look convinced.

"Perhaps, my lady, this should wait until we are certain we have secured the castle, if-"

"No. We must do it now. Our presence elsewhere will not change the outcome, and if we fail in that regard..." she nodded towards the bleeding man over Renard's shoulder, "...I do not wish to fail in this one too."

Kill him! Kill him! Kill him!

Is this me?

I don't want to be here.

Make him suffer! He needs to suffer!

He is the seed of your damnation.

The disembodied voices flew around her in a giddying carousel.

It was only when she stared directly into Renard's eyes, that their wretched clammer hushed.

How strange.

"He is insane; we can believe nothing he tells us," Renard said.

She concentrated on the candlelight dancing in his eyes. The voices quietened, fading back into the shadows.

Is this what Morlaine suffers? Constantly?

"I know, but what else do we have?"

Other than her visions. Her *sight* telling her to go to Magdeburg for her other monsters would be there when that doomed city's walls fell. And they would kill the woman

Renard... probably had some feelings for.

"I need to know what he knows," she closed her eyes, expecting the voices to return in that darkness, but they didn't, "so that we can find the Red Company, else we have to go to Magdeburg and..."

"And?"

She opened her eyes, "That will be difficult."

Have you lain with Hilde yet, Ulrich?

Another voice whispered, though a more familiar one.

She stepped around Renard.

It was not the time for such foolish thoughts.

Bulcher watched them through dark slits. Still grinning. Still bleeding, though the blood flowed slower. And, as Renard rightly said, still insane.

How do you even make a madman suffer?

And if he did not suffer, like Wendel didn't suffer, could she ever sate vengeance, that shrieking and bellowing creature that forever clawed and ripped inside her?

Bulcher's lunatic giggles weren't going to feed that thing.

So, what to do? What to do?

The sticky dagger in her right hand started spinning again.

Cut and cleave... cut and cleave...

She bent her knees, lowering herself to Bulcher's eyeline.

Flyblown's mark sizzled on her thigh.

"How did you find the Red Company, my lord?"

"By listening to the whispers in the wind, honey flower, 'tis where you find all the most useful things."

She dropped to her knees.

"Rumour and gossip?"

Bulcher's eyes went with her.

"When you crave certain things..." he licked his blooded lips, "...they have a way of finding you."

"What things, my lord?"

"Power. Wealth. Pleasure."

"And they found you, did they?"

"Oh no," Bulcher shook his head hard enough to wobble his many chins, "they are shy and tricksy. But the means to find them. If you look. They will come. Most are useless, but between the grit, if you sift carefully, you can discover stuff that gleams."

"The Red Company?"

"Among other things. I heard whispers. I looked. They made themselves known..." Bulcher's grin stretched his face far enough to send more blood dripping down his chins, "...we did business."

Behind her, Renard moved. Shuffling his feet. A sound she recognised. He wasn't happy.

She placed her left hand on the blubber of Bulcher's right thigh. The skin was corpse-white in the candlelight and slick beneath her fingers. She'd expected him to be hot and clammy, but Bulcher's flesh was cool. They were on the other side of the room from the fire, and she supposed it must be chilly sitting with your britches around your ankles.

Flyblown's mark was almost pulsating.

"How do I find them," she asked.

"Why would you want to, my succulent damson?"

"So that I can kill them."

Bulcher stared down at her for a moment. Then, he threw

back his head and laughed.

She placed the point of her dagger against the top of his knee and began to move it along his thigh. Not hard enough to break the skin but sufficient to leave a vivid red scratch in its wake.

Bulcher lowered his head. His laughter subsided to a chuckle and finally a couple of breathy snorts before silence descended. He watched the blade's progress towards his still engorged *thing* with interest.

"Tell me," she said, her gaze fixed on the two dark slits gazing down at her rather than the blade. Or the *thing* it was heading to.

"Or?"

"Or I hurt you. Like the demons you sent hurt my father. Like they hurt the women and children of Tassau. Like all the innocents who died a year and two days ago. Because of you."

"But you cannot hurt *me*, child."

"Trust me, my lord," she paused the dagger's progress to push it into the blubber of the *Graf's* huge thigh.

The only sound to escape Bulcher, as steel parted flesh, was a single, drawn-out whistle.

She kept pushing in expectation of a scream, a struggle or, better still, a pleading, begging cry to stop.

But *Graf* Bulcher made no other sound.

And when the whistle stopped, he was still smiling.

Behind, Renard's feet shuffled some more.

She pushed the dagger in as far as it would go. Blood bubbled from the wound to darken Bulcher's pale flesh.

And still, he smiled.

"You cannot hurt me, my fawn; I am unlike other men."

"No?" the dagger made a wet plopping sound when it finally came free of Bulcher's thigh.

"No... have you not realised? Has the light not yet dawned, my sweet and succulent cherry? I am not a man at all. I am a god!"

"A god? That is... quite a claim..." her eyes flicked to the blade; she watched a fat bead hang from the tip until it fell to splash into the blood pouring from the wound in the *Graf's* thigh before returning her gaze to Bulcher's. He looked faintly bemused.

"It did take me many years to accept the truth, but one must always learn to come to terms with the undeniable, even in the face of lesser beings... absence of belief."

"And what makes you think you are a god, my lord?"

"I feel no pain."

She raised an eyebrow, "None at all?"

"Absolutely none. 'tis a gift from the divine."

She began moving the blade up the *Graf's* leg once more.

"We shall see."

"You can do as you wish. I will feel nothing. And I will not die, as gods are, of course, immortal. You, on the other hand..." Bulcher sniggered.

"Tell me, where can I find the Red Company," she forced her eyes to drop to Bulcher's *thing*, still erect, its purple head... staring back at her before her eyes bounced back to his, "I won't ask again..."

"Why, I shall tell you then! Neither of you are leaving Thasbald alive, so I'm sure Saul won't object. And he did lie to me about you. Which is very naughty..."

She paused the blade. A bloody line ran through the stab wound to the top of Bulcher's thigh; she hadn't noticed how hard she'd been pushing.

Control. I need to keep control.

"How?"

"There is a man in Hamburg. If anyone wishes to use the services of the Red Company, you go through him."

"This man's name?"

"He has many. I believe. In Hamburg, he is known as *Herr* Licht. In other places, he has other names."

"And where would I find him in Hamburg?"

Bulcher frowned, "It doesn't matter, my bouncy rabbit of delight, you are never going to visit Hamburg. 'tis a ghastly place, though splendid for making money. But as you are not looking to make money, I am doing you a service by-"

"Humour me," she dug the blade into his thigh and twisted it.

Bulcher didn't react.

Can he really feel no pain?

As absurd as it seemed, Bulcher hadn't shown the slightest discomfort at anything she'd done so far.

How do you make a man who feels no pain suffer?

She started moving the blade towards Bulcher's *thing* again.

"Herr Licht has an establishment off the Schaar Markt; 'tis small, discreet and not well signposted, as you might expect, given the line of work. Ostensibly, Licht is a shipping agent, but that is not his, shall we say, primary source of income," Bulcher tilted his head before enquiring amicably, "Are you intending to slice my cock off, angel?"

"If you don't tell me what I wish."

And probably anyway.

"Well, that would be a new experience. And you don't get so many of them at my age," Bulcher craned his neck forward as his squeaky voice quietened to a conspiratorial whisper, "but it will grow back, you know."

"You're quite mad, aren't you, my lord?"

Bulcher smiled happily.

Behind her, Renard shuffled his feet in agitation, "My lady."

She held up her free hand to quieten him.

"My lady!"

Flyblown's mark stung and smarted. What was wrong with the damn thing?

Her head snapped around, "What?!"

"Of course, he is insane..." Renard fingered the pistol in his good hand as he urged her towards him with the stiff fingers of his bad one "...all vampires are mad..."

Chapter Twelve

Bulcher turned his eyes on him, as much of them as he could see at the bottom of those dark,stagnant slits anyway.

"Her, I will have some delights with before I feast, but you, cripple, I think I'll just feed you to the dogs," the *Graf's* smile was stretched and amiable, "they'll enjoy your gristle and bone much more than I would."

He kept the pistol levelled and summoned Solace again.

She frowned and remained knelt at Bulcher's feet, her blade not far from the cock poking out from beneath the *Graf's* vast belly.

"His face, my lady..." he said when she stayed where she was. Her eyes had a glassiness he didn't like, as if her mind inhabited some other place. Certainly one where she hadn't noticed the scab forming on the cheek she'd sliced open earlier. It was healing before their eyes, the flap of skin slowly curling upwards as the monster's flesh reknitted itself with unnatural speed.

Her own demons had their claws buried too deep for her to recognise the demon sitting in front of her.

If he possessed two good arms, he'd use the other to drag her away, but he didn't, and he dared not risk putting the pistol aside. The leather lashing Bulcher's wrists and ankles to the chair did not seem as secure as they had a few minutes before.

"His face is healing!" he warned.

Solace blinked, and a little life returned to her eyes.

"You're not going to stop now, are you, sugar blossom? You can see how much fun I'm having!" Bulcher giggled and nodded at his hard cock, "you know you want to touch it; you always have…"

Solace recoiled and scrambled backwards till she sat sprawled and panting at his feet, staring at the *Graf*.

"You are a demon?" she asked, voice hoarse.

"Only occasionally, but don't fret, the rest of the time…" Bulcher beamed, "…I'm a sunny delight!"

Slowly, Solace stood up.

Bulcher watched with interest. The leather binding his wrists tautened, the chair's wooden arms creaked.

"Don't…" he warned.

"Can you find a killing shot, cripple? I think not. Your hand is shaking too much."

"I can kill you."

Bulcher giggle turned into a snarl as he leant forward, "If I thought that for a moment, I wouldn't have let you tie me up!"

He was close enough to be confident he could put a lead ball into the monster's forehead. However, the thought of what would happen if he did manage to miss inevitably made it a more challenging shot than if he'd been aiming at something inanimate and harmless.

"Although, I am a god, not a demon!" Bulcher blurted as if

struck by realisation, "So you cannot kill me anyway!"

The *Graf* relaxed his shoulders and slumped back into the heavy chair.

"Why are you here?" He wanted to keep the demon talking if only to distract him long enough to think what to do.

"Well, that's quite an imponderable question for this hour, don't you think?" Bulcher said, voice amiable again.

"Why are you in Thasbald? In the middle of a war? Why not somewhere safer in the south."

The *Graf* yawned, "War is where the money is. And the fun. All the commodities I deal in are best served here, where there are plenty of customers for them. And besides, tis my home. It has been for an exceedingly long time. And home is where the heart is! You know, I much preferred her questions. Having a pretty lass threaten your bollocks with a blade turns out to be far more stimulating than a cripple pointing a pistol at you. Who knew! The things you find out, eh? Even after centuries…"

"And the wives?"

The yawn became a grin, sly and knowing, "A man needs a wife. But when you're a god…"

"You're not a god; you're a monster," Solace almost growled like a dog on a leash at his shoulder. The dagger started spinning in her hand again.

"Is there a difference? Either way, a god must be worshipped, and to be worshipped in this world, you need silver, you need power, you need influence…" the heavy shoulders rolled as Bulcher flexed his head one way and then the other, "…the cunny is just a bonus."

He could feel Solace trembling next to him, her fury palpable. This wasn't how she'd imagined her encounter with *Graf* Bulcher going. And he suspected she'd done an awful lot of imagining over the past year.

But then they hadn't known he was a vampire.

"Your kind hide in the shadows," Solace spat, "how has no one found out what you are?"

"And what do you know of my kind? Our mutual friend Saul is hardly a shrinking violet, is he? Sometimes, hiding in plain sight is the safest thing to do. Besides, I am a god – I may have mentioned that already – I can do as I wish, and the world will bow and scrape before me regardless."

"Not all of it..." Solace said.

"We shall see about that" Bulcher's grin widened again, almost consuming his face. As the *Graf's* leg twitched, the ghost of a grimace momentarily competed with the grin.

And the leather strap around his left ankle snapped.

Bulcher's eyebrow arched as he stretched out his newly freed limb, "If you're going to try and kill me, best do it now. Once I'm out of this chair..."

"You don't die that easily," Solace threw her arm across him in case he had any wild fancy to put a lead ball in the monster's head before the *Graf* freed himself and ripped their throats open.

"No. I don't die easily at all, my little sausage..."

"You are going to suffer. You have to suffer!"

"So much anger! But don't worry, I have a cure for that..." Bulcher nodded towards his lap and winked.

Then he flexed his right leg. For a moment, the strap held,

and the chair groaned. But only for a moment.

"Ah, that's better..." Bulcher's right leg stretched out, massive, bloated thigh wobbling in the process.

"My lady...?"

He glanced at Solace. She remained at his side, head jutting forward, jaw protruding, face so contorted by the things coursing through her he barely recognised his mistress.

"If he gets free..." he stated the obvious when Solace said nothing.

"*When* I get free..." Bulcher's left hand flicked up, and the leather binding his wrist to the arm of the chair tore like paper, "...you're going to be my wife, for a little while at least, you lucky, lucky morsel..."

"My lady?!"

"Oh, haven't you got the balls to shoot me without her permission? What a whipped little cripple you are."

"You have to fucking suffer!" Solace took half a step towards Bulcher, face glowing red, eyes bulging.

The *Graf* smiled as if faced with a petulant but ultimately loveable child.

Bulcher's face changed, as he'd seen demon's faces change before, white, bloodless, a slash of a mouth filled with wicked fangs, black inhuman eyes imprisoning all the colours of the world in their depths, long and thin, though Bulcher's still sported bags of fat that seemed to pulsate and move separately from the rest of his features.

However much Solace wanted Bulcher to suffer, the only death you could visit upon one of these monsters was a quick one.

His hand shook. Solace screamed. Bulcher showed them his glistening fangs.

Master...

Solace took another step forward. Bulcher eyed her curiously.

Then snapped the last restraint holding him to the chair.

His stomach turned. His knees trembled.

If he didn't kill Bulcher now, they would both be dead, so to hell with what Solace wanted.

He pulled the trigger.

But, as we know, a pistol is not a reliable weapon...

*

The bastard was taunting her.

The evil, twisted abomination.

Another demon. Like all the others. A lunatic.

Sitting there, britches around his ankle, his *thing* poking up at her, grinning, and laughing and calling her pet names. When he should be begging, crying, pleading. When he should be suffering! For what he did, for what he caused to happen. All those lives, all that blood. For mines emptied of silver generations ago. The fool, the mad, stupid, sickening, monstrous fool!

And now, on top of it all, he was taunting her. Snapping the leather restraints one by one, showing her they were nothing, that she was nothing. It was all a game, a jest. He was playing with her, a cat with a mouse. A fat, evil, disgusting, obscene cat!

Fury boiled.

She'd felt it before, many times. But never this strong, never this overpowering. The closest she'd come to this was when her dreams had taken her into Madge's mind as the mad woman waited to fire *The Eagle's Claw* to avenge her own father's death under Styx's iron hooves.

Renard was calling to her. Shouting at her.

No matter.

Nothing mattered.

The blade spun betwixt fingers and palm.

Bulcher's blood darkened the steel, soiled her hand. She wanted more. She wanted to fucking bathe in it.

And here he was. Taunting and smiling and... and... aroused!

Part of her wanted to throw herself at the monster. Another held her back. Not out of fear or sense but because he had to suffer, and she didn't trust herself to do it. She didn't believe she could do it. He wasn't just a monstrous man after all; he was a monster.

But if he didn't suffer, there would be nothing to fill the emptiness, the nothingness. The ache in the void would continue unabated. Swelling, growing, and consuming until nothing remained of Solace von Tassau bar the shadow where she walked.

"If he gets free..."

Renard's voice floated from somewhere, distant beneath the roar filling the candlelit room. She was only vaguely aware of her own screamed words.

"You have to fucking suffer!"

Which was when the monster showed his true face.

And the fury became fear.

But she had sworn never to show these things fear again.

Only Bulcher's right wrist was still bound, not that it was that keeping him sitting gloating on his throne.

She took a step towards him on watery legs.

Renard said something else.

Kill him!

No, he must suffer.

Or he'll kill us.

Please, he has to suffer! It's the only way. If-

She raised the spinning blade.

Bulcher bared his fangs, wicked, thin and sharp as the dagger in her bloody hand.

The demon snapped the last restraint.

There was a flash and a scream behind her. Something thumped onto the floor.

Bulcher rose.

This face was long and inhumanly ashen, the fat drooping from it as if held in bags too flimsy to contain it. The chair fell backwards. He seemed even larger, taller, wider. And his *thing* was still pointing at her.

The *Graf* reached out, unfurling corpse-white fingers, "Come, Solace, be mine, as you are meant to be..." something that might have been a smile twisted itself around the fangs, "...come, kneel before your god, come, show your husband-to-be due homage..."

She risked a glance behind her.

Renard writhed on the floor, clutching his face.

His pistol had misfired.

She was on her own.

She raised her dagger.

"Think you can catch me, Bulcher?"

The monster stood between her and the door; she'd sent her men down to deal with the Thasbald soldiers, and Renard was incapacitated. Possibly blinded, possibly dying.

Bulcher took a step towards her. Or tried to. It seemed even vampires had problems when their britches were around their ankles.

As he stumbled forward, she rushed in and drove the dagger into his chest, spinning away as he tried to envelop her within his enormous, flabby arms.

"I'll have to settle with you suffering in Hell!" she spat at the creature as she staggered backwards.

Bulcher stood there, swaying, liquid eyes looking down at the dagger in his chest. She'd rammed it into the hilt, and a black flower blossomed around it, darkening the *Graf's* silk shirt.

She backed away till her legs pressed against the bed.

The *Graf* shuffled around to face her.

Why isn't he dead?

Slowly, Bulcher's hand rose to the blade's hilt sticking out of his chest.

With a grunt, he started pulling it free.

If they don't die instantly, they don't die.

She'd missed his heart.

Or the surrounding fat armoured it so well the steel blade hadn't been long enough to reach it.

Behind Bulcher, Renard was groping for the table where

his second pistol rested.

The clatter of her dagger hitting the floor pulled her eyes back to the *Graf*.

"I said..." Bulcher kicked himself clear of his britches, "...kneel, wife..."

"I'd rather die."

She wanted to reach for the fencing dagger at her hip. Except it wasn't there. She wore the maid's uniform she'd gone up to Karoline's previous chambers in. She hadn't thought she'd need another blade. Which she supposed showed you could never have too many knives.

He rolled his shoulders, "All in good time."

Behind Bulcher, Renard found the second pistol. He was now trying to make his eyes work.

"Now I'm going to have to put right all the mischief you've made in my home, so I won't have time to deal with you straight away but don't worry, I've never shirked from teaching my wives exactly how they should behave..."

Renard raised the pistol, face contorted with the effort; even from the corner of her eye, she could see how much it shook.

Her blade lay on the floor by Bulcher's discarded britches. If Renard didn't kill him, she'd have to hope the distraction would be sufficient for her to grab the dagger. And do a better job of finding the bastard's heart with it.

But he needs to suffer!

Yes, he did. But she wouldn't be able to make any monsters suffer if she died here. Or worse.

Bulcher was still talking.

"...so, be a helpful little sweet pea and hold your hands out for me to tie up..."

A strip of leather from one of the torn belts swung from the *Graf*'s left hand. He was slapping the wobbling flesh of his bare thigh with it. She hadn't seen him pick it up.

She edged along the bed as if trying to make for the door; Bulcher swivelled with her. Renard sucked in a breath, steadying himself as he peered through red, bleary eyes.

"Why don't-" she began, but before she could finish, Bulcher dropped the belt. Moving with the speed of a demon rather than the fat old man he pretended to be, he twisted around, scooped up the huge throne-like chair as if it were made of twigs and hurled it across the room.

The chair smashed into Renard. The pistol went off, but wherever the shot ended up, it wasn't in Bulcher. Wedged between wall and chair, Renard didn't move.

She tried for the dagger, but Bulcher spun back around and grabbed her.

"No! No! No!" he boomed, dragging her to the bed by her hair.

She kicked and clawed, but every blow bounced off the *Graf*, who threw her onto the bed.

"I guess I'm just going to have to tie you up the hard way..." he leered, face once more human, though no less terrifying.

She tried to spring off the bed, but he caught her with a swiftness no human man of his size could and slammed her back down.

"Now stay still, or I'll have to pin you down, and I'd much

prefer to save that fun for when I've got the time to deal with you properly."

She cast around for something to hurl at him, but nothing more fearsome than a pillow was within reach.

The only other weapon in the room was Renard's sabre, but that was in its scabbard, under both Renard and the chair.

Is he dead?

He wasn't moving.

Of course he isn't.

Worry about him later.

He survived falling into a frozen moat in the middle of winter. A chair wasn't going to kill him.

Bulcher loomed over her. She tried rolling away, but five cold, fleshy fingers caught her ankle and yanked her back.

"You are a frisky one, aren't you, darling girl? I'm going to enjoy making you one of my wives..."

Her heart pounded as he reeled her in. His *thing* still... still... bobbing. There was a stink to him, underneath his perfumes, something rank and sickening, something dead and rotting. Gorge rose. Clawing up her throat.

But she would no more show one of these monsters that than she would her fear.

She swallowed it as she struggled.

"I really am going to have words with Saul, I almost missed out on you. Silver has more worth, of course..." he leaned over and grabbed her hair again, pulling her towards his face.

She tried to claw his eyes, then rip open the unnaturally

healing wound on his cheek. Bulcher didn't even blink.

"Now a kiss for your husband-to-be, just a little one, then I really must go and kill your friends, my darling bud..." he paused and straightened, a thoughtful look on his face despite the blows she landed on it, "...and my current wife, she'll have to go, too. We can't be legally married while she's still around, though not before Saul has-"

Bulcher's words dissolved into a gurgling noise in the back of his throat as his eyes, at the bottom of their dark slits, rolled upwards.

For a second, he tottered, then toppled forward like a felled tree.

She rolled away, just avoiding his huge body crashing on top of her.

She sat panting, staring at the crossbow bolt protruding from the back of Bulcher's head.

Her eyes eventually moved from Bulcher's motionless form to the doorway, where Hilde stood.

"Did I do the right thing?" Hilde asked, lowering the crossbow she'd left in the other room.

She looked at the girl for a moment, chest heaving.

Then nodded.

"Thank you..." she managed to say.

Despite the voice screaming in her head.

He was supposed to suffer, you stupid bitch!!!

Chapter Thirteen

"You look like shit," Lucien told Renard, peering over Hilde's shoulder as she fussed over... her man.

"Admittedly..." the mercenary hitched a thumb at the whale-like corpse face down on the bed with a crossbow bolt protruding from the back of his head, "...not as bad as him, though."

"Thanks," Renard winced as Hilde extracted something from his cheek. Her retainer would have a few new scars to commemorate this night.

"Your work?" Lucien asked.

It took her a moment to register he meant *Graf* Bulcher.

She shook her head, then nodded towards Hilde.

Lucien whistled and patted Hilde's shoulder, "Nice shot."

"Thanks! Remember it next time you think about pawing my arse," she said without looking away from Renard.

"What happened?" Lucien asked her.

"He was a demon."

"He was wha-"

"What is happening downstairs?"

"We told them we were witchfinders as you suggested and... erm..." Lucien's head swivelled back and forth between her and the corpse on the bed, "...they went a bit quiet..."

Renard tried shooing Hilde away, "How many of them know about Bulcher...?"

They looked at each other.

Lucien scratched his stubble, "Any that do might not take too kindly to the idea of witchfinders..."

"Perhaps they've run away..." Hilde offered, still trying to dab Renard's face with a damp cloth.

"They haven't attempted to break down the door?" she asked.

Lucien shook his head, "Do you mind if I throw something over his lordship? That great flabby arse is a bit off-putting."

She nodded.

"What do we do now?" Renard asked from behind Hilde's fussing.

Leadership came with many downsides. People assuming you always knew what to do being one of them. It wasn't a problem when she did know what to do, but people began to expect it. Be careful what you wish for.

Currently, she had little idea of what to do.

The goal of finding Bulcher, getting him alone and killing him as slowly as possible had consumed her. Everything else had been vague notions and half-baked promises. Now Bulcher was dead; he hadn't suffered, but at least she had some intelligence to help find the Red Company.

And all she wanted to do was curl up and sleep.

Despite spending most of the day curled up in a box.

"My lady?" Renard asked.

She wanted to tell him that she was an eighteen-year-old girl who'd never even been kissed, so what made him think she knew?

Apart from the months of telling him she knew what to do, of course.

She rubbed her temples. Her head hurt.

Poor you!

But at least Flyblown's mark no longer burned.

"We can't stay locked in this tower all night..." she tried to look assured, "...we should go back to the others. We need to deal with Bulcher's people in the Great Hall."

"Deal, my lady?"

"Don't fret, Ulrich; I promise I won't hang anybody."

"No, of course not," Renard struggled to his feet. He had to grab hold of Hilde to keep himself there. His face was singed and bleeding; he held his side, too, "But how do we deal with them?"

"They need to accept Karoline as their mistress now Bulcher is dead."

A frown fought with Renard's features, "How do we do that, given we've..." his words trailed away as his eyes drifted to the giant lump under the sheet Lucien had covered the *Graf*'s corpse with.

It'll be ashes soon. You should cut something off before we leave...

"Don't worry, I can be very persuasive."

It's a fair walk back to the Great Hall, so there will be ample time to think of something.

"But..." Renard frowned. And then immediately winced and rubbed at his battered face, "Bulcher has a son, the one he told your father he wanted you to marry. Leopold. He is Bulcher's heir; he is now the new *Graf*, Karoline has-"

"Leopold doesn't exist."

Renard frowned again. And winced.

"He doesn't?"

"That's how Bulcher did it. Someone would eventually notice a man living for centuries. But a son replacing his dead father, why, that's the most natural thing in the world, is it not?"

Renard neither frowned nor winced. He just looked blank.

She tried again.

"I can only guess the details, but I assume it worked like this. The *Graf* has a son no one ever sees. A soldier permanently away... soldiering, for instance. Bulcher would go away somewhere on business, visit a distant relative, sit on a mountain and talk to God, or something, *anything* that would keep him away for a year or two. Tragically, he would drop dead during his absence, and his son would return to take up the title. Thus, to the world, the same man has not ruled Thasbald for centuries."

The frown returned, but at least no wince accompanied it this time.

"And the son is always the identical fat old man as the father?"

"A chip off the old block!" Lucien snorted.

"I don't know. Perhaps Bulcher could alter his appearance a little, make himself look younger. Wendel could change his face, after all. All I know for sure is that Leopold, who is far away fighting border skirmishes with the Turks, does not exist. Vampires can't produce children, only sire more of their own kind. Leopold is a figment. Which makes Karoline the heir to Thasbald."

Renard made a little noise in the back of his throat, which she took as agreement before he could think of any more questions.

"Go and bring Karoline down," she said to Hilde before turning back to Renard and Lucien, "Tell the others we will be leaving soon and be prepared to fight our way out, if necessary. We cannot allow ourselves to be bottled up in here."

When the three of them just stared at her – well, Renard stared and swayed – she barked, "Now!"

Hilde and Lucien turned for the door; Renard stayed where he was, "My lady, I-"

"I will be down in a little while, please, I need a moment. Possibly two."

Renard lingered, his face red and peppered with cuts, crumpling in concern.

"Come, Ulrich," Lucien called from the door, "we can talk about firearms maintenance on the way down. A prudent man always takes proper care of his pistol..."

The crumpled look of concern gave way to a shake of the head and an eye roll.

"Go, please, Ulrich; there is nothing here that can hurt me now."

Apart from yourself... she suspected Renard wanted to say, but he nodded and shuffled after Lucien.

Leaving her alone with the corpse.

She stood at the end of the bed for a long time before ripping the sheet off the body. She wanted to look into Bulcher's dead, empty eyes but had to make do with his exposed arse, great rolls of fat and a smattering of warts.

There was a lesson there somewhere.

She could try and roll him over, but she'd have no more luck with that than she would a dead cow.

Bulcher's flesh had already developed a grey hue, wrinkles deepening like a desiccated grape. Soon, he would be nothing but ash.

She waited for something to happen without knowing what it might be. What it should be.

Rage. Relief. Joy. Comfort. Release. Something.

But vengeance, her vengeance, at least, seemed to be a tree that bore little fruit.

Time passed, so she stopped counting it.

If he'd suffered... if I'd made him beg... if... if...

But she hadn't. Hilde killed him. He'd died in a heartbeat; he'd known no pain. She knew Hilde had done the right thing, and the monster may well have killed them all if she hadn't, yet if she could feel one thing in the emptiness that filled her, it was resentment.

Hilde took my vengeance from me, just as she is taking Renard from me...

Despite recognising the thought's stupidity, she could not dampen that one solitary spark in the darkness.

Eventually, she moved around the bed, eyes not straying from the crossbow bolt protruding from the back of Bulcher's head.

"You took everything from me, and now I have taken everything from you..."

The words rang hollow, a child taunting the deep, endless night.

She had another slice of vengeance, but the nothingness

remained. The void within. The darkness beckoned, it wanted her to step deeper into its embrace so she could do what must be done, but what would remain of her afterwards? Would she consume the emptiness, or would the emptiness consume her? Would she use the darkness, or would the darkness use her?

A shiver ran through her. A feeling. Of sorts. Was that something? Anything?

Time was passing.

She placed a hand on either side of Bulcher's head and turned his slack face to hers. He already felt like dried meat beneath her fingers. The head twisted easily enough, but a series of clicking, cracking noises accompanied the movement as if his neck bones were breaking.

Dark, empty eyes stared back at her once she crouched down.

She didn't know what she hoped to see, but whatever it was, it wasn't there.

No pain contorted Bulcher's features. He'd died so quickly he hadn't even had the time to look surprised.

"My father died on a spit above a fire because of you…"

Bulcher didn't react.

No shame, no remorse, no fear. Nothing. His eyes were as empty as the void within her own soul.

She didn't know how long she stared into those lifeless eyes. She had a sense of time running through her fingers, but it felt no more real than anything else outside the room where the bitter fruit of her vengeance lay dead and cold. She wanted to pull up a chair and watch the bastard turn to grey ash. But that was an indulgence too far, even if she thought it might provide the salve vengeance had so far failed to deliver.

So, she pulled out her dagger and hacked off one of the bastard's fingers.

She was already heading for the door as it joined Wendel's ashes in the pouch hanging from her neck.

*

By the time he reached the bottom of the stairs, his face and good hand felt afire, but at least his head no longer spun.

Lucien watched him all the way down in case he stumbled. Either to catch him or laugh at his expense.

"How is our lady?" the mercenary asked as he gingerly lowered himself onto one step after another.

"She's fine..."

He had a pretty good idea Solace was a long way from *fine*, but his newfound pains made him even less inclined towards conversation than usual.

They found Lebrecht, Gotz and Usk huddled together, weapons drawn on the stairs, far enough back that the door was out of view around the spiral. Lebrecht sat on a step, Usk had his back against the curved wall as he sharpened a dagger. Gotz was the lowest, wide enough to block the stairs alone with his bulk.

"Anything, my lord?" Lucien asked Lebrecht.

The young nobleman shook his head.

"We briefly heard some noise a while ago, but nothing since. Been quiet for a long time." Gotz added. The old soldier's eyes rose enquiringly to the ceiling.

"Bulcher's dead. He was a demon," he replied, grateful to

find some wall to slump against.

Gotz whistled, Usk stopped sharpening, and Lebrecht's expression of astonishment might have been amusing in other circumstances.

"A demon? But he can't be!" Lebrecht spluttered.

The young nobleman seemed to struggle with the idea that a member of the nobility could also be a blood-sucking fiend. Those of lower birth were probably less sceptical about the aristocracy guzzling blood.

"You can go and see the body, my lord," he muttered, tiredness crashing over him, "it will turn to ash shortly."

"And Lady Solace?"

"On her way down."

Lebrecht nodded and stood up, "And then?"

"We take Lady Karoline to the Great Hall so that she can meet her new subjects..."

Gotz cocked a bushy eyebrow, Usk gave his blade another lick of whetstone. Lebrecht just stared.

He shrugged, "She knows what she's doing."

He knew no such thing, but it hurt too much to think of anything more persuasive. His good hand throbbed, his face stung, his chest and ribs ached from where the chair hit him. It was a hefty piece of furniture, and Bulcher hurled it with unnatural force. He'd be lucky if nothing was broken. And as he knew he wasn't lucky...

He ran his damaged hand down his damaged side and tried to keep the wince on his damaged face to a minimum.

"Accusations of witchcraft give most people the runny shits," Lucien mused, "show the fine folk of Thasbald their *Graf's* head turning to ash and they might be prepared to accept anything."

"Assuming none of them knew about it," Gotz said.

"Complicity and innocence," Lucien shrugged, "are interchangeable concepts when it suits all parties."

That chair must have hit his head, too, as that could have passed within spitting distance of wisdom if it had originated from a different mouth.

Usk nodded down the spiralling stairs, "How do we get through our friends on the other side of the door.

"We try talking again, as our lady suggested, and explain the benefits of siding with the righteous," Gotz said.

Lucien grinned, "...and when that doesn't work, we kill the devil-worshipping cunts."

"And if it's killing," Usk asked, "who goes through the door first?"

"He's too rich, he's too old, and he's too broken..." Lucien's finger jabbed towards Lebrecht, Gotz and him in turn, "...so, that just leaves me and thee, son."

Usk wrinkled his face and nodded, "Guess I can't get any uglier..."

"If they are good Christian men, they will listen to reason," Lebrecht glanced up at Lucien, "...perhaps it would be better if I tried to talk to them this time."

"Be my guest, my lord. But, if they were good Christian men, they wouldn't have pledged their fealty to a demon in the first place, don't you think?"

Lebrecht didn't answer. Neither did anyone else.

They sat in moody silence for a long time until the sound of feet on stone stirred them.

Solace appeared around the turn of the stairs, Hugo at her

shoulder, the rest of their party presumably behind them.

"Well?" Solace's voice sounded assertive, but her eyes looked distant and haunted.

"There was no response when Lucien tried to negotiate with the Thasbald men," Lebrecht said, "I thought it best I try next."

"And if they ignore us again, we go and kill the buggers," Lucien added.

Solace nodded, "Do it."

"My lady?" he asked as Lebrecht squeezed past Usk and Gotz.

She took a moment to focus on him as if he were far away instead of beside her. Then she smiled, "All is well, Ulrich…"

Her bloody fingers moved to the pouch around her neck. Usually, she kept it tucked out of sight; now, it hung atop her maid's dress. It bulged more than before. Blood flecked the leather.

The sound of Lebrecht hammering on the door pulled his eyes away.

"I say, you men, we wish to talk…"

Lucien smirked; Usk sighed and drew his sword. The rest of them listened.

"Your master has confessed his wicked sins, in the name of our Lord, Jesus Christ, I implore you to lay down your weapons and allow us free passage, else face His wrath…"

"Didn't know the pup was on such good terms with the Almighty…" Lucien muttered, earning him a disapproving look from Solace.

More hammering on the door.

"Answer me! I am Lebrecht of Gothen; I command you to answer me!"

"If they ain't gonna answer to God, sonny..." Lucien said, readying his pistols.

A few moments later, Lebrecht's head poked around the curve of the stairs, "If they are still there, they are quiet as mice."

"C'mon, *Herr* Usk, let's rouse some mice... the rest of you, come out fast behind us. As they don't appear inclined to talk, don't worry about pleasantries..." Lucien glanced over his shoulder and flashed a grin, "...best you stay here till the dirty work is done, my lady."

Solace said nothing but slid the dagger from its sheath on her wrist once more.

Lucien and Usk went down to the door; Lebrecht followed them. He exchanged glances with Gotz to decide who should be the last of them out.

"Age before beauty, lad," Gotz said as he squeezed past the old soldier's belly.

Behind him, Hilde peered over Solace's shoulder, shooting him a smile, but the stairs carried him out of sight before he could acknowledge it.

Lucien and Usk were at the door by the time he caught up with them. He drew his sabre and waited until Gotz huffed and puffed his way down behind him.

"Ready, gentlemen?" Lucien asked.

If the Thasbalders waited for them in the corridor with cocked guns, it was going to get very messy, very quickly.

"Once I open the door, we go, and we don't stop till they're all dead. Or we are. Understand?"

"Get on with it," Gotz spat on the steps.

Lucien nodded at the door.

Usk leant his sword against the wall and gently pulled back the iron bolts top and bottom before lifting the wooden bar. With the door unlocked, they readied themselves.

From where he stood, he could hear nothing but his own heart above the creaking leather of the men around him. Armed men were likely waiting for them on the other side of the now unbarred door.

Another opportunity to die.

They were coming thick and fast.

Despite it being cold enough to mist their breaths, a bead of sweat rolled down his temple, stinging some of the cuts from the pistol that had exploded in his hand. He'd been fortunate not to lose fingers or an eye.

What else might he lose beyond that door?

He ran his thumb along the familiar worn leather strapping around the hilt of his father's sabre.

So long as it wasn't his honour, it didn't matter.

Usk had his sword back in his hand, the other on the door's latch, his shoulder against the seasoned oak. The Gothen soldier would go first, and he would go low so Lucien and Lebrecht, who'd come after him, could fire their pistols at whoever was waiting. By the time he and Gotz came through, men on both sides might already be dead.

Tomos Usk looked back at Lucien. The mercenary nodded.

His mouth was suddenly dry, as if the moisture had been drawn from it to slicken his skin with sweat.

I might never see Solace again.

I might never see Hilde again.

Curiously, he was not sure which of those possibilities troubled him more.

Usk pushed the latch and barged the door open. The young soldier, whose face was never pretty at the best of times, roared a scream and piled into the corridor in a running crouch. Lucien, bellowing too, went straight through the door after him, pistols up.

Lebrecht jumped the final few steps, his own pistols raised.

He followed, sabre ready, feet flying down those last steps and out into the corridor.

No guns fired, no steel crashed against steel, and no men screamed.

The Thasbalders had no screams left to give.

They were already dead, their bodies scattered, bloody and broken along the corridor.

Behind him, Gotz stuck his head through the door before muttering, "Fuck…"

"Who killed them?" Lebrecht asked as they fanned out from the door.

"Bosko and his men?" Usk prodded the nearest corpse with the tip of his sword.

"No…" his mouth had, somehow, become even drier as he stared at the body Usk stood over, "…it wasn't Bosko."

He was sure neither Bosko, nor any of his men, had ever ripped anyone's throat out…

Chapter Fourteen

"Are these the men you saw?"

Pale-faced and open-mouthed Hugo gave the barest of nods, "I... I think so..."

"You said there were six?" Lucien asked, looking back over his shoulder.

"There were..." the boy screwed up his face, "...well, maybe only five, but definitely more than..." his eyes skipped from one corpse to the next, "...four."

Gotz, with some contortions, bent down and prised a pistol from the fingers of one of the dead men, "This one hasn't been fired either."

"We would have heard shots," Lucien said.

Gotz straightened up, "Would have thought we'd have heard men getting their throats torn open, too..."

"Not sure if this one had his throat torn open," Lebrecht said, staring at the bloody pulp of one of the corpse's head. Blood and brains still trickled down the wall.

"This one didn't, either" Usk pushed the head of a bearded middle-aged man. It flopped from one side to the other.

"Neck's been snapped," Renard said, "I've seen that before. When The Wolf's Tower fell..."

The same suspicion circled out in the dark periphery of her own mind, where the light of logic and sense never reached.

"Why kill Bulcher's men instead of rescuing him?" she asked, voice low.

"Maybe they..." Renard's shoulders slumped, "...I don't know."

"Saul the Bloodless is not here."

The words fit her tongue well; she thought them true. Her *sight* or wishful thinking? Sometimes, she fancied they were much the same things. Still, Flyblown's mark had started tingling again, though less fiercely than when she interrupted Bulcher's twisted nuptials.

Renard asked the obvious question, "Then who is?"

"It seems Bulcher was not the only vampire in Thasbald," she said, resisting the urge to rub the five welts on her inner thigh.

"But-"

"Why kill Bulcher's men? Why not rescue him?" They were back to the original question.

"My lady," Lebrecht interrupted them, "we should not linger."

"Agreed,"

"Perhaps it would be prudent to simply leave."

She cocked an eyebrow, "Leave?"

"We do not know what we face here. With Bulcher dead we-"

"No. I need his money. And I promised it to your men."

"Perhaps we should not overreach, as for my men, they-"

"I do not break my promises, my lord. To my enemies or my friends."

She waved them forward.

Usk and Lucien at the front, Hugo and Gotz at the rear behind Hilde, Karoline, and Elin.

Karoline kept red, raw eyes straight ahead to avoid the four corpses. The blood pooling on the stones was harder to miss. She clung to Elin's arm, though her maid appeared even more terrified. Hilde, however, eyed the dead men with interest as she stepped over them. The girl carried the crossbow she'd killed Bulcher with and seemed more than prepared to use it again.

Every little helps...

Thasbald was silent save for their footsteps on the wooden boards. Besides the four dead men, nothing seemed out of place for a castle at night.

Save *everything* felt wrong.

The cold clawed her, the shadows drifted like restless ghosts, the silence hung like a shroud. Her *sight* babbled and bubbled. The incoherent, manic gibbering of something forever huddled in the darkest corner with its face behind its hands.

Something is wrong... something is wrong... something is wrong...

She remembered it well from the night The Wolf's Tower fell.

It had slept for most of the last year but was peeking through its fingers tonight. And it didn't like what it could see.

"Is anything different?" she asked Renard.

He frowned as he shot her a glance.

"This is the way you came from the Great Hall earlier?"

"Yes... nothing's different..."

She shook her head when he looked enquiringly at her.

The stone and wood weren't different; why would they be? No, it wasn't Thasbald that was different; it was her perception of it. And her *sight's*.

Her hand brushed the top of her thigh.

Flyblown's mark smarted as if its five gashes were freshly slashed into her flesh.

Perhaps Lebrecht was right.

Don't overreach.

Bulcher was dead. He'd given them information about the Red Company. Maybe they should flee.

But I need Bulcher's wealth!

Just like she'd needed the bastard to suffer.

The darkness seemed to thicken, as in Karoline's bedchamber. Just imagination, of course. However, the way everyone's breath steamed wasn't. It was getting colder.

Fires had burned down; they were in the depths of winter, and the sun was long gone. So, nothing unusual in that.

Nothing at all...

She shivered as she walked.

No one spoke. Not even Hilde. Another oddity.

Her hand found the pouch around her neck. Heavier now. She could feel the lump of Bulcher's finger, yet to turn to dust.

Nothing, nothing, nothing... I feel nothing...

She dropped her hand and pushed the thought away. She had other concerns, for now.

They were on a staircase. She didn't remember entering it. Nobody else seemed concerned, so she supposed they must have. Mind wandering. Again. Not good. Concentrate.

The shadows are too heavy. Flyblown's mark is smarting. The temperature has plummeted. The sight is jabbering in the corner.

Death is coming.

Another thought to shake away. Death was always coming.

We all die a little every day, don't we? From the moment we're born, death is coming, death is waiting, death is patient.

And if we die a little every day, shouldn't we try really hard to hold onto whatever makes us feel alive?

Where were these thoughts coming from?

Concentrate!

She tried concentrating. She tried not to glance at Renard either. And then not at Lebrecht.

She was failing to do a lot of things tonight.

The bastard should have suffered!

She blinked.

They were in another corridor.

She couldn't recall them leaving the staircase.

Shadows pressed in. Lights had burnt out. That was all.

Leather rasped, metal scraped, wood creaked.

Hearts beat, breath exhaled, bone moved.

What do I have that makes me feel alive?

Renard walked at her side, eyes narrowed. Concentration? Peering? Pain?

He'd lain with her.

She remembered.

She never forgot.

The memory sometimes made her tingle.

We die a little every day.

Why am I thinking about that now?

Death is coming.

The shadows hang too thick.

Hold on to what makes you feel alive.

Her hand moved of its own accord. For once, not to the pouch around her neck, where Bulcher's index finger now sat amongst Wendle's grey ash.

But to Renard's hand.

She didn't want vengeance. She didn't want to make anyone suffer. She wanted to be the girl she'd been a year and two days before.

The price of vengeance is not paid in silver...

She reached.

Hold on to what makes you feel alive.

Her fingers found his.

Flyblown's mark burned.

The sight howled behind its hands.

This is not what I want.

This is what I want.

They must suffer; they must!

How else do you fill the emptiness carved by loss, grief, and pain?

She gripped his hand.

Renard faltered. He sucked in a breath.

So did she.

They stopped.

Ahead of them, in the shadows, death stood waiting.

*

Solace took his hand to stop him, but he'd already seen

the almost spectral figure before them.

The woman stood unmoving in the centre of the corridor, hands crossed in front of her stomach, head slightly lowered, eyes raised.

The shadows hung deep. Little pockets of oily light guttering around the remaining rushlights offered little against the great, deeper blackness of the winter night, but it wasn't so dark the woman could have just appeared.

He swore he hadn't seen her step from the shadows; one moment, the corridor had been empty, the next, this woman stood half a dozen paces ahead of Lucien and Usk.

Although she was not a woman.

Fair-haired, with striking, sharp features, pale skin darkened by the blood smearing her lips and chin. Slim, without being slender, she wore a white gown, loose where it was unsoiled, sticking to her body where blood drenched it. The left sleeve ripped away, the exposed arm bloody to the elbow.

She flashed feral white teeth at them. It put him in mind of a smug fox sauntering out of a hen house after a most satisfying evening of slaughter.

"Welcome to Thasbald..." the monster said.

"Who are you?" Lucien asked, both pistols raised.

"You know who I am."

Solace shouldered her way between Lucien and Usk.

He cursed under his breath and did the same.

"You are death..." Solace said.

The creature tilted her head. Blood dripped from her chin onto her cleavage, "Indeed..."

Solace took another step forward, "...but not for me..."

His legs filled with lead. He didn't want to go near the demon. The fact she had the appearance of a woman made her seem even more obscene and profane than the demons of the Red Company.

Of course, Morlaine was a woman… but… well… she was different. He liked to tell himself.

Wherever his lady went, he followed. That was his deal. His penance and his privilege. A man whose honour lay in tatters should have no complaints about the places his betrayals led him. He took another step, his father's sabre held out wide, cutting edge towards the demon.

The thing's eyes moved to him, just for a breath, but long enough to almost turn the lead in his bones to water.

I stood before Saul the Bloodless and defied him.

I felt Alms' graveyard breath on my cheek.

I chased Wendel, knowing I could not stop him.

So, why does this woman frighten me more?

The blood-soaked dress, he hated noticing, clung wetly to her breasts, the nipples large and… apparent…

Is it simply because she is beautiful as well as terrible?

Could the thing that frightens a man the most be his own desire?

His thumb found the worn leather around the hilt of his father's sword. Smooth, familiar, comforting. His eyes, however much his legs wanted to run away, refused to look elsewhere.

"He is dead, isn't he, child?" the demon asked, eyes, thankfully, sliding back to Solace.

"Bulcher?"

"Him."

"Yes."

"You killed him?"

Solace held up her chin. He usually thought he had little idea what went on behind her eyes, but if she felt any fear standing but a few strides from a creature she knew could kill her in an instant, she wasn't showing it.

"Tell me why?" the demon lifted her blood-splattered chin to mirror Solace.

"He did me a great wrong."

"Vengeance, then..." the demon's tongue ran over its blood-slickened lips, "...did it taste sweet? In the darkness, I have often wondered."

"He deserved to die. He received justice for his crimes. That is all that matters."

"But did he suffer?"

Solace took half a step backwards as if slapped.

The demon laughed, throaty, deep and wet.

"You know what I am, don't you?"

Solace nodded, "You are a demon. A vampire."

"You have seen the like of me before?"

"Too many times. I know your kind."

"And yet..." the demon's eyes flicked to the rest of their company, "...you have not tried to kill me? You have not turned your guns and blades on this..." she ran hands down her soaked dress, leaving their smeared imprints on the fabric, "...abomination..."

"Bulcher made you like this, didn't he?"

Bloody hands fell to her side, then a hiss, "Yes..."

"What is your name?"

"Why do you care?"

"Bulcher tried to marry me once."

"You had a fortunate escape."

"He killed my-"

The woman twisted away and walked back into the shadows.

"Wait!"

"Go now, and you will live," the woman said as the shadows consumed her, "or stay and find the death everybody else in this place deserves."

"What is your name?! Who are you?!"

When Solace made to run after the demon, he grabbed her wrist despite the pain that lanced up his bad arm. She could have pulled away from his numb fingers. Instead, she held onto it as if anchoring herself to prevent a storm-swollen river from sweeping her away.

The figure paused, no more than the white patches of her gown and her blonde hair visible in the darkness, "People once called me Samanta... but now..." a laugh, small and bitter, "...I have been nothing for so long, I barely remember what 'tis like to be... anything."

The pressure on his bad hand eased as darkness consumed the creature.

"What-"

A scream cut Lebrecht off.

They all twisted around, but there was nothing to see. It hadn't belonged to any of their party, but it had come from behind them, not from the direction the demon had gone.

"What... is going on?" Lebrecht asked. Karoline was crying again, or Elin was. Given how much they clutched each other, it could be hard to tell.

"We were wrong..." Solace's eyes turned forward again, "Bulcher didn't murder his wives once he was done with them..."

Another sound broke the still silence. This time, it was not a scream but a shriek of laughter echoing around them like demented thunder.

"...he did something far worse to them..."

Part Two

Widows

Chapter One

Thasbald Castle, Electorate of Brandenburg, The Holy Roman Empire - 1631

"How many brides did Bulcher have over the years?" Renard asked.

"Six or seven..." Lucien crumpled his face, "...so they told me..."

"But we don't know how long he was a vampire," she said, "He could have been doing this for centuries."

"But he couldn't have turned them all into demons," Renard said.

Another scream split the night. Distant and terrified before something cut it short.

"Couldn't he?"

Renard looked glumly back at her.

As they stood together in the corridor, another rushlight spluttered and died.

They'd brought the two lanterns the guard at the door to The Silver Tower had, but they didn't stop the shadows from thickening further.

"Who..." Karoline swallowed, "...who was that woman?"

"I'll explain later."

There was a time and a place for telling the recently widowed their demonic deceased husband would have tried to turn them into one of the undead, too, once the first flush of marriage faded.

But this wasn't it.

She started down the corridor.

Renard hurried after her, "Are we leaving?"

"Not until we've got all we came for."

"But-"

"No buts, Ulrich, we need Bulcher's silver."

Footsteps creaked in her wake; she trusted all her company followed.

"The demon offered us safe passage if we left," Lucien caught up to her other shoulder, "we should take it."

"Really?"

"You saw what she did to those Thasbalders?"

"I've seen what these monsters can do at close hand several times..."

"Then you know why we should leave better than me."

She glared at Lucien. For once, he wasn't grinning back at her.

"I had not thought you one to give up so easily, Captain."

"I know when to fight and when to retreat. First rule of soldiering, that."

"And we should abandon the rest of our company then?" she pulled up short and turned on him sharply enough to make him step backwards. Everybody else came to a halt behind them, "Captain Bosko? Sergeant Paasche? All those Gothen and Vadian men who came here with us?"

In the distance, a pistol shot echoed.

"It might be too late for them, my lady..."

"Well, we shall see..." she leaned in closer and dropped her voice, "...if we are to defeat the Red Company, I need Bulcher's silver and gold..." When Lucien continued to stare at her, she added, "...if I am to make you rich, I need Bulcher's silver and gold."

That made the mercenary's lips purse, "And how much gold and silver does Bulcher have stashed away here?"

"A grand hoard," she said without hesitation, "he told us before he died. He has been collecting wealth for centuries. All those noble wives, all those estates, all those inheritances, plus whatever else he has been up to. Profiting from the war, I would guess, from what he said. He only wanted to marry me because he believed untapped silver remained in my family's old mines in Silesia..."

"Centuries..." Lucien mused.

"You can collect an awful lot of silver over centuries."

Uncertainty flickered in the mercenary's eyes.

"We find our men, we take Bulcher's fortune, we leave..."

It sounded ever so simple when she put it like that.

"Where is-"

"There's no time for questions," she set off again, "you either follow me or not; the choice is entirely yours..."

Renard stayed at her side.

Again, she did not look behind her. Again, footsteps echoed hers.

"Bulcher said nothing about-"

"I know."

"Then-"

"Bulcher's hoard is in the vaults below the castle."

Renard's eyes lingered on her as they walked. They were approaching more stairs.

"You know that...?"

"Yes."

Did she?

It sounded right. Where else would you keep your treasure but the safest part of your castle?

Flyblown's mark still smarted. The sight still gibbered.

The demons in the darkness preoccupied them, but it still felt true.

As they descended the stairs, Lebrecht took his turn.

"Is this wise, my lady?"

"We are going to find your men, my lord."

"Well, yes, but..."

"And Bulcher has enough wealth to meet my needs and yours."

"Mine?"

"You can build many bridges with the silver you take home."

Lebrecht didn't sway as much as Lucien had at the mention of money.

She put a hand on his elbow and stared at him for as long as she dared, given they were descending an ill-lit staircase in a demon-infested castle, "Lebrecht, please..."

She didn't add with words that she'd be ever so grateful if he did whatever she asked, but she hoped that's what the turn of her mouth and the set of her eyes whispered.

With Lebrecht, after all, she had more than silver to tempt.

He smiled and seemed to flush... then stumbled and half fell down the next few steps.

She thought she was beginning to come to terms with the tricky business of getting men to do what she wanted by turning them into tongue-tied idiots. Although the wind fell from her sails a little when she realised Lebrecht's slip was due to the blood-slicked stairs rather than her womanly charms.

This wasn't the time for seduction or negotiation.

She waved Usk and Lucien forward.

The two soldiers slid past her and down the stairs. Renard and Lebrecht stayed with her.

Renard's expression was disapproving. Whether due to her trying to seduce Lebrecht into doing her bidding or lying to Lucien about Bulcher telling her where he had stashed his treasure, she didn't know.

Lebrecht was staring, too. But not disapprovingly. She thought.

Was this a suitable moment for flirtation?

She smiled at him, eyes lingering for a heartbeat before letting them slide away.

Renard shuffled his feet in the way he had when he was unhappy about something. Even with the blood covering the stairs. There was a lot, smeared all the way down until the steps met the corridor below and darkness consumed everything.

Usk reappeared and summoned them down.

The source of the blood sprawled half a dozen paces away from the stairs, which opened into what appeared to be a large but disused dining room, with sheets thrown over the furniture.

"Who is it?" she asked as she approached the body.

"Not one of ours," Lucien said, crouching over the corpse, "though hard to tell for certain as there's not much of a face left."

Lucien wasn't exaggerating. Something had clawed the man's face off; his chest ripped open, too. From the blood trail, it looked like his killer dragged the body downstairs before depositing it here.

"Come on," she rolled an impatient hand, "we can do nothing for him."

Lucien's knees cracked as he straightened.

Back by the stairs, Karoline or her maid were whimpering at the sight of the bloody corpse.

She waved a hand again to get people moving.

Do I still need Karoline?

Usk pulled a sheet from the nearest covered piece of furniture – an overly ornate chair – and laid it over the corpse.

"Come, my lady," he called to Karoline.

They wouldn't get anywhere soon if they had to cover all the dead they came across.

"Wherever we're heading," Renard said in a quiet, urgent hiss, "if it isn't out of the front gates, we can't take those two with us..."

They watched as Karoline and Elin tiptoed towards the corpse as if it were a sleeping beast that might gobble them up if they woke it.

Renard was right, but she could spare no one to take them to safety any more than she could spare anyone to watch over the two women.

"Bosko can look after her when we find him."

"If he is still alive."

Another good point she wanted to ignore.

As soon as Karoline and Elin managed to negotiate the corpse without fainting, she waved everybody on. Once they reached the Great Hall, she would have a better idea of what was happening and, she sincerely hoped, what they should do next.

"Someone's there!" Karoline jabbed a quick-bitten finger into the gloomy dining room.

Hilde, who walked behind the two young women, swung her crossbow where Karoline pointed. Lucien levelled his pistols.

Nothing moved.

The flickering rushlights along the wall made faint shifting shadows of them play across the sheet-covered furniture.

"A trick of the light," she said, turning away.

"No!" Karoline insisted, "Someone is there!"

Some of the sheets draped over tall pieces of furniture could, with a bit of imagination and a fair dollop of stupidity, look like ghostly apparitions in the untrustworthy light.

Usk took a step forward, peering into the gloom.

She grabbed his arm.

"Leave it!"

"I think something *is* there..."

She followed Usk's gaze but saw nothing.

Imagination.

She glanced at Renard. He shrugged.

No one else had ever crept through a castle surrounded by monsters, so she trusted no one else's judgement.

She tugged at Usk's sleeve; the big soldier reluctantly lowered his sword and let her pull him back to the scant light.

"Tick... tock... tick... tock..."

They swivelled back to face the darkness in unison.

"Who's there?" she demanded as Renard rushed to put himself between her and the shrouded room.

Nothing moved.

"Tickety-tock... spickety-spock..."

"Answer me!"

"...I'm nothing but a clock!"

The voice, thin and high, came from the opposite side of the room. She could just make out what might have been a grandfather clock covered in a sheet.

"All vampires are mad..." Renard muttered.

When the voice didn't come again, she hurried her company forward.

"The light!" the voice shrieked, loudly enough to make Elin jump and Karoline squeal, "Kill the light!"

Once more, they stood trying to make out something amongst the shadows.

The voice belonged to a woman, but not Samanta. Another of Bulcher's brides?

"This one doesn't seem to be doing anything?" Renard said.

"Never let an enemy get behind you; first rule of soldiering, that," Lucien said before she could reply.

"One should never get trapped behind your enemy's lines

either," Lebrecht shot straight back.

It didn't seem the most opportune time to discuss military strategy.

"Keep going. If anything comes out of that room, shoot it."

The men nodded. Hilde lingered, crossbow still raised, then came after them.

From the shadows, the sound of sobbing serenaded the echoes of their boots every step of the way.

*

It seemed a lot longer back to the Great Hall than he remembered.

He asked Hilde if they'd gone wrong. She told him not to worry whilst looking worried herself.

They found candles to add to their two oil lanterns, lighting them from a dying rushlight. The pools of light were growing smaller, and he was grateful for the illumination, even though they only held the dark back a fraction.

How long to dawn?

He had no idea.

Not that much daylight would find its way inside. Even by the standard of old castles, Thasbald had few windows. He hadn't thought that strange earlier. He really should pay more attention to things...

They found no more bodies as they moved along corridors, down stairs and through rooms. Whilst all looking similar, nothing was in the slightest bit familiar.

He became increasingly sure they were lost.

Then there was the voice.

The one they'd first heard in the disused dining room.

A faint disembodied sobbing that only registered above the

squeak of floorboards and boots when they paused. Occasionally, he caught a word or two tangled within the weeping. Fragments of nonsense as far as he could tell. He assumed everybody else could hear their companion, but no one seemed much inclined to talk about her.

Every time he checked behind them, he saw nobody, but whoever she was, she must be trailing them.

He'd thought her another demon, but the possibility it was some distraught, disturbed child nagged him.

He didn't want to leave another child to the bloody mercies of vampires, as he had back in The Wolf's Tower?

He fell back from Solace's side to walk beside Hilde.

"I'm not the only one who can hear that girl crying, am I?"

He'd spent enough sleepless nights listening to plaintive sobbing, punctuated by heart-stopping screams, for the question to be a serious one.

Hilde slowed and looked over her shoulder.

"No, you're not the only one."

A gut-wrenching wail rolled out of the darkness.

"Should we-"

"No," he put a hand on Hilde's elbow to hurry her along before they fell behind everyone else.

They came to another staircase.

"We go down?" Solace called back to Hilde.

"Yes... I think..."

Solace pushed her way back through the others, Lebrecht trailing in her wake. He eyed the corridor, expecting some waifish, tear-stained child to stumble out of the shadows, begging them to save her.

But nothing came bar the sound of distant crying.

He blew out a breath that steamed instantly.

"Do you know where we're going?" Solace asked.

"We keep going down," Hilde knew the castle better than any of them but was far from an expert on Thasbald. And in the dark...

"If you're not sure, say so," he said, "'tis easy enough to take a wrong turn in a strange place."

Uncertainty flickered over Hilde's face alongside the light from Solace's candle.

"Oh, for..." the rest of Solace's sentence was lost as she wheeled away muttering.

Lebrecht turned and went after her. Was there something slightly puppyish in the way he trailed after her?

"Don't worry about it, lass," Gotz said, sucking at one of his remaining teeth, "I've often led people astray."

"Sorry..." Hilde pinched a strained smile, "...I knew the way going up to Lady Karoline's chamber but coming down... everything looks the same!"

He fought competing urges to hug Hilde and hurry off after his mistress. In the end, he just kept staring into the darkness behind them.

"I... want... to... go... home... now..." the voice wailed; each word punctuated by thick, wet gulps.

"So do we all, girl, so do we all..." Gotz gave Hilde's shoulder a squeeze before hurrying them along. Solace and Lebrecht were already leading them down the stairs.

He hesitated.

When faced with a herd of prey, the predator often tried to isolate the weakest and separate it from the protection of numbers.

And what were vampires, if not predators?

Still, his boots lingered.

"Where is your home?" he called.

No reply came. But the sobbing faded to what might have been sniffs.

"What is your name?"

Silence.

"Ulrich?" Gotz and Hilde waited at the top of the stairs. The others had already gone down, and he could see only the bobbing glow of their lanterns and candles.

He walked backwards towards the stairs, still trying to make out a figure in the shadows. A few rushlights flickered at the far end of the corridor, but they cast no more light than distant, isolated stars.

One blinked out for a heartbeat or two before reappearing.

Something had moved in front of it.

Or someone.

A child. Lost and alone?

Had he seen any children in Thasbald? A couple of stable lads around Hugo's age. But no one younger.

He lingered atop the first step.

Another rushlight blinked out of existence. Then reappeared.

"Who are you? Show yourself?"

Nothing.

Even the crying stopped.

But someone was there.

"Ulrich..." Gotz pulled on his arm.

Hilde was watching him closely.

He found a hollow smile and nodded.

The three of them hurried down the stairs after the others.

"What's wrong, Ulrich?" Hilde asked as they caught up with the rest of their company.

It was a question that could take a while to answer, given almost everything currently seemed wrong.

So, he shook his head and carried on down the steps.

He could feel Hilde's frown without looking at her.

"Does this seem familiar to anyone?" Lucien asked as they faced another dark corridor.

Only Gotz answered.

"I'm starting to think this castle is a lot bigger on the inside than on the outside..."

"We keep going down; that's where we want to get to..." Solace said, heading off.

The way out of Thasbald would be below them. But he had a nasty feeling that wasn't where his mistress wanted to go.

His place was at Solace's side, and it would be, he knew, to the day he died. Which might well be today. But again, he lingered, looking back up the stairs. Hilde stayed with him. Neither carried a candle, and no lights burned in the staircase.

Did a slight figure dressed in white stand at the very top?

"Is it following us?" Hilde asked.

"It?"

"One of the monsters."

"I don't know if it is a monster."

"Then what?"

The words, *a lost child,* hovered on his lips.

Back along the corridor, their company's light receded. Solace was not waiting, even for him.

Just as he made to hurry Hilde away to catch up, a wet, half-choked voice floated down the stairs.

"I want... to... to... go home..."

He found he had a boot on the first stair before Hilde grabbed him, juggling her crossbow in one hand to do so.

"No!"

She was right, of course. The girl was almost certainly a demon. Like Bulcher, like Samanta. But something so hopeless, so forlorn, so... so damned lost in that voice, pulled him towards it.

Perhaps some demonic magic. Or simply the guilt he carried since he ran from the doomed children of Tassau. The guilt he heard in the dark of the night as the ghosts of sobbing children, the guilt that had made him spend Solace's silver to buy sanctuary for Madleen's daughter Seraphina in Madriel.

Guilt could do terrible things.

Guilt could make you do stupid things.

"Please..." the hopeless, forlorn, lost voice of a girl sniffed, "...do you know the way home...?"

And guilt could also separate the weak from the herd.

Shrugging Hilde off, he started back up the stairs...

Chapter Two

First, that girl, Hilde, gifted Bulcher a clean, quick death the bastard didn't deserve, and now she'd managed to get them lost. Even through her haze of annoyance, frustration, fear and uncertainty, she knew she was being more than a little unfair, but she needed to lash out at someone!

Had The Wolf's Tower been so uniform, so similar from corridor to corridor, from stair to stair?

To her, every stone, every piece of wood, every corner and every step had been different. As familiar as family, as unique as old friends. Even blindfolded, she would have known precisely where she was from the creaks, sighs, draughts, and scents. But this place!

Everywhere was the same!

The latest corridor intersected another to form a crossroads. A few rushlights still flickered here and there in sconces, but their greasy light was succumbing to the darkness without servants to replace them. And all the servants, along with most of the rest of the household, were locked in the Great Hall and kitchens.

She'd planned to denounce Bulcher to them, present Karoline as their liege and persuade them serving her was preferable to burning at the stake for witchcraft and the worship of demons. It had been a less than complete plan, but now that demons were at large in Thasbald, she required another.

Now, she needed not only the Thasbalders' acquiescence but their assistance, too. Together, they might be enough to hunt down Bulcher's widows. However many of them there were, they were not the Red Company.

She'd replaced one dubious plan with another, but she would prevail; God had not saved her only to fail.

Although if they didn't find their way to the Great Hall soon...

She was about to ask Hilde if she had the faintest inkling about which way they should go when the sound of boots came from the corridor ahead. Lucien and Usk put themselves in front of her as a wide-eyed man emerged from the darkness. After bouncing off one wall, he careened into the other, tripped over his feet, hit the floor and slid to a halt before their boots.

The man lay panting, looking up at them. Or at least the pistol Lucien shoved in his face.

"Please..." the man gasped.

Perhaps thirty, hair thinning at the front, long oily locks at the back, and hollow cheeks speckled with pockmarks, the man wore Thasbald livery and shook like a kitten someone had recently tried to drown.

He didn't look much like a demon.

She pushed between Lucien and Usk.

"What's your name?"

The man blinked at her before looking at Lucien and Usk, clearly confused about why one of them wasn't asking the questions.

"Answer her, man," Lebrecht said, coming the long way around Usk.

The man preferred the look of Lebrecht as he answered the nobleman instantly, "Audrius, sir, Audrius Wirth."

"And why are you in such a hurry, Audrius Wirth?" Lucien asked, pistol still hovering above Wirth's forehead.

"Them, sir."

"Them?" she asked.

Wirth twisted around and jabbed a finger at the darkness behind him, "Them... they're out!"

"Who are out?"

When Wirth turned back to them, his eyes seemed almost large enough to pop from their sockets as he spluttered, "*Them!*"

This wasn't getting them anywhere.

She gestured to Usk to get Wirth back to his feet. The big Gothen obliged, none too gently, before slamming the man against the wall.

"Now..." she peered around Usk, who had Wirth warmly by the throat, "...start making sense."

Wirth's eyes once more darted to the men, apparently still confused as to why the blonde girl in the maid's dress was doing the talking.

She slapped his face.

He whimpered and tried to squirm from Usk's grip.

"Talk to me, Audrius..."

The man-at-arms stilled. His eyes fixed on her, finally.

"Who are they?"

"I... don't know."

"You don't know?"

Wirth shook his head. As much as he could with Usk's massive hand clamped to his throat.

"He... the *Graf,* keeps them below... I... we... are not supposed to talk about them... if he hears-"

"*Graf* Bulcher isn't going to hear anything ever again," she said.

"Save maybe the sound of Satan's pitchfork going up his arse," Lucien added.

"So..." she leaned in close enough to catch the stink of Wirth's breath, "...tell me what you're not supposed to talk about."

Wirth stared emptily back at her, Adam's apple bobbing up and down behind Usk's hand.

"Don't seem the talkative type," Lucien sighed.

"No use to us then," she said.

"What should I do with him, my lady?" Usk asked.

"We've no time for baggage; kill him."

Usk slid a dagger from its sheath with his free hand.

"No!" Wirth squealed, "I can talk! I can! *Please!!*"

Usk was putting the steel to Wirth's throat when she touched the burly Gothen's shoulder.

Would I have killed him?

She shook the thought away. There was no more time for niceties than there were for doubts.

She noticed Lebrecht watching her out of the corner of her eye, all pinched mouth and furrowed brow. Seemed he might have time for niceties and doubts. So long as he kept his mouth shut and did as he was told, he could have all the doubts he wanted. She'd deal with them later.

"Talk!" she said, voice sharp enough to make Wirth flinch.

Despite the musclebound young man with the misaligned face holding a blade to his throat, Wirth seemed more scared of her.

Good.

"I haven't been here long... I don't know much... but they said the *Graf* keeps people down in the catacombs..."

"What people?"

"Women."

"Who are these women?"

Wirth shook his head, carefully given the proximity of Usk's blade, "I don't know. I was told they were mad and dangerous and had to be kept locked up."

"How many women are down there?"

Another careful shake of the head, "I don't know. Honestly!"

"And now these women have escaped?"

"Yes."

Lucien leaned against the wall next to Wirth, "How?"

Wirth's eyes flicked around their company.

"You're the ones that seized the *Graf*, aren't you?"

Lucien looked at her, "Sharp fellow, this one..."

"Answer the question."

"Captain Damstra... he let one of them out."

"Why?"

"There wasn't enough of us to take back the castle, to free the *Graf*... Captain Damstra thought... one of the women... was less mad than the others... could be trusted to help..."

Lucien grinned sourly, "And how'd that work out for Captain Damstra?"

"She was..." Wirth's voice broke, and the words died.

"A monster?" she finished for him.

Wirth nodded.

"Samanta?" she asked.

"I didn't know her name. Damstra knew her. Thought she could help. I didn't know why. Thought she was just a woman, but Damstra told us not to ask questions. When we got to the Silver Tower, he took her chains off and ordered her to break down the door so we could rescue the *Graf*. She laughed. Then... then... it all happened so fast!"

"You escaped?"

"I ran. Been hiding since the screaming started..." Wirth looked from side to side, "More than one of them is out now!"

"Samanta freed the others..." Lebrecht said behind her.

She nodded.

"We have to get out of here!" Wirth insisted, "She killed four men in an instant! Her face... oh, god, it changed! I swear, it changed! I-"

She slapped Wirth's face again.

"Stop blubbing!"

Wirth started shaking, his knees buckled, and he slid down the wall to cower at Usk's feet.

She wanted to hit him again, tell him to be a man and stop snivelling. She'd seen worse than he had, suffered worse than he had, and she hadn't curled up into a ball like a frightened child.

No, you put a pistol under your chin and pulled the trigger...

"My lady..."

Lebrecht had hold of her wrist.

Had she hit the cowardly wretch again? Her palm stung. Maybe she had. No matter; he deserved it.

She stepped back. Karoline and Elin were staring at her, Hugo too. Gotz stood behind them, face impassive. She ignored them all.

Lebrecht hunkered before Wirth, "Listen to me, man, can you get us to the Great Hall from here?"

When Wirth said nothing, Lebrecht put a hand on his shoulder. The Thasbalder flinched, but the touch was gentle, "Please, Audrius. Help us, and we'll help you."

Wirth focused on the young nobleman.

"How...?"

"We know what these monsters are. But we need your help getting out of here. We know you had no part in this. *Graf* Bulcher was an evil man, but the sins of the master do not fall upon those who serve with good heart and honest intent. You did not know about the monsters, did you?"

Wirth shook his head, "No, my lord! I thought them stories... just silly gossip!"

"Then you have nothing to fear from us. Take us to the Great Hall so we can find the rest of our people, and we will leave this place of horrors."

Lebrecht stood and offered Wirth his hand.

After hesitating, the man-at-arms accepted and let the nobleman pull him to his feet.

Wirth was scared, but something about his fear grated. He was weak, and she had no use for weakness.

"Come on," she said, "take us to the Great Hall."

The weakling almost shied away from her, which set her teeth on edge. She would have shoved him down the corridor, but Gotz's voice pulled her attention away from the wretch.

"My lady... where are Ulrich and Hilde?"

*

"What are you doing?" Hilde hissed at him.

It was a good question.

His boots took him back up another couple of steps.

Sadly, he didn't have a satisfactory answer.

Instead, he told her to go, "I'll catch up with you."

"The hell you will!"

Hilde's shoes scuffed the stairs as she followed him.

He was putting her in danger. He thought that might stop his feet.

It didn't.

He peered into the darkness. The meagre glow from the few rushlights still burning in the corridor barely dusted the top of the stairs. But enough fell to reveal a slight and ghostly figure looking down at him.

"I want to go home..." a wet voice sniffed. Had he ever heard such hopelessness?

Yes, of course, he had. Every night he'd lain awake since The Wolf's Tower fell, tormented by his ruined arm and shoulder, plagued by the pain of his guilt, dishonour and shame. The children's voices. The children's tears. The children's pleas.

The ones he'd left behind.

"Where is your home?" he asked, mounting a few more steps.

"It's a place called..." the voice lapsed into silence punctuated by sniffs, "...I don't remember!"

He held out his bad arm before him at the sound of the girl's distress. His good hand still gripped his father's sabre, "It doesn't matter... we'll find it. Tell me, what's your name?"

"My name?"

"Yes. My name is Ulrich, this is my friend, Hilde..." he jerked his head at the woman pointing a crossbow at the faint silhouette atop the stairs.

"I am seventeen..."

He doubted she was that old. He took another step. Then, one more.

"No... not your age, your name?"

"That is my name. I am Number Seventeen. That is what He calls me..."

"He?"

"My husband. My lord. My master."

"*Graf* Bulcher?"

"Him."

The figure made no move. They were halfway back up the stairs now. He still didn't know what he was doing.

"He's dead."

"We know."

"We?"

"All of his numbers."

"His... wives?"

"His brides. He calls me Bride Number Seventeen... I want to go home. I don't want to be here anymore!"

Seventeen? It seemed Bulcher had more wives than those Lucien found out about.

"Before you were Seventeen... you had a name?"

"Yes."

"Do you remember it?"

He climbed more stairs. Hilde did, too. The girl, he couldn't, wouldn't, think of her as Seventeen, shuffled back so only the upper half of her was visible in the gloom.

"It was so long ago. I want to go home."

"How long have you been here?" Hilde asked from his side.

"I don't know. We keep our own time. Tickety-tock, I'm a clock!"

She kept backing up a step for each one they took forward.

"Please... can you try and remember your name. Your real name."

"That girl's dead..." a coldness descended upon her voice.

"No, she isn't. She's still there. What's your name?"

The shuffling feet stilled.

"Judita... her name was Judita."

"You are Judita."

"No. I am Seventeen."

They reached the top of the stairs. Judita had backed up, closer to where a couple of rushlights still guttered and danced. Her face was in shadow, but he could see light fringing blonde hair. She wore a loose white dress, like Samanta's, though hers didn't appear soaked in blood.

They paused.

Judita didn't look or sound like a demon; she looked and sounded like a frightened girl.

"How old were you when you came here?" Hilde asked, perhaps the same thought crossed her mind.

"I married him on my twelfth birthday," Judita said, head

and voice lowering.

The youngest a girl could marry, so long as she had her father's permission. And what father could refuse *Graf* Bulcher?

When he exchanged a glance with Hilde, Judita said, "You should not come any closer. He did not feed us often. He liked us weak... I am sorry, but can you please take me home..."

Judita turned her back on them and shuffled away.

He followed but did not close the distance between them.

"How many brides did Bulcher have?"

Judita's thin shoulders rose and fell. She did not turn around. "I do not know. He kept us apart. Mostly. Sometimes, someone came with blood for me. Pig's blood mainly. It keeps us alive, but... 'tis not what we crave. I never saw who. They just pushed a bowl through a hatch in the door. But it wasn't Him. I could always smell Him... Other times, He did come to see me. To... make a woman of me..." she stopped next to the two flickering rushlights and turned to face them, eyes narrowing against the feeble, greasy light, "...even though he made me something that is not a woman."

She swayed in front of them, hands wrapped around each other, long white-blonde hair falling half way down her back. Her skin colour was barely different from the soiled white dress she wore, save for the vivid red rings circling her eyes. He fancied if she stood before a brighter light, it would shine straight through her. Pitifully thin, with arms and legs like sticks, her teeth were too large, and her cheeks too hollow.

Had she always been so emaciated? Or had Bulcher's diet of pig's blood, to keep his brides alive but weak, reduced her to this?

Two questions forced their way forward. Just how hungry were Bulcher's demon brides?

And how many of them were at large in Thasbald...

"All I know," Judita said, "is that I am Number Seventeen. And I have been here a long time..."

"You never met any of the others?" he asked, thumb finding comfort in the worn, familiar leather twisted around the grip of Old Man Ulrich's sabre.

"Yes, over the years. Occasionally, He liked to make a woman of more than one of us at the same time. Sometimes, he brought others, sometimes, he did... bad things..." a smile, small, hard, and bitter, contorted Judita's ashen face, "my master was a man of many appetites. All of them excessive..."

She lowered her face and examined the pale bones of the fingers before her.

"How old-"

"Please, no more questions," Judita's eyes shot up, "Take me home!"

"But I don't know where your home is, Judita..." he said.

She smiled, "'tis so long since I have heard that name. Thank you."

"There is-"

The smile faded, "I have no time. Please. Take me home," when he said nothing, she added, "My home is with God now, if He will still have me."

"Are you asking us to-"

"Yes. I am... I would prefer to see the sun again and let the light take me home to God. But I fear I cannot last till dawn. I wish to do terrible things. To you. To anyone. And if I do that, I will never be able to go home because God will not want me. For all my sins, I have never taken a life..." her mouth twitched into something between a smile and a snarl as she raised her skinny arms out to her sides, "...so, please, Ulrich, take me home."

Judita closed her eyes.

She looked like a girl but sounded impossibly old, immeasurably tired.

Her outstretched hands trembled, her lips quivered. Tears rolled down her cheeks, glinting in the feeble rushlight.

"Please..."

Her voice strained as if her arms held back walls inexorably closing in upon her rather than thin air.

Her face twitched, and for an instant, it changed, only for a breath, but still long enough to see what lived beneath the skin of the skinny girl before them.

He lifted his father's sabre and stepped forward.

"You do not have to be this, Judita."

"I am what He made me..." the old voice said from the young girl's mouth.

"Everything is a choice."

"And this is... mine..." again her face changed; this time, it seemed to flicker back and forth between the tear-stained girl and the sneering monster.

He hesitated, fearing the monster would prevail.

Even weak and half-starved, he didn't doubt Judita could rip his throat open.

Kill her.

The sabre, so familiar, suddenly felt heavier in his hand.

She is not a child.

"I know someone," he said, "a demon like you. She does not kill; she controls the thing inside her. She cannot walk in the sunlight, but she does not walk solely in the darkness, either..."

Judita peeled an eye open.

"That is not me. My master made me weak."

Master...

"Our masters do not make us, Judita."

"No?"

"No. We make ourselves."

She smiled at that.

She was a pace or two out of his sabre's arc. At this distance, she could kill him before he could even raise his father's steel.

"Do it," she said.

He tried to speak, but she wasn't talking to him.

Behind him, in quick succession, a twang, a snap and a hiss.

The crossbow bolt took Judita cleanly between the eyes.

The girl crumpled to the floor.

A smile upon her face.

Chapter Three

No one had seen what happened to Renard or Hilde; no one noticed they were missing until now.

How did I not notice?

Renard always stood at her shoulder. At least whenever the slightest possibility of danger threatened.

"We should go back and find them," Lucien said.

"We need to get the Great Hall," Lebrecht said, equally unequivocally.

Hilde wasn't dead. She couldn't be. The *sight* had shown her the girl's death, and it hadn't been in Thasbald Castle. And wherever Hilde was, Renard would be, too. So, he was likely safe.

Indecision tugged her one way and the next. She didn't know if being decisive was the first rule of soldiering or not, but she thought it must be close.

"They'll catch up with us at the Great Hall," she said, hoping the decisiveness in her voice was loud enough to mask the churn in her stomach.

"My lady-" Lucien began.

"They are fine. Trust me," she nodded at Wirth.

Usk gave him a shove when Bulcher's man did nothing.

"The Great Hall," Usk barked, "now!"

It took a second shove to get Wirth going, but when he started moving, with Usk upon his shoulder, the rest of them fell into line.

"You know they are not in danger?" Lucien leaned into her as they walked.

"Yes," she said without hesitation.

When the quizzical look lingered on his face she gave him a significant glare, "*Trust* me."

"Oh..." Lucien straightened up.

Wirth led them down another barely lit corridor followed by an equally gloomy staircase. When they reached the bottom, the corridor was broader, the walls lined with oak panelling. More lights remained burning.

"This looks more familiar," Lucien said.

"Seen this before, too..." Gotz said a dozen paces along the corridor.

Blood.

Smeared against the wall.

The wood panel was cracked as well as bloody. Something had hit it with considerable force.

Something like a head, she suspected.

For a moment, voices floated in the distance. Laughter, too, but it vanished before she could focus on it.

"You heard that?"

Lebrecht nodded as he hurried Wirth along.

Several times, she checked over her shoulder in the hope of seeing Renard appearing behind them.

He is not going to die here.

She felt no certainty about that.

But what if he did?

Others stood with her now. But Renard's absence cut keenly. How could she do this alone?

He is not dead!

She fixed her eyes on the corridor ahead and swore she would not look for him again.

But what if he is!?

The corridor met a larger one still.

Wirth pointed, "The Great Hall is along here..."

Lebrecht nodded, "Yes, I recognise it now. He is right."

Wirth looked back at them with twitchy eyes, perhaps wondering what they would do with him now he had served his purpose.

At the end of the corridor, a final set of stairs led down towards the Great Hall.

Lebrecht put his shoulder in front of her and waved Lucien and Usk forwards. Usk moved without hesitation; Lucien checked with her first. She nodded.

She watched with Lebrecht as the two soldiers edged down the stairs, weapons drawn. Behind her, Hugo held one lantern beside Karoline and Elin, who clutched the other. Gotz, as was often the case, she'd noticed, lingered at the back.

Lucien and Usk reached the bottom of the stairs.

The silence hung deep. Both men hunched forward as they peered into the shadows from behind their weapons. Lucien had a pistol in each hand and Usk his sword. They glanced at each other before Usk waved them down.

The doors to the Great Hall remained closed, but none of their company were in sight.

"They were supposed to guard these doors with their lives," Lucien said, head still swinging back and forth when she joined him.

She cast an eye about the floor, "No blood or signs of a fight."

"Guess they didn't defend them with their lives then..."

"We should leave while we can," Lebrecht said.

"Not without what we came here for."

Or Renard! A distant voice wailed in the back of her mind.

"This place is infested with demons, my lady!" Lebrecht insisted, nostrils flaring.

"We don't know how many."

"But-"

"tis not easy to turn someone into a vampire; most die. However many brides Bulcher accumulated over the years, 'tis not likely more than a couple became like him."

Lebrecht's eyes narrowed, "How do you know that?"

"I have become an authority on the subject over the last year."

Their new companions didn't know about Morlaine, and she thought it better it stayed that way.

She looked around the empty, shadowy hall.

We could do with her help here...

But the demon left them, not prepared to do whatever it took to destroy the Red Company. There was no point wishing for what you did not have.

Her eyes flicked over the faces of her companions, whose expressions ranged through blank, concerned and terrified.

Always better to make the most of what you actually had at hand.

She moved to the doors of The Great Hall. Lebrecht came after her.

"What are you doing, my lady?"

"Bulcher is dead. Lady Karoline is the *Grafin* now. Thasbald must pledge allegiance to her."

"And if the people of Thasbald take umbrage at the killing of their lord?"

"Bulcher was a monster," she stopped half a dozen paces from the doors, "they will be relieved someone has done what they did not dare to do themselves."

"And if they were part of this?"

"They will jump at the opportunity to demonstrate their innocence by pledging themselves to Karoline."

"But-"

"Tomos, Gabriel, see if you can find any trace of our friends," she said.

The two soldiers nodded and moved to check the surrounding corridors for a sign of their missing comrades.

Lebrecht appeared to be struggling to keep his annoyance in hand. She smiled and held his eye, "Please, trust me, Lebrecht."

When that didn't ease the broody look, she found his hand and squeezed it. Lebrecht's eyebrows rose, his expression softening to a smile.

Yes, that did the trick.

Feet scampered across the flagstones behind them.

"My lady..." Hugo said, his cheeks red from the cold or shyness. As his cheeks were usually red when he spoke to her, regardless of the temperature, she suspected the latter.

"Yes?"

"I... I don't think you should open those doors."

Another one.

"Trust me," she said, wondering whether it more or less

likely people would if she kept saying it long enough.

Before she could approach the doors, Hugo grabbed her arm and thrust the lantern before them, "Look!"

At first, she had no clue what Hugo was pointing at, even when Lebrecht sucked in a deep breath. The realisation the darkness spreading across the floor in front of the doors wasn't a shadow dawned slowly.

Given the way Karoline screamed, it seemed most of their party had been quicker than her to see the blood flowing under the doors to form a large, slick puddle.

"Keep her quiet!" she told Elin, though the maid was already trying to comfort her mistress.

"I suspect there won't be too many people refusing to pledge allegiance to Karoline after all," Lucien commented, eyes moving from the blood to her.

"How many people did you lock in the Great Hall?" she asked.

"A hundred, at least," Lebrecht said, looking like the blood in his face had rushed to join that on the floor.

"More," Lucien said, "closer to two hundred.

"'tis very quiet in there..." Hugo offered.

Usk and Gotz reappeared.

"No sign of anyone- *Jesus!*" Gotz exclaimed, pulling up short.

After a while, she noticed that people were looking at her.

Careful not to slip in the blood, she walked to the door.

"You're not thinking of opening that, are you?" Lucien asked.

She ignored him.

Instead, she put her ear to the wood.

Hugo was right. It was very quiet in there...

"Is there another way out of here?" she asked, ear still pressed to the door.

"Through the kitchens," Lucien said, "we locked and guarded that one too."

She looked at Wirth, "Any other ways?"

The Thasbald man-at-arms continued to stare at the blood trickling under the door until Usk nudged him.

"I don't know."

"You don't know?"

"There was talk of secret passages the *Graf* used to... move about..." Wirth's shoulders moved up and down, "...these doors and the one via the kitchens are all I know for sure..."

"So, if there was another exit that Bulcher's Brides knew about...?" Lucien said.

"They couldn't have killed everyone..." Lebrecht's words hung in the air as they all stared at the blood still flowing around her feet.

"There's only one way to find out," she hammered her fist against the door, the blows echoing in the high, gloomy rafters.

"We need to find out?" Gotz asked.

"If there are enough demons in this castle to have slaughtered everyone in the Great Hall, we cannot hope to take the castle."

"Then best we leave!" Gotz suggested.

"We need Bulcher's silver."

"Comes a point when shiny metal loses its lustre."

She looked sharply over her shoulder at the old soldier,

"You don't have to stay. None of you do."

Silence came from both sides of the door.

"But if you don't want to run," Lebrecht asked, "and we can't overcome them, what can we do?"

She hammered on the door a few more times.

"Talk. We are not their enemies."

Gotz's overgrown eyebrows rocketed upwards, "You mean these blood-sucking demons who seem to have slaughtered Thasbald's inhabitants?"

She flashed him a dark smile.

"Precisely..."

From the other side of the door finally came a noise. Footsteps.

Splashing on wet stone...

*

"You're quite a good shot..."

"Quite?"

"A very good shot."

"Helps when your target isn't moving."

"I suppose..."

He stood at Judita's feet. They were as small and delicate as a doll's. He couldn't pull his eyes away from them. Although that might have been because he found it more comfortable than looking at the smiling face of the child they'd killed.

"Why did you shoot her?"

"To save you from doing it."

That dragged his attention away from Judita's tiny feet.

"You would have to have gotten closer to use your sword," she rolled her shoulders, "seemed safer for me to do it in case she..."

He wasn't sure if he believed that.

"You should have left it to me."

"I'll let you kill the next one."

Hilde's cheeks glistened in the guttering rushlight. When she noticed him staring, she juggled the crossbow with one hand to wipe a sleeve across her eyes.

"The rushlights are smoking," she explained, "they're about to go out."

"Better reload that bow before they do," he went back to the dead demon's feet, "we might need it again."

Hilde made no move to reload the weapon, "We should catch up with the others, too."

"Yes," he agreed.

His place was at Solace's side. He shouldn't be here. Although, of course, being at Solace's side was why he was here. Killing children. Or at least something that looked like one.

Strange, Judita sounded like a child when she cried but a world-weary crone when she spoke.

Despite himself, his eyes stole back to Judita's face. She was still smiling. A thin trickle of blood darkened her face. It had already dried to a black crust on her linen skin. The only thing to suggest she was not a human child.

"She said she married Bulcher when she was twelve," Hilde said, "she still looks twelve. How long ago did-"

"They don't age from the moment they are changed. It could have been a year ago; it could have been centuries..."

"No, I meant she was twelve when she married. She still looks twelve. She couldn't have been married long before..."

"Bulcher killed and changed her."

"Yes. Bastard..."

Hilde thrust the crossbow at him, which he just about managed not to drop along with his sabre, before crouching over the corpse. She closed the girl's dead eyes with a caress.

She muttered a short prayer, too softly spoken for him to make out even in the deep silence of Thasbald's night. When Hilde straightened up, she said, "Rest with our Lord, Jesus Christ, Judita..." then she yanked the bolt out of the girl's forehead with a wet crack.

"Haven't got many," she explained, cleaning the blood off on her apron.

He handed her the crossbow back and decided he preferred looking at Hilde than the dead girl.

Hilde cranked the bow and replaced the bolt with quick, strong hands.

"You've done that before, haven't you?"

"My big brother taught me," she paused to flash a brief and sad smile at him, "I was always shit at being a girl."

"Dunno..."

The smile came again; this time it lingered.

With the crossbow reloaded, they turned away from Judita. Leaving her on the floorboards felt wrong, but they had nothing else to offer. And he'd walked away from living children before now...

He was, he was ashamed to admit, grateful to Hilde. If she hadn't shot Judita, he would have killed the demon, but the thought of that fixed smile on the girl's head as it bounced on the floor. He had enough ghosts haunting him already.

"She is not how I imagined these demons to be," Hilde said as they began to retrace their steps.

"I think they can be as different as mortal people."

"You told her you knew one that could control the demon inside them?"

Neither Solace nor he had talked about Morlaine. Lucien hadn't either as far as he knew.

"We have met a number over the last year," was all he felt safe saying.

"Are they not all evil?"

"Was Judita?"

Hilde's brow furrowed, "I felt sorry for her. Is that wrong?"

"Compassion is never wrong. Just sometimes misplaced."

"And in her case?"

He shook his head as they descended the stairs. Behind them, the final rushlight flickered out.

"She never asked for what Bulcher did to her. However many of his brides – his widows now – are still in Thasbald; I doubt any of them asked for it either."

"Why would a man do such a thing?"

"We can ponder the nature of evil when we get out of here."

"Well, even if we achieve nothing else, we've stopped him."

"Yes," he agreed, "that's something, I suppose..."

They paused together at the foot of the stairs. There was no sign of the rest of their company.

If we get out of here.

"They didn't wait for us..." Hilde peered ahead as if checking Solace, Lucien, and the others weren't just hiding in the shadows.

"Probably didn't notice... I should have said something..."

"Why didn't you?"

"I heard a child crying, and..." he shrugged and hurried along the corridor; Hilde kept pace with him, cradling the crossbow. And looking at him.

He hadn't said much to Hilde about what happened to him the night The Wolf's Tower fell, how he'd dishonoured himself, betrayed his oath, helped the demons enter the castle and finally abandoned the women and children of Tassau to slaughter.

After Solace told their company her version the night before they arrived at Thasbald, Hilde had few opportunities to ask him questions. Partly because they had been busy and time short, but mainly because he changed the subject or found an excuse to be somewhere else whenever she tried.

"Why-"

"We need to be somewhere else," he said, lengthening his stride.

As always, Hilde's little legs were no impediment to her keeping pace with him.

No more questions followed, but he felt her eyes continually drawn to him.

They walked until they reached a spot where another corridor crossed with their own.

"Which way?" he asked

Hilde peered down each of the three barely lit options in turn.

She wrinkled her nose, "They all look the same to me."

"Great..." he sighed, "...lost in a castle full of demonic brides."

"Demonic widows," Hilde corrected, "and if you hadn't..."

He scowled.

She patted his arm. The reassurance of the gesture somewhat undermined by the fact Hilde had to juggle a loaded crossbow to do it.

"Be careful with that thing," he warned.

"Never shot anyone I didn't mean to yet," Hilde winked, "well, apart from the time-"

"I don't want to know."

Hilde giggled, stretched up and kissed his cheek.

Given their predicament, this didn't seem a suitable moment for such things. Therefore, it came as something of a surprise when he found himself kissing her lips in return, all cares, including those about the loaded crossbow, forgotten.

She kissed him back, pushing herself hard enough against him for him to have to take a step backwards and keep going until a wall got in the way.

Later, he had no idea how long they kissed; it seemed both a heartbeat and a lifetime, and when they parted, they were both panting. She still held her crossbow, awkwardly in one hand, he his father's sabre. Fortunately, they had managed not to stab each other. Though he became aware, he had been poking her with something.

Hilde's eyes sparkled in what little light remained, "I'd wager there are a lot of empty rooms hereabouts..."

"You..." he sort of laughed, sort of snorted, "...cannot be serious?"

"Why not? We may not live to see the dawn..."

The only worthy response to bob up was that his place was at Solace's side.

He knew little of women, his experiences generally fleeting and occasionally tragic, but he felt confident that wasn't going to go down well, so he plumped for the next one within grasp.

"'tis not appropriate."

Hilde laughed.

He took the opportunity to slide away from her along the wall, albeit stiffly.

The laughter eased into a sigh.

"We cannot... cavort! Not while our friends are in danger!"

"The same friends you abandoned for a demon's tears?"

This was teetering on the brink of becoming one of those conversations he really hated. In truth, he hated most conversations, regardless of the subject, but this one appeared particularly hazardous. He had an awful feeling she might start talking about emotions.

"We may never have another chance."

"We're not going to die here," he summoned her with a flick of his bad hand and headed down the corridor that seemed marginally brighter than the others.

"How do you know that?"

"I'm a born optimist..."

That made her laugh again.

It was an alien noise in the gloomy, freezing corridor.

They passed several doors. All closed. He wondered if they were bedrooms. He wondered if Hilde wondered the same thing.

My place is beside Lady Solace!

She had his oath. One he could not abandon without the loss of the last fragments of his honour.

He was cold and tired. There was a fair chance he would soon be dead. Every time he closed his eyes, he expected to see Judita's forlorn smile upon her pale, dead face, accompanied by the screams of terrified children, the weeping of innocents.

What did Solace care about him?

She was leading him to their deaths in her crazed pursuit of vengeance. He was nothing to her. Sometimes, he thought he caught her looking at him in a way that made him think he might be more than just a retainer, a sword, the last of her people, a means to an end, a tool to use, a weapon to break. *Something.*

But it never lasted, and he knew he was only fooling himself.

They were not friends. He was nothing to her, even though he would lay down his life for her in a heartbeat.

And here was a woman who wanted to...

The corridor ended in a door. Opening it, he found a spiral staircase, or at least the first few steps of one; the rest was but a wall of darkness.

"We need a light," he said, looking back at the nearest rushlight.

"You know I'm in love with you, don't you?" Hilde asked.

Which wasn't the answer he'd been expecting.

There were several answers to that question. All of them seemed unsuitable, so he settled upon the quickest.

"Yes."

"That isn't something I say lightly, you know?"

A conversation. About emotion. Oh, dear.

"I'll get a light."

He headed back to the closest rushlight still burning. It was awkward for him to carry in his bad hand, but Hilde needed both hers for the crossbow, and he wasn't sheathing his sabre. The holder had a wooden base, pockmarked by woodworm and an iron shaft into which the rushlight, the dried pith of rush soaked in fat, sat. The light was feeble, less than a wax candle, much less than an oil lantern, but cheap. And lighting a building the size of Thasbald Castle was expensive. Greasy smoke curled away from the feeble flame.

It didn't weigh a lot, but his arm still protested the burden. As it did whenever he insisted it did anything. He fixed his numb, stiff, uncooperative fingers around the wooden base and turned back to the stairs.

The corridor was empty.

Hilde was gone.

Chapter Four

She listened to the approaching feet.

It sounded like someone was walking through water lying on stone.

She glanced at her own feet. It wasn't water.

"I want to talk to you!"

The footsteps stopped.

Then came a scratching noise.

She imagined fingernails (long and undoubtedly bloody) scraping down the thick, seasoned oak of the Great Hall's imposing double doors.

Another sound.

A high-pitched whine. But not from the Great Hall this time.

She shot a look at her companions. It was Wirth. Usk had him by his collar, the only reason the man hadn't bolted by the look of it. She pressed a finger against her lips. When Wirth carried on whining like a whipped dog, she slashed the finger across her throat.

Usk grinned and made a show of reaching for his dagger. Wirth went white.

And shut up.

The scratching continued, like the fingers and thumbs of both hands moving back and forth as if playing a harp.

"I wish to talk to you," she repeated.

The scratching stopped.

Nothing took its place.

She looked the door up and down. Thick oak planks reinforced with iron studs and bands of black metal. It wasn't some ornate piece of showmanship. It had been built to hold. To keep people out or keep people in. Could it withstand a single demon who wanted to take it down? Possibly. But Flyblown's mark smarted like she'd been branded. There was a lot more than one vampire behind that door.

She'd thought Bulcher couldn't have turned more than a handful of his wives into demons. Now, she was having second thoughts about that.

She resisted the urge to step backwards.

"My name is Solace von Tassau. It has taken me a year and two days to come here and kill your husband. I am sorry it took me so long..."

The scratching resumed. But this time, with light, delicate strokes.

"*Graf* Bulcher was a monster; he took everything from me. He had my father murdered, destroyed my home, killed my people, stole what belonged to my family. I suspect he did the same thing to yours. To all your families. He wanted me to be his bride, too. If he had, I would be like you now. And we would all be locked in the dark together."

A knocking sound joined the scratching. A faint tapping, a knuckle gently rapping on the wood.

"*Graf* Bulcher was a monster. I killed him. I am hunting other monsters, too, the ones he employed to destroy my home. The Red Company and their leader, Saul the

Bloodless. Perhaps he used them to hurt you, too..."

The door rattled hard enough at the mention of Saul's name to make her take half a step backwards.

Another noise. Palms slapping against the door?

She imagined multiple women on the other side of the Great Hall's doors, hands and fingers on the wood.

"*Graf* Bulcher was a monster. I killed him. I gave him justice. I gave you all justice. Now I wish to talk to those he wronged..."

The door reverberated. Scratches, knocks, taps, slaps. Her mouth dried. Just how many women had Bulcher cursed? What had he done to them?

Her eyes fell to the blood pooling around her feet.

And what had become of the people she'd locked inside the Great Hall?

"My lady?"

Her attention moved to her companions.

Some had edged away, some had stayed firm, weapons drawn. She would have expected Renard to be at her shoulder. But he was gone.

What if he is dead? What if one of the brides had killed him?

He is not dead! I do not believe that. I do not!

It was Gotz who'd called her.

"I knew a man once," he said, "a Frenchman named Basile, a light-fingered fellow, a magpie of a man who could never pass a bauble without trying to steal it. Spent a lot of time in prison and a lot of time avoiding getting hung. Told me of a place he'd been locked up in one time, I can't remember where now, but they kept the troublemakers in tiny cells, isolated from each other. Too far for a voice to reach through thick stone. But not so thick noises wouldn't carry. Tapping, knocking noises, on walls and pipes..." his eyes shifted the shaking door, "...and doors..."

"You think they're talking?"

Gotz's big shoulders moved up and down.

"If they're not," Lucien offered, "then they're just insane."

Could Bulcher have kept them down there for so long they'd forgotten how to talk other than in this code? A secret language of the damned.

"Samanta spoke well enough," Lebrecht said.

"But we don't know how long she was down there or how long they were."

"Why are you even trying to talk to them?!" Karoline's question, asked with her hands almost clamped to her mouth, wasn't quite a shriek, but it wasn't far off.

She offered only a reassuring smile by way of an explanation. Karoline's usefulness was likely over, so she felt no need to waste more on the girl.

Turning back to the door, she rapped a knuckle on the oak.

"Be quiet!"

The noise stilled like wind fading in the woods.

"Can any of you talk?"

A long silence. Then, "I can talk, sister, I can remember..."

Each word that came through the thick wood of the door was a wet, bleeding rasp.

"I am Solace, the *Freiin* von Tassau. Who are you?"

"I am Number Twenty-Nine."

"That is not a name."

"That is all He gave me. He took everything else from me. Even my before name. I was his Twenty-Ninth Bride. Now I am His Twenty-Ninth Widow. Thanks to you... 'tis all that remains..."

"You are more than that."

"I am nothing. We are nothing. There was darkness. Now there is blood."

"Is... is anyone alive in there?"

"We starved for time without end. Now we feast."

"Have you killed everyone?"

"You waited a year and two days for your vengeance, Solace, the *Freiin* von Tassau..." the voice dripped beyond the door, "...we have waited so much longer for ours..."

"My vengeance is not complete. My vengeance has barely begun."

"We wish you well, sister..."

A volley of knocks rattled the door.

She pressed a cheek against the wood, feeling the vibrations in her bones, in her teeth, in her soul.

This could so easily have been me...

"I need your help..."

The knocking subsided.

"You did that which we could not. You killed He that damned us. For that, we will let you keep your blood. If you leave this place now. There is no other assistance we can give."

"Yes, there is. I want two things for killing your husband."

"Our years are long, sister. Our patience, however..."

She shuffled her feet. Blood splashed.

"My lady..."

That was Lebrecht. She thought. She wasn't really listening. She held out a hand.

"Do you have my men?" she asked.

"The ones from outside? Yes."

"Are they alive?"

"Yes... we saved them."

Saved them?"

"For later."

"I want them back. Alive."

Knocks. A rapid series of taps. A scratch or two.

"You have nothing we want. Save your blood."

"I killed your husband, sister. Does that not earn me anything?"

"Yes," the demon's voice seeped through the door, "It earnt you your life."

She glanced back at her company, whether for inspiration or to offer reassurance she couldn't say.

Lucien edged behind Usk and Wirth,

No expression on his face, he pointed at the Thasbald man-at-arms...

Sharply, she returned her attention to the door.

"What of the people we locked in there?"

"You want them, too?" Number Twenty-Nine laughed, the first time the demon expressed any emotion.

"Are they all dead?"

"Their blood washes the guilt from these stones."

"It was Bulcher who made you wh-"

"They served Him! They helped Him! Some from grandfather to father to son!" the great door began shaking in time with Twenty-Nine's words as the demon showed herself capable of other emotions, "They imprisoned us. They did his bidding. None lifted a finger to help us. They are all guilty!"

"But my men are innocent."

The door rattled on its hinges, dust shaking free from the old planks to float about her. It stopped just as she expected the doors to fly off, flattening her beneath thick, old oak.

In the still that followed, all she could hear was her heart.

Could the demons hear it, too?

"No men are innocent..."

The voice didn't belong to Twenty-Nine. This one sounded older, bone-weary; each word a chore, a block of stone shifted with brute force and hard sweat.

"No one is without sin," she conceded, "but they have done you no wrong. They serve me, they helped kill the monster, Bulcher. They deserve your thanks."

Silence.

Then tapping and scratching.

A discussion?

When it ceased, the second voice asked, "You wanted two things, sister?"

"To destroy my enemy, I need an army. To buy an army, I need silver, I need gold. Bulcher was rich. He stole from all your families, I believe, as he stole from mine. I want Bulcher's wealth."

A chuckle floated from beyond the door, "You have bones, sister, yes, you do."

"Who are you?" she asked the second voice.

"I am Five. I am the oldest bar one, but she is elsewhere. I have been here for... I do not know how long. I came here on the 14th of March, the year of our lord 1393... I remember that day. I have forgotten so much, I have lost so much, but I remember that cursed day well enough. Tell me, sister, how long have I been here?"

She counted in her head, before breathing, "Two-hundred and thirty-eight years..."

"Two-hundred and thirty-eight years... so, very, very long... and I believe that is the first time anyone has made me laugh in all those years..."

The door shook as if many hands slapped against it.

"This is a funny one, sister..." Twenty-nine snickered.

"What use do you have for silver and gold, sisters? You require only blood."

"He fed us pig's blood, for the most part," Five said, the words clunky and hoarse, as if she had to drag them up one at a time from some dark, disused well, "it kept us weak. Sometimes He brought us... other meat. A treat for the favoured among us, a punishment for the meat. Not often. But enough for us to yearn for it, to beg for it... to do *anything* for it. Now... now we are free... and we have an entire world to feast upon..."

*

"Hilde!"

He ran back along the corridor, struggling to keep hold of the rushlight with his left hand's numb, reluctant fingers.

The only response was the hollow echo of his own cry accompanied by the thump of nailed boots on the floorboards.

He skidded to a halt where they'd been standing together

moments before.

There was nothing to see.

He'd turned his back for only seconds. Surely, if someone (or something) had snatched Hilde, he would have heard the scuffle. Wouldn't she have fired or swung or dropped her crossbow?

All the doors along the corridor were shut. If something had dragged her into another room, even if she and her assailant had been silent, hinges would have squeaked, a door would have creaked.

Wouldn't it?

He headed for the stairs. If Hilde wasn't in sight and none of the doors had opened and closed, she could only have gone into the stairwell beyond a narrow stone arch.

He envisaged a demon coming silently behind her the second his back turned, clamping a hand over her mouth and using its unnatural strength and speed to pull her into the stairwell before she could even react.

His stomach lurched at the thought, while simultaneously knowing its inevitability.

Everybody I care about dies.

He hurtled into the stairwell, twisting first to check the stairs spiralling down then the ones going upwards.

Hilde had one shoulder against the wall and one eyebrow raised, crossbow cradled in her arms.

"I thought I'd check the stairs for you," she said nodding to the descending steps behind him, "we should keep going down."

Relief dissolved into anger.

"Don't go off like that!"

The grin faded; the eyebrow edged higher. "You mean like you did? Is that something only men are allowed to do?"

"I had a reason."

"So did I..." she slipped past him and turned into the downward spiral, "...the only difference is I know why I did it, you..."

She plunged into the darkness, forcing him to scurry after her.

"Why?"

"Because boys are rubbish..."

"What is that supposed to mean?"

Hilde might know why she was acting so foolishly. He didn't. He guessed it might have something to do with him walking off when she told him she loved him, girls put a lot of stock in things like that, after all.

Hilde's declaration might give him some pause for thought if they weren't lost in a deserted castle filled with demons. At the very least. But for now, it was a complication he didn't need. All that mattered was keeping her alive. Until then, she could be pissed at him all she liked.

Out of the flickering darkness, another door appeared. Beyond it, the stairs continued downwards.

"Let's try this one," Hilde awkwardly juggled the crossbow while fumbling with the latch.

"I should go first," he said.

"You don't have enough hands, besides..." she peered back at him, "...how many demons have you killed today?"

"Hilde..." he warned, but she'd already flung the door open.

"Oh, shit!" she took a sharp step backwards.

"What is it? he demanded, shouldering past her onto another dimly lit corridor identical to the one on the previous floor.

"More doors..." she stretched to put her chin on his shoulder, "...do you think these might be bedrooms too?"

He spun around to face her, "What's wrong with you?"

She looked down at herself and then back at him, "I've always thought myself rather ungainly and somewhat dumpy."

"Do you not understand how much danger we're in?" he stared at her before spluttering, "And you're not in the least dumpy!"

"See, Ulrich, see!" she beamed, "If you try really, really hard, you *can* say the right thing!"

"We have no time for such foolishness!"

"I have no idea how much time you, I or anybody else has. All I know is that we're still breathing and should make the most of it."

"By getting out of here alive!" he said.

"So we can die another day?"

"That's better than dying today."

"Depends on what you do today first."

"Jumping into bed and... and... *fornicating?!*"

Her eyebrow shot up again. Did all women do that, or just the ones he knew?

"Do you think that is something I do lightly, Ulrich?"

He turned, flicked his sabre ahead of him and started walking. There was no point talking to the woman. She'd clearly become touched!

"Don't you think we'd be better off carrying on

downstairs? We need to get to the ground floor, after all," she called after him.

He stopped. Then walked back to Hilde, to lean on one shoulder again, this time in the stairwell doorway.

She didn't stand aside.

"I'm scared," she said, "and I just killed something that looked a lot like a child. I also love you. I may have mentioned that already."

"Is that why you're acting peculiar?"

"I am peculiar. So, Ma was want to tell me, anyway."

He lowered his chin towards her. She raised hers towards him. The steam of their breath merged.

Weariness descended. As it often did since he'd been broken a year ago. His hand throbbed from the exploding pistol, his face stung, his bad arm swung between numbness and sparks of pain in its usual feckless, indecisive way. Lead filled his bones.

Perhaps Hilde was right.

Why carry on?

He'd asked himself that question many times since leaving the ruined Wolf's Tower two months ago, even when the alternative wasn't anywhere near so comely as the one standing before him now.

The answer, though, was always the same.

"I have obligations, Hilde; I cannot... hide in the dark with you."

"You mean Solace?"

"She is my mistress; she has my oath."

"Only your oath?" the skin around Hilde's lips tightened, her eyes narrowed.

"What else have I to give?"

"She is very beautiful. If you don't look into her eyes too closely anyway."

He frowned; he'd always thought Solace had pretty eyes that sparkled on occasion, but that was neither here nor there.

"I don't know what you're talking about."

"She isn't for you, Ulrich. Her kind are a breed apart from the likes of you and me. We are little better than horses or hounds to nobles like Solace and Lebrecht, something to be used until the point we have no more use, then we are cast aside..." she moved closer, eyes fierce, "...a dog might give its heart to their owner, but dogs are stupid..."

Several competing responses collided in his head.

He glared at Hilde while their dust settled until only one remained.

"I owe her my life. All I have to offer in return for it is my oath."

"Is that what you believe?"

"'tis the truth."

"Ulrich, I see the way you look at her..."

He leaned on his father's sabre, its tip pressing into the floor. The rushlight in his bad hand weighed more by the minute. Part of him wanted to curl up on the ground. Another part to find the dark room Hilde offered and forget about everything else in the universe for just a little while. Instead, he shook his head, knowing he would do neither.

How did he explain the bond between Solace and him? It was an impossible thing. Perhaps poets and bards could, but he didn't have the words. Whatever it was, however, it wasn't what Hilde thought she saw.

I love her and I hate her.

But it was more complicated than that.

Save her and you save yourself.

And they did not have the time for him to explain it, even if he could.

Honour is the only thing that cannot be taken from a man. He can only give it away...

"You know you will die on this lunatic quest of hers to find the Red Company and this Saul the Bloodless creature, don't you?" Hilde asked.

"Very likely."

"Do you think she will cry for you afterwards?"

"I don't follow Lady Solace for her tears. Or her love. Or for silver, or glory, or righteousness."

"Then why do you?"

He almost told her.

To save myself.

Instead, with an effort, he lifted his father's sabre, slipped past Hilde and stepped into the darkness once more.

Chapter Five

She looked back at her company.

Renard still wasn't there.

It made her stomach turn, it made her heart heavy beyond reason, it made her feel... less.

Without him at her side, she felt weak, uncertain, slow-headed and thick-thumbed. She didn't know why. He was but a single man and a broken one at that. But the thought of doing what she had to do, facing the future and all the horrors it held without him, made her want to give up. Unlock the great doors before them and let the Brides of Bulcher drink her dry.

She placed her forehead against wood worn smooth by countless hands over countless years.

He is not dead. And even if he is, I will continue, I will endure, I will do all that I must do, and I will prevail. God saved me for a purpose.

The frigid air she sucked in bit her nostrils. It smelt of wood, of iron, of frost. But most of all, it smelt of blood.

Feet sloshed behind her.

She turned and opened her eyes.

Lucien.

"You have a sly plan?" she asked, hopefully.

He placed a hand on her shoulder, big, rough. She wished it were Renard's; despite the fact he rarely touched her, she always found it reassuring on the odd occasion that he did.

Reassuring was probably the right word....

When the mercenary leaned in, he whispered a single word in her ear.

Trade.

Then he walked back to the others, leaving a trail of bloody footprints behind him.

"Do you have anything we want, sister?" Twenty-Nine asked. It was hard to tell from a disembodied voice coming through a thick oak door, but she thought Twenty-Nine sounded less hostile than Five. Less mad, too.

Two-hundred and thirty-eight years. Locked in the bowels of Thasbald castle, seemingly as an amusement for *Graf* Bulcher.

She shuddered. Even with the blood of the dead pooling around her feet, she couldn't help but feel sympathy and pity for the creatures on the other side of the door.

But sympathy and pity weren't going to deliver her vengeance.

Back turned to her company, she whispered to the door, "I have some of the men who did you wrong, who served your husband, who kept you in chains. I'll exchange them for my men."

"How many?" Twenty-Nine asked.

She resisted the urge to look at Wirth, "One here, four others elsewhere. From Bulcher's Household Guard. Did they do you wrong?"

"Yes!" Five hissed, the door shook in agreement, "His favourite pets got to play with His toys when they were good..."

Her mind didn't want to linger on what that meant, but it

quietened the distant qualms she had about giving men to demons.

"I will bring them to you."

"We can get them ourselves," Five said.

"It will be dawn soon. Some might escape. They will run from you but not from me. There are others here, too, on the walls. I will bring them all, in return for my men, in return for silver."

"We don't need your help!"

"I wish to give it. I would have been like you if the world turned only a little differently. I have Lady Karoline with me, his latest bride; she would have been with you before long. We are your sisters, too. We want to help you. And I want you to aid us. Bulcher is not the only monster in this world. Help me destroy the others, please... I cannot change what happened to you. But I can avenge you."

"The Red Company?" Twenty-nine asked.

"What are they to us?" Five snorted.

Taps and knocks shook the doors.

"Bulcher sent them to fetch me to him to make me his bride; I believe he has now dispatched them to kill Karoline's family so he could inherit the estate. We cannot be the only ones..."

The noises subsided to scratches. Then nothing.

The silence lasted so long she thought her strange audience concluded before Twenty-Nine's voice broke it.

"No... you are not."

She pressed her forehead against the door.

"Then give me what I need to avenge us *all...* and stop them from destroying more lives, as they have destroyed ours!"

She felt as much as heard the scratchings on the far side of the wood, placing the palm of her right hand, fingers splayed wide, as taps and knocks joined the scratches.

Finally, a voice again. Five's this time, "Give us the one you have, as a sign of your good faith... sister..." she could imagine a sneer upon the face she couldn't see. Distrusting, suspicious, expecting betrayal.

"And you will give me my men?"

"Some. The rest when you have brought us all those who sinned against us."

"And the silver, the gold, the coin?"

"We will discuss it further. Once you have proved your word..."

Am I going to send a man to his death?

She didn't look around.

And then more to theirs?

The door was silent. No voices. No noises.

I must do whatever is necessary.

They were testing her.

I must do what needs to be done.

To see if she would deliver upon her promises.

The price of vengeance, after all, is not paid in silver.

They were waiting for her.

Where the darkness beckons...

Slowly, she turned back to face her company.

As she moved towards them, the congealing blood sucked at her feet as if reluctant to let her go.

"What did they say?" Lebrecht asked.

She'd hoped the voices had been too quiet for the others to

clearly follow.

"They have your men, Lady Karoline's, too."

"All of them?" Karoline's red-rimmed eyes widened.

She shook her head at the snivelling girl, "I don't know."

"We haven't found any bodies..." Lucien said, "...out here."

"They said they're alive."

"And the people we locked in the Great Hall?" Lebrecht asked, looking as pale as Karoline.

"Some... possibly..."

Hugo stared intently at her. She fancied the boy's ears might be sharper than everybody else's.

"We have to get them out!" Lebrecht turned to the doors as if he intended to march in and rescue them. Or die very quickly, which seemed a far more likely outcome.

"How many of them are there?" Gotz asked, working on a tooth stump as he eyed the door like it was a rabid dog.

"Too many to fight," she said.

"So, we do nothing?" Lebrecht demanded, "I'm not leaving my men with those... monsters!"

"Neither am I."

Behind her, doors creaked and groaned.

Several of her companions jumped backwards, weapons raised.

She didn't turn around. She didn't look over her shoulder. She knew what would be there.

Nothing.

A black, empty void.

The vampires would have extinguished every light.

There would be only darkness and the world that hid within it.

She looked at Wirth, "We're going to do a deal with them."

And it beckoned...

*

They descended in silence.

It was heavy.

As was the rushlight. And his father's sabre. And every pain-filled step he forced his abused body to take.

He wanted to lie down. Somewhere warm. With Hilde.

But he pushed himself forward. He kept going down. Holding the rushlight sent spasms fizzing up his left arm. Holding his father's sabre made his burnt right hand sting and throb.

Solace needed him.

He should be at her side. She had his oath. She had saved his life. He loved her, and he hated her. If he were to ever regain the honour he'd cast aside to save his life the night The Wolf's Tower fell, it would be at his mistress's shoulder.

Save her, and you save yourself.

Yet, for the first time in a year, part of him whispered something else.

He thought it the weak part of him. The part he hadn't realised existed until he betrayed his oath and helped Saul the Bloodless and his monsters into The Wolf's Tower. The part that had wanted to live.

Women make you weak.

Another of Old Man Ulrich's sayings.

One he hadn't really understood.

Perhaps until now.

Fear makes you weak.

Greed makes you weak.

Stupidity makes you weak.

His father told him that, too. Those he understood.

But women?

Now, part of him wanted to slink away from his duty, from the tattered bloody remnants of his honour, to lie with the woman whose feet echoed behind him.

And maybe he understood what Old Man Ulrich meant a little better.

Though, perhaps *desire* was a more fitting word.

The world wasn't full of women he would walk away from his duty for, so it seemed somewhat unfair to blame the entire gender.

Out of the gloom, a door appeared, and the steps finished.

He stopped before it.

"What are you thinking?" Hilde asked. Her voice sudden and jarring enough to make him start. The rushlight's flame fluttered in his hand, their shadows danced on the walls around them.

"We should probably open it."

"I wasn't talking about the door."

"Oh."

"So, what are you thinking?"

He frowned. He couldn't see his thoughts' relevance to their current predicament. He still didn't think women made you weak, but they were undeniably peculiar creatures, all the same.

"Nothing."

He examined the door some more. Old and damp, rot seemed to have seeped into the bottom. It didn't look sturdy, even he might be able to kick it open.

"You must be thinking something?"

He suspected she might be annoyed if he said he was thinking about the door.

"No. Isn't your mind ever empty?"

"No. Never!"

She sounded annoyed.

He stifled a sigh. That wouldn't help either.

"We need to concentrate on staying alive, finding the others and getting out of Thasbald."

"Unless Lady Solace decides differently."

"She is in charge."

"How did that happen?"

"How did what happen?"

"How did Lady Solace end up giving the orders? She is younger than I am. And she is a girl!"

"She is the *Freiin* von Tassau."

"The world is full of women with fancy titles. Most of them spend their lives popping out babies and doing what they're told, just like normal women. Nobody gives a damn about their opinion, let alone take their orders. What makes *her* different?"

This time, he couldn't stifle the sigh. He placed the rushlight on the step. He hoped there was light on the other side of the door; he wasn't sure how much longer he could carry the rushlight, which reminded him how weak, pathetic and broken he'd-

"See!" Hilde announced.

"See what?" he peered over his shoulder up at her.

He was unsurprised to find a scowl.

"You don't care about my opinion, just hers!!"

"She has my oath. I am in her debt."

"Yes, that's as maybe, but what about everybody else? They don't. Lebrecht is the heir to the *Markgräfschaft* of Gothen; he is a *Markgräf* in his own right. Why does he follow her orders?"

Old Man Ulrich, he recalled, had a word for a man who always did a woman's bidding. A pretty one's anyway. It was a word he'd sneered in disgust whenever he talked about how women made a man weak.

Cuntstruck.

He decided it best not to share that piece of his father's *wisdom* with Hilde.

"Dunno, ask him."

"Seems... peculiar to me."

"She thinks God saved her life for a purpose. To destroy Saul the Bloodless and the Red Company. When someone believes in something enough..." he shrugged and instantly winced at his shoulders protest, "...they can bend the will of the world to their own."

"I guess I don't believe in anything enough then," Hilde sighed, "All the world does is rain on my little ginger head."

The wince turned into a smile.

He looked over his shoulder again, "That's probably a blessing."

She squarely met his eye, "Dunno about bending the will of the world, but it'd be nice to get my own way once in a while."

He quickly went back to the door.

She's talking about you...

"If there's anything you don't like the look of on the other side, don't be shy with that crossbow."

"I'll do my best not to shoot you..."

"Reassuring..."

He pushed open the door.

Nothing needing a crossbow bolt awaited them.

The darkness was absolute; the stink of dank old earth washed over him. What little the rushlight illuminated was either water, stone or stone stained by water.

"We came down too far; we're below ground here."

Hilde rested her chin on his shoulder again and wrinkled her nose, "Not much chance of a comfy room down there, I suppose..."

I wish she'd stop doing that.

He carefully extracted his shoulder from beneath her chin.

"What do you think is in there?" Hilde asked.

The mundane and the mad, he thought. The bowels of castles tended to be places where lords stored their provisions and made people disappear.

"Nothing good..."

The weight of the darkness was palpable, a wall of nothingness you might never escape from if you ventured too far into its embrace, too far from the world of men.

Nothing could make him walk down there. He doubted even a dozen oil lanterns could press back the darkness more than a pace or two.

Nothing other than Solace telling me to, anyway...

"Let's go back up."

Hilde nodded and turned around. Then froze.

Footsteps echoed from the stairs above them.

She looked questioningly over her shoulder at him.

They didn't sound like the booted feet of soldiers.

But they were coming towards them.

The memory of meeting the demon Alms on a tight spiral staircase in The Wolf's Tower tightened his throat.

Master.

The staircase was narrow and steep, hard to fight, hard to run.

The footsteps were soft, perhaps a slipper scuffing the stones.

Mistress.

He shoved that stupid thought away. He had a mistress, and he wouldn't ever betray her, even to save his own worthless skin. Not again.

He touched Hilde's arm and jerked his head at the door and the darkness beyond. It seemed something could make him step into it after all.

Hilde's eyes widened; she wanted to enter that void no more than he did.

Move, he mouthed silently.

She squeezed past him and through the doorway.

The footsteps kept coming. Your ears could play tricks on you in places like this, echoes and imaginings. He didn't want to guess how close the owner of those feet was to appearing around the curve of the stairs, but it wouldn't be long, and the glow of the rushlight would soon give away their presence.

Someone whistled. Three notes, ascending.

If it hadn't already.

He scooped up the rushlight, wincing at the spasm it sent up his bad arm and stepped after Hilde.

Despite expecting the night's weight to extinguish the flickering rushlight, the uneasy flame revealed crude stone walls slick with damp. He shut the door as best he could, certain the hinges hadn't squeaked before.

There was no means to lock it on this side, not that he thought the half-rotten wood could withstand a demon's blows even if it had. Once closed, it would at least conceal the rushlight's dancing glow.

And they would hear it opening.

He fumbled his father's sabre into its scabbard and gratefully exchanged the rushlight into his good hand.

Move, he mouthed again.

They could just about trot side by side down the corridor together, the cracked stone floor held puddles in the ill-fitting gaps. Green stains washed the walls, he had to bow his head a fraction to keep it from smacking the ceiling.

This is an ancient place...

Castles were often things that had grown over centuries, sometimes atop much older fortifications or structures. This felt much older than the grim towers above.

Their boots slapped in unison upon damp flagstone.

The world was as black behind them as before them; the rushlight illuminated little more than a few paces in either direction.

But he didn't hear the door open or any footsteps save their own.

In front of them, another door emerged.

A gate of iron bars as thick as his wrist, each so encrusted with rust all the straight lines had dissolved into bumps, crevices and nodules.

It hung open. A lock of clean black iron lay on the floor, a key still inserted.

On the wall, two unlit tar torches rested in equally rusted metal rings fixed to the weeping stone.

"The dungeons?" Hilde asked, looking like she wanted to point her crossbow in both directions at the same time.

"Uh-huh..." he said, lifting the rushlight to ignite a tar torch. It hissed into life, the darkness recoiling from it like a startled cat.

He moved to the torch on the other wall and lit that, too.

The emboldened light cut further into the dark.

It illuminated the patterns stained into the walls by centuries of dripping water and the black puddles they'd been walking through but little else.

"What do we do?" Hilde asked.

"Can't stay here," he placed the rushlight on the floor before pulling one of the torches free.

"Perhaps they've gone..." she eyed the way they'd come, but the door was too far back for the restless light of the torches to reach.

"Perhaps..."

"We could wait here a bit," the way she peered through the rusty gate suggested she didn't want to go on any more than he did.

Maybe the demon hadn't been as close as he'd thought. Maybe they'd exited the stairwell on a higher level.

In the distance, hinges wailed in protest as a door swung open

Or maybe not.

Hilde's eyes widened.

If the demon hadn't been aware of them before, they would be now the two torches announced their presence.

"Go..."

He pushed her through the gate and hurried her on.

Their feet slapped on the stone, uncannily loud.

But not so loud as to hide the sound of someone whistling.

Three notes, ascending...

Chapter Six

Audrius Wirth struggled and thrashed, but Usk had both the man's arms pinned behind his back, and no amount of struggling and thrashing would break the big soldier's grip.

"You can't send me in there!" Wirth begged, but her will was like Tomos Usk's grip. It wouldn't be broken easily.

"Can I not?"

"They are monsters! They will kill me!"

"What do you know of them?"

"I told you," Wirth sobbed, "Nothing!"

"I've lived my entire life in a castle," she said, her voice even, eyes never leaving his, never touching those gathered around them, "apart from the last year, after my home was destroyed and everything I loved taken from me by *Graf* Bulcher and creatures like the ones in there..." she nodded to the doors of the Great Hall.

Wirth's whining subsided to a pant, his struggling eased.

"So, I know."

"Know what?" Confusion vied with fear on Wirth's face.

"No matter how big a castle is, 'tis always a small place. People know people's business. Who is in love with who, who cursed who, every grudge, every grievance, every smile, every joke, every longing, every lust, every ambition, every dream, every nightmare..." she moved close enough for her toes to touch Wirth's and the rankness on his breath to wash over her, "...and every damn secret!"

Wirth tried to hold her gaze, but his eyes kept trying to slide away. Because he was lying? Or because she scared him?

Both, she suspected.

How did I become someone to fear?

It seemed such a ridiculous idea a laugh almost squirmed from between her lips, but she caught it in time. It was one thing to be feared; it was quite another to be thought mad.

"How could Bulcher have imprisoned them here and you not know about it? How could Bulcher not walk in the daylight and drink blood and you not know?" she meant to jab a finger into Wirth's chest, but somewhere betwixt thought and deed, the finger became a fist, "How could Bulcher be transforming his wives into undead demons and locking them up for his pleasure and amusement and nobody fucking know about it?!"

The next thing she knew, she was the one with her arms pinned behind her back. Lucien was making soothing noises in her ear, the kind you might make to calm a skittish horse.

And Wirth had somehow gotten a bloody nose...

She flexed her right hand. The knuckle hurt.

"Are you going to say something about a captain needing a clear head being the first rule of soldiering?"

Lucien chuckled and released her, "'tis heartening you've been paying attention to my wisdom…"

She nodded at Lucien as he stepped back into the circle of pale uncertain faces ringing them.

And resisted the urge to punch Wirth some more.

Instead, she licked the scraped skin of her right knuckle,

"You can explain to them that you didn't know anything. You can explain how you didn't know you were helping a madman turn women into monsters, how you didn't know you were helping Bulcher to damn their immortal souls."

She stood to one side and jerked her head towards the doors, "Perhaps they'll be more inclined to believe you than I am."

"My lady..." Lebrecht said.

She ignored him and found Usk's eye.

"If you want your friends back, take this piece of shit and throw him through those doors."

Tomos Usk didn't hesitate, he just lifted Wirth off his feet and took him to the Great Hall as if carrying a squirming child.

A terrified, screaming child.

Lucien went with Usk, but the big man didn't need any help with Wirth, so the mercenary started opening the doors.

"Solace-"

Gotz cut Lebrecht off.

"That man is a weasel, my lord. Lady Solace is right; I can smell it on him. He knew what was happening here; they all did. Remember how most of em couldn't look us in the eye before Karoline's wedding? They knew damn well and were happy enough to go along with it in return for comfort and safety. And whatever else Bulcher blackened their souls with."

Lebrecht didn't appear entirely convinced, but she stilled his qualms with a touch upon the arm and a flashing smile.

Then, she followed the others to the door.

Wirth was still struggling, but it had little evident effect.

"Throw him in," she said once Lucien unlocked the doors and shoved them open.

Wirth screamed.

He knew what was coming.

He'd have seen what happened to his comrades after they freed Samanta, but his terror ran deeper than that.

He knew exactly what hid in the darkness awaiting him.

Wirth's heel slipped in the blood, and he half went down.

"Please! Please! I didn't know!"

The pleas dissolved into screams as Lucien took one of the soldier's arms, and together, he and Usk sent him sprawling into the abyss of the Great Hall.

The sound was pathetic.

Unlike in the storybooks and tales of old, men rarely died with rousing speeches or cries of defiance upon their lips. Begging and sobbing were far more common.

So she was discovering.

Wirth did both as he skidded across the floor of the darkened room.

Something tugged distantly at her, but she ignored it.

If you shun mercy and compassion enough times, does it wither and die like an unwatered plant?

She sucked on her bottom lip as the question echoed away unanswered, forcing herself to keep watching.

The light of the few candles still burning didn't penetrate deep into the Great Hall.

Wirth was little more than a shadow as he scrambled, blubbing, to his feet. Lucien and Usk filled the gap between the half-open doors, but Wirth was preparing to hurl himself at them anyway.

Until a hand appeared out of the darkness to clamp long, bloody fingers upon his shoulder.

Wirth shrieked and tried to twist away.

Another hand came around his throat. The soldier's heel slipped on the bloody floor.

The darkness sprouted more hands and arms, figures, pale and ghostly, emerged. Wirth's ankles were pulled out from under him, and he went down onto the blood-washed flagstones.

He twisted onto his belly, arms flailing, trying to find something to hold. Figures took his legs and dragged him into the blackness.

Her last ever memory of Audrius Wirth was a pitiful elongated shriek, the whites of his bulging eyes and the trails cut through the blood by his grasping fingers.

Then, nothing.

She slipped between Lucien and Usk's shoulders to stand on the cusp of darkness.

The stink of spilt beer and cooked meats floated like ghosts; the greasy aroma of spent rushlights and dead candles, stone and damp, sweat and blood, shit and piss, the remnants of the living, the remnants of the dead.

"Have your vengeance, sisters..." she said to the black cavern before her, "...now give me my men!"

Only silence replied.

Boots moved on the bloody floor. Lebrecht, at her shoulder, sword drawn, peering into the abyssal darkness in front of them.

She eyed him sideways.

He returned the glance, disapproval writ large.

Yet he hadn't tried to stop her.

Might he refuse her anything?

"'tis difficult to find men who act with honour in these times..." he said, eyes sliding back to the darkness, "...let alone monsters."

"What choice do we have, really?"

The darkness stretched out. The Great Hall was large enough for echoes and chills to swirl around them. But just because it was too dark to see anything, she was not so foolish as to believe it empty. Here, the darkness paid attention. The darkness listened, the darkness watched.

Were the things that hid within its cloak judging her? Or did they just play with her? The games of the mad, the games of the damned.

She took a pace further into the hall.

Behind her, leather and metal shifted uneasily.

She thought of telling them if the Brides wanted them dead, they already would be.

The heat in Flyblown's mark ebbed a little. Did that mean she was right or wrong?

Perhaps she should ask that wraith the next time he appeared.

"We have a deal. Give me my men. And I will give you what you want in return. Then we talk about silver. We agreed."

Out in the darkness, something moved. Then stilled.

Lebrecht came to her shoulder again. Venturing deeper into the night at her side.

"Solace..." he said.

Solace... the room echoed.

"We are being played for fools..."

The echo became laughter.

They were being played with. But not for fools, she thought.

"Be quiet!" she snapped at Lebrecht.

The laughter faded.

Silence descended.

She fancied Lebrecht was looking at her like a puppy given a kick when it'd expected a cuddle.

She didn't look to check. Although she could not have walked far into the Great Hall, she was sure if she looked over her shoulder, the flickering candles beyond the door would be no bigger nor brighter than cold winter stars.

Monsters prowled out of sight, watching, weighing.

Strangely, no fear quickened heart or dampened brow.

She couldn't fear the darkness if she wanted to defeat it.

She could not run from it if she wanted to destroy the demons that lived within it.

Any tool, any weapon, any means.

You can only defeat the darkness if you embrace it.

Around her, frozen and silent, the darkness beckoned.

So, she stepped into it...

*

Another door appeared. This one thick iron, a patina of rust streaked the black, but it was far less corroded than the gate they passed through before.

It, too, hung open.

Hilde raised her crossbow and peered behind them.

He'd left one of the tar torches in its ring by the rusted

gate.

They could still see it, but it seemed an awfully long way away.

And every now and then, something moved in front of it.

Their shadow.

That occasionally whistled mournfully in the dark.

Three notes, ascending.

A key protruded from the heavy iron door's lock.

"We could lock it after us?" Hilde suggested.

"Might well be the only way out."

"Then perhaps we shouldn't go on?"

He edged her through the door, snatched the key and pushed the door shut. Or tried to.

The thing was solid iron, and he could do no more than provoke a few derisory groans from its hinges. It would take several men to open and close the thing.

He gave Hilde an apologetic look.

Sadly, he didn't even count as one man these days.

He dropped the key into his pocket.

Best nobody else could lock it while they were inside.

The corridor widened a little, with more tar torches dotting the walls. He touched his own against each, letting more restless orange light seep into the corridor as they spluttered into life.

Between the torches, more heavy iron doors sat either side of the corridor, all open, but he had no desire to stick his head in any of them. Each had a small hatch in the bottom, presumably for sliding food through to the unfortunate guests.

"This is where he kept them, wasn't it?" Hilde asked,

displaying more curiosity than him.

"Yes..."

Before she could peer around one of the rusting doors, he hurried her on.

Behind him, nothing moved but the light.

Had the torches deterred whoever followed them?

Vampires couldn't walk in daylight, but as far as he knew, artificial light presented no insurmountable problems. It certainly hadn't for Morlaine or the demons of the Red Company, anyway.

"What do you think he locked them up here for?" she asked slowing again at the next door as he touched the flame of his torch to the one fixed to the wall beside it.

"Conversation..."

Hilde scowled at him.

He turned his shoulders over, "Who knows, they're all mad."

"They?"

"Vampires."

"How do you know?"

He offered a thin smile, "Experience."

Instead of moving on, Hilde peered behind them.

"We seem to have lost our shadow."

"Perhaps," he added when she looked at him, "Mad and sneaky. Come on, let's keep moving."

Rather than doing as he said, Hilde turned to face the darkness before them. The shifting light didn't reach far; within a dozen paces, that heavy darkness waited patiently for them.

"How far do you think this goes?" she asked.

"Only one way to find out," he took a couple of steps before stopping when Hilde didn't follow.

"It's likely a dead end."

"As I said…"

"But it's a prison, isn't it? More secure if there's only one way in and out."

"Perhaps…" he conceded, looking back at the way they'd come. No shadowy figure lurked between the pools of dancing light around the tar torches, no footsteps, no whistling.

"So, if we keep going, we're going to end up even further from where we want to be."

Where he wanted to be right now was as far away from their shadow as possible.

"We can't go back."

"Why not?"

"Our friend."

Hilde hoisted crossbow and eyebrows in tandem.

"Last resort."

"But-"

"Hilde, just because you've killed two monsters with that thing tonight, don't fool yourself 'tis easy to kill them."

"More experience?"

"Yes."

"So running is always better?"

Do you run, or do you stand?

He shuffled his feet, splashing black water.

She gave him one of her curious looks, the kind he noticed she gave him a fair few of, the ones that seemed to say *I've no idea what's going on in your head, but I'm going to find out.*

"Come on..." he tried to move her forward again.

Hilde, however, had other ideas.

"Bring your torch in here," she slipped around the iron door and into the unlit room.

He rolled his eyes and muttered under his breath.

"I heard that..." Hilde called back.

The second time, he just rolled his eyes. After a final glance to ensure they were still alone, he followed her as far as the doorway.

The room was a little larger than he expected but just as cold and dank.

A large bed, a dressing table, a flecked mirror, a chest.

Things you might expect to see in any lady of substance's chamber if you ignored the damp bare walls and lack of windows. The thick iron manacles hanging from one of the walls, in his admittedly limited experience of ladies' chambers, however, were not. More manacles hung from each corner of the bed.

There were no candles or lamps in the room, though rust-crusted rings to hold torches sat on either side of the door.

Hilde put the crossbow on the bed before opening the hefty wooden chest in the corner and rummaging inside.

He hovered by the door, head moving back and forth between the corridor and the room.

"What do you think?" Hilde asked, holding out what he first thought to be a large dirty rag. Only as Hilde got closer to the light did he realise it was a dress, or at least, it had been once. Ripped, blackened by mildew and stained with what looked like blood. He would have felt bad about giving it to a dog to sleep on.

"It doesn't suit you."

"All the others are the same," she nodded at the chest.

"I guess Bulcher didn't lavish his dead wives with gifts."

When Hilde threw the soiled rag onto the bed to explore the dressing table, he was surprised it didn't disintegrate.

"He was generous enough with the jewellery," Hilde held up a pearl earring and a gold necklace she'd found on the table.

"Vampires are mad and the nobility are mad," he muttered, "what do you expect from someone who was both?"

Hilde put the jewellery back on the scoured tabletop, stared at them, then swept them back up and dropped them into her apron pocket.

"Well, that's what we're here for, isn't it?" she scooped up a couple of other pieces, "Stealing."

"Better hope whoever owns them doesn't treasure them..."

Hilde moved back to the bed and retrieved the crossbow. She indicated the manacles hanging from the wall, "What were those for...?"

"I shudder to think."

He leaned out into the corridor. Satisfied no one was in sight, he went back to Hilde. Then frowned and leaned back out again.

He counted six lights receding back along the corridor.

Hadn't he lit more torches.

"What?" Hilde asked, thumbing the crossbow.

Actually, he was sure he had?

"We should go."

Hilde picked up something from one of the cell's dim corners. A wooden bowl. She tipped it towards him. It was stained almost black inside.

"Blood."

"Pig's blood. Judita said."

"Must have a lot of pigs here," Hilde crumpled her nose and threw the bowl aside. The clatter echoed around the dank little room.

He winced and leaned back outside again.

Five torches flickered between the stretches of darkness.

"We have company... let's go."

"Why?"

"What do you mean why?"

Hilde shrugged, "If we're not going to get away from them. Perhaps we should talk, find out what they want?"

He glanced at the blood-stained bowl.

"I can guess what they want."

"If they do, shouldn't we fight on ground of our own choosing?"

"You've been hanging around Lucien too much."

"First rule of soldiering, that..." she grinned.

He didn't return the smile.

Run or stand?

He hated to admit Hilde had a point, but they weren't going to outrun whoever was behind them, but he hated the idea of having to face one of them, too.

Not that he feared for his own life; he would die at a demon's hands eventually. But he didn't want to see Hilde die first.

Madleen had been bad enough, and he'd hardly known

her. Hilde, he knew better. And wanted to know better still. He resisted glancing at the bed.

"What are we going to do?"

Do you run, or do you stand?

"Not stay in this stinking hole," he said.

"And when we're outside?"

"I'll decide when we get there."

Hilde pulled a long face and nodded, "Plenty of time to think of something, huh?"

"All the time in the world..." he agreed.

Once they were back in the corridor, he slipped his torch into a ring on the wall and drew his father's sabre before turning to face whoever was following them.

Chapter Seven

Something touched her fingers.

She half jerked away from the contact until she realised it was Lebrecht's hand, taking hers.

"What are you doing?"

The young nobleman stood next to her, a suggestion in the darkness, the distant light from the doorway catching in his eye as he looked at her. Otherwise, he was just another part of the night.

"Going with you."

"You don't have to; this is something I must do."

"Yes, I do."

"I know your men are-"

"Yes, they are."

Something between the tone of his voice, the feel of his skin on hers and an unquantifiable, unnameable certainty whispered Lebrecht's care for his missing men was not his only, or even his primary, concern.

She should send him back. Though, if the Brides killed her, few of her company would leave Thasbald alive. So Lebrecht might as well die at her side as with Lucien and the others.

The Brides, of course, were not going to kill her.

Were they?

Flyblown's mark smarted. Her *sight* chattered.

She took that as confirmation.

Surrounded by a frigid darkness from which monsters watched, it provided scant reassurance.

Still, she stepped further into it without hesitation.

Lebrecht, still holding her hand, did the same.

Things moved.

She saw nothing, but faint sounds betrayed movement. The hiss of fabric, the squeak of shoes, other noises she could not name. But nothing threatening. Not yet.

"I've come for my men!" she called out again.

A rustle. A sigh.

Nothing more.

Lebrecht held her hand tighter but made no attempt to pull her back when she continued.

Her foot touched something.

When she prodded it with the toe of her shoe, it rocked back and forth.

Her foot moved around the object... until she realised what it was.

"What's wrong?" Lebrecht's voice floated out of the darkness to her left.

She swallowed.

"There's a head on the floor."

Carefully, she pushed it to one side.

"It's not connected to... anything..."

Laughter lilted in the distance.

Followed by a sharp shushing noise.

The laughter faded.

"Solace-"

"No."

She wasn't going back.

She walked on. Slowly. When other things brushed her feet or legs, she didn't explore them; she could guess well enough what they were from the stickiness underfoot and the ripe animal smells permeating the frosty air around them. Shit, piss, blood, freshly slaughtered meat. The memories of terror that linger after the living are released from their torment.

Ahead, orange points of light glowed like feral eyes in the night. The last embers of the Great Hall's hearth.

As she watched, several blinked out before reappearing. Things moving between her and the fire's remnants.

She stopped. The floor was slippery and littered with obstacles. Sooner or later, one or both of them were going to trip, and she didn't much care for the idea of rolling about on a blood-soaked floor with the dead.

"Talk to me!"

A tapping sound was the only response. Metal on stone. A knife upon flagstone?

Then nothing.

She twisted around. The doorway was closer than she expected, brighter, too. Was Lucien harvesting candles and lanterns to light her way? If so, only a little reached her. She checked Lebrecht. Was there a fraction more to see than before? The vaguest outline of a man in a world where light did not venture.

Her head shot forward.

Things moved nearby.

"Sister..." a voice hissed, "...you bring us a man..."

The voice was neither of the brides she talked to through the door; deeper, smokier, it made her think of satin stretched over cheese wire.

"I bring you no one. I come for my men."

Lebrecht's hand twitched minutely; perhaps he objected to her describing them as *her* men.

"Many men came to us," another voice said, each word expressed so slowly it was almost a sigh. "He brought them. It amused Him. Our humiliation."

Something landed with a splat at her feet.

"That is part of one of them," the cheese wire voice said, "a part precious to him, a part well known to me..."

"Do you want us to take part of this one, sister?" a voice she recognised, Five, high-pitched and teetering on the precipice between laugh and scream.

Lebrecht's hand tightened a lot more at that.

"No. He is mine."

"You have nothing, sister. We have nothing. In our world and yours, we are but things, commodities, trinkets. We are leverage, we are a clause, we are means to an end. That is all we are," scorn dripped from Five's words. As did madness.

Was she really so sure she wasn't going to die here?

"I am more than that. And so are you."

"You are nothing. We are nothing."

"There are people who love me; there were people who loved you. Even when you have nothing else, you have that."

Something moved before her; the air playing across her face became even colder.

"Do you think we would have ended up here if anybody loved us? That we would have been given away to a man like Him?" Five's breath, if that was the correct word, stung her skin as if the creature exhaled tiny daggers of ice, "the only good thing He ever did was kill my father..." a bark of laughter made her flinch, but she refused to step back, "...served him right for being such a greedy bastard."

The reek of blood filled her nostrils. The distant orange pinpricks reappeared as Five moved to one side. Standing before Lebrecht, the demon sneered, "And what of you, man? Would you sell your daughter for your gain? To a creature like Him? Would you? Would you?"

Little thudding noises accompanied each question; Five's blood-stained finger stabbing into Lebrecht's chest. To the nobleman's credit, he stood his ground.

"No. Never."

Silence.

Five shuffled back in front of her, eclipsing the hearth's last embers once more.

Cold saliva speckled her face as Five spat, "Don't believe that shit. All men lie..."

"He is an honest man."

"He'd sell you for a scrap of woodland, a fishpond and half a dozen head of cattle. Men have only two uses for us, sister. You should never forget that."

She stepped forward. Lebrecht's hand tensed around hers. Five did not step back. Cold flesh, the stink of blood, old, musty fabric, scents she couldn't name, strange and exotic. Her forehead found the monster's. Hair, soft and wild, teased her skin.

"Bulcher wanted me for his bride. My father refused him. Refused because he recognised his evil, and because he wanted better for his daughter. He wouldn't have sold me at any price, whatever Bulcher offered. So, Bulcher had him killed, my people slaughtered, my home destroyed. My father was a good man..." she hissed in the creature's face, "...and he loved me!"

She felt the demon's slow, cool breath upon her lips.

She felt the sting of her father's palm on her cheek.

She felt his hurt and anger as he turned his back on her and walked away for the final time, towards his death, thinking her insane, thinking her a murderer.

Hating her.

You don't possess foresight, Solace, just ignorance. Your mother was a sick and troubled woman... and clearly so are you...

"He loved me..." she said again, though, this time, the words were little more than a sigh beneath the echo of the last thing her father ever said to her.

"He lied," Five tilted her head, "they all lie. There is no love in this world. Only different ways to hurt."

"That isn't true," Lebrecht said, "I am sorry for what befell you and your... sisters. None of you deserved that, but this... this place is not the world, and love is not a lie."

Five chuckled hard enough for spittle like the spray of a winter sea to dampen her face.

"Do you love her, boy? You hold her hand like a lover does. But I smell the stink of your lust, dried to your loins, scumming your skin, corrupting your soul. You're no different," Five's voice dropped to little more than a growl, "love is just another way to hurt us..."

Around them came a ripple of noise, metal on stone,

knives on flagstones. She imagined the demons circling them, crouching, watching, bloody knives in bloody hands, bloody lips drawn back into bloody sneers.

It wasn't a comforting image.

"Yes, I love her..."

Her head snapped in Lebrecht's direction as his hand tightened on hers.

She found that wasn't comforting either, though she didn't know why.

"...and I will never hurt her."

Five's cold breath faded as the monster stepped back.

"We are vampire. We live long and heal quickly, but we hurt the same as you. He taught us that. Do you know how many ways exist to hurt a woman? He was very inventive. More than most, more than you, no doubt. Pain amused him. Aroused him. He enjoyed our endless sufferings. I don't say you are the same, boy; you might not even enjoy doing it. But you'll hurt her regardless. That wretched thing between your legs will make you..."

A hiss seeped from the darkness, dead air escaping through bared teeth.

"We are not here to discuss love or pain," she said, raising her chin against the dark and the things hiding within it, "we are here to do business. I want my men. We had a deal."

"He liked to deal," the cheese wire voice came out of the night, "he dealt for all of us, with our fathers. And he betrayed them all..."

"I am not Him! I am your sister, and I want my men so I can destroy those who served Him!"

Silence.

Long and drawn.

Does he love me?

The voice was distant and plaintive, the voice of a girl who died a year and two days before. That girl cared about such things. But she was dead and gone, and love was just another lever to use. Five was wrong. Solace von Tassau wasn't the one love would hurt.

Assuming they both got out of here alive, of course.

Finally, Five's voice rolled out of the darkness. She hadn't heard the creature move, but the voice was retreating.

"Blood for blood, sister, can you do that?"

"I've done that."

"I will give you half your men; bring us the others who hurt us, and you can have the rest."

"Agreed."

"But if we do not have them by dawn..."

A man's scream echoed around the pitch-black hall.

Followed by laughter.

*

The figure emerged out of the gloom.

A woman.

She stood by the furthest of the tar torches. Gingerly, she pulled it from its metal ring on the wall and tossed it into the nearest cell before closing the door as if it were made of wicker instead of thick iron, sealing off the torch's glow.

"Samanta," Hilde said from his shoulder.

Indeed, it was. Pale and ghostly in the flickering light. White dress splattered with blood.

"Why are you following us?!"

Samanta walked to the next torch; with a pained expression of distaste and narrowed eyes, she plucked it from the wall, threw it in an empty cell and closed the door on the light.

She approached them, the darkness following in the wake of her dress' tattered, dirty hem.

Hilde raised her crossbow.

Another torch went into a cell.

"Why are you following us?" he asked again.

Samanta answered with a whistle.

Three notes, ascending.

One more torch disappeared. Leaving only the two where he and Hilde stood.

Samanta stopped, folding her hands before her, long white fingers entwining.

"Light does not belong here," she said tilting her head slightly as she added, "and neither do you."

"We are lost."

"I told you to leave."

"We are lost."

"And you think I am not?"

He wasn't sure how to answer that.

Samanta's eyes, icy blue in the remaining light, flicked to Hilde.

"Lower your toy, child. If I wanted to kill you, you'd be dead."

"I'm not the trusting sort," Hilde replied, "especially with the blood-soaked."

Samanta peered down at herself. The gown was provocative, showing her shallow cleavage. Blood smeared her chest as it did her dirty, once-white dress.

"I got a little carried away. Forgive me. But, on the fortunate side, for you two, I have eaten well. Which is a rare thing. He liked to keep us hungry. Keep us weak."

"But now he is dead."

"Yes!" Samanta smiled, eyes widening, "'tis a rather liberating feeling, I must say."

"I killed him," Hilde said, "with this toy."

The smile faded, "I don't intend to turn my back on you."

"You've seen him?"

"Oh, yes... one likes to be sure, to see with your own eyes even when you feel it in your..." Samanta's shoulders rolled, "...wherever."

"What do you want?" he asked, fighting the urge to put himself between Hilde and the demon but knowing the crossbow was more likely to save them than his sabre. Not very likely, but, still, there were times to be a gentleman and times to be pragmatic.

"Want?"

"You just happen to be following us?"

Samanta smiled. He found the fact she had a fetching smile almost as unsettling as the blood smeared around the fetching smile.

"Come, walk with me..."

Hilde stiffened beside him as Samanta approached. The demon's eyes narrowed against the flickering light of the tar torches as she drew close.

He lowered his sword; when Hilde kept her crossbow levelled at the demon, he reached out with his bad hand and carefully pushed the weapon down. Samanta watched him curiously as he winced at the effort to make his ruined limb do something useful.

"Are you going to ask us to kill you, too?" Hilde demanded, taking a step backwards.

"No, I don't think so. I am not so broken as poor Judita," that disturbingly fetching smile danced across Samanta's bloody face, "well, not quite, not yet…"

With that she slipped between them and walked on into the dark corridor.

Hilde looked like she couldn't decide whether to scarper in the opposite direction or shoot the demon in the back of the head.

Samanta stopped to look over her shoulder at them, "Oh, I've shown you my back…"

That smile again, before she glided on into the darkness.

He sheathed his father's sabre and took one of the flaming torches from the wall.

Hilde's eyes widened. He jerked his head in Samanta's direction, then hurried after the demon.

He didn't know why he did as the monster asked.

But he was almost certain it had nothing to do with her fetching smile…

Hilde looked like she didn't have a clue what he was doing either.

Rather than struggle for an explanation, he fixed his gaze on Samanta's back, her bloodied white gown swaying in time with her hips.

If the monster wanted them dead, they'd be dead, however handy Hilde thought herself with that crossbow, so they might as well see what she was about.

Of course, death wasn't the only unpalatable option when dealing with demons...

They walked largely in silence, save for the clip of their boots, the hiss of the torch in his hand and Samanta's occasional whistle. Three notes, ascending.

They passed more iron doors, most open, though not all.

"Have you considered the possibility she intends to lock us up down here?" Hilde asked out of the corner of her mouth.

Samanta laughed before he could reply, "At least you will have the bed together you desire if I do..."

Hilde's eyes widened.

"Their senses are very keen..." he explained.

"Very," Samanta confirmed from the edge of the torchlight without breaking stride.

"Where are you taking us?"

"Home."

Samanta stopped by a cell door; beyond, the corridor appeared to end with another black iron door cut by ripples of rust.

The demon stood in the open doorway, side on to them. She smiled and stepped inside.

"Is this a good idea?" Hilde asked.

"I don't think she means us any harm."

"Aren't all vampires mad?" she asked."

"So I've been told..." he said.

When he made to follow Samanta, Hilde put herself in front of him.

"I don't like this..."

He could understand that. They were walking into a

subterranean cell with a blood-splattered demon who had killed several people already tonight. There was a lot not to like.

He didn't think the *she would have killed us already if she wanted to* line would work. So, he borrowed one of Solace's instead.

"Trust me."

"Trust... you?"

And keep that ready, he mouthed silently, pointing at her crossbow.

Then followed Samanta inside.

Of all the things he thought he might find waiting for him, what did was not one of them.

Samanta waited in the middle of a marginally larger, slightly better-furnished version of the cell they visited earlier.

Naked.

He stood. Possibly gawping.

Samanta smiled fetchingly again. However, it wasn't her smile that grabbed his attention this time.

Skin, frost-pale from head to toe, breasts small but perfect, waif-slim but perfect, legs long, shapely and perfect; in fact, pretty much everything was quite-

A pain so sharp he momentarily thought he'd been stabbed seared through his ribs. He yelped and found not a dagger but Hilde's elbow in his side.

"What do you think you're doing?!" Hilde glared at him.

His eyes flicked between the two women before settling back on Samanta.

"Erm... what... are you doing?"

Samanta's smile grew brighter. As well as on her face, blood speckled the tops of her small but perfectly perfect breasts, too. Otherwise, she was unsullied.

"Changing."

The demon kicked away the bloody dress crumpled around her feet with a flick of a foot that, if he had the opportunity to study closely, he was confident he'd find as perfect as the rest of her.

Samanta held his eye as she turned away from them, a smile lingering with the look. The demon crossed the damp cell to a hanging closet in the corner.

Her arse, he was unsurprised to discover, was round, peachy and absolutely per-

Hilde's elbow found his ribs again.

She glared at him, eyes wide, nostrils flared, lips pressed. The kind of expression reserved for someone who'd messed up badly.

What? He mouthed.

Hilde shook her head, rolled her eyes and pointedly looked away. If she hadn't been holding a crossbow, he was fairly sure she'd have crossed her arms over her chest and started tapping her foot.

He glanced down.

She *was* tapping her foot.

Have I done something wrong?

He wanted to point out he hadn't known the demon would be naked. And he certainly hadn't asked her to strip. Yet, somehow, Hilde clearly thought he'd done *something*. He would have scratched his head in puzzlement, but it would have hurt his wasted arm too much.

"Why..." he turned back to Samanta rummaging in the hanging closet, "...why are you changing?"

"It isn't suitable for travelling," she flashed another smile over her shoulder, "'tis the blood. I suspect people would find that off-putting. Wouldn't they?"

"Usually."

"Yes, I thought so," Samanta disappeared back into the hanging closet.

"You are planning to travel... somewhere?"

"Oh, yes."

"Where?"

"Wherever you're going," Samanta held up another white dress, only differing from the one she had just kicked off in that mildew speckled it rather than blood and gore, "what do you think?"

"Why do you want to go where we're going?"

"Because we're going to be friends, and friends always go places together, don't they?" Samanta tilted her head and smiled in a manner he suspected a lot of men might find alluring from a naked woman. Then started dressing.

Beside him, Hilde's glare grew hotter than the tar torch in his hand...

In the Company of Shadows

Chapter Eight

"Start with the men guarding Karoline's chambers you took prisoner."

A ring of faces stared back at her.

Swoon sat on the floor, hugging his knees, still shaking. Wickler stood behind the younger man, face bloodless, the candlelight reflecting off the sweat coating his shaven head, eyes fixed on nothing, a deep gash across his right cheek. Blood still oozed from the wound. The freed Vadians huddled together. They all looked a decade older than the last time she'd seen them. Bosko was beside her, though his eyes remained on Karoline, his daughter.

She almost told him to go and hug the girl. It would make them both feel better.

"You're going to give them to those monsters?" Lebrecht asked.

"Better than leaving our men in there, wouldn't you say?"

Lebrecht pursed his lips but didn't answer.

"Lucien?"

The mercenary nodded and quickly left with Gotz, Usk and Hugo. None of the recently freed men appeared capable of doing anything for now, but that couldn't last. They only had until dawn, and she'd need them all to find and detain any other members of Bulcher's household who hadn't been in the Great Hall.

They had emerged from the darkness, one by one, stripped of their weapons but unharmed other than cuts, bruises, and hollow eyes. The cuts and bruises would all heal soon; the hollow eyes, she feared, would take much longer.

"What happened?" she asked Bosko, steering him away from the others.

"Huh?" he grunted, still staring glassily at Karoline.

"What happened?"

"Screaming..." he shook his head, eyes moving to the once more closed doors of the Great Hall, "...terrible screaming..."

"And then?" she asked when he fell back to silence.

"We stood outside. Not knowing what to do..." he pinched the bridge of his nose, "...there was banging on the doors. Voices. Pleading, begging, crying. For a while. Eventually, everything lessened."

"That was it?"

"There was laughter, too..." he shook himself as if trying to cast something off his back, "from... *them*."

"The Brides."

"Is that what they are?"

"Well, widows now. They want vengeance on those who helped Bulcher... make them what they are."

"Heaven help us."

"We help ourselves. How did they capture you?"

Bosko pulled a face and shook his head, "One minute we were gathered around the door not knowing what to do... then... these... monsters appeared. Out of nowhere. White gowns soaked in blood. So fast, so strong. They overwhelmed us before we could raise our weapons. When they didn't kill me, I thought they were going to drag me down to Hell for all my sins..." his eyes flicked towards Karoline, but he caught himself, and they bounced back to her so quickly she might have missed what he was doing if she did not know the girl was his illegitimate daughter.

"And in there?"

"It was dark. It smelt of death, like a battlefield, like a slaughterhouse. They put us... somewhere. A small room. They told us to be quiet or we'd die like the rest. I just prayed... and prayed. Until the Lord heard me and they dragged me out to return me here."

It wasn't the Lord who saved you...

"Were all the others in that room?"

"I think so."

"Could you find it again?"

"No," another shudder ran down Bosko's spine, "Are you thinking of trying to rescue them?"

"It would be suicide for all of us. No, we will give them what they want."

"You are giving Christian souls to the Devil's minions to feast upon, my lady!"

"As I did for your life, Captain. Would you rather I hadn't?"

Bosko lowered his eyes.

She'd saved his life, but he would eventually see it as another sin to burden his soul alongside his illegitimate daughter.

Sin, when she thought about it, was a damned peculiar business.

"Get the men into shape, Captain; we only have a few hours."

"How many are there?"

"I have no idea. You saw no one else before the Brides took you?"

"No."

"Then probably not many besides who we have and the ones killed by the Brides outside Karoline's tower.

"We could... just leave..." Bosko's voice tremored. It seemed he was in the mood to collect more sins. This time, the sin of cowardice.

"I am not leaving our men here," she said, her voice even and cold where Bosko's had faltered.

And I'm not leaving Bulcher's silver either.

"These creatures, they are evil. How can we trust them?"

"I don't know if we can, but whatever they are now, they were not always like this. Bulcher made them. None of them asked for this. Once, they were innocents, like Karoline, and he corrupted them. And every man and woman in Thasbald helped him. Do not cry for them, Captain; cry for the women those *creatures* once were. The creature Lady Karoline would have become if I had not met you on the road. And I didn't meet you by accident, I assure you. We do God's work."

He nodded.

"What about weapons?"

"Lucien will bring those we took from the prisoners and dead; we will find more. You have till they come back to prepare."

"Yes, my lady..."

Bosko drew himself straight and went to talk to the others.

She felt her own shoulders sag as soon as he turned his back.

I am not a monster...

She lifted her chin as Lebrecht rejoined her.

She looked at him.

Hug me, please...

He looked at her, his expression uncertain.

If you can't hug me, tell me I'm doing the right thing.

Lebrecht didn't hug her. He didn't tell her she was doing the right thing.

"We should not be doing this," he said instead, "we are cutting a deal with the Devil, and that will never end well."

"We use the weapons we have."

"And if they release the rest of our men, then what?"

"We take Bulcher's silver."

"And then?"

"Then?"

"We leave?"

"We will have all we came here for."

He nodded at the door, "And them? Once they have killed all those they believe wronged them, they will... return to womanly pursuits?"

"Womanly pursuits?"

"How many souls will they damn if we leave them here?"

"That... is not my concern."

"So only the demons that destroyed your family matter?"

"I can't right the world, my lord."

"Their blood will be on us."

"How do you suggest we kill them?"

"How do you suggest we kill the Red Company?"

She ran a hand through the short tangles of her hair, "I'll think of something."

"Damn well think of something now then!"

His eyes were wide, and he was breathing harder than he needed to. Fear or anger? Perhaps both.

"Did you mean what you said?" she asked.

"What I said...?"

"That you love me."

Lebrecht moved his feet and fidgeted with the pommel of his sheathed sword, "I don't see what-"

"Do you?"

He swallowed, "Why else do you think I am here? Why else do you think I betrayed my father?"

"'tis what I hoped."

He smiled at that.

It makes you easier to use...

The thought provoked a pang of something she couldn't or wouldn't name.

She found his hand. He squeezed it.

She stretched up and kissed him lightly on the lips.

It was not at all unpleasant.

When her heels returned to the floor, his cheeks were flushed. She suspected hers were, too.

"Trust me, my lord," she whispered, "all of this is meant to be. Including you and I."

Another pang. Sharper, deeper.

But it didn't show on her face.

And that was all that mattered.

*

"You can't come with us."

"Why?"

A looking-glass hung upon the wall. Old, tarnished, cheap. The demon's reflection mottled and distorted within a chipped frame darkened with mould. Samanta flicked at her long blonde hair as she peered into it.

"You are a demon."

"I will not tell anybody if you don't," the reflection smiled that fetching smile in the mirror, then Samanta spat on her fingers and tried to rub away some of the blood from her face.

"You cannot walk in the daylight."

"Then I shall ride. In a carriage! Like a princess!"

He exchanged a look with Hilde. From her expression, she clearly thought the solution to their current situation rested with the crossbow in her hands.

Samanta turned towards them; her smile faded as her eyes moved between them.

"Do you not want to be my friend?"

"It's... well... just-"

"You are a monster," Hilde's voice cracked, "You have no place in this world!"

Samanta sat down on the edge of the bed, still wiping blood from her face.

"I know what I am. But I remember what I was, too. Just..." she ran a palm over the crumpled bed sheets, before bending to pick up one of the black iron manacles and the chain attached to each corner of the frame, "Do you know what he did to me, in here? What he did to all of us?"

Some of the anger drained from Hilde's voice, "I can imagine."

"You think you can?" Samanta turned the manacle over in her hands, "Most of my sisters are mad. Many cannot even speak any more. Their minds are gone. I... survived, I think. And I survived because I told myself one day I would escape this horror. One day, I would be a real person again. One day I would not lie alone in the dark waiting for the sound of footsteps and praying that, this time, they would not stop at my door. That one day, I wouldn't be alone anymore. That one day, I would have friends. Like I did before I came here. Before He turned me into this... one day... one day..."

She dropped the manacle, the clatter of metal on stone rang as her eyes rose to meet his.

"And that day is today."

"I'm sorry for what happened to you. But I know what you are. You... you are dangerous."

"Sometimes he came on his own, but mostly not. Some things he did himself. But he liked to watch more than... participate..." Samanta indicated the room's solitary chair, a heavy throne-like thing against the wall facing the end of the bed. It was much like the one they tied Bulcher to in Karoline's bedchamber, "some of the men were his soldiers. Some were not. Some were what he called his *talented fellows*. I think torturer would be a more accurate description. Sometimes, he brought special friends who we would have to entertain while he watched..."

"But you are strong, fast, how...?" Hilde asked.

"He starved us of blood to keep us weak. He kept us in

pieces. And he always put soldiers outside. If one of us ever tried... some did... and their screams echoed for days. Weeks, even. Sound carries surprisingly well down here..."

"I am sorry."

"'tis not your fault."

"Still."

"I won't hurt you. You are not like them. I can tell."

"You can?"

"You can see the cracks in a man's soul if you know how. See all the way down the black. Some men are full of horrors. Some men are but a void. You are neither."

"I am broken," he said quietly.

"We are all broken, 'tis how we keep those damaged parts together to form the whole, that is the important thing..."

They stared at each other, and he could not shake the feeling she really could see down through the cracks inside him.

"Well!" Hilde said, "That's all by the by, but 'tis not getting us anywhere."

Samanta's blue eyes moved to Hilde, "Some of His special friends were not men. They were like him. Like me."

Her eyes returned to him.

"Some of them were from the Red Company..."

"How-"

"I have been listening to you. Vampires have exceptionally keen senses..."

"You've been following us?"

"I wanted to know who you were, why you are here, why you did what you did. I want to believe there are still good people in this world. Even if I am no longer one of them."

"You think we are good?"

"I am not so foolish as to think you can divide the world neatly into light and dark. But I have seen nothing but the dark for so long, however much I may have yearned for the light. You... neither of you... are like... *them*. That is enough."

"What do you know of the Red Company?"

"They served Him. Or He served them. They did his bidding, and he theirs. They were close. They came here. Not often. But often enough. He let them take entertainment with us. They were cruel. Mostly. Not so inventive as Him, but..." she prodded the manacle with her foot, "...they provided no relief from our torment."

"Name them?" he demanded.

"You doubt me?"

"The world is built from lies."

"Ah, a cynic!"

"Name them?"

"I did not learn all their names. Our introductions were not... formal. But one was tall and covered in tattoos. His name was Jarl. He liked me to say it. *Lord Jarl... Thank you, Lord Jarl*, he always made me say while he... amused himself. Although I wanted to do nothing but scream. The only other one whose name I learned was their leader. He never hurt me, but he scared me the most. He has the bluest eyes I have ever seen, and once you stare into them, you start to think if you can just look long enough, they will reveal all the madness in the world."

"His name?"

"Saul. Saul the Bloodless."

Had he mentioned Jarl or Saul since they left the Silver Tower? He didn't think he had.

"Do you know how to find them?"

"Perhaps..." she said, slyly to his way of thinking.

"Friends don't play games with each other, Samanta."

"We are friends then?" the demon's eyes brightened as she sat up straight.

He tried not to notice how Hilde's darkened in unison.

"Are you willing to help us?"

"Oh, yes!"

"You will need to talk to our mistress; she makes the decisions."

"The one with the short hair who talked to me before."

"Lady Solace, yes."

"But she wore a servant's dress?"

"She is not a servant."

Samanta's brow crumpled, "How can a girl be in charge? Has the world changed so much while I have been here?"

"Not so very much, I would imagine. Lady Solace is not... typical."

The demon leaned forward slightly, "Will she be my friend, too?"

"Lady Solace... makes her own decisions about people."

"'tis a long time since anyone thought of me as a person," Samanta jumped to her feet, "shall we go and find her?"

"We were heading for the Great Hall before we..." he glanced at the still surly looking Hilde, "...got lost."

"I will take you there then and introduce myself to her properly!"

Hilde eyed the demon warily as she approached, "And

what of the rest of your kind? Do they want to be our friends, too?"

"Most of them are too broken for anything. All they want to do is kill and feed."

"And you released them all?"

"We deserve a little vengeance."

"And what happens after vengeance is done?" Hilde asked, "What have you unleashed upon the world?"

The thought that was a question she could equally ask of Solace squirmed across his mind.

"What did the world care for me?" Without waiting for a reply, Samanta shied away from the torch, squeezing past them both and back into the corridor.

He exchanged another glance with Hilde. Each one seemed to earn him an incrementally more challenging glare in return.

"Tell me more about your lady?" Samanta asked after they left the cell. She was standing against the wall, circling a strand of long blonde hair around her finger. She was smiling again. At him. Lips slightly parted, cool blue eyes fixed on him.

He got the feeling Hilde's glares would not soften any time soon.

"You can find out for yourself," he looked left to the end of the corridor and the iron door barring it, right to the way they had come and then back at the demon. Who nodded to his right.

"After you," Hilde said.

The demon inspected Hilde's crossbow before pushing herself off the wall, "Why not? We're all friends now..."

Samanta glided down the corridor, still curling hair about her finger. He decided to pass on the opportunity to share another look with Hilde.

Instead, he found his eyes resting upon the sway of Samanta's hips.

He swallowed.

"Tell me," blue eyes appeared over the demon's shoulder, "what does your mistress want here?"

"Primarily to kill your husband."

"Which she has done..." another twist of hair around the finger, "...yet she has not left?"

"She also seeks knowledge of the Red Company so that she may destroy them."

"They did her wrong, she said."

"Yes."

"What did they do?"

She continued looking at him over her shoulder as they walked, her steps as smooth and confident as they were when she was paying attention to where she was going.

"Destroyed her home, murdered her father, killed everyone she knew."

"She was not the first to suffer so, I believe."

"How did you come to be here? he asked.

"It does not matter. All that does is that He is dead, His people are dead, or soon will be. His house has fallen. Vengeance is done."

With that Samanta walked on.

Hips still swaying, he couldn't help but notice.

He followed.

And Hilde followed him.

In the Company of Shadows

Chapter Nine

Lucien and the others fetched the prisoners and their weapons without incident.

The Thasbalders looked glassy-eyed and confused; one sported a bloody nose fresh enough to still be dripping.

She wanted to turn her eyes away, but that was a luxury she couldn't afford.

"What do you know of Bulcher's brides?" she demanded of them.

None replied.

But the averted eyes and shuffling boots spoke volumes.

Should she say anything more?

Not to assuage any guilt about these men, but to reinforce the decision in the eyes of her company.

In the end, she decided against it. Time wasn't on their side.

"How many men were on duty during the feast?" she asked.

More stony silence.

"How many men were outside the Great Hall?" she asked, in case they hadn't understood.

"Bitch," one of them spat a gob of phlegm at her feet.

Lucien's boot came down hard on the back of the man's calf. The soldier crumpled to the floor.

"Manners, boys..." Lucien growled.

She lowered herself to her haunches to find the soldier's

eye.

"Things have changed whilst you've been detained. Your master is dead; the women he kept imprisoned in the dungeons are free. And they are hungry..."

The colour drained from the man's face. One of his comrades mumbled something under his breath.

It seemed she did have time to talk after all.

"Tell me what you know. Tell me something that makes you useful to me... or I will give you to them."

"I know nothing, I swear!"

"You knew nothing of all those women Bulcher damned and locked in his dungeon to amuse himself with... *really?*"

"I swear it, on my mother's life. We just guard the castle, nothing more!"

"And you never went down there? Any of you?"

"No. Only the *Graf* went into the catacombs; he allowed no one else. On pain of death! We never-"

"This man's name is Aznar," a voice said, "and he is a liar."

Her head snapped up. It was the blonde-haired demon they met earlier. Her heart leapt, not at the sight of the creature, nor Hilde who stood behind her, but because Renard was with her. She wanted to scramble to her feet and hug him as the worry she'd kept dammed since he disappeared broke into a torrent of relief.

But, of course, she didn't.

It would not be seemly.

She rose and limited herself to looking enquiringly at Renard, who nodded at her. Neither he or Hilde appeared under duress, so she assumed the demon, Samanta, did not present a threat. Around her, the rest of her company turned to stare at the demon, who glided towards them on silent feet.

"His name is Aznar," Samanta repeated, "I saw him numerous times. All His Household Guard, his Favoured Men, were regular visitors. He wasn't the worst, but still..." the demon came to a halt by her side next to Aznar who glared back up at them.

Samanta bent her knees in front of Aznar.

Renard returned to his familiar place at her shoulder.

It made her feel... she wasn't quite sure what the right word for the feeling that swelled within her was. But *whole* came the closest.

"We were never allowed to show our real faces to you. Were we? Even though He starved us of blood to keep us weak. Even though we could sense it pumping and throbbing inside of you. Even though you were... as close as close could be. Because He was always there. Watching. Waiting. Looking for an excuse to hurt us more..."

Samanta leaned closer to Aznar, "Would you like to see my real face?"

"I... don't know what you're talking about!"

The demon's hand shot out. Aznar gasped as she seized his throat.

"Perhaps if you'd ever seen our true faces, you would never have done the things you did. After all, who would want to fuck this..."

Samanta's face changed. And in a heartbeat, she was no longer a pretty young woman in a dirty white dress. She had seen it before, the snow-white skin mottled with blue pulsating veins, the sharp, too-long face, the oversized eyes, the slash of a mouth filled with fangs. Still, it was a shocking transformation to witness.

Cries, curses, gasps, the scuff of boots, the clank of weapons. A scream, Karoline or Elin, presumably.

One of the Thasbald soldiers shouted, "Strike the monster down! They are ungodly; we must destroy them!"

"Strange, you never said such a thing when you served a monster, Ferdinand?" Releasing Aznar, Samanta rose, "Strange you never said that when you came down into the dark to be with us?"

Ferdinand flinched and tried to back away as Samanta stepped forwards, "Strange how we never heard you protest. All we heard was your whistle. The one you and your fellows used so we'd know you were coming for us..."

Samanta's human mask fell back in place as she puckered her lips and whistled.

Three notes, ascending.

"How I feared that sound. How many times I imagined I heard it echoing in the dark. Knowing pain and humiliation was coming, but not who it was coming to. I always prayed it would not be me, even though I know God turned his eyes away from me a long time ago."

Samanta stepped back and looked sideways at her, "I find it difficult to whistle with my true face. 'tis all those teeth. Not the biggest handicap, I confess, but still..."

She pulled her attention away from the demon to her company. Fear, horror, repulsion, and disgust were the most obvious expressions on the faces looking back at her. And those that weren't were mostly murderous.

Only Renard, Lucien and Gabriel Gotz were expressionless.

If she ordered them to take the prisoners to the Great Hall now, she wasn't sure they would.

On the other hand, if she told them to kill Samanta, the bulk her company would do it without question. Regardless of the consequences for either their comrades inside or themselves.

When she turned back to Samanta, she found the demon eying her curiously.

"You should not have shown your face," she said.

"Perhaps. But we must be honest with friends, particularly new ones."

"We are friends?"

"I hope so!" Samanta beamed, the look about as far away from the monstrous thing the demon had been a few moments before as she could imagine.

"My lady!" one of the Vadians, Gerwin, cried, "Keep away from that thing!

Gerwin, an earnest young man who cursed little and prayed a lot, appeared ready to take Samanta's head off her shoulders. His time in the lightless abattoir of the Great Hall hadn't done much to enamour Samanta's kind to him either.

She held a hand towards Gerwin while running her eyes back and forth along her company, "Nobody does anything. We are negotiating for our comrades' lives. Rash actions may cost them dear."

"These things are an abomination! An affront to God!" Swoon barked, sweat glistening upon his face under the candlelight. He wasn't prone to outbursts; normally, he said little more than his shadow, but now the cords in his neck stood proud, eyes bulging even more than they usually did.

Lebrecht and Bosko should be controlling their men, but both watched in cold-faced silence.

"You have nothing to fear from me; I have decided you are all my friends!" Samanta threw out her hands and smiled before turning to their prisoners, "Well, apart from you lot, you're all going to die horribly."

"Please!" one of Bulcher's Household Guards begged. Usk put a blade to his throat to quieten him. Another of the men started crying, and she could almost feel the uncertainty flickering around the room along with the candlelight.

"These men would come with Him..." Samanta began, "...He enjoyed our suffering. Sometimes, it was punishment; sometimes, purely for pleasure. I'm not sure if there was any real difference..."

The demon turned to Renard; Hilde stood at his shoulder, crossbow levelled at Samanta, "Give me a blade, please."

Renard looked at her.

"If I wanted to hurt anyone, I wouldn't need a knife."

When she nodded, Renard pulled a dagger from his belt, reversed it and handed it to the demon.

Around her, feet moved uneasily.

"When I came here, many years ago, I was like her..." the pale-faced Karoline visibly flinched as Samanta nodded at her, "...a little older, but an innocent, nevertheless. I am innocent no more. He... *Graf* Bulcher... made me his wife, took my dead family's estates and then, soon after, killed me and put His curse inside me. Making me like Him. Making me the thing you saw. I am different now. But I am also the same..."

Samanta pushed back the left sleeve of her soiled dress, then slashed Renard's blade across the milky skin of her forearm. The demon winced as a bloody ribbon erupted in the dagger's wake.

"I bleed as you do, I hurt as you do, the pain I feel does not differ from that which you would know if you pulled sharpened steel over soft flesh," Samanta wiped the blade clean on her skirt and handed it back to Renard, Hilde's crossbow moved in time with the demon's movement.

"The thing He put inside his dead brides has many facets. One is that we heal quickly and die extremely hard. That might sound like a blessing, albeit an ungodly one. But when your husband enjoys nothing more than seeing you suffer, I can assure you, my new friends, 'tis very much a curse..."

The demon held out her arm sideways, watching the blood trickle thickly down to fall in fat drops on the floor. Each patter of blood on stone punctuated the uneasy silence as Samanta looked at each of them in turn.

"What can heal can be cut again. Or burnt, or flayed, or crushed, or impaled, or broken or... well, just about anything you can imagine."

Samanta moved her bleeding hand over the kneeling Aznar, who squirmed as bloody droplets exploded on his forehead.

"Do you remember the day you broke each of my fingers

and toes in turn for your master's amusement, Aznar? I do. And the next day, when they healed, you came back and sliced each one off. I do remember the way He giggled as I screamed. But you said nothing other than, *"And now the next one, my lord?"* and every time He said yes, you got about it without hesitation or qualm. Taking off each one with shears. Snip. Snip. Snip."

Samanta cast her eyes around the room, raised her right hand and waggled her fingers, "They grow back, in case you were wondering. Hard to believe, I know. Found it quite unsettling myself the first time, I can tell you."

"We know how vampires heal," she said.

"Yes, I dare say you do..." slowly, the demon walked along the short line of prisoners, "I know all of you. You were His Favoured Men. You got the good jobs. Shall I recount all the fun we've had together?"

None of the men met her eye as she passed them.

"I remember. After all, there's precious little to do day after day alone in the dark to take your mind off the pangs of hunger ripping through your body than remember. I did try to remember the good things I had before He took them all away from me, too, but as the years dragged by, they receded so far that I found it increasingly harder. On the other hand, the pain and humiliation always had the clarity of the new. 'tis funny, no matter how many times you have part of yourself removed, it always does seem new..."

The demon's attention turned to Swoon, whose oversized Adam's apple bobbed up and down under Samanta's gaze, "Yes, I am an abomination, my new friend. I never asked to be or wanted to be; I was never given a choice. Perhaps I am an affront to God, too. But I never turned my heart from God, though, I suspect he turned his from me over those long, long years. But if I am an abomination and if I am an affront to God..." her eyes returned to the prisoners, "...I am not the only one in this room..."

The demon walked backwards from the prisoners until she stood at her side once more.

"And if that doesn't help persuade you to be my friend..." Samanta smiled with sudden, disconcerting warmth, "...I know where my husband kept his silver..."

*

He tried not to look at Samanta.

Dragging men to their deaths at the hands of blood-guzzling fiends should have proved a sufficient distraction.

Still, he found his gaze continually creeping back to the demon.

Morlaine was probably the most beautiful woman he had ever met yet she had stirred no attraction in him. In fact, she'd repulsed him, at least initially. He'd seen only a monster, not obviously different from the ones who brought damnation down on Solace and him.

Whilst still uneasy around her, by the time she left them at Ettestein, he knew her cloth was of a different cut to that of the Red Company's demons, but he'd still not viewed her as a woman.

Samanta, however...

Something about her drew his eye. *Demanded* his eye. Something in the turn of her lips and the sway of her hips, something in the depths of her eyes and the curves of her... well, she had various of those.

He was more than aware this wasn't an opportune moment for casting an appreciative eye over a woman. If there ever was an opportune moment for casting an eye over a woman with dead men's blood smeared over her face.

They were sending men to their deaths, they were cutting deals with insane demons who could slaughter them in an instant, and his mistress faced dangers from every side, including their own, judging by some of the mutterings from their company, particularly the Vadians. His focus should be on protecting Solace, nothing else. However intriguing he found them.

Then, of course, there was Hilde.

"I don't trust that bitch..." she breathed in his ear.

"They have very keen hearing," he reminded her.

"Good, she ain't my friend. Happy to call her worse to her face. Either of them."

Samanta was opening the doors to the Great Hall.

She was going to speak to her sisters to try to obtain their men in return for the Favoured Men they held.

"I doubt you'll find anyone else. Some of my sisters have been out hunting themselves..." he overheard the demon tell Solace.

He watched Samanta till the darkness of the Great Hall swallowed her. Once she disappeared, a collective sigh of relief rippled through their company.

Apart from Hilde, who just muttered, "Bitch," again.

Bulcher's Favoured Men huddled on the floor circled by their own men-at-arms. One was continually pleading his innocence to deaf ears, one denouncing them all for consorting with witches and demons, while the other two sat grim-faced but quiet.

It was the silent ones that worried him.

They were well-tied and unarmed, but it never paid to underestimate desperate men.

He stayed close to Solace's shoulder. And Hilde stuck to his.

His only concern was keeping his mistress alive. And Hilde.

Yet his mind kept returning to Samanta. The way she moved, spoke, looked. He wanted to know more about her. He wanted to know more of her. He wanted...

In the name of the Lord, what is wrong with me?

Had the demon cast a spell over him? Some dark, insidious glamour to make him desire her? He couldn't imagine why any woman, particularly one that had been locked in a cell and tortured for decades, might want to cast a glamour on him. But, of course, women were strange and unknowable.

He glanced at Hilde.

She peered back at him curiously.

He thought it no more likely that Hilde could read his mind than Samanta had cast a spell on him. Though he wasn't entirely prepared to discount either possibility yet.

"What do you make of her?"

Solace turned to him.

"I-"

"Mad and dangerous," Hilde jumped in, "We shouldn't trust her."

His mistress favoured Hilde with a thin smile, "Ulrich?"

"I... she is a demon... Hilde is probably right."

"Probably?" the two women asked in unison, though in different tones.

"I feel sorry for her."

"They are all worthy of pity. Or at least the women they once were do. But the creatures they have become..."

"We should kill them all," Hilde said, raising her crossbow as if volunteering for the job.

Solace gave Hilde an *if-I-want-your-opinion* kind of look.

"I think she wants to help us," he said, unsure if he knew any such thing.

"So do I," Solace said.

Hilde's face stretched in disbelief, "You can't-"

"Haven't you somewhere else to be, girl?" Solace asked.

Hilde's face darkened.

"No."

Lucien saved Hilde from being told she did in fact, have somewhere else she could be by sauntering over.

"You want us to see if we can find more of these bastards?"

"How long to dawn?"

Lucien scratched at something beneath his thinning hair, "A few hours still..."

"Let's wait for Samanta; I don't want to split our company till Bulcher's men are dealt with."

Lucien scratched harder, "Could just throw em in now..."

"Wait," Solace insisted.

"I'm good at waiting. Gotta know how to be patient, first rule of soldiering, that. Lot of sitting on your arse doing bugger all, while you wait for someone to kill or the brass to pull their fingers out of-"

"Thank you, Lucien."

"You're welcome," the mercenary shrugged and wandered off, now scratching vigorously behind his ear.

"We can't trust that monster!" Hilde said.

"Lucien's never let me down yet," Solace shot back.

"But-"

"Hilde..."

"But-"

"Go and check on Karoline."

Before stomping off, Hilde muttered something under her breath.

"She is quite feisty, isn't she?" Solace commented once Hilde was safely out of earshot.

"She's scared, like everybody else. It's how she shows it," he said, wondering if Hilde would be acting *quite* the same if Samanta hadn't shown him her nude body and started offering her friendship.

"What do you think of her?"

"She's strong-willed and demanding, but... I quite like her."

Solace stared at him, "I meant Samanta."

"Oh... erm... she..." an image of the demon naked in the restless light of a tar torch hurtled unbidden from the shadows, "...grabs the attention."

Solace gave him a curious look, as if unsure she heard him correctly.

To be fair, he wasn't entirely sure he'd heard himself correctly, either.

The demon's return saved him from further explanation.

A hush dropped on the room as Samanta crossed to them.

Even the Favoured Men pleading for their lives fell silent.

"Well?" Solace asked.

Lucien and Lebrecht joined them.

Samanta ran her eyes up and down both men, "Would you like to be my friend, too?" she asked them.

Lebrecht seemed to swallow his tongue. Lucien's response was more predictable. He eyed the demon's tits, nodding appreciatively before announcing to her, "I am no other than Lucien Kazmierczak, the famed soldier, adventurer and lover, renowned from Ghent to Gdansk for his friendliness. I expect you've probably heard of me even after being locked in a dungeon for so long?"

"We're discussing people's lives here," Solace snapped.

"Doesn't mean we can't be friends," Lucien replied, winking at Samanta.

The demon beamed back at him.

"What did they say? Will they exchange our people for Bulcher's Favoured Men?"

"The deal was everyone remaining in the castle before dawn, but in good faith, they will release your people in return for these Favoured Men and three more. By dawn."

"You said you didn't think anyone else remained in the castle?"

"Well, I could be wrong."

"And if we don't find three more?"

"My sisters will keep your people."

"I can't allow that."

"And if you do not leave Thasbald by noon, none of you will ever leave it."

Solace's jaw tightened, her eyes narrowed, her chin raised,

all by the smallest of increments, but enough to tell him she fought to keep her anger and frustration in check.

"There's nothing you can do to help us," he asked the demon, "as our friend?"

"The original deal was for everyone still in Thasbald; now you only need three. But they will give no more concessions. Number Five is somewhat... intransigent by nature."

Samanta's eyes moved to the Favoured Men, "Best you hand them over so we can start searching Thasbald without delay."

"We?" Solace asked.

"I am happy to help. As a friend."

"If we hand these men over," Lebrecht said, still eyeing Samanta warily, "we will have nothing to bargain with."

"You have nothing left to bargain with now," Samanta jumped in before Solace could reply, "'tis only that they consider Lady Solace their sister that has kept you all alive thus far."

Solace pursed her lips, then looked at Lucien, "Do it."

"My lady," Lucien nodded and twisted away, signalling to Usk, Wickler, Swoon and the Vadians to get the Favoured Men to their feet.

"Perhaps-"

"No," Solace cut Lebrecht off, "they deserve all they're about to get."

She kept herself stony-faced and silent as the four Favoured Men were hauled to their feet. One shouldered into Corcilius, and tried to make a run for it, but Usk managed to grab the man's collar and yank him back.

Whilst everyone else in the room watched the Favoured Men dragged, kicking and screaming, towards the Great Hall, his own eyes alit upon Samanta, partly because he had no great desire to watch men crying and begging for their lives, regardless of their crimes, but mainly because the demon's strange magnetism continued to demand his attention.

A faint smile curled her lips while her eyes sparkled like chips of blue ice in the winter sunlight. Smears of blood still darkened her pale skin in places. It should repulse him. It *did* repulse him. But it offered a dread fascination, too. Like something he knew was dangerous to touch, but that very danger created a compulsion to do the exact thing you knew you shouldn't.

One of the Favoured Men was screaming. A God-awful sound in the otherwise silent, high-ceilinged room filled with lingering shadows and hesitant light. Yet his eyes stayed on the demon and the ghost of a smile dusting her blood-smeared lips as the men who'd helped Bulcher abuse her for so long were dragged off to their fate.

What is wrong with me?

Why am I so fascinated by this monster?

Slowly, Samanta's gaze slid from the doomed Favoured Men to him.

He wanted to look away in the manner of men throughout time caught staring at a woman when they shouldn't be. But his eyes had other ideas.

Samanta's smile grew, the right side of her mouth curling up a fraction higher than the left, which made the gesture, it seemed to him, carnal and knowing.

For a moment, her tongue slid along her bottom lip. Then her eyes returned to the Favoured Men, the first of whom had just been hurled into the Great Hall.

By the time the second went in, the screams of the first were rolling out of the Great Hall.

But he wasn't thinking about that. He was thinking how Samanta turning her eyes from him caused an almost physical pain to momentarily convulse him.

It took a force of will to pull his gaze from her.

Despite his breath misting at the end of his nose, a heat rose within him, hot enough for beads of sweat to break across his brow.

He screwed his eyes shut and sucked in a deep lungful of cold, greasy air. It didn't help much. Nor did the shouts and pleas of the third Favoured Man thrown into the Great Hall.

Beneath the shouts and cries coming from inside came a multitude of tapping sounds. Like a swarm of insects rising. Hungry insects.

How many brides did Bulcher have?

It doesn't matter. There's only one of them that does.

He swallowed and opened his eyes.

Samanta watched the Favoured Men go to her sisters. Her chest rose and fell rapidly as if she were panting, though, unlike everyone else, her breath did not frost.

Again, he forced his eyes away. Scouring the room for something to anchor his gaze to keep it from stealing back to the demon.

Lucien and Usk were bundling the final Favoured Man into the Great Hall. Aznar. Who'd once snipped off Samanta's fingers and toes with a pair of shears for his lord's entertainment.

He was weeping.

Aznar managed to get a foot up on the frame of the Great Hall's door and pushed back against the two soldiers to prevent them from casting him into a darkness reverberating with insectile tapping.

Lucien and Usk pulled him back and tried to throw him through the open doors, but Aznar half twisted away and fell sprawling to the floor. Hands tied behind his back, Aznar struggled to rise to his knees in the doorway... then screamed as arms struck out of the shadows to seize him and pull him into the Great Hall.

Lucien and Usk took sharp steps backwards before the doors slammed shut, completely cutting Aznar's fading cries off.

Leaving the room in silence.

Apart from Samanta's giggle.

She clapped her hands together like an excited child.

"What a night this is turning out to be!"

Pretty much the entire company stared at the demon with varying expressions of distaste plastered across their faces.

Except from Hilde.

Who was staring at him.

And he had no idea how to describe her expression...

Chapter Ten

"Would you like to be my friend?"

Karoline recoiled as if slapped.

"I think we could be very good friends!"

Karoline would have bolted, but her back was already against the wall, limiting her escape routes.

"I used to embroider. Mother said I was especially good! Do you embroider? I might be a little rusty now after... so long."

"A little..." Karoline managed to croak. She clung to Elin's forearm so hard her knuckles were as white as her maid's face.

"Perhaps this is something we can discuss later," she said, trying to ease Samanta away from the petrified Karoline, "we do have more pressing concerns at the moment."

The demon frowned at her, "We do?"

"We do."

"Oh, well, I suppose..."

Solace took the demon's arm and steered her away.

"She seems ever so nice; do you think she wants to be my friend? I find it difficult to tell; the things you forget being away from people, it'd surprise you."

She thought Karoline more likely to befriend a rabid dog but made a positive noise in the back of her throat all the same.

"You said you would help."

"I did?"

"Now that we're friends."

"Oh, yes. You do anything for a friend..." the demon's brow furrowed again, "...don't you?"

"Where possible."

"Why, I'd be delighted to, my dear new friend, Solace!" the demon slipped a cold hand inside her arm as they walked.

She lowered her voice a tad, "You will show us where your husband's silver is?"

"I will...?"

She tried her best to suppress her sigh.

"You-"

Samanta giggled and patted her hand. The demon's nails were still dark with dried blood, she couldn't help but notice.

"I'm just teasing!"

"Samanta, we don't have a lot of time."

"Oh, tosh, I have an abundance of time. And teasing is what friends do, isn't it? Merry joshing and hearty pranks and... and such like!"

"Your sisters will kill our people in a few hours if we do not find-"

"Oh, they won't kill them that quickly," the demon waved a hand at the closed doors of the Great Hall, "they're very sated after their slaughter."

All vampires, as she now knew very well, were mad, but she couldn't tell if Samanta was genuinely as batty as a bag of frogs or whether the creature was toying with her for reasons of malicious glee or malevolent purpose.

"Are you going to help us or not?"

"I am!" the smile faded as the demon's features hardened, "Trust me, I am as eager to get out of this place as you are... and you *will* take me with you, won't you?"

"Yes," she said without hesitation, "of course."

"Ulrich told you I know Saul the Bloodless, didn't he?"

Renard had hurriedly recounted his meeting with Samanta. She wasn't sure how a creature locked in a dungeon for decades would know how to find the Red Company, but she was prepared to grasp any straw.

"I can give you your men, I can give you my husband's silver, I can give you the Red Company..."

"And in return?"

"Be my friend."

"And that is all?"

"Is it so hard to believe someone who has endured all that I have might value friendship above all other things?"

She moved a hand towards the Great Hall, "Are they not your friends?"

"We are bound by suffering and our husband's curse, but they are not friends. They, poor things, are largely insane. I am not."

"Are you sure?"

"Why do you think Captain Damstra chose me to help him free our lord? 'tis because they considered me trustworthy, malleable, controllable. They considered me sane."

"And yet you killed Captain Damstra and his men and released your sisters to slaughter Thasbald's household?"

Samanta held her gaze, eyes twinkling in the candlelight, either with mirth or malice.

"And what would you have done if you wore my shoes,

Solace?"

When she didn't reply, the demon smiled a faint knowing smile.

"Give me what you say you can, and I will be your friend for life."

"My life," Samanta asked, "or yours?"

She thought there was a fair chance neither would be particularly long but said nothing. Better not to start a friendship with too many lies, after all.

She called Renard over. For once, his short ginger shadow did not come with him, which pleased her for reasons she could not articulate.

"Samanta is going to show you where Bulcher kept his ill-gotten wealth. See how much there is and how much time it'll take to get it out. Then help search for the men we need to exchange for ours."

Renard's eyes flicked to Samanta, whose broad, beaming and somewhat unnerving smile again shone brightly.

"Given the shortness of time, wouldn't we be better off doing that the other way around?"

Her voice lowered another notch, "The silver is more important."

"It... is?"

"We will have other groups searching for Bulcher's people, but I want the silver secured. Take only people you trust."

Again, Renard's eyes slid back and forth between Samanta and her, "I don't trust anybody, my lady. Save you."

The demon tittered.

"I will stay here. In case there is a problem with my sisters."

"Your... *sisters?*"

"I don't want them changing their minds."

"And you could stop them changing their minds, my lady?"

"I could. Now go and be quick."

Renard did his usual trick of looking exceedingly unhappy before gathering together the members of their company he presumably distrusted least.

Samanta went with them, whistling.

As far as she could see, Renard hadn't invited Hilde, but she went anyway.

She divided the rest of the men and sent them off to hunt for any of Bulcher's remaining people in Thasbald.

Only Karoline, Elin, Bosko Lebrecht and Edrich, one of Bosko's men-at-arms barely older than Hugo, remained with her.

She'd have preferred Bosko and Lebrecht to have gone too, but Bosko refused to leave his daughter/mistress, and Lebrecht refused to leave her.

They'd found a chair for Karoline. Elin stood at her side, and Bosko paced up and down in front of them.

"We shouldn't be here," Lebrecht said, not for the first time, eyeing the doors to the Great Hall, "if they decide to come for us..."

"If they come for us, my lord, it wouldn't matter how many of us are here..."

"That is not reassuring..."

"I am not trying to be."

"It would be safer to go outside; we could ready the coach for Lady Karoline and our horses and leave if things go badly. Wickler's party are searching the walls anyway..."

"I'm not sure anywhere is safe in Thasbald."

"Here, we are the thickness of a door away from Hell, my lady."

She looked at Karoline, slumped on a chair like a flower denied water, drooping forward, petals limp, leaves curling.

"Very well, take her. But if she starts demanding her luggage, put her over your knee."

Relief softened Lebrecht's face, "Let us get going; this place makes my skin crawl."

"You go, I will stay here."

"My lady!"

She held up a hand, "I am quite safe."

"No, you are very much not!"

"They didn't kill me when we went into the Great Hall; they're not going to kill me now. We have a deal."

Lebrecht loomed over her, anger and concern competing to twist his fair features, "These are the Devil's minions; you cannot trust their word!"

"If I thought that, we all would have left long ago."

"I will not leave you here."

"If Lady Karoline is being unreasonable, you may, as I said, put her over your knee. However, trying the same trick with me would be most ill-advised..."

"Solace-"

"Go, my lord. See to Karoline's safety. If she stays here any longer, she may very well expire from terror. She has been through a lot. Too much..."

He followed her gaze to where Karoline hunched forward, panting like a trapped animal; Elin crouched beside her, one arm around her mistress, while Bosko hovered, a picture of helplessness. Young Edrich stood next to them, back ruler-straight and eyes front as if on ceremony.

Lebrecht's back straightened similarly, "I am not leaving you here alone."

"See Karoline settled in her coach, then come back. I am quite capable of looking after myself. She is not."

When he glared at her, she stretched up and kissed his cheek, "Please, my lord..."

It took a little more cajoling, but the kiss broke all resistance.

Is that all it takes?

Bosko and Karoline needed far less persuasion.

The Vadian Captain insisted she came with them, too, but she thought the insistence somewhat half-hearted. Bosko wanted to be away from here as much as his daughter did.

Karoline squeezed her hands with surprising fierceness as she whispered, "Thank you."

Whether she was thanking her for saving her from her marriage and inevitable damnation as one of Bulcher's Brides or for letting her escape the demon-infested bowels of Thasbald castle, she really couldn't say, and Bosko whisked the girl away before she could ask.

Lebrecht pressed a pistol into her hand, "Don't do anything stupid."

"As if I would, my lord."

With the rest of the party heading for the door, Lebrecht swayed as if atop a high windy cliff. Then he stooped and kissed her. And not on the cheek.

It was warm and pleasant, and a curious tingle ran

through her, but the moment passed, and his lips were gone before she could bring her mind to bear on the matter.

"Stay safe, my lady," Lebrecht said. He no doubt meant it as a manly farewell, but it came out more of a burped splutter.

"I will," she said.

He turned and hurried after the others, nailed boots echoing after him. He looked back and waved, then disappeared, leaving her alone.

Well, almost alone.

"Ah, young love, such a sweet thing..." a voice said from the lobby's darkest corner.

"My Lord Flyblown," she nodded as one shadow detached itself from the rest, "I've been expecting you."

"You have?" Flyblown sounded amused, "I'm not becoming predictable, am I? I do so prefer to keep people on their tippy toes."

"Not so much predictable as overdue."

"Hmmm, that makes me sound like a loan repayment. How disagreeable. Money is such a base and crude concept. The world was a kinder place before whatever bright spark thought up that tawdry idea."

"I'm sure it was."

"You can trust me on that," a feral grin stretched Flyblown's sharp, not quite finished features.

She shivered. The temperature had dropped noticeably. The candles were dimmer, too, or perhaps just further away. Flyblown brought the darkest portion of the night with him.

"Did you know Bulcher was a vampire?" she asked.

Flyblown examined his fingernails. They were long, yellowed and sharpened to points again, "Well, there were some *rumours*, but I try not to pay attention to tittle-tattle, as you know."

"And you didn't think to pass that on?"

"Oh, but what if it had been wrong? How much less you'd think of me!"

"I wouldn't be thinking of you at all if Bulcher had killed me."

Flyblown turned the shadow-laden hollows of his eyes towards the Great Hall, "Oh, he wouldn't have killed you. Well, not in the conventional sense..."

"And I suppose there were rumours about his brides too?"

Flyblown shrugged, "One or two... though very vague, as I recall."

"Are there any other bits of *tittle-tattle* you're not telling me?"

"Oh, most definitely. It is preferable that you remain focussed."

"I do sometimes wonder what I am receiving as part of our arrangement, my lord."

"Receiving? Why, I would have thought that rather obvious..." he ran long fingers down his long body, "...you receive me!"

She smiled. Patiently.

"Do you believe I can trust Bulcher's brides," her patient smile widened a fraction, "...from whatever gossip you may have heard?"

"Trust? By the ancient gods of blood and fire, of course not!" Flyblown stooped to lean in close, his icy breath tingling her skin, the musty scent of the crypt teasing her nose, "Despite everything, they are still women, you know!"

She blinked. She'd yet to determine whether Flyblown possessed a sense of humour. But given she hadn't worked out exactly what he was either, that was probably not a priority.

"My *sight* has not warned me that I can't, and your mark upon my thigh has cooled somewhat. Not that I am certain what that mark tells me if anything."

"Instinct is worth listening to, especially when one is as blessed as you."

"Thank you for your help, my lord, 'tis as valuable as ever."

"My pleasure, my dear. I must say, things are progressing swimmingly."

"They are?"

"Oh, yes. You are building your army, your enemies are falling, and, importantly, you are doing whatever is necessary. Most commendable..."

Flyblown purred the last few words, putting her in mind of a giant toothy cat whose current contentment was the only thing preventing it from trying to eat you.

"So, if everything is going so terribly well, why are you here? To pat my knee and tell me how special I am?"

"I'm here to ensure you see every possibility. It is what I do. Among other things..."

"Possibilities?"

"The world abounds with them. It is surprising how many can be overlooked. Of course, not every possibility will work, but that should never stop one from attempting them."

"I suppose not."

"Like young Lebrecht, you have him wrapped around your finger. He'll do almost anything for you now. Just imagine how pliable he'll become once fully wrapped around a more appealing part of your anatomy?"

Although she opened her mouth, she couldn't think of anything meaningful to say.

Flyblown chuckled. The way she'd imagine people of a certain nature might chuckle if they'd just witnessed a death they found mildly amusing.

"My Lady of the Broken Tower, what I am saying is what I have said before. You must do whatever is necessary..." Flyblown turned his eyes to the doors of the Great Hall.

"An army to fight an army."

"Ah, if it were only that easy."

"They could be useful. And they hate Saul the Bloodless as much as I do."

"Indeed, they do... Now, let us see if you've been paying attention. Why do I want Saul stopped, and The Red Company destroyed?"

"You said..." she wrinkled her forehead, everything seemed such a long time ago, "...he was an affront to the world, to the natural order, and the balance of things."

"What an excellent memory you have."

"You said he had dangerous dreams. And Henry Cleever said my brother has foreseen where those dreams will lead."

"The possibilities of them, yes. But Saul has not been the only one meddling with the natural order of things..."

"No?"

"Vampires are solitary creatures, for the most part. That is how they have survived. Few and far between, they have existed alongside mankind since the dawn of time by inhabiting the darkest shadows and deepest cracks. They are not intended to be collected..."

"Bulcher's widows?"

Flyblown nodded, "He did not simply make them and keep them for his own peculiar amusement. He profited from them, too."

"Profited?"

"A vampire's blood is powerful. You have some experience of this, yes?"

Morlaine's blood saved her in Madriel after she'd all but killed herself escaping the Man from Carinthia.

"Yes."

"It heals the sick and can extend a human life a little beyond the few allotted fleeting decades."

"And people pay for this?"

"You sound surprised."

"But... people are being burned at the stake all the time for witchcraft... why hasn't-"

Flyblown interrupted her with a snort, "Not the kind of people who can afford Bulcher's *medicine*."

"But... people would notice kings that don't age, wouldn't they?"

"Few kings could afford Bulcher's prices either. These are the people who rule from the shadows for the most part. The powers behind the crowns. And if a King recovers from illness, 'tis merely divine intervention. A matter for rejoicing, not the witchfinders."

"And you didn't try to put a stop to it?"

Flyblown's teeth flashed in the candlelight, "I have put a stop to it…"

"Why didn't you-"

"Knowledge is dangerous, and too much of it can warp one's thinking. If you knew this place crawled with vampires, you may have baulked from what needed to be done or sought more allies before attempting it. Bulcher is dead. His reign of greed and debauchery is over. The rich and powerful will have to suffer the malign influence of disease and time like the rest of the human race. The clock has been reset, the natural order restored. Almost."

"Almost?"

"Yes…" Flyblown's musky, dry meat scent washed over her as he leaned forward to whisper in her ear, "…almost…"

*

"How do you know where this silver is? Bulcher kept you in a cell?" Hilde demanded of the demon as she trotted along at his shoulder.

Samanta led the way as they descended into Thasbald's dark, dank bowels again.

"My late husband enjoyed many peculiar entertainments."

"What does that mean?" as much hostility dripped off Hilde's words as water dribbled down the stonework.

Thasbald stood in the centre of a vast wetland, and a lot of those wetlands seeped through the castle's deep roots like rot up a bad tooth.

"You'll see," was the demon's only response. Then a whistle. Three notes, ascending.

It was starting to grate on him; he couldn't imagine what hearing it on your torturer's lips as they approached must have been like. He never thought he would feel pity for a demon.

His eyes fell to Samanta's arse. The soiled, rotten skirts clung to it as she walked, rustling in time with her steps.

Pity was not the only thing he'd never expected to feel for a demon.

This is ridiculous!

It most certainly was. But his eyes had other ideas.

He tried thinking about being in the dungeons of a castle filled to the rafters with insane, bloodthirsty, demonic killers. It helped, a little.

Another thing to add to the night's list of unexpected things.

Behind him, Lucien and Hugo's boots splashed on the wet stone.

He wished more of their company were with them, but they couldn't spare many from the hunt for whatever survivors might still lurk in Thasbald.

"How much further?" he asked.

"Not far," Samanta looked over her shoulder and smiled at him.

He could almost hear Hilde's bristles rising.

They were heading down another corridor, much like the one that housed the Bride's cells, though this one lacked iron doors, just heavy wooden ones.

"What's behind these?" Lucien asked.

"Supplies."

"Supplies?"

"He traded commodities. All things have value, even more so in war. He sold to whoever paid the most. Grain, flour, leather, coal, gunpowder, weapons, iron, cotton... if you can think of it, 'tis likely down here somewhere."

"Beer?" Lucien asked, hopefully.

"Oh, I'd imagine so. Soldiers like beer, don't they?"

Lucien slapped his hands together, "That they do, lass, that they do!"

"How deep does this go?" Hugo's faltering voice piped up.

"All the way down to Hell..."

"Oh..." Hugo said. And shut up.

Lucien tried one of the doors, but a black iron lock sealed it.

"Do you doubt me?" Samanta stopped.

"Blessed with a curious nature," the mercenary winked.

The demon walked back to Lucien. He and Hugo shuffled aside till their backs pressed against the damp walls; Hilde held her ground and glared at Samanta as she passed. At least she didn't raise her crossbow.

"Let me show you..."

"You have the keys?" Lucien stood aside.

Samanta's eyes narrowed against the tar torch Lucien held.

Then she took that heavy black iron lock and plucked it from the door as if it were but a low hanging apple from a tree.

The sound of the iron snapping mingled with a low-pitched whine coming from the back of Hugo's throat.

The demon looked at Hilde, "And before my friend with all the questions asks, I couldn't do that during my years He kept me captive. He starved us of blood to keep us weak..." she dropped the lock to clatter on the rough stone floor, "...but now I am not starved of blood..."

"Useful girl to have around," Lucien sniffed, pushing the door open and disappearing inside.

Samanta put her back against the wall and stared at him.

He juggled the tar torch in his hand. It wasn't big enough to hide behind, but he did his best.

Lucien soon reappeared. Chewing something, "Barrels of salted eel," he explained, "Anyone want some?"

Everybody shook their head.

Apart from Samanta.

She was still too busy staring at him.

"Suit yourself, 'tis pretty good."

"Anything else in there?" he asked as they resumed walking, and Lucien continued munching.

"Lots of shit," the mercenary said, between cramming more salted eel into his mouth, "if every room is as loaded as that one, there's enough here to supply a sizeable army."

"I've got another question," Hilde piped up.

"Oh, the surprise..." Samanta said.

"If Bulcher kept you weak, how'd you kill those men bringing you to free the *Graf*?"

"Damasta gave me blood?"

"Whose?"

"One of his men's."

"He let you kill one of his men?"

"No. He opened a vein for me to drink while the rest stood outside my cell. Enough to give me the strength to break down the door to Karoline's tower for them and hurl myself at you while they came behind me," Samanta shrugged, "Damasta excelled at cruelty and loyalty. But when it came to cunning plans... not so much..."

They walked on. Past a lot of doors and down another spiral staircase.

The air became colder and moister.

Wasn't it supposed to get hotter the closer you got to Hell?

Earthy dankness tainted every breath.

His eyes still kept stealing to Samanta.

Hilde's remained locked upon him.

"We don't know where she's leading us?" Hilde insisted as they entered another lightless corridor.

Her voice was low, but he didn't doubt the demon could hear them.

"Solace trusts her."

"Well, that's alright then."

He eyed her, "I trust Solace's judgement."

Hilde didn't spit in his direction, but that was all you could say for the look that came back at him.

Hilde was right to be wary, of course; Samanta, as demonstrated with the lock, was strong enough to kill them all in an instant. But he went where Solace told him. That was his penance; that was his curse. And if she didn't understand that... well, it wasn't like they were married.

His eyes slipped to Samanta's rear again.

He really had to stop doing that.

Instead, he concentrated on the clip of their boots on damp stone and the torchlight's play on the pitted, stained ceiling. Less interesting, but far safer.

He probably should spend some time thinking about why

he felt so drawn to the demon, but he suspected that would only encourage his wayward eyes to misbehave.

Unless the problem has pulled a weapon, it's usually best to ignore it till it goes away...

When the world inevitably tumbled into darkness and despair, and all hope crumbled to bitter ash, at least he'd still have Old Man Ulrich's ale pot wisdom to fall back on...

"What are you smiling at?" Accusation dripped from Hilde's words.

He sighed. Inwardly.

"Just thinking of my father."

"Oh, right..." scepticism replaced accusation.

"I often think of him in difficult times. He had the knack of taking a bad situation and making it infinitely worse. I always find that a comfort..."

Lucien laughed. Then started choking on salted eel. He found it almost reassuring that his father still had some of his old magic left, even in death.

After some hearty back slapping and not turning too blue, Lucien declared himself fit enough to continue.

They cut the chatter after that, which was a relief in more ways than one. He didn't like the way sounds echoed down here. Although no different than any other enclosed space beneath the ground, he couldn't shake the feeling that Thasbald took every noise and transmuted it into some distant maniacal giggle.

The next set of stairs were longer, screwing down into the dark earth.

At the bottom was a locked door. Heavy iron.

It proved no barrier to Samanta.

The door opened not onto another corridor but something more akin to a cavern chiselled out of the bedrock. The sound of running water came from several directions. Their torchlight didn't reach the ceiling, whatever it did touch, glistened with moisture.

Lucien whistled.

The whistle echoed off into the distance.

Whilst sounding a little bit like maniacal giggling.

Samanta strode off into the shadows.

"She could be leading us *anywhere*," Hilde said, in case he hadn't heard her the first time.

They passed barrels and crates. Formless covered piles. Shadowy stacks and dark heaps. Sacks and trunks. Crude stone columns and roughly hewed arches climbed into the darkness.

"Is that a boat?" Hugo asked, peering into the gloom.

"Probably to get across the river to the underworld," Lucien said.

"Eh?" Hugo frowned, "What's the underworld?"

"Ignorant youth," Lucien said. Then clipped the boy around the ear.

"Ow!"

"Cut it out," he snapped.

He didn't like this place, and this was certainly no time for foolery.

Their footsteps slapped the rough stone. If he listened hard enough, it sounded like more than five sets of feet. Somewhere this big could hide a lot of feet. And who knew what a madman like *Graf* Bulcher might have hidden in his dungeons alongside supplies, silver and undead wives.

Another door loomed out of the shadows. Rust-washed iron with several locks. The sturdiest so far. So sturdy, in fact, that it took Samanta a couple of goes to force it open.

On the other side, more stairs descended.

"Should we have brought more torches?" Lucien asked, looking at the spluttering greasy flame he held.

"Don't worry, there are more down here," Samanta said, already disappearing into the unlit spiral stairwell, "he liked us to see at the end..."

Hilde shot him a glance, her expression more one of curiosity this time.

These stairs were deeper than the last, and the bottom door even heavier and more secure. Samanta let out a small grunt to break it open. At this rate, she could only be a few more doors away from breaking into a slight sweat.

The door opened onto a narrow, low-ceilinged passage lined with roughly hewn stone slabs. It reminded him of the secret tunnel Solace and he, along with the other survivors of the Red Company's attack, tried to use to escape from The Wolf's Tower.

He scanned the ceiling. There were no evident cracks, despite there being an awful lot of castle above their heads...

The passage wasn't long and soon delivered them to another door; two unlit torches sat in brackets on either side. Lucien lit them both from his, ignoring Samanta's look of distaste as the flames took and the shadows retreated a few paces.

On the other side of the door, something howled.

"What..." Lucien froze, torch still touching the one on the

wall he had just lit, "...was that?"

"Come, let me show you," Samanta said after plucking off the two iron locks on the door and pushing it open.

"After you," Lucien said, once the demon went through.

He passed his torch to Hugo and drew a pistol. Then went in after Samanta.

Inside was a small, unlit, unadorned room containing nothing but another door in the opposite wall.

And a naked, filthy, snarling woman.

She came flying out of the shadows, demonic face contorted in rage, fangs bared, eyes bulging.

He raised his pistol to shoot the creature, but Samanta grabbed his wrist to force the gun down.

Only when the demon's snarl became a yelp, and her head snapped back did he notice the collar around her neck and the thick iron chain fixed high to the opposite wall.

The chain prevented her reaching the door.

The demon stood, straining upon the chain, teeth snapping at him, grubby hands clawing at him but falling short, black broken nails slashed the air in front of his face.

"Ulrich, meet Number One..." Samanta said, her fingers, long, cool and smooth, still wrapped about his wrist, "...my husband's first love..."

"Why... why is she down here?" he asked.

"You'd have to ask Him that. I expect she's much cheaper to keep than a guard dog, which might have had something to do with it..." Samanta slowly uncurled her fingers, though her eyes lingered on his, "...in addition to all His other faults, He was something of a miser, too."

Number One howled and clawed, the cords on her neck

straining to break the collar. Red raw skin caked with blood where the tightly fitting iron bit deep peeped through the dirt. Wild tangles of muddy brown hair fell almost to her waist, ribs protruded from her emaciated form, and scabs covered her arms and legs.

"Starved of blood, too?" he asked.

"Not enough to break iron, but enough to break bone. And enough to keep people away from that door," Samanta nodded across the room, then moved along the wall to where a wooden wheel sat, linked to the iron chain around One's neck via several pulleys set into the ceiling. A lock prevented the wheel from turning, but Samanta ripped it free.

How much had she drunk to give her this strength, and how long before she needed more? Questions he'd never asked Morlaine.

Samanta slowly turned the wheel, the chain shortened, and One staggered back into the far corner, hissing and clutching the collar.

As the demon retreated, he ventured into the room, allowing the others to enter behind him.

"Fuck me..." Lucien said from his shoulder. Hilde went to the other side. Hugo loitered wide-eyed in the doorway.

Once Number One was in the corner, Samanta crossed to her.

"Don't come any closer," the demon warned.

Number One spat and hissed at Samanta, who slowly took the wretched remains of Bulcher's first wife in her arms and held her. For a while, the creature struggled, clawing at Samanta's back with black torn nails, even trying to sink her fangs into her fellow demon's shoulder at one point as arms and legs thrashed.

Samanta refused to let go, cooing soft words he couldn't hear as she rocked the wretched remains of Bulcher's first wife until the struggles abated and a muffled sobbing replaced her screams.

"Loosen the chain, just a little, please," Samanta asked, not looking back at them.

When he remained rooted to the spot, Lucien handed his torch to Hugo, too, and moved to the wheel. Releasing the mechanism's brake allowed the demon enough chain to slowly lower Number One to the damp stone floor, where she sat, cradling her.

Samanta pressed her forehead against Number One's, whispering all the time.

He felt the tug of Hilde's eyes.

What's she up to?

She didn't need to say it, the suspicion was writ large behind the raised crossbow.

Hilde tensed.

Looking back, he found Samanta working on Number One's collar. It didn't take her long to snap the lock on the thing and pull it free. As it clattered and skidded across the room, One sobbed.

Smoothly, Samanta rose to her feet turned her back on the demon and crossed the room.

Holding out her hand, she said to him, "Your sword."

Hilde stiffened some more.

"Ulrich..." she growled as he slid his father's sabre free and handed it to Samanta. She could rip iron apart with her bare hands; if she wanted to kill them, she didn't need a sword.

Number One climbed to her knees. Under the long, tangled hair, the face of a young woman had replaced the nightmarish demonic features beneath the encrusted dirt. Only where the tears ran was the young woman's face clean.

Samanta held his father's sword at her side.

"Are you sure, sister?"

Number One nodded and closed her eyes.

The sword flashed, and the demon's head hit the stone floor before her body toppled sideways.

Chapter Eleven

"Kill them?"

She glanced at the door to the Great Hall.

"Do not worry, My Lady of the Broken Tower," Flyblown reassured her, "they cannot hear us."

"Kill them all?"

"Well, you don't have to be entirely clinical. If one or two were to escape, well..." bony shoulders rolled beneath his cloak, "...it would not matter terribly."

"It wouldn't?"

"One or two more insane, blood-crazed vampires on the loose won't make much of a difference given the lamentable state of the world. Well, unless they were to eat someone you care about. But that's by the by. A whole host of them descending on humanity, however..."

"Harder for you to remain secret."

"Quite. And that won't do."

"And that's more important than the lives they might take?"

"Vastly. There's a natural order. We've discussed it previously. Do pay attention. Were you a slovenly student? One would imagine so."

"I want the Red Company, I want Saul. I have no reason to kill Bulcher's Brides."

"Apart from the fact they are insane, blood-crazed killers who will wash out of here on a crimson tide."

"I didn't know you cared so much about innocent lives?"

Flyblown sniffed, "Of course I do; such things keep me awake at night..."

She pinched the bridge of her nose, "My priorities are Bulcher's wealth and finding the Red Company. Preferably before they head to Magdeburg-" she frowned at Flyblown, "I don't suppose you actually know where they are now and aren't telling because... I have to prove myself or something?"

"Nope."

"My lord..."

Flyblown swished a finger back and forth over his heart, "Honest."

She peered at him.

Did he look shifty?

"Even if I knew how, I don't have the time," she said.

"Trust me, you do not want them following you once you leave here."

"Why would they?"

"Oh, I don't know..." Flyblown made a languid circling motion with his right hand, "...possibly because you plan to steal all their gold and silver..."

"No, I'm not. I shall negotiate for it once we have shown good faith by giving them the last of Bulcher's people."

"They won't give you any."

"They don't need it, they're demons!"

"So was *Graf* Bulcher. And they're not demons, they're vampires, there's a difference. Slow pupils, why do I always end up with the slow pupils..." somewhere in the shadow-filled hollows of Flyblown's face, eyes may have rolled upwards.

"I believe we can do a deal."

"And if they say no, you can't have any of the wealth their late husband largely stole from their families or earnt from their blood; what will you do, hmmm?"

"I could ask them to join us."

"Join you? An army of lunatic women who have been locked up and tortured for decades, centuries in some cases. How do you think the world will react to such a merry band traipsing about the country?"

"There may be some difficulties to overcome," she raised her chin and held Flyblown's half-concealed eyes, "but you need an army to fight an army."

"Indeed. But they do not constitute an army. And they will get you all killed. They have been starved. For years. For decades. For centuries. Beyond these walls is an ocean of blood. Even the ones who don't howl at the moon won't be able to control themselves for more than a day or two. They will kill, and they won't care one jot who they kill. My Lady of the Broken Tower, trust me, that is an unbelievably bad idea."

"Perhaps..." she conceded.

"So, when they tell you they won't share their silver, what will you do?"

"They will."

"What will you do if they tell you they won't share their silver? Humour me, please."

She bit her lip, and her gaze slid away before she mumbled, "I'd probably try and steal it..."

"Ah, by all that's unholy, at last!"

"But-"

Flyblown thrust a finger against her lips. She tried not to jerk her head away. It smelt like it had been somewhere rather unpleasant for a long time.

"Think of a plan. Just in case. You've already sent people to locate Bulcher's ill-gotten gains, so you must have considered the possibility. And if you go down that road, you will have to take care of them. You've already made enemies of the *Markgräf* of Gothen and the Swedish Army; trust me, you don't need any more..."

"But how-"

The finger pressed harder; the skin seemed to bulge around her lips as if water filled the digit.

"It is my role to nudge you in the right direction and to ensure you see all the possibilities open to you. It is not my role to tell you how to do everything. You must be able to think for yourself, my lady, because I cannot always be here to hold your hand. So, think about where you are, what is here, and what you can do with it..." Flyblown withdrew the finger and flashed another of his feral smiles, "...and then make sure you put all those misbegotten wretches out of their misery before you leave!"

"Solace!"

Her head shot around.

Lebrecht came hurtling towards her.

"My lord, is something wrong?"

The young nobleman skidded to a halt, forehead rippled by frowns, "No... well... you seemed... erm... strange."

"Strange, how so?" she glanced at Flyblown. Except there was nothing to see. He was gone.

"Was as if you were not really there," he laughed, high-pitched and nervous.

"It has been a long night, my lord. And the night likes to play tricks."

"Yes, of course," Lebrecht said, still looking at her as if she were some manner of curiosity.

"Is all well with Lady Karoline?"

"Yes. She is settled in her coach; Bosko and his man are seeing to the horses."

"You saw no one?"

"No one alive."

"They have been outside?"

"A guard, neck ripped open as if savaged by a dog," Lebrecht looked towards the Great Hall and lowered his voice, "I doubt anyone else remains alive in Thasbald bar us. I fear these creatures are toying with us. Like a cat before it bites the mouse's head off..."

"We search till dawn."

"And then?"

She shook her head and paced to the stairs. Lebrecht trailed after her, feet echoing in time to the wheels spinning in her mind.

"My lady?"

Lebrecht stood behind her as she stared up the steps. More candles had died, shadow hung ever thicker. Were all Bulcher's widows now in the Great Hall, or did some still stalk the rest of Thasbald? Were they watching and listening? Or were they too lost to their own madness to care what the last living things in Thasbald were up to.

She could talk to Flyblown without fear of them

overhearing because she was certain he only ever appeared in her mind, and even the sharpest of demonic ears could not eavesdrop on that conversation.

But anything else she said was in danger of being heard.

So, she would have to speak very quietly...

"I am frightened," she said, not at all quietly.

"My lady?"

"Do you really love me?"

"Is that what frightens you?"

She had to laugh at that. Looking over her shoulder at his concerned face, she wanted to laugh more.

"No, my lord, 'tis not that. 'tis the being surrounded by monsters that I find frightening."

"Well, yes..." he put a tentative hand on her shoulder; when she didn't jerk away from the touch, his fingers curled around it.

She placed her own hand atop his.

"Do you?"

"Yes. From the moment I saw you."

She thought that unlikely. Lust, perhaps, but love? No matter. It served her purpose.

She twisted to face him.

"We have a little time; let us go somewhere and forget about the horrors for a while."

Lebrecht's eyes widened to the point of bulging. Which wanted to make her laugh all the more. She was still a novice when it came to the business of seduction and wasn't sure whether driving Lebrecht's father to wanting to lock her in his highest tower counted as a success or not. But there was a time for laughing at a man, and this wasn't it.

So, she kissed him instead.

As before, it was not at all unpleasant. It warmed and sent tingles a tingling from her lips downwards. Her heart quickened as he returned the kiss. His hands found her waist, pulling her closer.

Pleasant. But was this it?

She had long dreamed of a handsome Prince of the Empire kissing her. Celestial choirs, bursting shafts of dazzling light, shaking buildings and dancing angels had often accompanied the kiss of her dreams.

Pleasant didn't quite seem worth the wait.

I wonder how Renard's lips would feel...?

She jerked away from Lebrecht.

"I'm sorry, my lady, I didn't mean-"

"Don't worry about my honour, we'll likely be dead soon..." she grabbed one of the remaining candles still aflame and, holding Lebrecht's hand, dragged him up the stairs.

"Is this something we should talk about? I-"

"No!"

She ran. He ran with her. The angels might not be dancing around them, but the shadows did. A jig in time with the candle flickering in her hand.

Did anything watch them from the other side of those dancing shadows?

Watching with curious, hungry eyes?

She didn't know.

And, for a moment, she didn't care.

She just ran. His hand in hers.

Feet thumped on floorboards.

She wanted to laugh. Feeling strangely alive in the dead castle.

Was that wrong?

Of course, it was wrong. The world was wrong. At least hers was. But who cared? No one. The people who loved her were dead.

Renard aside.

And he didn't love her anyway.

And Torben.

Who she'd never been sure had been capable of love in the way most people understood.

Even before he sold his soul to Saul the Bloodless to save their lives. And become something he thought he'd always wanted to be.

It didn't take long to find a bedroom.

There were a lot of rooms with beds in a castle.

It was small but not mean.

She held Lebrecht off long enough to light what candles came to hand.

"I want to see," she breathed.

Then he was kissing her.

She let him.

It wasn't unpleasant, after all.

And the tingles were curious.

As for the warmth inside her...

She pulled him to the bed.

He stopped to try and get his boots off. He was a gentleman, after all.

She yanked him onto the bed.

He tried to undo his weapons belt.

She dragged the blankets over them and curled a hand around the back of his neck to pull him close. He gave up fiddling with his belt to kiss her throat.

Oh, that did tingle most interestingly...

She placed the flat of her hand against his chest.

"Stop."

He was panting. A hand was investigating her skirts. That felt interesting, too.

But he stopped. Which was for the best. She didn't want to have to get her dagger out.

"Now..." she breathed in his ear, "...we can talk without being overheard..."

*

After Samanta broke off the locks to the second door, she told them to wait before slipping inside. He thought her hand shook a little, and the locks harder to break.

Hugo was staring at the naked, headless corpse.

"Have some respect for the dead, lad," Lucien's elbow nudged the boy, "...if you have to gawp at something, gawp at her head, not her tits."

"I ain't!" Hugo looked like he wanted to bolt out of the dank, stinking little room.

He glared at Lucien, who shrugged and started picking at one of his remaining teeth.

Samanta came back with sackcloth, which she spread over Number One's corpse after she placed the head with the rest of the body.

"You knew her?" he asked.

"No more than I knew anyone here. We were all no more than passing ghosts to each other. He liked to inflict pain..." the demon pursed her lips, "...and being alone can be the most unbearable torture of them all."

Samanta went back through the door, summoning them with a flick of her wrist.

"There are more torches on the wall," she told them once they followed her through.

As Hugo began lighting them and the light pressed the darkness back, Lucien whistled.

Although the room was only five or six paces wide, it stretched back beyond the torchlight's reach. Wooden chests of varying sizes lined each wall. Several were open, each filled to the brim with coins.

Lucien moved to the nearest and plucked out a handful of silver thalers, letting them trickle through his fingers in a metallic waterfall back onto their fellows.

He scooped up more, "Are they all filled with-"

"Yes. Silver, gold, coins, ingots, bullion, plate, ornaments, jewellery, anything you can name. So long as 'tis made of silver or gold. This, my friends, is the reward of centuries of avarice."

"Fuck buying an army..." Lucien straightened his back, "...there's enough here to get the bloody empire!"

An ornate wooden chair, gilded with gold, sat with its back to the door, facing Bulcher's hoard. Samanta gently lowered herself into it.

"My late husband's ambitions went further than that. He wanted to buy the whole world. A fancy I always doubted, for to buy means giving something to obtain what you want, and He only ever allowed wealth to enter this room, never leave it."

A leather cuff hung from each arm of the chair.

She took the right one and rang her fingers over it.

They were definitely shaking now.

"He never let his wives leave here either..."

Samanta shuddered and dropped the cuff.

"All his wives' lives ended here, more or less. I believe a couple killed themselves before he decided it time to bring them here. They were the lucky ones..."

He walked into the room and turned his back on the riches to stare at Samanta. Hilde, as she usually did, followed him. Hugo lingered by the door, wide-eyed and skittish. Lucien plonked his arse down in a chest piled to the rim with coins.

"What happened?" he asked when Samanta said nothing, staring into the darkness beyond them.

"I never knew what he was. I knew he was evil, but that was a simple deduction. Everybody here was distant, strange, cold. I didn't understand it. I couldn't work out what I'd done. Why people didn't like me. Why nobody wanted to be my friend. Of course, it wasn't that. They just knew I would not be around for long. Perhaps looking at me was too much like looking in the mirror...

He hurt me, he used me, he... did as he wanted. I thought him unspeakably cruel and cried myself to sleep every night. I prayed I could go home. That he would die. That some handsome prince would come and rescue me.

None of those things happened.

I spent eight months as his wife. After a while, he started coming to me less. I thought perhaps I'd annoyed him by not catching with child, though he never talked of any desire for them.

I grew progressively sick, weak, pale, listless. I only found out later he put a sleeping draught in my wine so he could feed from me. I had the strangest nightmares, but, of course, in reality they were memories not nightmares. The monster in my dreams was real. It was my husband...

I asked for a physician once, he slapped my face and told me nothing was wrong with me. I never asked again.

Then, one day, he announced my father was dead. A hunting accident. If I had not been so shattered with grief, and weak from blood loss, I might have thought it odd, as my father did not care for hunting.

He seemed happy. He stood and watched me cry. He offered no comfort, no words, nothing. He just stood. Smiling.

Later, a lawyer came. My father had no male heirs, so I would inherit our estates. Or rather, my husband would. That was why he was so happy..." Samanta cast an eye over the caskets of silver and gold, disappearing into the gloom, "He had what he wanted. And he had no more use for me. Alive anyway. A week after the lawyer left and everything legally became His, He brought me down here..."

The demon turned her head, "Boy," she said to Hugo, "there should be something hanging on a hook next to the door. Bring it to me."

Hugo looked like he wanted to be told not to do anything the demon asked. Instead, he nodded at the boy.

The something was two pieces of polished bone, connected by a metal thread that glinted in the flickering light. Hugo handed it to Samanta at arm's length and immediately scurried backwards to the door as soon as she took it.

The demon took a bone handle in each hand, raised it to her eye level and pulled them apart until the metal tautened.

A garrot.

Her eyes fixed on the wire as she spoke.

"He brought me down here, one hand clamped around my arm in case I tried to run away. From my room, the one He put yesterday's bride in, all the way down, down here, I never saw another soul. I assume that wasn't an accident.

He never said a word all the way. He just wheezed in my ear, panting. Not from exertion, he never really got out of breath despite his size, that was an affectation, like the way he wobbled and struggled when he stood up. As a vampire, he had no trouble breathing, no trouble moving; he wanted the world to see only a fat old man, not the thing that lived inside that disguise.

No, the panting was excitement. He was about to do the thing I think he enjoyed even more than making money..."

She twisted the garrot back and forth. Threads of gold and silver seemed to be spun around a steel core.

"When he opened that door and introduced me to his first wife, I screamed. But even then, I didn't try to run. I'm not sure I even could have. Eight months of having my blood stolen had left me too weak to do much anything. He held me, fingers digging so hard into my arms as she snapped and snarled at my face, a dog on a chain whose dinner was just out of reach.

He told me if I was a good girl, I might be as useful as his first wife one day..."

Samanta's eyes remained fixed upon the wire. Gold and silver were soft, pliable metals, hence the steel beneath.

He pulled Number One's chain back enough to make her retreat several paces. He told her he had a treat for her if she was good. He ordered her to kneel and beg. She did. And her face returned to normal. She wasn't a monster at all. Just a young woman. Like me.

He had a knife; he held my arm out over her. She was crying and begging. Begging for blood, begging for me to run away, begging for Him to kill her. I was screaming, struggling, but... He was too strong. He slashed my forearm open and laughed as my blood rained down on Number One.

Her face changed again to... that other one.

He laughed as she threw herself at me, but the chain pulled her back.

"Don't be greedy! Bad doggy! Bad doggy!" he shouted.

He made me watch as she scurried around, licking my blood from the floor.

"See," he slobbered in my ear, "see what fun we're going to have, what jolly, bloody fun!"

After pulling Number One away from the door, He dragged me in here..."

Her eyes rose from the garrot to sweep across them, save for Hugo, who still loitered in the doorway behind her.

"It was dark. At first. He forced me down in this chair and bound my wrists to these cuffs. Then he lit the torches on the wall. He wanted me to see. He wanted all those he brought here to see. All his gold, all his silver, all his shiny, special toys that he had collected over the centuries."

Samanta held up the garrot, letting it dangle from her right hand.

"He wound this around my neck and slowly strangled me as he explained how my family's wealth would soon be down here with all those who went before me. He told me what my future held as this sliced open my throat. How no one would miss me, his sickly young wife who'd proved such a disapointment... I listened to Number One howling in the antechamber as she smelt the blood running down my neck as the wire cut into my flesh..."

She stretched out the garrot once more, then placed the wire, silver and gold twisted about steel, against her throat. Closing her eyes, she shivered.

"He kept loosening the wire, and I would gasp, I would cry, I would beg. He stood behind me. I could smell him. His sweat, his scented oils, the something beneath all that which I could not name. Around me, the world span; the gold and silver reflected the flames cavorting to my torment. Above it all, I sensed his excitement, just how much he was enjoying hurting me... and even through my pain and terror, I pitied him... what kind of man enjoyed doing such a thing?

In the end, of course, he showed me he wasn't a man at all...

As the darkness closed, he stepped before me and let me see his true face. The one I recognised from my *nightmares*. The one he intended to curse me with, He'd cut his palm. Dark blood bubbled from too-white skin. He watched with those inhuman eyes, where the colours danced in their depths, and he pressed his bloody palm over my mouth while twisting the garrot with the other.

Watching, watching, watching me with fascinated eyes, so large and black I could see myself reflected in them, swirling amongst threads of gold eddying within their deeps... then... I was gone..."

Samanta shuddered, and the hand holding the garrot flopped to her lap.

"When I awoke, I was down with all the other Brides. When I awoke, I was no longer Samanta; I was a number. When I awoke, I was the thing I am now," again her eyes moved amongst them, "this thing you fear and despise..."

No one said anything. Hilde had dropped her eyes, Lucien placed his hands on either side of him to bury in silver, Hugo shuffled his feet. He did... nothing.

"I am sorry," he said when the silence became too painful.

"So am I... You all despise me, you hate me, you fear me. It was only the thought that one day I might be free of this place, that I might find friendship and companionship that kept me sane, stopped my mind from collapsing like so many of my sisters. Through all those years, all those decades of pain and loneliness. But when I look around you and your friends. I now see that such a notion was... rather foolish... given what I now am... so, like Judita and Number One, there is only one freedom left to me..." Samanta lifted the garrot and held it towards him, "...'tis said things are never so bad after the first time..."

"We are not going to kill you," he said without hesitation. Out of the corner of his eye, he could see Hilde. It looked like she might have appreciated some consultation on that statement.

"But you hate me?"

"Why would we hate you?"

"Because I am a monster."

"You are what you chose to be. The same as everybody else in the world. So, choose not to be a monster."

"I do not believe everybody else will see the matter quite so simply."

"I can only speak for the people in this room."

He looked around the room.

"I've fought alongside some right cunts," Lucien sniffed, "never stopped me trying to keep them alive or accepting a beer off em, and a lot of em done worse than you, for a lot less reason, lass."

"I used to run with a gang of brigands; they robbed and murdered anyone who came down their road," Hugo said, clinging to the door frame, "I thought them, my friends, so... so... you ain't any worse than that... really..."

He glared at Hilde when she remained silent.

"As long as you don't try and eat anyone..." she eventually said, meeting no one's eye.

As ringing endorsements went, he doubted he'd ever heard three more piss-poor efforts.

He was still trying to think of a way to frame their words more kindly when Samanta tossed the garrot aside and jumped to her feet.

"Great! We're all friends!" Samanta beamed, "What shall we do with all this loot then?"

In the Company of Shadows

Chapter Twelve

They found no one else alive inside the main castle, but Wickler's party came across three guards in one of the outer towers, all blissfully asleep. They'd also discovered a stable lad hiding with the horses.

"I told him to piss off," Wickler said, jaw set firmly, eyes challenging, "I've done some shit in my time, but I don't kill children."

She'd patted his arm and said he'd done the right thing.

Whether she would have done the same if he'd only found two guards asleep in the tower, she didn't know.

Would she have given a child to Bulcher's widows?

I am not a monster...

Of course, she wasn't.

She stood in the courtyard, cloak drawn about her. She'd changed back into her travelling clothes, grateful to be out of the maid's dress, even if it did have some of Bulcher's blood splattered over it.

She touched the bag around her neck, already the finger inside felt dry, if she pressed hard enough, she thought it likely it would crack.

"'tis nearly time, my lady," Renard said, appearing at her shoulder.

The sky to the east above Thasbald's outer wall and towers flushed pink.

It was a few minutes till sunrise.

Time to feed the monsters.

"Are you going back in there again?"

"I have to talk to them."

"And then?"

"Come outside as soon as the sun is up, Lebrecht will tell you the rest of what we need to do."

"My lady?"

"Walls have ears."

And there are only so many men I can take to bed to talk to...

She looked at Renard and smiled.

It can be difficult to know exactly how your own smile looks without the aid of a looking-glass, but she thought it a strange one all the same.

The perplexed expression on his face suggested he thought so too.

"Can we trust Samanta?" she asked, as much to break the silence as anything else. The curious combination of instinct, *sight* and Flyblown's mark told her they could. Or at least they could this time. What she might be like out in the world was another matter.

What would Morlaine say?

"I believe so..." he said, "...as far as we can trust any insane, blood-thirsty demon."

"We will have little time to do this. Without her assistance..."

"She wishes only to be free of this place. To have the life Bulcher denied her. How realistic that desire is... I do not know, but I think 'tis genuinely held. And I am usually inclined to think the worst of everybody."

Before she could say more, Tomos Usk came hurrying down the steps into the courtyard, "My lady, the doors of the Great Hall are opening..."

She sucked in a deep breath. It was cold enough to sting, but at least it was clean out here.

Inside, there was dirty work to do.

She nodded, gave the brightening eastern sky a final, longing look, and went back into the dark, gloomy innards of Thasbald castle.

The three captured soldiers were on their knees before the black chasm of the now-open doors to the Great Hall.

She wondered how young the stable lad had been for Wickler to turn him loose; these kneeling soldiers were no more than boys. They all looked younger than her, anyway.

They weren't part of Bulcher's Household Guard, his Favoured Men. These were regular men-at-arms. The ones who got to stand out on the walls in the cold and the rain, rather than those who participated in Bulcher's sick games with his cursed wives.

Still, they wore Bulcher's livery, lived under Bulcher's roof, and took Bulcher's coin. This place was so wrong, the evil within it so obvious; she couldn't believe anyone here was ignorant of what was happening. Turning a blind eye to evil didn't make you innocent; it made you complicit.

"What are you doing?" one of the soldier's cried as she nodded, and her men hauled them to their feet.

Should she say something? Should she ask them questions? Should she assure herself of their guilt?

She wasn't judge. She wasn't jury. She wasn't executioner.

And they were simply a means to an end.

"Take them," she said.

She was doing what was necessary.

Because the price of vengeance wasn't paid in silver.

The men – she was trying hard to think of them as men rather than boys despite their callow features, wide eyes and pimples – didn't fight and struggle as Aznar and the Household Guards had. It took only a couple of shoves in the back to get them moving into the Great Hall. They were as scared as anyone might with their hands tied behind their back and surrounded by armed men with hard eyes and sharp metal turned in their direction, but they didn't look like they knew what was waiting for them in the darkness.

She followed them to the threshold of the Great Hall.

"Please, what is this?" one of Bulcher's men (yes, yes, they were men), twisted to demand. Not of her; she was just a girl, after all, but of Lebrecht, who looked like he should be in charge.

"This is... what is necessary," she answered for Lebrecht.

From within the darkness of the Great Hall, tapping and banging noises rolled out of the chilly air along with the stink of blood and death.

"Do it!" she said.

And they shoved each boy – no, no, man! – into the expectant darkness.

One stumbled and fell; the other two staggered forward but kept their footing.

For a moment, they teetered on the margin between dark and light... then the shadows sprouted limbs, pale and slender, to wrap around each of the boys (no, damn it, men!) and pull them screaming into that dark abyss.

The tapping and banging grew in volume to accompany the screams.

Until all abruptly stopped together.

The hard eyes of the men with sharp metal, she noted, were mostly refusing to look at her.

She walked past them to stand where those boys (men!) had awaited death a minute before.

When she checked over her shoulder, Renard was making to follow her; she waved him back, Lebrecht, too.

They had other work to do.

They had lit lanterns and tar torches to better light the lobby. Alone and apart, she turned her back on the light and her eyes to the darkness within the Great Hall.

"I have fulfilled our bargain!" she called, "Give me my men..."

A few taps that soon faded to nothing was the only reply.

"We have a deal, sisters!"

She took a couple of steps forward, the sticky floor pulling at her feet every time it parted company with the ground.

"Don't make me come in and get them!"

That produced a volley of rattles and bangs in response. Laughter, most likely. The derisory kind.

Then, silence again.

But they were close. She could feel them. The weight of their eyes, the weight of their hunger, the weight of their madness and suffering.

"Talk to me, sisters! We have business to do!"

Nothing.

Then.

"I can smell a man's desire on you..."

She twisted around. The words had been whispered in her ear.

A figure stood against the light.

No taller than her, black hair piled atop her head, bare shoulders, a dark dress, the colour lost to the shadows, bloody splashes mottled her skin. Insufficient light penetrated the Great Hall to make out the demon's features clearly.

"I know it well," Five said, "how I hated that smell. That organic, musty, needy little stink. We have so many curses 'tis hard to know which is the worst, but our heightened sense of smell... it can be quite a burden..."

Five's voice was husky; it had made her think the demon was ancient, but from what she could make out in the shadows, she looked little older than her.

"I can imagine..."

"Can you?" Five moved in a circle around her, shadowy eyes seemingly never breaking from hers. The way the demon made no sound upon the blood-slicked flagstones suggested she was bare footed.

"A nose is as much a curse as a blessing in this world."

"You don't know the meaning of cursed, sister."

She turned on the spot in time with Five to keep the demon in sight. Others moved in the deep, dark shadows, shapeless forms almost, but not quite, indistinguishable from the night that had taken up residence in Thasbald's Great Hall.

Outside, the newborn sun might be bursting light upon the world, but it was still midnight here.

"I had everything I loved destroyed. Your lives are not the only ones Bulcher broke."

"And yet you still breathe, sister. And yet you still walk under the sun, sister. And yet you are not a hated and despised monster consigned to the shadows, sister."

"No. I may breathe and walk under the sun, but I am still dead. 'tis only vengeance that keeps my heart beating."

Five stopped.

"Vengeance…"

"You understand vengeance, don't you, Number Five?"

"I have dreamed of little else for… eternity. Yesterday, it was no more a dream than any other day. Then you came, sister, and we were freed."

"I didn't free you. I didn't know you existed."

"Our sister, who they thought the meekest and most controllable of His brides, released us, and we have slaughtered those who despoiled us, abused us, used us," something glinted in the faint light that fell this far but no further from the Great Hall's open doorway. Teeth. Five was smiling, "but there are more in need of slaughter, don't you think?"

To fight an army, you need an army.

Flyblown warned her the Brides were too dangerous to use. But what more potent weapon was there to kill a demon than another demon?

"I do, sister. Saul the Bloodless and the Red Company."

"Men…" Five exhaled.

An accompaniment of identical taps. Metal on stone. All in unison. Applause?

"More monsters than men, sister."

Five stopped pacing to lean in sharply enough to force her to have to overcome the instinct to jerk away from danger.

"All men are monsters, sister..."

The tapping increased in volume without changing its rhythm.

The creatures beyond the light were expressing approval.

"They are not," she said.

Five's head tilted from side to side, the demon's nose no more than a finger from her face.

"If you had known what we have known, sister. If you had seen what we have seen. If you had felt what we have felt, you would not say that. We have all seen the Devil, sister, and we know the Devil has many forms and comes in many guises, but here, in the dark, in our solitude, in our misery, in our pain and humiliation, we have all learned the same single, immutable truth..." Five came close enough for her to taste the blood on her breath, "...the Devil always has a cock!"

The wet sound of flesh slapping stone replaced the metallic tapping.

Bloody palms hitting a bloody floor.

"Not all men are like Bulcher or those that served him."

Five snorted dead air in her face, "You think not?"

"I know not. And it wasn't only men who served Bulcher, was it? There were women in this hall, too,"

"Indeed, but none of them came down to our cells to play His games with us. The women of Thasbald were as enslaved as we were."

"And yet you killed them, too."

"And yet we made them free, too. We made them strong;

we made them so no man could ever hurt them again," Five's fingers curled around the back of her head, "we made them like us."

"You turned th-"

"Yes! Not all will be born again, just as not all His brides were born again. Death is greedy, but some will, some will awake soon, and they will take their place."

She tried to pull away, but Five's grip was too strong.

"You've inflicted your curse on them like Bulcher did on you. That makes you no better than him!"

"We are not Him! We do not do this for sick, twisted amusement like Him. We do this for a greater purpose! 'tis a sacrifice for the common good."

"What purpose?"

"To break the Devil's hold upon the world."

"Men?"

"Yes! In all my long years in the dark waiting for my pain, I realised it. Don't you see? 'tis so obvious. After all, the Devil is a trickster; dressing the naked truth in finery to blind us. The world's ills all come from men. War, famine, poverty, suffering, injustice, persecution. They are the bitter fruit of the world of men. But imagine, sister, what the world would be like if the Devil did not hold power. Can you? Can you imagine that world?"

Around them, wet, bloody palms slapped wet, bloody flagstones.

"Women are weak; women are *kept* weak. Even we, who are strong, were kept weak for the amusement of men. But no longer. Now we are free! Now the blood of men flows freely, too. And that makes us strong, sister, so very strong!"

The noise echoed around her as the pressure on her skull increased to the point she thought the demon intended to crush her head into a bloody pulp.

Maybe she blacked out for a moment because she found herself sprawled on the tacky floor with no memory of how she got there.

Five stood over her.

"I could make you strong, too, sister," the demon said.

"I am strong."

"All women are strong. That is why they keep us in chains. Why they make us think we are weak. Why they fear us. But you could be so much more."

"I have no desire to live in the darkness."

"The darkness only exists when we are too weak to see the world."

"Perhaps, but I see enough."

Five snorted, "You think you can defeat The Red Company as you are?"

"Yes."

"You won't..." the demon leaned in over her, "...you can only defeat what lives in the dark by living in the dark yourself."

Slowly, she eased herself onto her haunches. When she climbed back to her feet, she had to peel her hand off the blood-soaked floor.

Five moved back. A little.

"Join us, sister," the demon offered, "we can destroy our enemies and remake the world."

"You have big dreams," she said, wiping her palms on her

britches, "for someone who has spent so long chained to a bed."

"Where better to dream than when you float in chains with the filth?"

"Give me back my men."

"Your answer is no, then?"

Her hand found the hilt of her fencing dagger.

Five chuckled and turned away.

"My men!"

"Ah, of course. I nearly forget. I don't understand the attachment. But I suppose a deal is a deal," Five clicked her fingers.

Feet shuffled in the deep black depths of the Great Hall.

Her stomach unclenched a fraction.

Flyblown had been right. They wouldn't give her the silver she needed, and she would have to destroy them. One blood-crazed group of demons seeking to escape the shadows and reshape the world was enough.

She had no idea if it would work, but she wasn't leaving Thasbald without the silver, and she couldn't leave Five alive to dream her blood-soaked dreams either.

The sound of feet came closer.

She would wait until her men cleared the Great Hall before asking about the silver. Five might not give it, but the longer she kept them talking, the longer they had to take Bulcher's wealth.

Figures moved in the gloom.

Her eyes had adjusted to the darkness a little, which made her uneasy in a way she couldn't articulate.

The indistinct figures parted.

Something thumped on the floor at her feet.

Then something else.

She shuffled back and aside so the faint light of the doorway fell upon the objects.

A third head landed next to the first two.

Sergeant Paasche's, she thought, though, given the blood, poor light and contorted expression, it was hard to be certain.

The fourth was Harri. She recognised the jug-ears.

"We had a deal!"

"You got half your men back, sister. Half a deal is better than anything we ever received."

She watched in horror till the pile of heads on the floor numbered the missing men.

"Ola and Enni?" she heard herself ask, the barmaids from the *Eagle's Claw* who'd become friendly with Egon and Hector, two of the Vadians whose heads now sat at her feet.

"We have given them our blood. We shall see if they are reborn or not. Either way, the world of men shall not use them again."

The two young women *she'd* brought here.

"We could give you our blood, too, sister..."

"I don't want your damn blood!"

"Then you should leave now. We are sated. We are generous. Be gone. Men will never pollute Thasbald again," Five returned to the darkness, "and the whole world shall soon follow..."

She wanted to scream, she wanted to lash out, she wanted to kill the bitch.

Instead, she kept her eyes on Five and the other brides as

they faded back into the shadows. Then she stormed to the door, jaw set hard and nostrils flaring.

She had a castle to destroy.

*

"Always keep your powder dry..." Lucien nodded approvingly, "...first rule of soldiering, that."

Lead lined the room's walls and floor to stop sparks, high narrow windows provided ventilation while charcoal had been scattered to absorb moisture.

There was also a shit load of gunpowder.

"Shouldn't it be underground?" Hilde asked as the three of them peered in through the door.

"Too much damp here," he explained, "moisture ruins gunpowder, it needs to stay dry. Everything was dripping wet down below, remember?"

Hilde nodded.

Then she asked, "Why are we doing this instead of getting the silver?"

"I've got one good arm and you're a girl. We can't carry much."

"And I don't do heavy lifting," Lucien added, "I'm contractually excluded."

"Is there enough?" he asked, venturing inside.

"Depends on what you want to do with it," Lucien wrinkled his nose, "If you want to send this place to the moon, for instance, I reckon there's plenty."

"The moon will do," he said.

"We just have to set this off, with enough time for us to get out of Thasbald?" Hilde said.

"Without the demons figuring out what we're doing," he

said.

"While we scarper with as much of their silver as we can carry."

Lucien scratched his head.

They all looked at each other.

He shrugged.

"What could possibly go wrong?"

Lucien moved on to worrying something out of his left ear, "Always wondered what it's like on the moon..."

"So... what do we do?" Hilde asked, still standing by the broken door. Without Samanta's help, getting through the two heavy doors that sealed off the castle's powder store had taken a lot longer. Though it did give Lucien the opportunity to show off his lock-picking skills.

Lucien waved a finger, earwax and all, at one of the smaller kegs. "We open one of them little beasties, and use it to make a powder trail running from them big barrels to make a fuse. The trick is making the powder trail long enough to give whoever lights it time to leg it out of the castle before it blows while ensuring the trail is thick enough that it won't fizzle out."

"How'd you ensure that?" Hilde asked.

"It's quite a precise business with little margin for error," Lucien assured her.

Hilde pulled a face, "That means you're going to make a wild guess and cross your fingers, doesn't it?"

"Yep."

"And if you get it wrong?"

"We'll tragically have to say farewell to whatever poor sap ends up having to light it..." Lucien's eyes flicked between them, "...and don't look at me; I'm contractually excluded from blowing myself to smithereens, too."

"Best get started then..."

"Who *is* going to light it?" Hilde asked, staring at him.

"Guess it'll be me," he said.

"Why you? I can run faster than you!"

"No, you can't."

"Yes, I can!"

"You're a girl. You're not doing it."

Hilde's brow puckered, "I can light some powder and run. Don't need a cock for that."

"You're not doing it."

"But why you?"

"Because it's better than me doing it," Lucien said, easing the lid off one of the smaller kegs.

"But-"

"No time for bickering, Hilde. I'm doing it. There's nothing wrong with my legs. Solace should have got our men back now; we need to get the silver and blow this place."

He remembered almost collapsing with exhaustion heading back to Ettestein's gate towers with Morlaine, Sophia and her mad cousin. But that was over a month ago, possibly even six weeks. And he was much stronger now.

Really, much, much stronger...

They retreated to the stairs and let Lucien get on with it. The less he saw, the more he could convince himself the mercenary did in fact know what he was doing.

"I don't want you lighting this," Hilde said.

"Not that keen myself, but I'm here."

"Could get that demon to do it. I bet she's fast..."

"She's hauling silver for Solace."

"I don't trust her."

"But you want her to light the powder trail?"

"I'd be a lot less upset if she ends up on the moon with all of them other demons instead of you."

"I'm a good runner."

She gave him a look that suggested she'd seen him run.

"I'm faster than you or Lucien."

The look didn't alter much.

"Let's wait and see what happens; we should get news soon."

Hilde moved her eyes from him. Light filtered through the narrow windows, which at least meant the demons wouldn't bother them here. Presumably, *Graf* Bulcher hadn't spent as much time inspecting his gunpowder as his silver.

Most of Thasbald's windows were shuttered and closed for reasons that were now blindingly obvious, but the powder store needed to be ventilated.

"He kept a lot of gunpowder," Hilde muttered, with the air of someone begrudgingly prepared to change the subject.

"Valuable commodity. Even more so during a war. Looks like Bulcher was selling to all sides. A profitable business. I guess he could only marry so many women and murder their families at a time."

"How'd he get away with it?"

"Rich men get away with anything. If anybody noticed, I'm sure he had ways of dealing with them. Even the church. You saw the coin and plate he had down there."

Hilde nodded.

Then her eyes met his again, "Wouldn't take much of that to buy us a comfortable new life somewhere..."

Us?

"I follow where Lady Solace leads."

"Unto the gates of Hell?"

"If needs be..."

"I don't understand you, Ulrich."

That makes two of us.

Rather than her questioning eyes, he focussed on Lucien, who was proudly displaying his bum crack as he shuffled backwards towards them, bent over, pouring out the powder trail.

When the mercenary reached them, he gently put the powder keg down and gave his stubble a scratch.

"Problem?" he asked.

"Can't lay a powder trail down the stairs."

"And this isn't long enough?"

"Can you run as fast as a hare?"

"No."

"Then it isn't long enough."

"So... what do we do?" he asked, looking doubtfully at the stairs.

Lucien tapped his nose, "I'll have to take the powder line back up to the far end of the corridor and back here again. Maybe a couple of times. Like a snake."

"That'll work?"

"Like a charm. Unless a spark jumps to the next part of the line and ignites that, of course."

"What happens then?"

"You'll need to figure out how to run like a hare."

Lucien found something to chuckle about as he picked up the keg and started pouring out the next part of his powder snake back up the corridor.

"This isn't going to work," he rubbed his sore eyes.

"All the more reason to get someone else to light it then," Hilde insisted.

The powder store was on the castle's second floor, with only one way in. The walls looked like they'd been reinforced, but there was so much powder if it went up, some extra bricks weren't going to make a whole lot of difference.

How long would it take him, at full pelt, to get out of the castle from here?

A minute? Two?

Then climb in the saddle and ride far enough away?

Another couple of minutes.

He stared at Lucien's growing powder snake.

Did I come all this way to blow myself up?

Solace hadn't asked him to do this. In fact, he thought she would much prefer someone else did it, though, like the Almighty, Solace's plans were hard to work out.

But he couldn't ask anyone else to do it.

The sound of feet slapping up the stairs yanked him from his worries.

Hilde and he stepped back from the top of the spiral staircase in unison. She raised her crossbow, and he his sabre. Given all the gunpowder scattered about and his recent luck with firearms, it seemed best to leave his remaining pistol where it was.

Hugo skidded to an alarmed halt, arms outstretched.

"'tis only me!"

He eased Old Man Ulrich's sabre into his scabbard, careful not to catch any of the surrounding stonework, else a stray spark might ignite the powder.

"Is there a problem?"

He could tell from Hugo's flustered expression that there was.

"All Hell's broken loose! Lady Solace wants this done as soon as possible!"

"What happened?"

"The demons killed all the prisoners!"

He sighed and looked down the corridor to Lucien.

"How long?"

"Five minutes," Lucien called back.

"That long enough?" he asked Hugo.

The boy threw out his skinny arms, "If they don't kill us all first, it is!"

"They're attacking her?" he was already taking a step towards the stairs.

Hugo shook his head, "Not yet; she's trying to keep them bottled up in the Great Hall, but…"

Easier said than done.

"Go back to Lady Solace and tell her we need five minutes. Come back when she's ready to go, and everyone is out of the castle."

The boy made to turn away, then hesitated, "The way out is by the Great Hall. If everybody else is out of the castle, whoever lights this… the demons could be between them and the way out?"

"Go," he said, "we'll worry about that when we have to."

Hugo nodded and ran back down the stairs.

"There's nothing to fret about," he smiled at Hilde when he turned back to find her staring at him, "I have it on good authority that God has other plans for me…"

Chapter Thirteen

"You lying, murderous, fucking bitch!"

She hurled the tar torch she'd just snatched from a slack-jawed Gerwin into the Great Hall and watched it shedding sparks as it spun through the darkness.

It briefly illuminated a tableau that could have come from Hell itself. A carpet of corpses littered the floor amongst overturned tables and benches, around which wraith-like figures scurried. A few shrieks of fury came back in response to the unwelcome light, but nothing came hurtling towards her before they slammed the doors of the Great Hall shut, and she barked out orders to stack furniture against it.

"That won't hold them," Gotz said.

"It'll slow them though."

Another door led around the side of the Great Hall to the kitchens; she had that shut and barricaded, too. There would be other ways the demons could come, but they were the two most direct.

As Gotz, Swoon, and the Vadians barricaded the doors, she sent Hugo to confirm how long Renard and Lucien needed before the castle's powder store was ready to blow. She hoped it big enough to bring the whole fortress down on the demons' heads. The boys (no, men!) had told her it was a sizeable magazine and where to find it.

Hopefully, they hadn't been lying. Not that there was

much she could do about if they had, given she'd handed them over to Five and her mad Brides.

While the men worked, she made sure the big doors of Thasbald's keep were open and stayed that way. They faced east, allowing bright early morning sunshine into the lobby before the Great Hall. They rattled in the sharp breeze until Pavol found two thick wooden wedges attached to leather loops, which he fitted to each door to silence them.

Tapestries hung on the external wall of the lobby; ripping them down, she found narrow shuttered windows. They sat too far up for her to reach.

"You!" she shouted at the red-haired Vadian Pavol as he hurried past, "Find a way to get those shutters open, now!"

When he just blinked at her, she almost screamed, "The demons can't walk in the fucking sunlight!"

Pavol jumped and ran off to find something he could stand on to reach the shutters.

While the men worked, she collected oil lanterns.

All the time, she expected the doors to start bulging and demons to come pouring from the shadows.

The urge to remain in the bright morning light of the doorway was overwhelming, but she stamped on it and carried the lanterns to their hasty barricade.

"Douse it all in oil."

Gotz looked like he was going to tell her that wouldn't hold them either, but he started emptying the oil without comment.

She grabbed Swoon, "Get the rest of the horses out of the stables and saddled – and get Lady Karoline and her maid to help you if need be."

Swoon's over-sized Adam's apple bobbed up and down in alarm. Before his fleshy lips could grapple the word *How?* into submission, she yelled in his face, "I don't fucking care! If we don't get out of here soon, we're all going to die!"

Swoon's Adam's apple jumped so far up his throat it almost hit her in the eye, and then he sprinted out of the door like Five's demons and all their inbred cousins from Hell were on his heels.

She turned her attention to barking orders and swearing at the rest of her company.

The ones I haven't got killed yet.

There was no need to keep quiet about what she was doing now.

Or crawl into bed with a man to talk to him.

Two competing forms of guilt swirled around her like deranged bats. But guilt, like many other things, were luxuries she couldn't currently afford.

If this went wrong, she'd be getting the remainder of her company killed, too, and the only thing she'd be sharing with a man again was a grave. She needed to keep the demon's attention on what was happening outside the Great Hall, not elsewhere in Thasbald.

Of course, the danger in keeping a bear's attention was that you did such a good job of it, the damn thing charged you.

She grabbed another passing Vadian whose name it took a moment to remember and pushed him at the door, "Get outside and help ready the horses... Stengel! And make sure the portcullis and main gates are open!"

He gave her a look that suggested he was weighing up

whether to spit at her or punch her. Perhaps she wasn't the only one blaming Solace von Tassau for the pile of heads in The Great Hall, but if so, he swallowed it and headed off after a nod and a grunt.

As he disappeared, Pavol managed to pull the first of the shutters open, and a shaft of sunlight speared the far wall, illuminating the dust motes and smoke floating in its path.

She wondered what such a spear would do to a demon.

The barricades grew, oil poured over them, and the shutters opened in turn, each adding another spear of daylight. Out in the courtyard the horses were readied. Hugo returned, and she led him into the courtyard so he could whisper that Renard and Lucien's surprise would be ready in another five minutes.

She nodded, told the boy to stay near and say nothing else.

Back inside, she watched and waited.

Perhaps Five thought she was no particular threat and was content to leave her to rearrange Thasbald's furniture.

The passage of the shafts of sunlight creeping down the lobby's far wall marked the passing time.

"My lady!"

Lebrecht stood in the corridor doorway, entering the lobby opposite the Great Hall's doors.

She padded over to him.

The nobleman moved back into the shadows.

Behind him she found Usk, Wickler, the largest of the Vadian men-at-arms, a sour-faced Bohemian named Macek, and Samanta.

Plus, three large chests.

The men were red-faced, panting and slicked with sweat despite the cold. Samanta looked like she had just been to fetch an empty laundry basket.

"Problems?"

Lebrecht shook his head while trying to catch his breath.

She moved past the men.

"Are any of your sisters close enough to hear us?"

The demon stood transfixed, an expression of awe and fear pulling her pale face in different directions. It took a moment to realise it was the daylight pouring across the room that she was looking at.

She had to repeat the question before Samanta dragged her eyes away.

A single tear run down the demon's cheek.

She brushed it away, shaking her head, "No, I don't think so."

"You don't *think* so?"

"None are close enough to hear. I would sense them. I am certain."

Five lied to her and killed her men; could she trust Samanta wasn't doing the same?

She turned to Lebrecht, "Our men are dead. The demons lied to us."

Usk dropped his gaze, Macek muttered something under his breath, Wickler spat, but his eyes didn't move from Samanta.

Lebrecht, at least, didn't say the demons lied to *you*.

"We have to leave now; I've barricaded the Great Hall, and the powder room is set."

Lebrecht opened his hand towards the chests, "There's a

lot more down there..."

The glint in the young nobleman's eye, she thought, looked a bit like silver.

"The barricades won't hold them; I don't want to risk more lives..."

"I can get more," Samanta said, "I'll be much quicker alone."

"We can't wait long."

"Would more help you?"

She nodded.

"Then I will get you more, as a friend!"

"But-"

"I'll be quick!" Samanta was almost a blur as she shot off back down the shadowy corridor.

"Should bring down the roof on that one's head, too..." Wickler said, eyes lingering on the corridor after Samanta disappeared.

"Samanta didn't kill those men," she snapped at him.

"No, the other fucking monsters just like her killed my friends," the man-at-arms snapped right back.

"Wickler..." Lebrecht warned.

"My lord..." he said, still glaring at her.

"We can discuss our grievances later, Peter..." she said, returning his glare, "...but for now, let us do what we must to stay alive. And deal with *them*."

Wickler had a particularly intense stare. The kind that might make you think him the manner of man who'd have no qualms about slitting your throat if an argument went badly enough.

She held her ground and gave it right back to him.

For some men, a woman doing that to them would only make a bad situation worse. If Wickler was one of those men, he managed to suck it back in as he lowered his eyes first and nodded, "Yes, my lady."

"Get these into Lady Karoline's coach. But as quietly as you can, we don't want them knowing what we're up to. Understand?"

Usk and Macek mirrored Wickler's nod and they began moving the chests. It took two men to lift each one.

Once they were out of the corridor, she opened the third chest.

Silver glinted brightly back at her.

Enough to buy an army?

And enough for a man to sell his soul for, too... be careful, My Lady of the Broken Tower; silver can be a dangerous friend to have...

She looked up with a start.

The voice had been Flyblown's, but no pale-faced apparition stood in the shadows.

Slowly, she closed the lid.

How many of the men with her did she really trust?

If they got out of here, she supposed she'd find out soon enough.

"My lady!" Hugo was in the doorway, "Something's happening!"

She left the silver and went back into the lobby.

The doors to the Great Hall shook hard enough to send clouds of dust billowing out into the shafts of golden morning light cutting into the room. The makeshift barricade of oil-doused furniture rattled but held.

Not that she thought Five was trying to break it down; there were sufficient demons on the other side of that door to turn it to kindling in minutes. Maybe seconds.

No, Five wanted to frighten them.

To convince them to leave without further bloodshed?

Or because the bitch had started to enjoy yielding the fear instead of receiving it.

The door shook again.

The men around her exchanged nervous glances.

Lebrecht returned with Usk, Wickler and Macek, the first two chests of silver loaded onto Karoline's coach.

He shot her a questioning look. She made a hurry-up signal with her hand. Lebrecht disappeared with Usk to get the last chest. Wickler and Macek drew their weapons and joined the knot of silent men standing with her in the centre of the lobby.

"Stay steady, men!" she shouted, "those murderous bitches can't survive the sun's touch. They come through that door; they're going to burn!"

The door rattled again. Louder this time.

It was about as close as two heavy pieces of wood were likely to get to a hearty guffaw.

Keep playing with me, bitch; I've burnt your kind before...

She held a hand out to Pavol, who stared back blankly.

She jabbed a finger at one of the tar torches still flickering on the wall, and the red-haired Vadian trotted over and fetched her one.

The doors boomed again. Violently enough to make half the men jump and the other half take a step backwards.

Pavol's hand shook as he handed the smoking torch to

her.

Hers wasn't.

She walked slowly to the door. Her boots scuffing on the flagstones the only sound.

So, she filled the void with another.

She whistled.

As Renard told her Samanta had.

Three notes, ascending.

The door remained still.

Like a dragon holding its breath.

She stood before their makeshift barricade. On the other side, monsters waited, monsters listened.

She looked over her shoulder.

A wake of smoke floated behind her, lanced by the morning sunlight pouring in through the shutters. Wary, uncertain faces watched. Across the lobby, Lebrecht and Usk moved carefully with the last chest towards the door.

Timing.

Many decisions in life came down to when you chose to do them.

The margin between success and tragedy could be measured in any unit of time, from years to minutes. Her eyes returned to the door.

Sometimes, even seconds.

How long to wait. How soon to act.

Another sound came. Not the shake of the door being hammered but scratching and tapping noises. Nails and knives. On the other side of the wood.

Lots of them.

She counted to ten.

The scratchings and tappings slowly increased in volume as if a wall of insects pressed against the door.

She turned around.

Lebrecht and Usk had hauled the chest out into the daylight.

She looked at Hugo, splayed the fingers and thumb of her left hand and mouthed the word *five*, then pointed at the stairs. The boy nodded and hurried off to tell Renard and Lucien to set the powder alight in five minutes.

She swept her hand to the sunlit exit and mouthed the word *go* to the rest of the men.

Lebrecht would get them mounted and away from Thasbald.

She turned back to the door, which rattled and shook again.

She whistled another three notes.

Then held the torch against the oil-soaked furniture. It ignited with a pleasing *whoosh*.

She walked to the small barricade in front of the side door and tossed the torch onto it, setting that ablaze too.

Turning back, she found the lobby empty, except for Gabriel Gotz, thumbs finding room under his stomach to hitch into his belt.

"I told you to go," she said, standing beside him to admire the flames.

"Yep," he nodded, "you did, but thought you'd benefit from some company. As it happens, I am marvellous company."

"Really?"

"Uh-huh," he nodded, "how long you think that door's gonna hold?"

As long as Five wanted it to hold. The demon had a flair for the dramatic. Hopefully, it would be the bitch's undoing.

"Doesn't matter," she said, "we're leaving..."

"Erm... Solace..."

She turned to find Samanta standing in the doorway behind them, a chest bigger than the other three held easily in her hands, face screwed up as she squinted into the light.

Tugging Gotz's arm, they went to the demon.

She took off her cloak and handed it to Samanta once she put down the chest, Gotz gave her his gloves.

"Can you get to the coach?"

Samanta looked terrified suddenly but nodded.

"Get her there, then go," she told Gotz.

"But-"

"Do it," she said, "just make sure there are enough horses left for the rest of us. We'll be right behind."

She turned back to the demon, "Ready?"

Samanta pulled the hood over her head, "Yes. I can do anything for my friends!"

Gotz was eyeing her.

He knew as well as her that the men outside would rather the demon fried in the sunlight than ride away to safety with them. Maybe he did, too. But the demon, even without a massive chest of silver, would be useful.

And, after all, what were friends for, if not using to attain your goals?

"Take her to the coach," she said as the demon scooped up the chest of silver with no apparent effort.

"And see she comes to no harm," she added as they moved

across the lobby.

Gotz nodded.

Samanta let out a faint whine as they approached the door and the awaiting daylight.

"I won't be able to see much out there…"

Gotz patted her arm, "Stay close to me, girl, and I'll see you all alright. Plenty of women around who can vouch that's true enough."

She tried not to roll her eyes, though Samanta giggled nervously.

"Wait," she said as the demon tentatively approached the sunlight.

She scooped up one of the tapestries that had hidden the shuttered windows and draped it over the demon and around her face.

"Thank you!" Samanta said in a small voice, "You are a true friend!"

Gotz put his hand on Samanta's arm and gently ushered her into the fierce morning light.

She returned to the lobby.

Smoke was filling the room. And the big doors of the Great Hall shuddered and cracked behind their burning barricade.

She retreated to stand within the column of daylight spilling through the open doors and drew her daggers as part of the burning barricade tumbled forward, and the scream of splintering wood echoed around the rafters.

Biting her bottom lip, daggers spinning in her hands, she checked the stairs.

And waited.

*

"Lady Solace said five minutes," Hugo shuffled from one foot to the other as if the powder on the floor were already alight.

"Some things take as long as they take..." Lucien winked, "...else you fuck them up and they blow your balls off. And trust me, young gentleman, you don't want that happening before you've even had a chance to use em for anything useful."

Wisdom dispensed, Lucien disappeared back inside to finish whatever was required to make a powder room, and the castle around it, explode.

"We could set it off while he's still inside..." he eyed the now complete gunpowder trail snaking back and forth along the corridor to the powder store Lucien had instructed them not to go anywhere near.

"No," Hilde said firmly.

He shrugged.

Worth a try.

"She said five minutes," Hugo repeated.

"It hasn't been five minutes yet."

"It hasn't?"

"Nope," he said assuredly. He had no idea how long it had been but didn't want the boy getting any more anxious than he already was.

"Seems like it..." Hilde said unhelpfully.

"You two should go down. Get on a horse and put some distance between yourselves and Thasbald..." he glanced towards the powder room, "...on the off chance he knows what he's doing."

"No," Hilde said.

Hugo shook his head as well.

Some day, before I die, someone is going to do as I tell them...

"Well, we can't all sprint for the door together."

"Why not?" Hilde demanded.

Just the once. Just so I know what it feels like before I go to the Lord...

"Because... we'd be falling over each other, getting in each other's way... whoever does it will need a clear run."

"I'll do it," Lucien said, carefully picking his way towards them to avoid disturbing the powder snake.

"It's ready?" he asked.

"It's ready."

They all looked at each other.

"I'll do it," Lucien repeated.

"I thought you were contractually obliged not to blow yourself to smithereens?" Hilde asked.

The mercenary shrugged.

"Better I do it," he said, "I'm faster than you."

"How do you know you're faster than me?" Lucien demanded.

"Because I'm younger and you're fatter."

Lucien sucked in both a breath and his stomach, "Lucien Kazmierczak is not *fat!* He is *burly...*"

"You're fat. Your belly wobbles when you run."

"It does not!"

"You're doing that cock comparing thing again, aren't you?" Hilde snapped at them, "Why don't you two just get them out and be done with it? Then we can all see who's got the bigger one, and you can stop all this nonsense once and for all!"

Lucien's eyes widened, "There's no bloody competition, I can tell you that, lass!"

"I can light it," Hugo offered.

They all turned to the boy.

"I'm faster than all of you."

"No, you're not," they all said pretty much simultaneously.

"Yes, I am. But I ain't good at much else. Can't fight, can't ride, ain't clever... but I am fast... and I want to do *something*."

They looked at each other.

"Someone has to do it," Hilde said at last.

"I'll be right behind you," Hugo said, "just make sure there aren't any demons in my way, cos I'll be coming like I got a big dog snapping at my arse!"

He didn't like it, but Hugo was faster than them.

Lucien reached into the stairwell, picked up the candle in a black iron holder they'd left at the top of the stairs out of harm's way, and handed it to the boy.

"Our five minutes are up," the mercenary said.

Hugo put his shoulders back, chest out and nodded as he took the candle.

"Once we're through that door, count to a hundred, then light the powder up," Lucien told the boy.

"You can count to a hundred, can't you?" he asked.

"I can count to ten..." Hugo offered.

"Can you count to ten, ten times?"

Hugo screwed up his face and thought about it before

nodding, "Think so."

"Then you run like hell, right?" Hilde said.

"We'll be in the courtyard," he added.

Hugo grinned, "If you only have a hundred-count start, I'll catch up with you slowpokes long before that!"

"Right, let's get going..." Lucien pushed Hilde and him towards the stairs.

He looked back at the boy from the top of the spiral staircase.

Hugo beamed back, grinning from ear to ear, clutching the candlestick as if it were made of gold and had been given to him as a birthday present rather than to use to blow the castle – and possibly himself – to bits.

For the first time in the boy's unfortunate life, someone was trusting him to do something important and he was proud as punch about it.

Please, God, don't let it be the last thing he ever does, too.

He winked at the boy.

Then pushed Hilde in front of him and they were belting down the stairs.

"Think you can keep up, fatty?" he called to Lucien.

"Cunt," the mercenary shot back from behind him, already panting.

By the time he counted to one hundred, they were out of the spiral staircase and at the end of the corridor that led directly to the main staircase that would take them down to the lobby before the Great Hall and the doors opening onto the castle's courtyard.

Where they'd be horses saddled and waiting.

Hopefully.

Ahead, a dusting of light marked the main staircase. Otherwise, all was dark and shadowy. Thasbald didn't boast many windows, and those it did were mostly shuttered.

Doors flashed by. All closed.

The corridor was wide enough for Hilde to run at his side.

She was still clutching her crossbow; despite its weight, she seemed to be breathing easier than him.

He skidded to a halt at the top of the main stairs as Lucien lumbered after them.

"Don't wait for me," Lucien bellowed.

"Wasn't planning to," he spat out a coppery tasting gob of spit. Hilde was taking the stairs two at a time towards the sharp morning light flooding up from the lobby. He did the same.

The smell of burning wood filled the air as they reached the last turn of the stairs, and then, above the pounding of their feet on the steps, an almighty crack and crash. His heart and stomach went in different directions as he thought the powder store had gone up early, and he wouldn't even have time to berate Lucien for fucking it up.

But when the roof failed to fall about their ears, he realised the sound originated below, not from above.

He hurtled onto the landing of the last flight.

At the bottom of the wide wooden stairs, Solace stood alone in the lobby. Sunlight poured in through the open main doors and high, narrow windows he hadn't even known were there. The doors to the Great Hall hung shattered, and pieces of burning furniture lay in piles across the lobby.

And around the flames, figures moved, tentative and hunched, squinting at Solace from behind raised hands and splayed fingers.

"My lady!" he shouted, drawing his father's sabre and jumping from the last few steps to stumble and skid to his mistress' side.

She held a fencing dagger in one hand and a smaller blade in the other. And something that sat smack in between a smile and a sneer upon her face.

Hilde joined them, crossbow pointed at the demons.

Some snarled and snapped like dogs, several scurried upon hands and knees, most shied away from the flames, and none came anywhere near the parts of the lobby sunlight fell directly upon. Blood caked all of them, from matted hair to bare feet.

Lucien caught up with them.

"Fuck," the mercenary panted, drawing his pistols, "and I thought I'd woken up next to some frightening women in my time..."

Solace lowered her blades, "They can't hurt us; they are worthy of only pity... where is Hugo?"

"Coming," he said.

"Are you not going to say farewell, Five?" Solace shouted at the demons.

Several hissed back.

One, face obscured by tangles of dirty blonde hair, sat cross-legged on the floor, face in her hands weeping. Another kept jumping toward one of the beams of light slanting down from the windows above her hand to illuminate the swirling smoke, fingers outstretched.

If Five, the demon's apparent leader, was amongst them, she was not showing herself.

Unless she looked just as mad as the others in the daylight.

The sound of pounding feet came from the stairs, and Hugo, wide-eyed and grinning like a miser in front of a free meal, came hurtling down towards them.

It really was time to go.

Then, one of the demons, a waif in the bloody ruins of a once white dress, stepped into the sunlight between Hugo and them.

The creature screeched, thrashing wildly as what looked like steam erupted off her skin in spinning tendrils. He wasn't sure if the demon was trying to grab the boy or kill herself; either way, Hugo ducked and managed to dodge under a flailing arm, throwing off globs of steam like fat from a pan... but his foot slipped, and he went tumbling to the ground.

He was up instantly, but the stumble had taken him beyond the corridor of sunlight that stretched from the open doors and up the stairs.

The nearest demon was on him in a flash, face changing as she grabbed the boy and yanked him towards her snapping fangs.

A pistol barked – Lucien's – and a bloom of dark blood erupted on the demon's back. The creature staggered and snarled but still managed to sink fangs into the boy's shoulder.

Hugo screamed, knees buckling as he tried to make it to the safety of the sunlight.

A woman shouted *No!* as he stepped out of the sanctuary of the light to swing his sabre at the demon. It could have been Solace or Hilde. Possibly both. His place was at Solace's side, but he couldn't stand by and watch the boy being torn to pieces.

The sabre cleaved into the back of the demon's neck; a gout of black blood sprayed an arc across the room. The creature went down screaming, momentarily pinning Hugo beneath her, but the Bride weighed less than the boy did, and Hugo managed to slither out.

Another gun boomed, another bride screamed, and he turned in time to see one go down holding her face, but others were coming in a wave, terrible elongated faces, black bottomless eyes reduced to slits against the light, gaping fang-filled mouths, tangled, blood-matted hair.

A wave that moved with impossible speed through the smoke.

He jumped back towards the light.

And something shrieking and screaming hit him in the chest.

He went down on his back.

The heat slapped his face.

One of the Brides had thrown herself through the air and they tumbled backwards together, landing on the floor in the path of the daylight falling through the door.

He'd got his sabre up and against the bride's throat but had no room to swing the blade.

The nightmarish face filled his vision.

And it boiled.

The prominent blue veins in the white skin bubbled and

broke; steam rose off the Bride as she shrieked, her breath, hot and bloody, smacked his face.

The demon reared up, clawing at her own face.

Solace drove a dagger into the creature's eye.

The Bride fell sideways off him, and he scrambled to his feet.

He stood panting for a moment,

Hugo clutched his bloody shoulder, as he slumped into Lucien. While Hilde was frantically trying to reload her crossbow, Solace had turned to face the Brides. A snarling, hellish wall of teeth lined the edge of the daylight.

Dear God, how many of them were there?

Amongst the snarls and screams, voices cried out too. Some cursing, some pleading, some beseeching God for mercy, some begging forgiveness.

An occasional hand, white, bony, tentative, braved the sunlight, only to be immediately snatched back with a howl of pain.

"We must go now!" Lucien shoved Hugo at the door.

Hilde, crossbow loaded again, moved with him.

Solace stood, statue-like, staring into the faces of the damned.

He put his bad arm across her and pushed.

For a moment, he feared his mistress would resist, but she turned away, and they made for the door.

"Shit!" Lucien said.

A Bride had gotten behind the left-hand door and was trying to close it. Fortunately, both doors were wedged open. The Bride couldn't or wouldn't put her arm into the sunlight to pull the wooden wedge out, but she was strong enough to push the door slowly closed regardless.

And the column of sunlight cutting into the dark heart of Thasbald began to narrow...

Chapter Fourteen

That could have been me.
That should have been me.
The thoughts crashed and echoed around her as Renard bundled her towards the doors, towards the daylight.
Why wasn't that me?
Bulcher's Brides lined the sharp daylight like a crowd on a city street come to see a king pass in his gilded carriage. Save the only king they looked fit to cheer was the one who wore horns upon his head rather than a crown.

Contorted faces, some human, some demonic, some flickering between the two. Eyes scrunched to slits against the light or screwed completely shut. Every face was bloody, and tears cut streams through the blood on every face.

Not all the Brides lined their route to safety; others shuffled around the debris scattered about the doors to the Great Hall. One blank-faced girl who must have been about her age when Bulcher put his curse inside her stood before a couple of burning chairs, slack-jawed and dead-eyed, hands outstretched and turning over each other as if trying to warm herself. Another, no older than Karoline, sat cross-legged on the floor amongst the remnants of their barricade, cradling a severed head, rocking it like it were a baby she was encouraging to sleep. Another-

"Fuck!" Lucien shouted; the urgency of the curse dragged

her eyes away from the pitiful souls she could so easily have joined.

A Bride was pushing one of the doors shut.

Sealing me in, where I belong...

A thrum and a snap, and something whooshed by her ear. A crossbow bolt thudded into the Bride's back. Hilde really was a good shot.

The Bride screamed but kept pushing the door.

Another joined her. The wedges Pavol had found and slid under the doors to keep the wind from shutting them popped out, and the door slammed shut a couple of paces in front of their noses.

They all jinked right to remain within the protection of the sunlight.

The wall of Brides surged forward.

But the demons couldn't cross the sunlight to reach the other door. They were going to get out. Whether they could get far enough away before the powder room blew was another matter. But at least she wouldn't be entombed inside Thasbald with *Graf* Bulcher's Brides.

Then one of the Brides leapt across the sunlight and landed on the other side to start pushing that door shut.

Another tried the same trick as they reached the door; Renard's sabre all but cut the slender demon in two, showering them in dark, cold blood.

The second door screeched in unison with the demon pushing it; the column of light narrowed further, and then Renard was bundling her through the gap, blinking into the glorious, wintry morning sunshine.

She lost her footing and found herself sprawled at the

bottom of the steps on the courtyard's frosty cobbles as Hilde burst out behind them. Finally, Lucien and Hugo staggered through, the mercenary's face bright red, the boy's as pale as the demons pursuing them as he clutched his wounded shoulder.

An arm in a torn and bloody white sleeve burst through the opening and seized the boy's collar, yanking him backwards towards the closing gap between the doors, towards the darkness...

Without time to draw his sword, Lucien dropped the spent pistol in his hand and grabbed the boy. Screaming, Hugo's arms fixed around Lucien's neck, "Please!" the boy screamed, "Don't let me go!" as they were both dragged back onto the threshold.

Lucien managed to get a shoulder against the closed door and brace his legs as the bloody arm, boiling off steam in the sunlight, blindly tried to drag them through the door.

Renard charged back up the steps, taking them two at a time, sabre drawn. Hilde dropped to her knees, snatched the leather strap on the wedge and tried to yank it free. The wedge screamed in protest, Hugo screamed in terror, the Brides inside screamed in... pain, fury, madness, she could only guess. Lucien cursed. The cords in his neck standing out, one hand on the door, trying to keep them from the demons.

"Don't let me go!" Hugo sobbed.

"I'm not fucking letting you fucking go, you dozy little fucker!" Lucien roared in the boy's face.

Hilde, down on one knee, yanked the wedge again. Grunting with the effort as it popped from the bottom of the second door suddenly enough to send her falling backwards.

Without the wedge, the force of the Brides behind it, more interested in stopping the sunlight from getting into Thasbald than preventing them escaping, or too mad to know the difference, slammed the door shut, trapping the demon's steaming arm that still had hold of Hugo's collar. Until Renard severed it with a slashing blow.

Released, Lucien staggered away and tumbled down the steps still embracing Hugo to land at her feet.

"You didn't let go!" Hugo gasped, almost disbelievingly.

"Of course, I didn't fucking let go," Lucien barked, "now get your skinny hide off me. We're not fucking betrothed or anything!"

She grabbed the mercenary's hand and hauled him to his feet as Renard and Hilde pelted down the steps.

"How long?" she asked Lucien.

"Fuck knows!" the mercenary was already running for the horses.

Lebrecht stood in the centre of the courtyard with their mounts.

He looked... concerned.

"I told you to go!" she shouted at him, skidding to a halt.

"I told you to get out with everybody else!" he shouted back.

She snatched Styx's reins.

The stallion shot her a disdainful *and-just-where-the-hell-do-you-think-you've-been* kind of look before tossing his midnight mane and snorting steam.

Lebrecht vaulted onto the back of his own horse and

wheeled to face the main gates, "How long have we got?"

"Fuck knows!" Lucien roared again, hauling Hugo onto the front of his saddle by one arm, "Ride!"

She didn't wait, and Styx needed little encouragement. As soon as she dug her heels into the stallion's side, he was away, ears down and eating up the ground beneath his iron hooves.

Thasbald's outer towers flashed by in an instant, the wind slapped her face, and the low winter sun dazzled as they shot out onto the causeway.

"Run, boy! Run!" she wasn't sure if she screamed or laughed. Blood coursed through her veins as her heart pounded in time with Styx's hooves. Sunlight glinted off the surrounding water, turning the dark bogs and streams of the wetlands into ribbons of silver.

Light. Everywhere, beautiful light!

Ahead, she could make out Karoline's coach and the other survivors of their company. And her silver!

Bulcher was dead. She had coin for her army. She had leads to find Saul and the Red Company. The world was bright, the world was light!"

So long as she didn't get blown to smithereens when the powder store went up, of course.

And didn't think about the latest batch of corpses she'd left rotting in her wake.

How far did she need to go?

When she looked over her shoulder, she found that Styx had outrun others. She reined him in a little. After being cooped up in Thasbald's stables with lesser beings, the stallion wasn't overly keen, but she eventually slowed him enough for them to catch up.

"Shouldn't something have happened by now?" Lebrecht asked, squinting back at the castle as he came alongside.

"Patience, my lord," Lucien said, one arm wrapped around Hugo's waist to keep him from falling into the frost-crisped grass tufts lining the causeway. The boy had gone from white to green.

As Renard and Hilde caught up to them, a distant low thud emanated from the castle. Puffs of smoke escaped several of the thin, narrow windows down on the castle's eastern flank.

"Is that... it?" Renard twisted to Lucien, "We went to all that trouble for that? Your farts do more bloody damage than that!"

Lucien scrunched up his face, "Not one of my most impressive eruptions, I must confess."

She half turned Styx around to watch the smoke curl from the castle.

"What-"

Thasbald came apart.

The ground shook, and startled birds took to the air in squawking flocks. Thunder rolled over them, the horses whinnied in terror, Hilde's rising up on its hind legs and almost unseating her. Even Styx gave a snort and shuffled back a step or two.

Part of the top half of the castle soared upwards for a few seconds before crashing down in a cloud of black smoke. Towers tumbled inwards, walls fell, and huge blocks of stone flew outwards in all directions.

She hauled Styx around. The stallion needed no more

encouragement.

Ahead, Karoline's carriage waited, the rest of their company gathering together to watch the destruction. Out of the corner of her eye, something smashed into the wetlands, sending water spouting skywards.

This time, she didn't look back till she reached Karoline's carriage.

Bulcher's last widow stood on the causeway, as always, clutching her maid as she watched the carnage.

"Seems to have worked out well," Gotz smiled, leaning on the pommel of his saddle.

She checked over her shoulder as the others arrived. All had managed to avoid any of the castle landing on top of them.

After patting Styx's neck, she jumped from the saddle to see what remained of Thasbald. A few towers protruded above the spreading cloud of dust. As she watched, one of them wobbled drunkenly before toppling inwards.

"Think we got all of them?" Renard asked, peering back over his shoulder.

"We better have," she said, eyes narrowing, "we don't need any more enemies."

"Their leader?" Lucien was too busy admiring his handiwork with the excited smile of a pleased-with-himself little boy plastered over his face to look at her.

"Five? As far as I know. I didn't see the bitch at the end. I doubt she went out for a walk in the sunshine, though…"

She looked at the soldiers gathered around Karoline's coach. Usk, Wickler, Swoon and the Vadians like Pavol and Mesek. Men whose friends Five had killed, men who died because they followed her here, who died because they agreed to help her kill Bulcher and seize his castle and wealth, who died because she thought she could cut a deal with an insane vampire, who helped her send three boys (they really hadn't been men however much she tried to convince herself they had been) to their deaths.

And now Bulcher's castle was a pile of rubble, and all bar four (admittedly large) chests of silver coins were now buried beneath it, along with Bulcher's Brides.

Some of those men, she noticed, weren't watching the fall of Thasbald Castle. Some of them were looking at her.

And none of them were smiling.

"Where do you think she was?" Renard asked after dismounting. That girl, Hilde, at his side, crossbow hanging loosely from her left hand, her right, she couldn't help but notice, entwined with his.

For some reason, she wanted to spit.

She forced her eyes back to Thasbald. A few towers on the southern side of the castle remained visible, sun glinting off the conical roofs poking above the dust cloud. Nothing else could be seen, the dust and smoke masking even the outer walls and towers. Licks of orange flickered and flashed within the dust, columns of black smoke twisting heavenwards. Nothing else moved.

"Hopefully, she figured out what we were up to and tried to reach the powder store. With daylight falling on the main stairs, she couldn't take the direct route and... she ran out of time..."

"Maybe..." Renard didn't sound convinced. She wasn't sure she was either.

"Well, that was something you don't see every day," Gabriel Gotz moved to her side, his eyes moving from the remnants of Thasbald to her, "What are you going to do for your next trick?"

She patted Styx's neck, then climbed back into the saddle. Something shifted within the shadowy interior of Karoline's coach; a figure bundled in clothes hiding from the sun glimpsed through the almost closed shutters.

There was little to see, but she couldn't help wondering whether the demon inside hid from the sunlight or the sunlight refused to fall upon the demon. A silly notion. Of course.

She looked down at Gotz and made sure she spoke loudly enough for everyone to hear as she answered his question.

"My next trick?" she smiled darkly, "Kill the rest of my enemies…"

A Dark Journey Continues...

The Night's Road – Book Six

No Tomorrow

Follow Solace, Ulrich, and company's journey as they pursue Saul the Bloodless in *No Tomorrow* the next instalment of the Night's Road.

In the Company of Shadows

If you'd like to read more dark tales from the world of *In the Company of Shadows*, there are currently two free novellas (available as eBooks only) – *The Burning* & *A House of the Dead* – available. Both are set shortly before the events of *Red Company*. To get your free copies just visit andymonkbooks.com. or scan the QR code below and join Andy's mailing list for updates, news of forthcoming releases and bonus material.

The Burning

The madness of the 17th Century witch burning frenzy has come to the sleepy village of Reperndorf.

Adolphus Holtz, Inquisitor to the Prince-Bishop of Würzburg, is keen to root out evil wherever he deems it to be. His eye has fallen on young Frieda and he fancies she'll scream so prettily for him when the time comes.

Frieda has already witnessed one burning and knows from the way her friends and neighbours are looking at her that she will be next. She seems doomed to burn on the pyre until a mysterious cloaked stranger appears out of the depths of the forest...

The first novella of *In the Company of Shadows* expands the dark historical world of *In the Absence of Light* and the shadowy relationships between humans and vampires.

A House of the Dead

All vampires are mad...

The weight of memories, loss, the hunger for blood, the voices of your prey whispering in your mind, loneliness, the obsessions you filled the emptiness inside yourself with, the sheer unrelenting bloody boredom of immortality could all chip away at your sanity.

And love, of course, one should never forget what that could do to you...

Mecurio has hidden from the world for twenty years in the secret catacombs beneath the city of Würzburg known as the House of the Dead, a place of refuge for vampires away from the eyes of men.

He tells himself it is so he can complete his Great Work without the distractions of the mortal world. But it isn't true. Time is slowly stealing the woman he adores from him and he has hidden their love away in the shadows of the House of the Dead to await the inevitable.

When a vampire whose bed he fled from a hundred and twenty-seven years before, arrives in search of information, he sees the opportunity to do a deal to save the woman he now loves for a few more bittersweet years. But all vampires are mad, one way or another, and when you strike a deal with one you may not end up with what you bargained for...

Books by Andy Monk

In the Absence of Light
The King of the Winter
A Bad Man's Song
Ghosts in the Blood
The Love of Monsters

In the Company of Shadows
The Burning (Novella)
A House of the Dead (Novella)
Red Company (The Night's Road Book One)
The Kindly Man (Rumville Part One)
Execution Dock (Rumville Part Two)
The Convenient (Rumville Part Three)
Mister Grim (Rumville Part Four)
The Future is Promises (Rumville Part Five)
The World's Pain (The Night's Road Book Two)
Empire of Dirt (The Night's Road Book Three)
When the Walls Fall (The Night's Road Book Four)
Darkness Beckons (The Night's Road Book Five)

Hawker's Drift
The Burden of Souls
Dark Carnival
The Paths of the World
A God of Many Tears
Hollow Places

Other Fiction
The House of Shells
The Sorrowsmith

For further information about Andy Monk's writing and future releases, please visit the following sites.

www.andymonkbooks.com

www.facebook.com/andymonkbooks

Printed in Great Britain
by Amazon